DEVIL IN THE COUNTRYSIDE

CORY BARCLAY

www.CoryBarclay.com

First edition: December 2016

Cover Art by Vaughn Mir (wyldraven.deviantart.com)
Cover Design by Mike Montemarano (mikemontemarano.com)

ISBN-13: 978-1541048607

ISBN-10: 1541048601

This book is dedicated to my mom, dad, and brother, who have always supported me in any creative endeavor I undertake.

Table of Contents

*

By the early 1500's, European Christians were killing each other at an unprecedented rate in the name of religion. This was the age of the Protestant Reformation and the Catholic Counter-Reformation. And while across the ocean in North America witch-hunts were gaining traction, in certain parts of Europe the focus was often on a far different target – werewolves.

This story depicts one such actual werewolf investigation and trial —a particularly infamous one that took place in Germany, the birthplace of Martin Luther and the Protestant Reformation.

So although some characters and events are fictional, the subject matter is not.

*

PART I

The Case of Dorothea Gabler

CHAPTER ONE

HEINRICH

1588 — Near the town of Bedburg, Germany

It had been some time since Investigator Heinrich Franz had inspected a murder scene, and he relished the opportunity. As he removed his black gloves to inspect the body, a tingle ran down his spine.

The victim's body was situated near a tree, tucked away from any trails or passing eyes.

"Our killer wanted to make it difficult to identify the victim, but not to find her," Heinrich said to his right-hand man and bodyguard, Tomas.

He crouched over the body. Her exposed entrails had been dragged around the trunk of the tree, separating her legs from her torso. Her right foot was missing three toes, and her left arm was missing altogether. Her mangled face was a canvas for flesh-eating insects. He could only tell the victim was female by the tattered blue dress she wore and the stringy blonde hair plastered against her head.

Heinrich glanced at the dress. *Maybe it will help to identify her,* he thought, and then looked at her face. *Because that certainly won't.*

Heinrich prodded beneath the dress, but found no signs of defilement. The stench of decay was not yet overwhelming, but still strong enough to offend his keen nose.

"She's been dead for less than twenty-four hours," the investigator said. He turned to the frightened farmer standing behind him. "And you found her when?"

"This morning, sir." The farmer held a grimy cap close to his chest. "I was walking my dogs when the wind brought her smell right to me. Then I saw crows circling—"

"I didn't ask *how*," Heinrich said, "just *when*."

The investigator circled the tree and bent down to examine the torso with a magnifying glass. Flies and maggots crawled over her body and through her deep cuts. Heinrich put a finger to one of her small, exposed breasts. It was cold and clammy.

"She was killed in broad daylight, sir?" the farmer asked.

Heinrich ignored the man. He pocketed his magnifying glass, stood up with creaking knees, and wrestled his hands back into his gloves. "Judging by the size of her breasts and feet, I'd say she was no more than fifteen years of age."

"Just a child," the farmer murmured. He started fidgeting with his cap, and then stammered. "There wouldn't perhaps be any kind of . . . *reward* for finding the body, would there, sir?"

Heinrich gave the man an icy glare and spat on the grass. *Heartless swine,* he thought, shaking his head. *Trying to profit on the death of a child.* He started pacing in front of the farmer, and then stroked his chin and twirled his thin, wispy mustache. He stared at the man's fat, doughy face. He was middle-aged, with a patchy gray beard. His eyes were soft, and he looked harmless, but Heinrich knew that appearances never made the man, nor told the whole story.

"The real question I have," Heinrich said, "is what was a young girl doing out here alone, so far from any roads?"

"Perhaps she was lured here?"

The investigator eyed the farmer. "A fine observation," Heinrich said with a disingenuous smile. Then it vanished. "My next question is what were *you* doing out here so far from the trails?"

The farmer scratched his scalp, and then his face slowly distorted and his mouth fell open. He stammered some more. "Y-you can't believe that . . . that *I* . . ." he trailed off. "I told you, sir, I was leading my dogs—"

Heinrich nodded and Tomas came to the farmer's side and grabbed his arms. The farmer shouted and squirmed and tried to break free.

"You can't do this, sir! I came to you only trying to help!"

Yes, trying to help your purse.

Tomas looked pale and queasy as he wrestled with the farmer.

"Take him to the jail," Heinrich ordered. "I'll be by a bit later. Find out whatever you can."

Tomas nodded and turned away.

"And Tomas," Heinrich added. The soldier spun on his heels, and Heinrich stared into his eyes. "Whatever means necessary."

Tomas nodded again. "What are your thoughts, sir?"

Heinrich sighed and put his hands on his hips. "I'm thinking the Werewolf of Bedburg has returned."

The search for the Werewolf of Bedburg had gone cold over the previous two years. Prior to that, the terrible beast rampaged across the German countryside for a decade, unopposed.

When he vanished, no one knew why.

There hadn't been any definitive sightings since. Sometimes a peasant clamoring for fame would claim to have seen the beast, and it would stoke the flames of fear around Bedburg all over again. But these sightings were always unfounded—Protestant minorities trying to scare Catholics, or the other way around.

This latest discovery, however, could not be ignored. In the past, Heinrich had seen wounds as grotesque as those on the latest victim.

Finally, the hunt was on again, and Heinrich felt the hair stand on the back of his neck.

He made his way back to the town of Bedburg, and decided to postpone his interrogation until the morning, to let the farmer stew in the dank cellars of the jail for a while.

The investigator decided to stop in at the local tavern on the east side of town. He meandered through the muddy roads of

Bedburg until he came to a stone building with a brick-tiled roof. As he arrived, the sun was setting behind the trees to the west. He opened the front door and was greeted by a stale wave of heat across his face.

Inside, the place was bustling. Travelers and peasants and tradesmen alike sat at circular wooden tables, drinking, laughing, and telling stories to each other as they ogled the passing bar wenches.

A large hearth was lit on the left wall, and the bar was located opposite the hearth. Heinrich took a seat at the bar, next to a broad-shouldered man. He took off his gloves, rubbed his eyes, and ordered a mug of ale. Within seconds of sitting, a short-skirted, redheaded girl with freckles dotting her nose sashayed over to him and gave him a coy smile. She opened her mouth to speak, but Heinrich waved her off before any words came out. She frowned and stormed off to a nearby table.

"If you don't take her, I might have to."

Heinrich faced the big man sitting next to him. He had a leathery face, and a long, dark beard. His tunic was ragged, and he had scars on his thick arms. The most telling sign was his eyes—the hardened eyes of a man who had seen many horrors in his life. Heinrich deduced that the man was a soldier.

"Have at her," the investigator said.

The man let out a raspy, rumbling noise that sounded somewhere between a laugh and a battle cry. He took a large pull from the mug in front of him, belched, and then stuck out his hand. "Georg Sieghart," he said.

Heinrich paused, stared at the man's bear-like hand, and noticed an iron ring around his fourth finger. He took Georg's hand—the man had an iron grip—and said, "Heinrich Franz." Then, with his chin, he gestured to the ring on Georg's hand, and then to the redheaded girl nearby. "What would your wife think of that?"

A smirk formed beneath Georg's long beard, and he shrugged. "She wouldn't mind. Haven't seen her in some time."

He looked at Heinrich's hands, noticed a similar ring, and

said, "Is that why you resist the temptation of a good time?"

"You could say that."

Georg lifted his mug. "To chivalry," he said with a smile.

Heinrich bumped mugs with the man and took a large gulp. "Have you just returned from warring?"

Heinrich spoke of the Cologne War, which had ravaged the state for nearly seven long years.

"How did you know?"

"It's my job to know. You haven't seen your wife for some time, and you sit like a soldier."

Lines formed on Georg's forehead. "How does one *sit* like a soldier?"

Heinrich looked Georg up and down. "Slumped shoulders, but still with a disciplined posture. You hold your mug with both hands, as if it's going to run away, and your eyes dart around, looking for the nearest threat."

Georg frowned. "You've known me for two minutes, and you gathered all that? What are you, a Protestant spy?"

Heinrich looked over his shoulder and then leaned in conspiratorially. "I'm the chief investigator of Bedburg," he said in a low voice.

Georg frowned. After a moment, he grinned, and then he clapped Heinrich hard on the back and let out another deep belly rumble. "Well, Investigator Franz, you are only half right. I *was* a soldier, but not any longer."

"Wounded? Discharged?"

Georg finished his ale, and then he leaned close to Heinrich. "Deserter," he said with a straight face. "But don't tell your boss."

Heinrich couldn't be sure if the man was being serious. "And you're Catholic?"

"Of course. Born Jesuit. But I've killed enough Calvinists and Lutherans to last a lifetime. The Protestants may be heretical bastards, but from what I've seen and done, I'm not too sure we're much better."

Heinrich leaned back in his stool, somewhat startled at

Georg's bluntness. "Those words can get you killed around here."

Georg stared at Heinrich and frowned. "Should I be worried you're goin' to squeal on me, Investigator Franz?"

Heinrich paused. Then he smiled and patted Georg on the back. He decided he liked this man. *We need more people like him—not afraid to say what they mean—men with conviction.* "No," he said. "We need people with spines like yours. Our country is being overrun by gutless sods and weasels."

"That doesn't sound very Catholic of you, Investigator Franz."

Heinrich eyed the large man. "Who said I was Catholic?"

Georg's face lost its color. It wasn't until Heinrich began chuckling that Georg's face lit up. The big man grinned and said, "What are you investigating?"

"I'm trying to find the Werewolf of Bedburg."

"Ah. I heard the beast has returned."

"How? The newest victim was just found today."

"It's my job to listen," Georg said with a wink. He stood from his chair, stretched his thick arms, and groaned. "Word travels fast." He gave Heinrich another hard slap on the shoulder, and then began to walk toward the door of the tavern. "Have a good night, investigator."

Heinrich looked over his shoulder and called out, "What are you here for, Georg Sieghart?"

When the big man reached the door, he turned and had a mischievous grin on his face. "You're here to *find* the werewolf? Well, I'm here to kill him."

CHAPTER TWO

GEORG

Georg strolled half-drunkenly to an inn near the tavern. As he clomped through the muddy roads, he looked up and smiled at the yellow moon that lit up the cloudless sky. The usual commotion of horses and people was replaced by an eerie silence. The townsfolk stayed indoors and shuttered their windows, frightened of the news that a killer had returned to their town.

As he stumbled along, Georg wondered if he'd said too much to the investigator. In hindsight, he realized it wasn't smart to blab about deserting his military post to a complete stranger.

It's the alcohol's fault.

Georg also couldn't tell if the man was being truthful when he said he was the chief investigator for the lord of Bedburg, Lord Werner. If he was telling the truth, then Georg figured he'd see more of Heinrich Franz in the future. Also, it meant that the investigator would be his rival in the search for the killer.

Since leaving the army, Georg had followed the werewolf's bloody trail, first from the city of Cologne, and then west, to Bedburg. He thought he was closer to finding the beast than anyone else was, but then the murders stopped happening, and the trail went cold.

Now everything had changed.

He came to the small inn and wandered inside. A crackling fire warmed the lobby, and an elderly clerk stood near the far wall. Next to the clerk was a staircase that led up to the bedrooms.

"Claus," Georg said with a nod.

"Welcome back, Herr Sieghart. Find what you were looking for?"

"Always and never," Georg said, and shrugged. He disappeared up a staircase and went to his small room. When he plopped himself on his hard cot, his brain started swirling.

I'll need to find more work if I'm going to pursue this beast, he thought, laying his head down. *And I'll need . . .* he started, but darkness found him before he could finish his thought.

He had a horrible dream that night—the same nightmare he'd had nearly every night over the last few months. It always started differently than the time before, but always ended the same.

This time, he was in a dark village. Owls hooted from nearby trees. The rank odor of burning hair, wood, and flesh reached his nose. It lingered like an unwanted lover. He could hear screaming and shouting coming from nearby houses.

This was a Protestant village, and the people here were poor farmers and peasants. More importantly, these people worshiped the teachings of Martin Luther.

Georg fought for the city of Cologne and for the Catholic prince-elector, Archbishop Ernst of Bavaria. He was joined by Spanish troops, and the poor Protestants in this village were his enemies.

Men and women and children burned, and their death-woes pierced the sky as ashes billowed and choked the night air. Many of the women were burned as witches—without trial or proof—and their children were killed for being spawned from demons. The men were forced to watch their women being raped by the Spanish soldiers, before their own throats were cut. The bodies piled high. Then, to scare off other reformers, the village itself was razed.

Then the dream took a familiar turn.

Georg was ordered to kill a mother and an infant she carried.

There could be no witnesses to this awful, senseless massacre. Georg hesitated. Staring at the horrified mother, he was reminded of his own wife and unborn child. *What crimes could these two possibly have committed? Why must they die?*

And just before swinging his blade, the nightmare adjusted to his life at home, returning from the war, and the horrors he found there . . .

Georg jolted awake with a gasp. He was covered with thick sweat. He looked outside his small window and saw that the sun was rising. He decided he'd attend early Mass to try and find solace from his perpetual nightmares.

Hunting the werewolf had become the only escape from the life he once led. But sleep brought out the worst in him, as if God was telling him that he'd never be forgiven for the atrocities he'd committed.

After a quick meal of boiled eggs, Georg left the inn and headed to the nearby church. The early risers were preparing for their hard day ahead. Men pushed wheelbarrows to and from the farmlands, and cattle were set to graze the pastures. People kept to themselves.

The church was located in the center of town, easily accessible for all. It was one of the grandest structures in Bedburg, and had a huge, golden cross fixated on its pure-white gable, and a stained-glass front door.

People of all sorts attended Mass: old women trying to find answers for their sickly children; starving farmers; worried soldiers. Usually, Bishop Solomon ran the morning Mass. He was an old, Roman Catholic parish leader who gave enthralling sermons, issued indulgences, and gave confessions to the congregation. But today, a young man—no more than twenty years old—took his place.

The priest was Father Dieter Nicolaus. He had short-cropped hair, a black cassock, and a friendly, smiling face. His sermons were delivered in a calm demeanor, without the spitfire rhetoric or flying hand gestures that were trademarks of Bishop Solomon.

After saying opening prayers, Father Nicolaus gave a sermon about the evils of false prophets—such as Martin Luther—and of the murder from the day before.

"Remember, brothers and sisters, Satan comes to us in many forms—hidden, as he were, in the dark fur of a cowardly beast. A killer. A creature of the night, fueled by black magic. The poor girl from yesterday has been identified as a good, pious Catholic. Don't let her terrible death falter your belief in God. Let it strengthen your resolve. For He is everywhere."

The priest put his hands on the pulpit in front of him and cleared his throat. "The Protestant devil seeks to destroy good Catholics by any means necessary. In this case, he's sent us a terrible message: Believe in our evil teachings, or a horrible death will befall you. But do not fear, brothers and sisters. We will fight on, we will find this *beast*, and we will defeat him. God will show us the way. We will find our way through this tragedy, as we have before, and we will prosper in His glory!"

With his final proclamation, the congregation cheered and hollered. The speech seemed to give the scared townsfolk a renewed sense of faith. The smart priest had managed to link the murder of a young girl with the supposed tyrannies of Protestant practices. Georg wondered if the Lutherans and Calvinists spouted similar ideas—that the werewolf was an instrument of God, sent to punish the Catholics for their choice of faith.

After his sermon, Father Nicolaus shook the hands of his people, and then Georg walked up to him. "A riveting sermon, Father Nicolaus."

"Thank you, my son."

Georg was somewhat irked by a man half his age calling him *son*, but he let it go. "I was wondering if I might have a quick word?" he asked. "Nightmares have haunted me for too long, and I was hoping you could help me."

"Absolutely," the priest said. "Come to the confessional."

Georg followed Father Nicolaus to the back of the nave, and entered the booth. "Bless me father, for I have sinned," he began.

"How long has it been since your last confession?"

"Four months."

"And what would you like to confess?"

"I've killed many people in the name of God—innocent people. It has made me weary and detached from my faith. My family is gone. Can God still love me after all I've done?"

After a short moment of silence, the priest spoke. "A crisis of faith is common in every man, my son. Remember that God is everywhere, and He loves everyone. Obedience and perseverance are cornerstones of our faith. If you repent, He will forgive. The war you fight is a war on God, and you fight on the side of the righteous. Never forget that."

Georg nodded and let the words mull over. He was told to recite the Hail Mary prayer ten times, and then he thanked the priest and left the church.

CHAPTER THREE

DIETER

Father Dieter Nicolaus clasped his hands behind his back and watched as Georg Sieghart left the church. Then he turned and noticed a woman dressed in a habit and veil standing next to him. The nun was a middle-aged woman with a stern face. Her hands were folded near her stomach, and she was frowning beneath her white veil.

"Sister Salome," Dieter said, bowing to the nun.

"Father." The nun kept her eyes on Georg Sieghart as the big man walked through the stained-glass doorway, out into the sunny morning.

"I hope that man returns to Mass. He is a troubled man, with a troubled soul," Dieter said.

"A common sight in these troubling days," Sister Salome added.

"Indeed." Dieter stroked his chin, and faced Salome. "But he has a different air about him than most. He is not anxious, just conflicted. I'd like to learn more about Georg Sieghart. Where does he come from? What are his ambitions?"

"Do you believe he's a threat to the congregation, Father?"

Dieter was shaking his head before Sister Salome finished her sentence. "No, no, nothing like that. But I know every person who attends Mass—from the innkeeper to the tailor's son—yet I know nothing of him."

Sister Salome bowed and stared at the tiled floor. "I will find out what I can, Father."

The nun shuffled away toward the back of the nave, and disappeared down a hallway. Dieter followed her down the hallway, walked past her, and came to a large, oaken door. He knocked on the thick door, and a voice from inside said, "Come."

Inside, an elderly man with a sagging face and feathery, white hair around the crown of his head sat behind an elegant table. The man wore a purple sash over his black cassock, and a large cross hung from his neck. He scribbled on parchment, and didn't bother to look up from his desk as Dieter entered.

When no introduction was forthcoming, Dieter said, "Your Grace, I would like to speak with you."

"So what's keeping you?" the old man asked, still writing.

"It is about my sermon—"

"A very eloquent sermon."

"W-well, thank you, but it was quite uncomfortable, too."

Bishop Solomon sighed and finally looked up at the priest. His eyes were graying, his back was hunched, and his cheekbones were leathery and pocked from age. "What was uncomfortable about it? You aren't there to hold the hands of the people. In times such as these, it takes some words of distress to stir the townsfolk."

Dieter rubbed his temples. "I suppose this was different because I've paired tragedy against those we disagree with. It doesn't seem right."

Bishop Solomon snorted and said, "It is *very* right, my son. This attack was surely the work of Protestant monsters. Do you not find it odd that the killing comes just as the Cologne War slows to a crawl?"

The bishop stood from his chair. The bones in his body creaked as he came to his feet. Resting one hand on his table for support, he said, "We are winning this war, Dieter, and our enemies are trying to propagandize this tragedy to justify their own perverse, heretical agenda."

Dieter couldn't believe what he was hearing. *Does this man truly believe that?*

The priest cleared his throat and tried to find the right words. They came a moment later. "But do you really think a *werewolf* is the source of this girl's death? Has anyone ever *seen* one of these monsters?"

"I've seen the bodies of the victims, Dieter, and not just this girl's. No man could have inflicted such terrible wounds, by God's mercy." The bishop made the sign of the cross in the air. "And there have been witnesses, trials, executions. Yes, I very much believe that there is devilry at work here. And it is not your job to doubt . . ." the bishop trailed off, and then stared straight at Dieter with his piercing gray eyes. "Tell me, do you believe in God?"

Dieter scrunched his face. "Of course, Father. What kind of question—"

"And have you *seen* him before? In the flesh?"

Dieter opened his mouth to speak, but then closed it when he noticed Bishop Solomon's scowl.

"Well, what's your answer, Dieter?" the bishop asked. He didn't wait for a reply, but instead raised a finger to the sky. "Your job is to relay God's message to the laymen, and to offer guidance. Don't forget that."

Dieter wanted to say something—to argue—but he bit his tongue. He thought that comparing werewolves to God in the way Bishop Solomon had was a fallacy. But he also knew better than to argue with his superior.

The bishop waved off Dieter with a skeletal hand, and then he sat back down. He picked up his quill and looked down at his parchment. "Go to the market and feed the poor, my son. Clear your mind of this, and please don't come back with this nonsense again. Despite your vanity, you will preach the sermons that God wishes you to."

You mean the sermons that you *wish me to.* Dieter clenched his jaw and stared at the top of Bishop Solomon's head. Anger welled inside, but he managed to say, "Yes, Father." Then he spun on his heels and left the chamber. He went to the altar at the back of the nave, gave a short prayer, and then stormed past the pews and out of the church.

Outside in the cool morning, Dieter's frustration quickly subsided. Though the bishop's words stung—comparing Dieter's skepticism about the werewolf with a lack of faith—he was a man of the cloth, and not one to hold grudges.

Perhaps the bishop is right—do not doubt what you do not know. Dieter wanted to know the identity and motivations of the Beast of Bedburg just as much as anyone. He hoped those things would eventually come to light, but knew he needed to be patient in the meantime.

As the Bible taught that God worked in mysterious ways, it also taught that Satan was perverse—he brought evil and monsters into the world, and drove men mad with lust and depravity. The killings around Bedburg and Cologne over the last few years were proof of that. The entire war between the Catholics and Protestants was proof of that.

So much senseless death, Dieter thought. *And for what?*

As he ruminated, Dieter made his way from the church, down a small hill, and headed toward the heart of Bedburg. The sun seared the early morning fog and its rays burst through the clouds. Dieter marveled at the grand sight. Smiling, he passed by several tradesmen and farmers, and nodded to each one of them. Most of them returned with a nod of their own.

Dieter felt great satisfaction in his familiarity with the people of Bedburg. But as he made his way into the center marketplace of town, he saw someone whom he *did not* recognize.

While the farmers were setting up their tents of grain and fruits and vegetables, and the tradesmen set up their wares, and the butchers shouted their prices for their fresh meats, *she* stood out from all of them.

She was a beautiful girl in a pristine white gown, with curly hair the color of the sun, and fair skin that made her look angelic. She carried herself with grace and elegance, and Dieter stopped moving when he laid eyes on her. In a place full of dirty peasants—hands blackened from hard labor, tunics crusted with week-old filth—she seemed so out of place. She was a diamond in a field of coal, and Dieter was shocked that he'd never seen her before.

The girl skipped over to a fruit vendor and looked into a crate of apples, then rummaged through the crate, squeezing each one. Dieter felt the urge—the *desire*—to speak with her. As a shy priest and a man of God, he couldn't ever remember feeling that need before. And it happened so fast.

Dieter found himself walking in her direction before his mind realized what it was doing. He couldn't control his legs. His robe swept the dirty ground as he neared her, and he almost tripped over his own feet.

Once beside her, he cleared his throat. "H-hello, young lady."

The girl faced him. She smiled and had big, sad eyes. Dimples formed on her cheeks as she smiled, and Dieter's heart could have stopped right then and there.

"Good day, Father," she said, and curtsied.

"May I?" Dieter motioned toward the apple she held. His hands fidgeted as he reached out.

The girl was slightly taken aback, but then she nodded. "Of course."

Dieter felt the apple and stared into her blue eyes. She was probably no more than sixteen years of age. "You don't want this one," he said, and placed the apple back in the crate. He poked around for a moment and found two apples that felt firm. He handed them to the girl and said, "These two will do," and smiled. "They're just ripe enough."

"Thank you," she said. Her hand grazed Dieter's as she took the apples, and the hair on the priest's arm stood on edge. "You are very adept at apple-picking."

Dieter felt his face turn as red as the fruit he'd just handed over. "Er, well, I must be . . . for my vocation," he stammered, and immediately felt stupid for saying it. Then he gained his composure and cleared his throat again. "In fact, I was just about to go feed the less fortunate. Would you like to accompany me?"

The girl raised her eyebrows. "What a coincidence. I was just headed to do the same."

Dieter paid for the apples for the girl, and then the two walked to a grain-seller and bought two loaves of brown bread. They walked toward the southern outskirts of town, side by side.

"My name is Dieter Nicolaus," the priest said as they walked down the muddy road.

The girl held folds of her white dress in her hands, so the edges wouldn't drag in the dirt. "I'm Sybil Griswold," she said with a shy smile. "Pleased to meet you, Father Nicolaus."

Coming to the edge of town, Dieter and Sybil saw poor and homeless citizens gathering for their morning soup-and-bread routine. The southern end of town—near the farmlands—was where the unluckiest people in Bedburg stayed: the homeless, the mind-addled, the weak, and the decrepit.

When the poor folk saw a girl in a white gown and a man in a black cassock headed in their direction, with food in their hands, it must have seemed like a miracle. Dieter and Sybil were immediately swarmed and surrounded by tens of groaning, aching townsfolk. They all reached out and tried to touch and take the food, but Dieter organized them into a line. He was used to this process, and it made his heart and soul swell whenever he could help the people. Of course, he'd never done so with a beautiful angel by his side.

Within minutes, the food was all gone, and the poor folk dispersed. While handing out the bread, however, Dieter learned much about Sybil.

She was the daughter of a well-to-do farmer, living just outside town. "Not far from where we are, in fact," she'd said. Dieter could hardly believe it, seeing as that she looked like a queen's daughter.

She was also sixteen years old—as he'd guessed—four years younger than he.

"Why have I never seen you in church before?" Dieter asked as he handed out the last chunks of bread. "I would surely recognize your face."

Sybil looked to the ground. "My father doesn't attend church, so I don't either. We're usually working the land while Mass takes place. Today he let me go into town for a treat because this season has been good to us."

"Even on holidays? Specials occasions?"

Sybil shrugged.

Dieter frowned. "Does your father work you hard?"

Sybil had a blank look on her face. "Not any harder than the other boys and girls."

"And boys?"

Sybil glanced at Dieter. "What of them?"

"A pretty girl like you—you must have them lining up at your door."

Sybil shook her head profusely and blushed. "No, no, father doesn't allow that," she said, turning away.

Dieter stared at Sybil with a stern look in his eye. He decided that he would have to meet her father. He could tell that Sybil felt uncomfortable talking about him, and Dieter wanted to find out why. Not that it was any of his business, but he felt compelled, for some reason.

After handing out blessings to the poverty-stricken folk, Dieter offered to walk Sybil home. He didn't want her walking alone, and her farm wasn't far from town. She accepted, and before long they were in the grassy, hilly countryside.

Sybil's estate was huge, and standing outside the front door of her house was a middle-aged man with his arms crossed over his chest, looking quite displeased.

CHAPTER FOUR

SYBIL

Peter Griswold frowned and said, "Go inside, Sybil." He was a stout man with a deep voice. His skin was dark and leathery from years of laboring in the sun. He was also missing his left hand.

"But father—"

"Inside, young lady."

Sybil groaned and stormed past her father. She looked over her shoulder and took one last glance at Father Nicolaus before disappearing into the house.

The interior of the house was built of stone and wood. Besides the main cooking room, there were four separate chambers: two small rooms where Sybil and her younger brother slept, Peter's larger quarters, and a small washroom.

Sybil's brother, Hugo, poked his head out from behind his door. "Are you in trouble, Beele?" he asked. He was an irreparably shy eleven-year-old, with a shaggy head of brown hair and big, almond-shaped eyes.

Sybil faced him and smiled warmly. "No, Hue, everything is fine." Despite his nervousness, Sybil loved the boy more than anyone else in the world.

When she heard muffled voices coming from outside, she crept up to the front door and put her ear to the wood. Sybil knew her father was a stern man, and she hoped Peter wouldn't be too hard on the priest. Father Nicolaus seemed like a kind, gentle soul.

"What do you think you're doing, priest?" she heard her father say.

"Sir, it's not safe for a girl to walk home alone. You should know that. Have you not heard of yesterday's murder? A girl younger than your daughter was found dead, not far from here," Father Nicolaus said.

Murder? Sybil thought. Her heart started to race. She knew she lived a sheltered life, *But how have I not heard of such a thing?*

"I will take care of my daughter," Peter said.

"You can't protect her when you aren't *with* her," Father Nicolaus snapped. A long pause followed. "Look, sir, I am a man of God," the priest began again, calmly. "We fed the poor and I walked her home. There was no ill intent." Another pause, and then, "Are you a man of God, sir?"

Sybil could hear her father groan, and then he must have decided to stay quiet.

Father Nicolaus spoke again. "Are you a Protestant?"

"No," Peter said, "of course not. My family wouldn't last a day in this town if that was the case."

"So why have I never seen your family at Mass?"

"What I do with my family is none of your business, priest. I don't answer to you—"

"No, you only answer to God, as we all do. Don't you want to save your soul?"

Peter scoffed. "I'm busy trying to teach my children work ethic and the realities of life. We have no time for God in our daily work."

Sybil gasped and put a hand over her mouth. Even *she* knew what a bad thing that was to say to a priest.

Father Nicolaus sounded undeterred. "We all have time for God, Herr Griswold. He is all around us, after all. If I see your family at Mass in the coming days—which I hope to see—let's see if I can't change your mind about giving glory to God, even in your day-to-day routine."

Peter grumbled a few more times, and it seemed as though the

20

conversation was coming to an end. Sybil sprinted away from the door and into the living quarters, where she sat down on a chair and grabbed a spindle and thread.

A moment later, Peter stomped into the house. He put his hands on his hips and glared at Sybil. After a long moment, he asked, "Where did you meet him?"

"At the marketplace," Sybil said. "He helped me pick out apples."

"I want you to stay away from that boy."

Sybil's eyes narrowed. "He's not a *boy*, father. He's a kind, harmless man, and a priest."

"No man is harmless—not even a priest—especially not when my daughter is involved. You don't see the way men look at you, Sybil, because you're young."

Sybil stood from her chair, crossed her arms over her chest and stuck her nose up at her father. "He was just being nice. It isn't like he was trying to court me."

The air seemed to leave Peter's lungs, and he pointed a thick finger toward his daughter. "Don't even say that word . . . *court*."

Sybil threw her arms in the air. Her voice raised an octave as she said, "I'm not a little girl anymore! I can't stay here forever, and you can't protect me forever!"

"You'll stay here as long as I say."

Sybil tried to stay angry, but then her bottom lip began to tremble. She looked down at the ground.

Peter walked over to her and put a hand on her slender shoulder. He kneeled beside her, so they were at eye level. He tried to soften his voice and said, "Beele, I'm your father. It's my job to protect you. You don't know the terrible things that men are capable of, especially to a beautiful girl such as yourself. I would be lost if anything ever happened to you. You know that, right?"

Sybil nodded as tears welled in her eyes. "Is that why you lied, then? To protect me?"

Peter's neck jerked back.

"You lied and said we weren't Protestants. Why?"

Peter scratched the back of his head with his only hand. "So you were eavesdropping," he said with a sigh. "There are things you don't understand about the world—"

"Then make me understand!"

"Our people are not safe here, Beele!" Peter snapped. "Don't you see why we hardly ever venture into town? The Catholics hate us, they're winning the war, and they control the town. A few years ago it wasn't like that, but now it is, so we must be discreet."

"Father Nicolaus doesn't hate me," Sybil said in a low voice, still pouting with her arms crossed.

"Father Nicolaus doesn't know you. And he surely doesn't know you're a Protestant."

"No, but he knows we don't go to church. Can't he assume why?"

"He can't do anything without proof," Peter said. He stood to his full height. "Now, come, enough of all this. Let's start dinner, and tomorrow we'll begin the day fresh."

As he walked away, Sybil kept her eyes on him. She was a curious and observant girl, and she could tell by his body language that there was something else nagging at her father.

Why doesn't he mention the murder that Father Nicolaus spoke of? He says he wants to protect me, but isn't that something I should know about?

CHAPTER FIVE

HEINRICH

Karl Achterberg howled in agony as the fifth fingernail from his right hand was forcibly removed with rusty pliers. The farmer whimpered and collapsed to the ground, clutching his hand. Blood seeped through his fingers and down his forearm. He pissed himself, and the urine pooled at his feet.

The torturer, Ulrich, was a big man with a purple scar running down half his face. He grinned, seeming to take a grim satisfaction in his work.

"Wipe that smile off your face," Heinrich said to the punisher.

Ulrich frowned. "Is it so wrong to take pride in what I do, investigator?"

Heinrich shook his head. He'd kept the farmer in jail over night. Now it was morning, Heinrich was a bit hung over, and the man's screeching was giving him a piercing headache.

While Heinrich had been imbibing with his new acquaintance—the huntsman Georg Sieghart—a distraught mother had come to the coroner's chambers. She recognized the dead girl's tattered blue dress and identified her as Dorothea Gabler, the woman's daughter. Then she promptly fell unconscious at the grotesque sight of her beloved child. Dorothea was fourteen years old, and the daughter of two tailors.

Her mother had no idea why Dorothea would have been so far out in the countryside—their home was near the town.

The girl had gone missing two nights ago. Heinrich figured she was killed last morning, and discovered that afternoon by the farmer, Karl Achterberg.

Heinrich was certain that this farmer knew more than he was letting on. The interrogation had gone on throughout most of the morning, however, and Karl hadn't said much. The investigator contemplated using more severe interrogation techniques, as removing fingernails was more painful than permanent, and not very efficient in this case.

"Tell me something I can use, Karl, and this will all stop. Tell me something, and you can go home to your wife and son."

The heavyset farmer glared at Heinrich with a look of horror, as if wondering how the investigator knew of his family. He whimpered.

"Very well," Heinrich sighed. "Tomas?"

Heinrich's right-hand man walked into the cell. He tugged at a rope, and two large hunting dogs were led into the room, leashed together.

"Your prized hounds, Karl. If I open them up, are you telling me that I won't find the remains of Dorothea's missing left arm in their stomachs?"

Karl sputtered and his jaw dropped. "I . . . please," he began, and trailed off.

When no more words were forthcoming, Heinrich turned to Tomas. "Kill them."

Tomas hesitated and arched his brow at the investigator. Then he unsheathed a knife from his belt and held it to the throat of one of the dogs.

"Wait! Wait!" Karl shouted. "Please, don't kill them! I'll tell you what I know."

Heinrich nodded to Tomas, who sheathed his knife with a sigh of relief.

"Maybe now we'll get somewhere," Heinrich said. He took a seat on a stool in front of Karl.

Karl choked on his own spit and swallowed hard. His bloody hand trembled, and his eyes darted around the room. "There's a man—a neighbor of mine. H-he's a Rhenish farmer. He's quite wealthy and well-known throughout—"

"His name?"

"Peter. Peter Griswold. Some people call him Peter Stubbe behind his back."

"Why?"

"He's missing his left hand. No . . . his right." The farmer shrugged. "He's missing a hand."

Heinrich nodded, crossed one leg over the other, and rested his chin on one of his fists. "Continue."

"He's an evil fellow, my lord. I swear it. He practices black magic and rituals and steals off into the night. I've seen it, as God as my witness, I've seen it!" Karl Achterberg began to sweat from his forehead, brow, and from other unseemly places.

"Where does he go at night?" Heinrich asked, cocking his head to one side.

"I've never followed him, my lord. But he does evil things in his home. Ask around, and you'll see I'm not lying."

"What kinds of *things* does he do, Karl?"

"Evil things."

Heinrich felt his piercing headache return, and he breathed deeply to control his temper.

"He beds his own daughter, my lord," Karl said, as if he noticed the frustration on Heinrich's face.

Heinrich's eyebrows went high. He leaned in toward Karl, his face getting so close that he could smell the farmer's foul breath. "Incest is a grave accusation, Karl. Have you witnessed this act before?"

Karl tried to look away. His eyes darted around some more. "N-no, I haven't, my lord. But I've heard the stories! I'm not the only one who's heard them."

Heinrich breathed hard through his nose and studied the farmer's trembling face—his beady, sunken eyes; his perspiring neck and forehead; his fat, sagging jowls.

After a long pause, Heinrich abruptly stood and turned away

from the man. "Is there anything else I should know about Peter Griswold?"

"O-one more thing, my lord. He secretly follows the teachings of Martin Luther."

Heinrich spun around and faced the farmer again. "A Lutheran, you say? My dear Karl, why didn't you begin with that?" He smiled, turned to his bodyguard, and clapped Tomas on the shoulder. "I believe we should go talk with this man, Tomas. Don't you?"

Tomas nodded. "And what about the dogs, investigator?"

"And what about me?!" Karl whimpered.

Heinrich looked at the punisher. "Lock him up, Ulrich."

"But you said I could go home, my lord! Please, I've told you what I know!" Karl pleaded.

Heinrich ignored the wailing man and walked at a brisk pace out of the jailhouse.

Heinrich ate a quick lunch to ease his headache, and then he and Tomas took two horses from the jail and rode south, toward the farmlands just outside of Bedburg.

It was midday, so they traveled hard and fast down the muddy, winding trails of Bedburg's main thoroughfare. As they reached the edge of town, gray clouds began to swirl overhead. They made their way into the hilly countryside, asked around for directions to Peter Griswold's estate, and found it easily enough.

For a farmer, Heinrich decided, Peter Griswold had a large estate. There was a pasture with grazing cattle, a stable and barn behind the main house, and an extensive field of crops. His nearest neighbors were acres away, to the west and east. Heinrich assumed one of those neighboring estates was Karl Achterberg's.

A man was outside of the main house with a rake in his hand, finishing the day's chores. As Heinrich and Tomas approached, the man stood tall and leaned on the rake. Even from a distance,

Heinrich could notice his left hand—or lack thereof. Heinrich and Tomas dismounted a fair distance away, and led their horses toward the house.

The big man threw down his rake and ambled their way. He stopped them at the edge of his fields, and crossed his arms over his chest. "Can I help you?" he asked, sounding annoyed.

Heinrich took off one of his black gloves and held his hand out. He smiled, and said, "Hello, Herr Griswold. I am Investigator Heinrich Franz, and this is my associate, Tomas."

Peter hesitated, looked at Heinrich's hand as if it carried a disease, and finally took it. His grip was suffocating. "To what do I owe the pleasure, investigator? It's nearly nightfall."

"We are investigating the murder of Dorothea Gabler. I'm sure you heard of her brutal murder from yesterday?"

"Who hasn't," Peter said. "It's a tragedy. Though you said it was the Gabler girl? I didn't know that. Sybil will be devastated."

Heinrich paused and studied the man's face. It was blank—expressionless. "Indeed. Sybil is your daughter, I'm assuming?"

Peter nodded.

"Were they friends?"

"Somewhat. They were close in age."

Heinrich slipped on his black glove and put his hands behind his back. "Well, so that I don't waste your time, I'll get right to it." He cleared his throat. "We have some disturbing news that might implicate you, in some way, to young Dorothea's death."

The farmer's face tightened. "What in God's good graces are you talking about?"

"Well, I've heard that you might be a practitioner of . . . what was it again, Tomas?"

"Black magic, my lord."

"Right. Black magic. I've also heard that you are a follower of Martin Luther, which, as you know, is quite frowned upon these days."

Peter shook his head. "You have some gall to make those accusations, *sir*. Where do you people get off? I don't practice

27

magic—of any kind—and I don't follow Luther, goddammit. That's the second time someone's accused me of that today."

Heinrich put a hand forward. "Please calm down, sir."

"Calm down?" Peter shouted. "Where do you get your lies from? Who is trying to tarnish my good name? I am a loyal citizen of Bedburg, and I have a reputation to uphold."

"Your accuser's identity is part of our ongoing investigation," Heinrich said, looking down at his own boots. "But you said someone else called you a Lutheran today? Who might that be."

Peter opened his mouth and looked to the sky, as if thinking. "Dieter . . . something or other," he said. "The young priest. He walked my daughter home this morning."

Heinrich reached into his tunic and produced a piece of parchment and a quill. On the paper he had written *Dorothea,* and now he drew a line next to the name and wrote *Sybil Griswold—friend,* and *Dieter—priest.*

Peter scratched the stubble on his chin, wrinkled his forehead, and after a long pause he started nodding. "Ah, I see what's going on here."

Heinrich cocked his head to the side. "Sir?"

"This is that slick bastard Karl Achterberg's doing, isn't it?"

Heinrich shared a look with Tomas, but the soldier just shrugged.

"What if it is?" Heinrich pried.

"That goddamn goblin has been after me for as long as I can remember."

"Why is that?"

"Because he thinks I dishonored him," Peter said. "Why would I ever want to mix my land with his tiny farm? He's a disgruntled quack."

Heinrich twirled his wispy mustache in his fingers. "What do you mean by 'mix your land,' sir?"

"He's my neighbor."

"I'm aware."

"With all due respect, investigator, have you been living in a tree?" Peter sighed heavily. "Everyone knows how desperate he was to marry his sod of a son to my beautiful daughter."

Heinrich looked down at his parchment and started writing. "He wanted to arrange a marriage between his son and your daughter? How long ago was this?"

"About a year ago. And yes, with that marriage he'd have been entitled to *half* my farm. That ass. Sybil is far too precious to me, and my family is doing fine without that fool. And now he uses that incident to spout outlandish claims about me. Really, Herr Franz, a practitioner of black magic?" Peter started to chuckle.

Heinrich closed his eyes and frowned. He rubbed his temples and thought, *Goddamn farmers. Did Karl Achterberg really believe he'd be able to frame this man over his petty marriage dispute? I should harvest that man's organs.*

The investigator cleared his throat. "I'm sorry to waste your time, Herr Griswold. But one last question, before we go, if you don't mind. Where were you two nights ago?"

Peter looked past Heinrich and stuck out his lips. "I was at the marketplace with my daughter, 'til late. We were selling some vegetables."

With that, Peter Griswold bid the investigator a good day, and went into his house.

Heinrich watched the farmer enter the house. He caught a glimpse of a fair-skinned, blonde girl peeking from the door as it was closing.

"What do you think about these farmers, Tomas?" Heinrich turned to his bodyguard.

Tomas shrugged. "I don't know, sir, I'm not an investigator."

"Humor me."

Tomas stepped from one foot to the other, and cleared his throat. "I'd say they're stringing you along, my lord."

Heinrich nodded. "I'd say you're right, my good man."

*　　　*　　　*

An hour later, Heinrich was back at the jailhouse, staring at a bloody table of matted fur and intestines. In front of him, Karl Achterberg's hounds were carved open, and Heinrich peered inside their open stomachs.

Since Karl Achterberg had sent Heinrich on a wild chase, the investigator reneged on his deal.

He didn't release the man's dogs.

Unfortunately, it was for naught, as Dorothea Gabler's missing left arm was not in either dog's stomach.

CHAPTER SIX

GEORG

As night fell on Bedburg, Georg Sieghart looked up to the cloudy sky and realized that winter was fast approaching. A cold wind swept through the city, and light rainfall speckled the ground, turning the streets muddy and damp. Georg wrapped his large wool overcoat tightly around his body as he slogged through the roads, sniveling.

Even with the shoddy weather, the big man had a smile on his face for the first time in ages. It was a smile that even rain couldn't wash away. He put his hands in his pockets and felt the cold reassurance of silver coins jingling against each other.

As he neared the tavern for his nightly consumption, the last stragglers of the day emptied the roads and shuttered their doors and windows, preparing for the inevitable storm. Georg rounded a decrepit building and listened to his boots slap against the muddy road. He dipped into an alley with an awning overhead, and was dry for a moment. As he reached the end of the alley, he narrowed his eyes and felt his heart drop to his stomach.

If nothing else, Georg Sieghart was a tracker and a hunter, and he knew when he was being followed.

It was the faint sound of another pair of boots slogging through the mud, slightly out of sync with his own. It came from behind him, at a hurried pace.

Georg made sure not to give himself away. He kept his same stride and stared forward at the wet ground. Then he abruptly changed his course and started zigzagging around buildings, cutting corners sharply.

The wind and rain drowned out the footsteps from behind him, and he rounded the corner of another building and put his back against the wall and nestled his head against the cold stones. He unsheathed a long knife from his belt, and waited with bated breath as his heart thumped in his chest.

After a long moment, the footsteps grew louder.

Then the footsteps stopped, and all Georg could hear was the rain falling against the mud, and his own heart beating faster and faster in his ears. Adrenaline coursed through his veins, and he breathed deeply, three times.

Holding his breath, he leaped out from the corner to face his pursuer, dagger held taut in his hand.

A dark, hooded figure stood motionless at the other end of the building, just ten paces away. He was a small man, but Georg couldn't make out much more than that.

They both stood silent, with the rain dripping down their bodies.

Then the hooded figure jumped away and sprinted off to the left, away from Georg's sight and around the side of the building.

Georg took off running after the man, reached the end of the building, and sidestepped cautiously around the corner.

He was met with nothing: no sword-point waiting to run him through, no hooded figure. It was as if the person had vanished into the rain. More likely, he had disappeared in the maze of labyrinthine alleyways and roads.

Georg's mind raced as he decided if it was worth giving chase. He sighed, waited for another moment, and sheathed his knife. For now, he just wanted a drink to celebrate his day.

He'll know where to find me, Georg thought.

As he walked the rest of the way to the tavern, he couldn't help but glance over his shoulders, eyes darting in all directions. But he didn't see the hooded figure for the rest of the trek.

*　　*　　*

A tidal wave of warm, stale air sailed into Georg's face as he walked into the tavern. The place was already bustling with commotion and lively patrons. On a night when a storm was imminent and the working men didn't want to return to their wives and families, this was clearly the place to congregate.

The fireplace was lit along the left wall, and men surrounded it and rubbed their hands to dry off and warm their bones. The tavern's round-tables were occupied with drunks, and they all seemed to fancy themselves as master storytellers. The barmaids and wenches perused the tables and sat on laps, whispered into ears, giggled at the drunken, stupid jokes, and put up with getting their asses slapped as they walked away.

All in all, it was a regular night at the tavern.

One woman that caught Georg's eye wore a short skirt that showed off her pale thighs, and her corset was wrapped tightly around her slim body. Her fiery red hair bounced on her slender shoulders as she sauntered over to a table of three men.

As if on cue, one of the men slapped her ass as she walked by, and the redhead immediately spun and kicked out viciously, striking her high-heel straight into the man's chest. The man gasped, lost the air in his lungs, and plummeted off his chair, hitting the wooden floor with a thud.

The other two men were taken aback, shocked, and then they quickly broke into a fit of laughter. The fallen man tried to act angry, but he was too flustered, and his friends were laughing too hard, so he just ended up looking embarrassed and ashamed as he struggled to his chair. The redhead said something to the emasculated man, and the man nodded glumly, his eyes cast downward.

Georg had met the redhead the other night, and he'd grown to like her. "Ah, sweet, vicious Josephine," he said to himself, chuckling.

"Are you going to stand in the doorway all night, or are you going to drink? Come on and close the door. It's colder than my mother's tits out there."

Georg turned to the voice, which came from the bar. He

33

smiled. It was the same strange investigator from the night before.

"Ah! It's the spy," Georg said, walking over to the bar with a grin on his face. He slapped the investigator hard on the back, and the thin man coughed. "How are you this evening?"

Investigator Franz controlled his cough, and then looked Georg up and down, as if studying his goofy smile. "I'm assuming not as well as you," he said.

Georg took a seat next to the investigator, reached into a pocket, and slammed a handful of silver coins on the table. "Next round is on me."

Investigator Franz took a sip from his mug, raised his eyebrows, and then made his hands into a steeple on the table. "Ah, empty pockets one day, buying rounds the next. A true soldier of fortune. Where does such fortune spring from?"

"From the well of blood, my friend. Skinned myself three wolf pelts and a pair of antlers today," Georg said with a smile. "So I'm out of poverty—at least for the next few days."

Investigator Franz looked shocked. "You trapped the wolves yourself?"

Georg made a face that seemed to ask, *Is there any other way?* "Of course," he said. "The tanner gave me a fair deal for the hides."

"And you were alone?" The investigator's face was creased with wrinkles. He started twisting his thin mustache. "What about the beast?"

"What about him? What do you think I was out there looking for?"

Heinrich paused, opened his mouth, and then closed it. He raised his mug of ale. "You are a braver man than I, my good hunter."

A moment later, the barkeep, Lars, walked over to Georg and presented him with a mug. His eyes lit up when he saw the silver coins in front of the hunter. Lars was a tall, light-skinned man with short blond hair, and a beard to match. Georg flung the barkeep a silver coin, and Lars went back to his conversation with a stout man sitting on the other side of Investigator Franz.

Georg took a long pull from his mug, belched loudly, and then wiped some drops from his beard. "So, how goes the investigation?"

"I can't talk about that," Heinrich said. "It's ongoing."

Georg shrugged, and both of the men were quiet for a time, people-watching and drinking their drinks.

Obviously wanting to get something off his chest, Investigator Franz finally said, "I've hit a couple dead leads. But I have some others."

Georg wasn't convinced. He smiled, drained the rest of his ale, and said, "How much would I have to pay you to stop chasing the werewolf?"

Investigator Franz frowned and stared at the hunter.

"You are my competition, after all," Georg clarified.

"I can't do that."

"Can't, or won't?"

"Both. I work for Lord Werner, Georg, and can't stop until this . . . *thing* is found and killed." He stopped and looked around the tavern. "Why are you so obsessed with this creature, anyway?" He nodded toward the silver coins sitting in front of Georg. "It seems you can make a good living trapping and hunting."

Georg grunted. "I could make a living, but where's the glory in that? Imagine being the man who butchered the Werewolf of Bedburg. He'd be a hero."

"I plan on being that man," Investigator Franz said.

"Not if I find him first."

Georg could feel the investigator's eyes boring into him. He suddenly felt tired, and he stared down at his empty mug and said, in a low voice, "I have a personal vendetta with the beast, you could say."

Lars walked over and put another drink in front of Georg.

"Ah," the investigator said, "so the truth comes out. A vendetta—how so?"

Georg groaned, and then looked past Investigator Franz. "That Josephine sure is a fiery one, ain't she?"

The investigator turned and gazed at the woman. He shrugged.

Georg stared at another girl, smiled, and then looked at Heinrich "Want me to buy you one of them?" he asked, nudging his chin toward a busty brunette. "My treat. Have a little fun. I've got the money."

"No, that's quite all right. Save your money."

Just then, the big man sitting next to Investigator Franz and conversing with Lars stood from his chair. People turned in his direction when he spoke with a booming voice. "How can you say that, Lars? The man is a staunch Catholic! Sigismund will do great things for Poland. You just watch." He ended his spiel by thrusting a finger toward Lars.

"International politics, how great," Georg muttered to the investigator, shaking his head. King Sigismund III, the newly crowned king of Poland, faced frequent Protestant incursions, and his support amongst the Catholics was a hot topic of debate.

But as Georg drank his ale and minded his own business, Investigator Heinrich Franz suddenly spoke up. "Well, what about Saul Wahl?"

A wave of gasps swept through the tavern, and all eyes were on the big drunk, and Investigator Franz. The angry man looked as though Heinrich had just spit in his mug. "You mean the *Jew*? Saul Wahl, the One-Day King?"

Investigator Franz nodded. "One and the same. Jew or gentile, a man's leadership should not rest on his religion, no?"

Georg put a hand on the investigator's shoulder, and whispered, "Heinrich, I don't think this is a good—"

"And what are you, some blasphemous heathen?" the loud drunk said. "The *pope* is our voice, in polity and sanctity. Anyone who says otherwise is a heretic and a cur, you filthy Jew-lover."

The large man's nose nearly touched the top of Heinrich's head, and his stale breath pushed past the investigator.

"I'm not a Jew-lover," the investigator said, "I am simply a man."

By this point, most of the conversations in the tavern had paused. People were backing away from the two men. The drunk Catholic was twice the weight of the investigator, and nearly a head taller.

"Want to find out how much of a man you are?" the big man asked, cracking his knuckles.

Investigator Franz shrugged and sighed. He started to turn away from the man, and said, "It's no matter—"

And then he was flying to the floor, away from his stool, with ale cascading over his head. The punch sent the investigator crashing to the ground, in a heap.

More gasps came from around the tavern.

The big man drove his foot into Heinrich's side, who was gasping for air and writhing in pain.

Georg's eyes went wide, and he grabbed the nearest hard object: his clay mug. He clenched the mug hard and slammed it into the side of the big man's head. The mug broke into a thousand pieces, and the dazed drunk went slack and flew into a nearby table, sending more mugs crashing to the ground. Ale spilled from the tables like small waterfalls.

Blood seeped from the big Catholic's head, and he was silent. Investigator Franz choked for breath, slowly bringing himself to his knees.

Georg stood between the crumpled Catholic and Investigator Franz, the handle of his clay mug still resting in his raised hand.

Heinrich got to his knees and started to say, "I should arrest you all . . ." but then he broke into a coughing fit.

Georg helped him up by his arm. "No, no, friend," he said. "I think it's best if you get out of here. Sleep it off, eh? You'll be fine in the morning."

Investigator Franz looked dazed, and his eyes were wild with anger. He stumbled into a stool, nearly fell onto another table, and made his way to the door. Before leaving, he declared that, "You're all criminal *fanatics!*" and he pointed at each and every person in the tavern, one by one. "Letting your religious ridiculousness dictate y-your . . . your conscience."

Georg slapped himself on the forehead. He helped push the investigator out of the tavern, and Heinrich went stumbling out into the rain.

When Georg turned to go back in for another drink, the redheaded bargirl, Josephine, was standing in front of him. She glanced at the dazed Catholic man on the ground.

"That man is an asshole," she said.

"Which one?" Georg asked.

Josephine looked up at him. She was prettier than he'd even recognized—sparkling green eyes the color of emeralds, big red lips, soft freckles dotting her nose. She smiled, and dimples formed on her rosy cheeks. "Both of them," she said.

Georg grinned dumbly back at her.

"That was nice of you to protect your friend, lumberjack." She grabbed him by the arm, and ran her soft hand down his rough forearm. "Though it was stupid of him to thrust himself into other people's business."

"He was drunk."

"Well, he should learn his place and not get into fights he can't win."

"I think he believes he can win every fight."

Josephine chuckled. It was a soft, airy laugh—sweet and sour at the same time.

Georg pulled at his beard and shrugged. Then he grinned again. "Yeah, you're probably right."

She nodded toward the stairs at the back of the tavern, and then smiled with her big red lips. "Come on, lumberjack. My business is one that I won't mind you . . . *thrusting* into."

Georg stuttered and stammered and lost all motor control. Josephine led him by the hand, practically dragging him, and they stepped over the dazed, prone Catholic, and vanished up the stairs.

CHAPTER SEVEN

DIETER

The next morning was dreary and gray. Rain kept falling and fog swirled through the streets. Father Dieter Nicolaus expected the weather to deplete his congregation at Mass. He'd become the regular minister, taking the aging Bishop Solomon's place, who seemed increasingly frustrated with life in Bedburg.

The bishop sealed himself away in his lavish chambers for nearly all hours of the day, presumably writing letters to other members of the diocese about the growing discord and insolence of the Lutherans and Calvinists in his city. While they remained subdued and quiet for the most part, the Protestant numbers seemed to be growing, in secret.

For Dieter, it seemed like only a matter of time before some kind of civil revolt took place in town, despite Castle Bedburg being a major hub for Catholic mercenaries in the region. Dieter feared what kind of bloodshed would result from an uprising, and it was his job, he felt, to quell the violent rumors that he heard from his people. He was a man of peace, and it was his duty to pass that notion onto others.

It was becoming harder and harder for the young priest to continue preaching the hate-filled sermons that Bishop Solomon made him preach. If anything, the sermons decrying the Protestants only seemed to strengthen their cause, and made them more rebellious.

There had been peace in Bedburg for nearly a year, but Dieter feared that peace was coming to an end, which is why he decided to reach out to Bishop Solomon before Mass. He hoped to change the old man's thoughts—or at least his public stance—on the hateful sermonizing.

As he walked through the empty church with his hands tucked beneath his robe, a young, shaggy-headed boy—just on the cusp of adolescence—ran out from the hallway that led to the bishop's chambers. The boy's eyes were red-rimmed and cast downward as he stormed past Dieter, toward the doors of the church.

The young adolescent was an altar boy, one whom Dieter recognized. The priest gave the altar boy a concerned look as they passed each other.

What is he doing here so early, before the first light of dawn? Dieter wondered.

Dieter shook his head and turned the corner to the hallway, continuing toward the bishop's chambers. As he turned the corner, Sister Salome was walking toward him, and they both hopped backwards to avoid running into each other.

"Sister," Dieter said with a nod.

"Father," Salome said, a solemn expression on her face. "I have the information you requested."

Dieter cocked his head. "Information?"

"About the hunter, Georg Sieghart."

"Ah, yes. I'd nearly forgotten about him." Dieter hadn't been able to stop thinking about Sybil Griswold over the past day, and it was quite a distraction. As much as he tried, he simply couldn't get her out of his head. "What have you uncovered?" he asked.

"Before he was a hunter, Herr Georg Sieghart was a pikeman and arquebusier in the Spanish Army of Flanders," the nun said. She had her hands clasped behind her back.

"He *looked* as though he had a military background," Dieter said, rubbing his chin. "Where was he stationed?"

"He was a mercenary fighting for the Duke of Parma, Alexander Farnese. He fought in and around Westphalia, and

40

together with Farnese he fought at the Battle of Werl against Martin Schenck, a general of Cologne's former archbishop."

"He fought against the Calvinists?"

Sister Salome nodded. "He was involved in numerous campaigns and battles, and helped raze many Protestant villages—including ones filled with women and children."

Dieter frowned and ran a hand through his hair. He felt somewhat perturbed at Sister Salome's ability to speak about the most disturbing things in such a matter-of-fact way. "So he is troubled for a reason. I can see why he'd question his faith."

"Moreover," Salome continued, "he deserted his army for unknown reasons. Upon returning to his family farm near Cologne, he discovered his wife and unborn son brutally murdered . . . supposedly by the Werewolf of Bedburg."

Dieter sighed. "God have mercy. Do you suppose it's true?"

Salome shrugged.

Dieter narrowed his eyes on the nun. "How did you come about all this information, Salome?"

"Herr Sieghart frequents a tavern, and the barkeep there is a gossipmonger of sorts. Lars, as he's called, will tell you anything for the right price. He says that Georg Sieghart comes to the tavern nearly every night, and when he's drunk enough, he either takes a . . . *lady* to the rooms upstairs, or he leaves to a nearby inn."

"So he enjoys drinking and whoring," Dieter muttered. "Not surprising for such a man."

Sister Salome nodded. "He is a sinner of the flesh, Father."

"And a conflicted sinner, at that." Dieter massaged his temples. "You give me much to think about Sister. Thank you for your hard work." The priest gently put his hand on the nun's shoulder, and Salome nodded and shuffled away.

Before she could get too far, Dieter called out, "One more thing, Sister. Are you sure he's a Catholic? If he deserted his post, can we be sure that he isn't a Calvinist or Lutheran spy?"

"I'm unsure," Salome said. "All I know is that he fought for

Archbishop Ernst of Cologne, in General Farnese's army, and he was a Catholic while under the archbishop's employ."

Dieter nodded, and Sister Salome disappeared around the corner of the hallway. The priest shook his head. *By God, his family was killed by the same beast that ravages Bedburg? How horrific . . . and how coincidental. How can he know it was the same killer?*

Dieter peered around the corner of the hallway and noticed that people were beginning to fill the pews. He'd have to wait for another time to plead with the bishop about changing his sermon's rhetoric.

Despite the dismal weather, Dieter was happy to see that it looked like his church would be full, even though everyone seemed to share a solemn look on their cold, wet faces. It had been three days since Dorothea Gabler's murder, and there seemed to be no leads.

The people are scared, Dieter thought, *and rightly so. They fear for their lives, for their children, for their families. The beast, after all, only seems to target good Catholics. How can I explain that to this congregation? How can I ease their suffering and terror?*

Perhaps the bishop is right. These people need a renewed hope—they need to know what it is they're frightened of.

Dieter squinted and gazed around the room, noticing many familiar faces: the regular tradesmen and farmers who came every morning; the hunter, Georg Sieghart, sitting near the back; the arrogant investigator standing next to Georg, his arms crossed over his chest, a fresh bruise on his face. The investigator and hunter spoke casually with each other, as if they were acquaintances.

Dieter's eyes lit up.

Sybil Griswold walked into the church, albeit without the rest of her family. As the priest looked closely, he noticed something strange about the young woman. Her face was not bright and radiant as before, but instead narrow-eyed, angry, and maybe even sad.

The look alone made Dieter's heart sink.

CHAPTER EIGHT

SYBIL

Before arriving at church, Sybil had been furious as she slogged through the muddy streets. Before the sun's first rays broke through the morning horizon, she sneaked out of her house, despite her father ordering her to stay away from Father Nicolaus.

She knew the consequences of her actions. Her father would be livid that she traveled alone in the morning, and even angrier that she disobeyed him. But she didn't care. She wanted someone to talk to.

How could my own father lie to me? Sybil thought. She understood why he withheld information from Father Nicolaus and the investigator, but why to his *daughter?* She hated being treated like a child and being kept in the dark.

It took three whole days before Sybil learned the victim of the murder was Dorothea Gabler. She cried hot tears, and they mixed with the cold, spitting rain on her face. The sun began its ascent as she neared the church.

Sybil felt she needed to find out why her father was getting so caught up in lies: once to the priest, once to the investigator, and now once to her. *Dorothea was my friend! We grew up as neighbors! I have the right to know what happened to her.*

The religious lies made sense—any Protestant practices were stigmatized within the community, and could ruin Sybil's family. But why had Peter lied to the investigator about being at the market on the day of Dorothea's death?

And why implicate me, by saying I was with him? Doesn't father know that it will only be a matter of time before the investigator realizes that no one can validate his story? And then what?

Sybil sat through Father Nicolaus' sermon with her knees drawn up against her chest. She tuned out much of the sermon, and she felt guilty for it, but her thoughts wouldn't stop swirling around in her head.

Besides, she caught the gist of it: The Protestant devils brought the beast upon the Catholics, to test their faith, during a time when the Catholics needed their faith most of all. They needed to be strong, resilient, and obedient to God.

It was depressing for Sybil. Her people were being demonized for something she had no control over—something she might not even believe in—and she was surrounded by people who leaned on every word Father Nicolaus told them.

I hope he doesn't truly believe the things he's saying . . . they're awful!

This wasn't the same gentle, kind-hearted man she had met at the marketplace.

After the sermon, Father Nicolaus came to Sybil with a warm smile on his face. His smile quickly turned into a frown when he noticed her sad expression.

"Sybil, I'm glad you made it to Mass. Are you well?"

"I am fine," she said with a shy shrug.

"I wish your father and brother would have attended, too."

"I don't think my father would have liked that much. And besides, he doesn't even know I'm here."

"You came without his permission?" Father Nicolaus asked, putting his hands on his hips.

In response, Sybil crossed her arms over her chest. "I am my own woman, Father."

Father Nicolaus began to say something, but then closed his mouth. He smiled, and rested a hand on Sybil's shoulder. "That you are. But it sounds like you didn't enjoy my sermon."

"*Enjoy* is hardly the word I'd use, Father. It was all so . . . harsh, if I'm being honest."

The priest sighed. "I appreciate you being honest, Sybil, and I suppose you're right. I could have toned down the fire and brimstone—"

A big man with a thick, dark beard appeared behind the priest and tapped him on the shoulder. Sybil recognized him from Mass. He had been talking to the investigator before the sermon.

"Father," said the big man, with a throaty voice, "I was hoping for another confession today. My nightmares still haunt me."

Father Nicolaus faced the man. "O-of course," he said, "right this way." Then he turned to Sybil. "If you'll excuse me, my dear."

Sybil nodded, and the priest walked toward the confessional booth, near the altar. The big man followed him.

Sybil gazed around the church, and noticed that most of the congregation had left the building or were busy talking with one another in soft whispers.

In the corner of the room, she noticed the dark-clothed investigator eyeing her.

That must be the same man who visited my father last night.

The man seemed to be inspecting everyone in the congregation, and he was holding and writing on a small piece of parchment.

Sybil stood up and walked to the man with her shoulders held high. The investigator ignored her, until she cleared her throat loudly. "Excuse me, sir," she said. "Are you the investigator who came to visit my home yesterday?"

The tall man had a wispy mustache and a perpetual frown. He had day-old stubble, a purple bruise on the left side of his face, and he looked down his nose at Sybil. "And who are you?"

"My name is Sybil Griswold. I'm the daughter of Peter—"

"Yes, yes, I connected the dots." The investigator's eyes narrowed, and he tucked his parchment inside his tunic. He looked her up and down, this time with a little less condescension in his stare. "My, you are a pretty thing, aren't you?"

Sybil's face flushed, and the man stuck out a gloved hand. Sybil shook it and curtseyed.

"Investigator Heinrich Franz," said the man. He gave her an exaggerated bow, and said, "What can I do for you, Frau Griswold?"

"Well," Sybil began. She felt her throat go suddenly dry and hoarse. "I wanted to t-talk to you, if you could be bothered. I overheard you talking to my father yesterday."

Investigator Franz gave her a humorless smile. "A little eavesdropper, eh? What is it you want to say to me, girl?"

"It's what my father said to you, sir. I don't think he was being entirely truthful, and I want to know why."

The investigator's eyes squinted. "*Why* is a good place to begin, Frau Griswold, for establishing a motive." The investigator continued to smile. "It seems that you'd make a fine detective, young lady. Please, continue."

Sybil's face was still red, and she stared at the tiled floor and started fidgeting. She put her hands behind her back so the investigator couldn't see them. "It's about what he said—about being at the market with me three days ago, before Dorothea's death."

Investigator Franz sat down at the nearest pew and nodded, his curiosity obviously piqued.

"Well . . . he lied. And I know it's not right to lie. We weren't at the market that day."

"Where were you?"

"He was out for most of the day—I'm not sure where."

Investigator Franz rolled his eyes.

"*But,*" Sybil continued, "I was at my farmstead . . . with Dorothea Gabler."

The investigator tried to hide the dark look that overcame him, but it wasn't very convincing to Sybil, who could almost *see* the cogs turning in his mind. "You were with the murder victim?" he asked. His voice became harsher and less cordial, and he reached into his tunic, as if ready to pull out his parchment. "That doesn't bode well with me, Frau Griswold."

Sybil shook her hands in front of her face. "No, no, it's nothing like that. Dorothea was my friend! She was my neighbor. We were playing at my house while my father ran errands. I don't know why he would say otherwise."

Investigator Franz started twirling the ends of his mustache. "People who lie about things, no matter how small the lie, have something to hide, Frau Griswold. So, tell me, is there something your father is trying to hide from me?"

Sybil paused, then slowly shook her head. This was not going how it originally sounded in her mind. "N-no . . . I don't believe so. My father would never harm anyone."

The investigator stared at her, or, rather, *through* her. "Tell me what happened next, my dear. When did Dorothea leave your home? This is important."

Sybil pursed her lips, thinking hard. "She left before sundown. But the odd thing is, as I watched her leave, she didn't go in the direction of her family's estate."

Investigator Franz leaned closer to Sybil's face as he pulled incessantly on his mustache. "Where did she go?" he asked, his voice suddenly sounding giddy with excitement.

"She went toward my other neighbor's homestead." Sybil looked into the investigator's dark eyes. "She was headed toward Karl Achterberg's family farm."

Investigator Franz leaned back in his pew and took a deep breath.

Just then, the front doors of the church swung open with a crash, startling everyone in the room. All eyes turned to a wide-eyed, frantic man with disheveled hair. He looked as though he'd just seen Satan himself.

"Please, God, oh sweet Lord! Come quick! Mercy on me— mercy—someone come! There's been another murder in the countryside!"

CHAPTER NINE

HEINRICH

For the first time, Heinrich felt he had a solid lead on the Dorothea Gabler case. He wasn't sure why Sybil Griswold would come to him with questions about her father, but he attributed it to teenage angst. His head spun as he tried to figure out what it meant that Peter Griswold had lied about his whereabouts during the day of Dorothea's murder.

After he parted with the girl, he drew a triangle on his parchment and wrote the words *Gabler, Griswold,* and *Achterberg* on the points, to signify that the families all lived near each other.

Heinrich, Tomas, and Georg Sieghart took three horses and rode south from Castle Bedburg, into the country and toward the newest crime scene. All the while, Heinrich felt like his brain was trying to leap out of his skull. He tried to create a timeline for the Gabler murder.

If what Sybil said was true, then on the day of the murder, Dorothea and Sybil were together at the Griswold house. Peter Griswold was absent, and he was certainly *not* at the marketplace, as he'd claimed, nor was he with his daughter.

Sybil was also best friends with the murdered girl.

So, what motive would Peter have of killing his daughter's friend, and in such a gruesome way? It doesn't make sense—unless lust was involved.

Lust and depravity are always possibilities in cases like these.

Before sundown, and before she was killed, Dorothea Gabler ventured from the Griswold estate to Karl Achterberg's estate.

Why in the world would she do that? What was her connection with the Achterbergs? There's some familial connection between the Achterbergs, the Gablers, and the Griswolds that I'm missing.

And was Karl Achterberg at home when Dorothea arrived? If not, where was he? Maybe someone in town can shed some light on the farmer's whereabouts.

It appears both Karl Achterberg and Peter Griswold were absent from their respective houses when Dorothea was alone in the country . . .

Heinrich knew that Karl Achterberg and Peter Griswold were not on good terms. That created animosity, but not necessarily a motive for killing Dorothea Gabler, for either of the men.

I need to know more, Heinrich thought, shaking his head. He felt a rush of anger swell within him, because he'd released Karl Achterberg, and now he had no further evidence to arrest him with.

It was Josephine. Her mangled corpse was on display just a few miles from where Dorothea Gabler's body had been found.

As Heinrich looked around the open landscape with his arms crossed over his chest, he asked himself, *What is so special about this location?* The land was hilly and green, with cloisters of trees dotting the horizon. It was a decidedly plain region, but in the distance were woodland areas—possibly where a murderer might choose as a base of operation.

Does one of those woods hide the secret to these killings?

Josephine's body was just as gruesomely damaged as Dorothea's had been. Her red hair was damp and stringy, plastered on her forehead. Her emerald eyes were staring up at the gray sky, horrified looking, and her red lips were parted in a silent scream. Her throat was torn out, but her limbs weren't dismembered like Dorothea's had been. Her half-naked body had been exposed to the rain and wind, giving her skin a shiny, alabaster appearance. A gaping wound around her stomach told an even darker story.

Heinrich kneeled close to the body and removed a glove from his hand. Her skin was ice cold. "She's been dead since last night," Heinrich said.

Georg stood over the body with his head slumped, looking as though he were about to weep. "Poor, poor girl," he mumbled. "She was so sweet. Too sweet for this dark world."

Heinrich continued his analysis. "She's still in one piece, which leads me to believe the murderer was in a hurry this time." Heinrich looked over his shoulder, and noticed a dirt road nearby. "Close to a trail . . . unlike Dorothea. It's as if the murderer wanted her to be found."

"Why?" Georg asked. "Didn't you say the same thing when looking at Dorothea?"

Heinrich shrugged. "Perhaps to make a statement? 'No one is safe out here.' That sort of thing."

Still crouched, Heinrich leaned closer to the body and inspected the most alarming wound: a cavernous hole in her stomach. He gagged when he stuck his head closer—the stench was unfathomable, and her intestines had been removed.

But that wasn't the worst part of the discovery.

Heinrich replaced his glove and his knees creaked as he stood. "I'm afraid," he said with a deep sigh, "that Josephine was pregnant."

Georg gasped, made the sign of the cross over his chest, and turned away from the body. "Oh, Josey. Good God. How can that be?"

Heinrich turned to Georg. "Given her profession . . ." he began, but then cleared his throat when Georg narrowed his eyes. "I'm not sure how far along she was, but the fetus was ripped from her body."

Tomas bent over and vomited on the bloody grass.

Georg threw his hands in the air. "God have mercy. Should we assemble a search party? I could track the infant down."

Heinrich scratched his head. "I'm afraid there's no way a premature infant could have survived the harsh weather from last night, if it had been alive to begin with. It's a lost cause, Georg. I'm . . . sorry." Then he tapped his chin. "Also, there aren't any tracks, which is . . . *odd*, to say the least."

"Are you saying a ghost committed this murder?"

Heinrich shook his head. "I'm saying that our killer wants to make a statement, but is still trying to hide. He will strike again."

What do these two murders have in common? Heinrich thought. *Both were young, virile women, unmarried and traveling alone. But one was a young farmer's girl, the other was a prostitute . . .*

The investigator turned to Georg. "Do you know if Josephine was Catholic?"

Georg nodded. "I heard it only in passing. She told Lars last night that she planned on going to Mass this morning, and wondered if the barkeep wanted to accompany her."

Heinrich's brows went high on his forehead. *A new suspect . . . but why would a barman kill his biggest moneymaker and asset?* It also made no sense—a running theme in this investigation. "A tavern owner and a prostitute attending Mass together . . . do you find that strange?"

Georg gave Heinrich a pointed look. "Everyone has to make a living, investigator. That doesn't mean they can't be pious and repentant at the same time. I would say a barkeep and a harlot have *many* reasons to atone for their sins. More than most."

"Perhaps." Heinrich made a clicking sound with his tongue. There was something else nagging at him, and he felt hesitant on bringing it out in the open, but it needed to be said, and he would judge the reaction carefully.

He inspected the brown-red grass surrounding the body. *Who would better know how to conceal his trail than a hunter and tracker?*

Heinrich stared at Georg. "And what about you, Herr Sieghart?"

Georg cocked his head to the side. "What about me?"

"When I left the tavern last night, I saw you hurry upstairs with this woman. You were the last one seen with her."

There was a momentary pause, and then Georg's eyes went

wild, and he let out a primal growl. He flew toward Heinrich before the investigator could prepare, and cocked his arm back. His fist smashed into the investigator's jaw, and Heinrich went skidding to the ground.

Heinrich's head hit the grass hard and a bright light tore through his vision. He tasted blood.

"You damn bastard," Georg shouted, standing over the investigator. He thrust a finger down at Heinrich, who spit blood on the grass and rolled to his back, groaning.

Tomas was on Georg within moments, ripping his sword from its sheath and pointing it at the hunter's neck.

"That drunk fool from last night was right," Georg continued, ignoring the sword at his throat, "you're nothing more than a rotten cur. Do you have an ounce of shame in that skinny body?"

Heinrich waved Tomas off. "Shame?" he croaked. "I seek the *truth*, hunter, and nothing else. I will do whatever it takes, ask whatever I must, to get it. I am an officer of the law, you boar!"

"Your law be damned," Georg said.

"Your God be damned!" Heinrich propped himself onto his elbows. He massaged his jaw and gingerly opened and closed his mouth. "That's the second time I've been struck in as many days, and it *will* be the last."

"Not if you keep flapping your unruly tongue."

Heinrich helped himself to his feet. He was dizzy, and could feel another bruise forming on his jaw.

Heinrich knew it was a foolish thing to have said, but the logic was simple. Every investigator worth his salt knew that there was a direct correlation between how a man reacted when accused of something, and his guilt. The more angry and defensive a man became when accused, the more likely he was innocent. A guilty man would have deflected and quietly shown the shame on his face. An innocent man would, well, punch the accuser in the face to defend his honor and virtue.

"I apologize," Heinrich said at last. "I had to see how you would react. And you . . . well, you played the part well." The investigator massaged his jaw again.

"*Played the part?* Are you mad? This isn't some *game*, investigator. Two women are dead. I could have loved Josephine. She reminded me of my wife—all fire and beautiful passion."

Heinrich squinted. That was the first time Georg had spoken about his family, even when Heinrich had pried for that information. The investigator decided he would have to learn more about Georg's family, if only to help strike Georg from the suspect list altogether.

"And what about you, you smarmy bastard?" Georg pointed at the investigator. "You saw me go upstairs with Josephine last night. What else did you do? Who's to say that you didn't wait for her to leave and kill her yourself."

Heinrich shrugged. "I went home to sleep off my drunkenness, as you suggested. And what motive would I have of killing this whore?"

Georg stammered, opened his mouth, and stared at the grass, as if he hadn't thought his allegation through. "She wasn't a whore," he mumbled, turning away.

After a lengthy silence, Heinrich walked up beside the hunter and put an arm around his shoulder. "Tell me," he said, "something that might lead me in the direction of Josephine's killer. I can't help if I have no leads."

Georg shrugged away the investigator's arm. "Well, I didn't want to say anything last night, but . . ."

Heinrich leaned closer with glinting, eager eyes.

"Someone followed me to the tavern last night. I never caught the culprit, or saw his face, but I did give chase."

Well, that's a foolish thing to omit, Heinrich thought. *Why would someone follow him? What's Georg's importance in Bedburg?*

The investigator spit more blood on the ground. "See if you're followed again tonight, on your way to the tavern. Don't take pursuit, but let me know if you were tailed. If we're lucky, we can trap this miscreant."

Georg shook his head. "That's not going to work. Lars

doesn't want you coming in and riling up his patrons, threatening them with arrests. It's bad for business."

Heinrich sighed and put his hands on his hips. "Well, are you still flush with funds from your hunt, or are you in need of money, my good hunter?"

Georg stared at the investigator and then nodded and looked down at the ground, as if he was ashamed.

"Then I have a proposition for you," Heinrich said. "What if I were to pay you to be my . . . liaison? Lars seems to be quite the back-alley tongue-flapper. What if you were to feed me information? For Josephine's sake."

The hunter pulled at his thick beard and shrugged. "I don't see any harm in that."

"Good," Heinrich said with a smile, and then slapped the hunter's back. He reached into his coat and came out with a handful of silver coins. "Then your first order of business is to find out what you can about Karl Achterberg's family."

"The farmer? How will that help Josephine?"

"One thing at a time, my friend. I believe all of this is connected, and that Dorothea Gabler's killer will lead me to Josephine's." The investigator nodded, and then strolled over to his horse. He started to mount, then turned to Tomas and motioned toward Josephine's body. "Tomas, clean this up. I don't want the public seeing this."

Tomas nodded.

Heinrich eyed Georg. "Meet me at your inn tonight with whatever you find out."

"How do you know where I stay?"

"It's my job to know," Heinrich said with a smirk.

"And where are you going?"

"To find answers, my good hunter."

*　　　*　　　*

An hour later, Heinrich Franz was at the doorstep of Karl Achterberg's house, which was built on the bottom of a hill less than half a mile from Peter Griswold's estate. Both houses were just a few miles from the two crime scenes.

Peter Griswold had not lied when he said that Karl's farmland was much smaller than his own, and they were such close neighbors that a marriage between Karl's son and Peter's daughter seemed like a good idea for the Achterbergs. Heinrich could understand Peter's reluctance to forge such a familial alliance: Karl's home was built in a windswept nook, at the bottom of the hill. His fields looked desperate, and his cattle looked malnourished.

Light drizzle started to come down during Heinrich's northern ride from Josephine's murder site. He shivered and pulled his coat tight as he walked up to the door. He knocked.

The door swung open and a middle-aged woman appeared in the frame. She was big, round at the stomach, with frumpy brown hair and a sullen look on her pocked face.

"What is it?" she asked, staring at Heinrich from head to toe. She crossed her arms over her formidable chest, and frowned.

"Are you Karl Achterberg's wife?" Heinrich asked, and then peeked at the parchment in his tunic, "Frau Bertrude?"

"What's it to you? If you're looking for my husband, he's not here."

"No, no, I'm not looking for him. I wish to speak with you and your son. I am Heinrich Franz, chief investigator to Lord Werner of Bedburg." He thrust his hand out and gave his best fake smile. Bertrude stared at the gloved hand as if it were a snake waiting to strike.

Over Bertrude's shoulder, Heinrich could see a young boy poke his head up, trying to see who was at the door. He was perhaps thirteen or fourteen, and was a frail thing, despite his hefty mother.

"Ah," Bertrude said, "so you're the man who mangled my husband's hand."

Heinrich cleared his throat. "Er, well, not directly. I simply seek the tru—"

Bertrude held her palm up. "Save it. I don't care what you do to that worthless fool."

"Worthless?" Heinrich asked with raised eyebrows. The rain started to pick up, and the investigator motioned toward the living room. "May I?"

Bertrude paused and then shrugged, stepping away from the doorway. Heinrich walked inside, which was warm but sparse. There were two closed doors at the end of the living room, and a hearth in the left corner. In all, it appeared that the Achterbergs hadn't had company in quite some time.

"So . . . where is your husband, if I may ask?" Heinrich rubbed his hands together.

"Do I look like his watch dog?" Bertrude sat down on a chair next to the fireplace.

Heinrich frowned. His patience was already wearing thin with this sour country bumpkin. "No," he said flatly, "you look like his wife. And wives usually know where their husbands are."

"Not me. Maybe he's hiding from you."

Heinrich couldn't tell if the woman was smirking or passing gas.

"What do you want with me and Martin here? It's nearly time for supper."

"I don't smell anything cooking." Heinrich noticed a pot in the corner of the room, but it wasn't even set to boil.

"It's nearly time for supper," Bertrude repeated.

Heinrich sighed and struggled to pull off his wet gloves. "I'm here on the matter of Dorothea Gabler's death."

"I thought that little sapling's case was resolved. Isn't that why you let Karl go?"

"Resolved?" Heinrich said. "Not in the least." He walked closer to the fireplace and reached his hands out to warm them. "Your estate doesn't seem in the best of conditions."

"Should I blame Karl for that, or you, for imprisoning him?"

"I beg your pardon?"

Bertrude waved at the investigator. "It's no matter . . . Karl is a weak, useless man."

"What do you mean by that?"

"Never mind," Bertrude said. "He can't support us, even in this dung heap. Like you said, our estate isn't in the best of conditions."

After a moment of silence, Heinrich turned to look at the boy, Martin. His eyes seemed strangely sad and tired at the same time. When Heinrich looked at him, Martin made sure to quickly stare at the ground, as if finding something interesting on the floor.

A bitter mother, a missing father, and a downtrodden boy, Heinrich thought. *I don't need to be an investigator to know a broken family when I see one. Perhaps Dorothea's murder has something to do with it.*

"I'll get to it, then," Heinrich said after the lull in conversation. He reached into his tunic and pulled out his piece of parchment and his quill. "It's come to my attention that the day before Dorothea's murder, she was seen at this house."

Out of his peripheral, Heinrich saw young Martin's eyes shoot up, as if shocked to hear that revelation.

"Who told you that?" Bertrude asked quickly—almost too quickly.

"Sybil Griswold," Heinrich said.

Bertrude scoffed and waved off the investigator. "Ever since our failed marriage between Martin and her, that little tramp has had it out for my family."

"Mother," Martin said in a shy voice, speaking for the first time. "Don't call Sybil a tramp. She's my friend."

"Keep quiet, boy," Bertrude snapped.

Heinrich faced the boy and asked, "Sybil Griswold was your friend? Even after you weren't able to marry her?"

"It wasn't her fault," Martin said with a shrug. "My father and her father don't like each other."

"I've heard," Heinrich said. "But you *do* like Sybil?"

Martin blushed. "Well, not like *that.*"

Heinrich twisted his mustache. He decided to try a different approach. "Was there someone else who you had feelings for, Martin?"

"Don't answer that, Martin," Bertrude said.

The boy wrapped his hands behind his back and kicked at the floor. Heinrich could tell the boy was eager to say something. Martin slowly began to nod, and Heinrich thought he saw tears forming in the boy's eyes.

"Dorothea," he said.

Bertrude growled. "Martin, not another word, you little heathen."

Heinrich scribbled fiercely on his parchment. He had Sybil's name written next to Martin's, but he slashed through *Sybil* and wrote *Dorothea* above it.

The boy never wanted to marry Sybil in the first place. Did Dorothea have the same feelings for Martin as he did for her?

As if reading Heinrich's mind, Martin's voice rose in volume and he said, "Why, mother? You know it's true! I loved Dorothea!"

Bertrude struggled, but she stood from her seat and pointed toward one of the closed doors at the back of the house. "Go to your room right now, boy!"

Martin scampered off, and then Bertrude turned her motherly wrath on Heinrich. "I want you out of my house. Now! I won't be answering any more of your questions."

Heinrich had a few choice words to say, but Bertrude cut him off. "I said *now*! Or I'll pummel your skinny hide so badly that even God won't recognize you."

Heinrich opened his mouth to speak, but decided he'd been pummeled enough over the past twenty-four hours, and that his face had no more room for bruises, so he turned and left.

CHAPTER TEN

GEORG

Following Josephine's death, a palpable hysteria swept through Bedburg. Her murder struck the community in a much different way than Dorothea's had: one was an innocent girl, the other was a beloved, beautiful woman, despite being a harlot. That fact only boosted her popularity with the lonely men of the city.

One thing that became clear following Josephine's death was that no Catholic was safe, and it scared the folks of Bedburg. The fact that Dorothea's murder was no closer to being solved pushed that sense of fear and uncertainty to a fever pitch.

As Georg made his way through the streets of Bedburg, he watched as peasants, merchants, and nobility alike spoke in whispers, walked a bit faster, and constantly looked over their shoulders. Laymen and priests preached on the open streets, damning the killings as works of Satan.

Georg strolled along the Erft River and passed Castle Bedburg, where the tone was more reserved than in the heart of town. Soldiers held worried looks and clutched their spears with white knuckles. One man was in the corner of the keep, vomiting from a hangover. Another soldier spoke softly to a comrade, saying, "I just saw her three nights ago—she was such a lovely lass."

The other soldier smiled. "The lovely lass with the lovely ass."

Georg felt a flash of anger flow through his body. He clenched his fists and kept walking away from the men, heading east toward the tavern.

It was nearly twilight when he arrived, and the streets were all but empty. It seemed Josephine's murder had enacted a self-imposed curfew throughout the town.

While the people outside the tavern were scared and nervous, inside the tavern was a different feeling altogether. The attitude was stuffy and angry and rebellious. Fists pounded on tables and voices shouted over each other. One man stood on his stool with a frown and yelled, "We have to do something about this! This damned monster took one of our own!"

A chorus of yells followed in overwhelming agreement.

Another man stood from his table and raised his mug. "Revenge for Josephine!"

"Our wives and children and families won't be safe until the Beast of Bedburg is dead!" said another.

Georg stared at the grim faces in the crowded tavern and shook his head. *Give fearful men some stiff drinks and they all become heroes*, he thought. But he couldn't blame them. He felt the same as the rest of the drunks.

He ambled to the bar and met the eyes of Lars. The barkeep came over to him and laid his hands on the table. "A right damn shame," he said, handing over a mug to the hunter.

Georg nodded. "She was a fine woman." He jutted his head toward the other people in the bar, who were now cheering and shouting their undying love for the fiery redhead. To Georg, it seemed that everyone had some compliment to say about the woman, but they all neglected to mention the darkest detail: that her unborn child had been torn from her.

Perhaps no one wants to take that responsibility—that their possible child has been taken from them . . . or perhaps they do not know. Surely that sly investigator only lets information slip when he wants it to.

Another man shouted an empty claim of revenge, and it finally sent Georg over the edge. He turned and faced the ravenous crowd, and bellowed, "And what, exactly, do you valiant knights have in mind? How do you plan on finding this monster and exacting your vengeance?"

The commotion came to a dead stop, and all eyes turned to Georg. A few of the men stammered, but then looked down, around, and any direction away from the large hunter. *What* they needed to do was clear, but *how* was a different question entirely.

One man stepped forward. He had been the first to stand on his chair and lament. He was about as tall as Georg, more stout, and had an eye-patch covering his left eye.

Georg pinned the man as a soldier. He knew the type—the swagger, the deep frown, the dark eyes—much the same way as Investigator Franz had pinned Georg when they first met.

"I propose we stage a hunt," the man said in a deep, gravelly voice. "If Lord Werner is going to sit on his ass, then it's up to us, the people, to quell this madness."

People started nodding their heads and murmuring. Soon, the murmurs rose to shouts once again.

It seems the knights have found their king.

The man grinned and gazed around the room. "Tomorrow, then, in the morning, we go hunting! Bring all the firepower we can muster—pitchforks, torches, guns—anything we can use."

"You don't think a hunt will raise alarm with Lord Werner?" Georg asked.

The man faced Georg. "I hope it does! We can claim it as a hunt to mark the beginning of winter and the end of autumn. Isn't that what this town does every year?"

Georg had to admit that the man was quick on his feet, and he had conviction. He reminded the hunter of . . . himself. Perhaps the man's idea wasn't as foolish as it sounded. But Georg still couldn't help but play devil's advocate. "So we hunt as many wolves around the country as we can find, and hope that one of them turns into a man once it's killed?"

The man frowned. "Do you have a better idea, Georg Sieghart?"

Georg raised an eyebrow. *This man knows me?* He eyed the

soldier from head to toe, and after a pause he stretched his arms out wide. "I suppose not."

More cheers erupted from the crowd.

The man with the eye patch smiled and sauntered over to Georg. "And it's not a wolf hunt, Georg. It's a witch hunt."

"How do you know me, soldier?"

"How could I not?" The man clapped Georg on the shoulder. "Everyone knows Sieghart the Savage. Do you not remember me?" The man frowned, said, "I'm hurt," but then smiled again and stuck out his hand. "Konrad von Brühl. We fought together when we sacked Westphalia."

Georg nodded slowly and shook the man's hand. "A bloody battle," he said, "but no one calls me Sieghart the Savage anymore, and I'd like to keep it that way."

"Fair enough. But it is true—you were a madman on the battlefield . . . and off."

"That time has passed." Georg looked to the ground and felt suddenly uncomfortable.

"Will you join us tomorrow?" Konrad asked.

Georg stayed silent for a moment, but finally nodded. "I will, but if you'll excuse me, I have ale to drink, and I'd rather drink it alone."

Konrad held his palms up in surrender. "Be the loner," he said. "You always were." Then he walked away to tend to his flock of eager comrades.

Georg watched Konrad walk away, then drank three mugs in succession. He turned to the blond barkeep. "You're a praying man, are you not, Lars?"

Lars washed out an empty mug with a rag, then threw the rag on the table. He shrugged. "I tend Mass when I can, sometimes before I open up here, sometimes after. Why do you ask?"

"Can you tell me anything about the Achterberg family?"

Lars walked toward Georg and stared at the hunter. He rested his elbows on the table, leaned forward, and made a steeple with his hands. "I might," he said, and then his gaze went to the empty table between them.

It took Georg a moment to realize the implication. He reached into his pocket and slid a couple silver coins across the table.

The barkeep nodded. "What is it you want to know? I'm not sure I know anything that isn't already public knowledge."

"Tell me what you can, maybe as far as five days back."

Lars stroked his chin. "You're here for that damn investigator, aren't you? About the young girl's murder?"

"I'm here on my own accord. Is my money not good here?"

Lars sighed, tucked away the coins, and put his hands on his hips. "Well, what's there to know? They're Catholic. Karl was accused of the girl's murder, and then released. But everyone knows that."

"What about Karl's family?"

Lars hesitated and scratched his scalp. "Well . . ." he said, trailing off. "I've seen his son at church. He's an altar boy. A bit too old to be one, if you ask me." He leaned closer to Georg and whispered, "I can only imagine what that old bishop uses the poor boy for."

Georg furrowed his brow. "An altar boy? Is there anything you can tell me about the family on the day of Dorothea's death?"

"Let's see," Lars said, taking his time. "Five days ago . . ." he began, and then his face lit up. He eyed the table again.

Georg groaned and slid more coins to the barkeep.

Lars hungrily pocketed the coins and cleared his throat. "Like I said, I either go to church early or late. Sometimes in the earliest hours of the morning I see the altar boy there. It's as if he sometimes stays the night." Lars shrugged. "Maybe he's forbidden from traveling at night, with all these murders taking place."

Georg started growing impatient. "And on the day of Dorothea's murder?"

Lars drummed the table with his fingers. "I think . . . ah, yes, five days ago you said? I do remember going for an afternoon prayer, before opening up here. The boy was being dropped off at the church, by his mother."

Georg leaned forward. "Did the mother stay with him throughout the day?"

"Oh, no," Lars said, "only for a short while. She left after a quick prayer, but the boy stayed."

Georg knew he was onto something, but he didn't know what. It would take a more powerful mind to add up these clues, someone whose "job it is to know." But he felt a sense of pride and worth just by getting possible clues from the greedy barkeep.

"Much obliged, friend," Georg said after a pause. He handed another coin to Lars and said, "For your troubles."

Lars nodded to the hunter, and his eyes gleamed as he palmed the coin.

Georg stood from his stool and left the tavern, heading toward the nearby inn.

CHAPTER ELEVEN

DIETER

In the early morning hours, Dieter Nicolaus plodded around the outside grounds of the church, sweeping away leaves that had gathered from the rain the night before. Then he tended the communal gardens, which he'd planted himself.

He was proud of his gardens. On the western wall of the church was a floral arrangement, with vibrant roses, fire lilies, and pink houseleeks. These were rugged flowers that would be tested by a difficult winter. On the eastern side of the church was the vegetable garden, full of beans and rye and wheat, that would help feed the church staff and Bedburg's poor community.

He smiled at the gardens, and then looked to the sky. It was an overcast morning, and would likely stay gray until the skies turned white with snowfall. Wrapping his robe tight around his body, Dieter made his way to the front of the church. Due to the changing seasons, he expected a big turnout at morning Mass.

He heard a faraway voice, and then turned and looked down the hill from the church's doors. Strangely, at least ten people were gathered near the base of the hill, surrounding a single man.

The man was thin, robed, and had long hair and a dark beard. He stood atop an overturned fruit crate, and his hands were gesticulating toward the heavens, as if beckoning God.

Curious, Dieter walked down the hill. He frowned when he realized what he was witnessing.

"We are *all* sinners, brothers and sisters, sons and daughters! Salvation can only come through His word, through righteousness of the Holy Spirit. No man, in his fallen grace, can lead you away from sin—only God can! And not everyone is assured a place in heaven, whatever you may have been told.

"Do not place your faith in the idolatries of Man, and the pope! You cannot *buy* your atonement, but must work faithfully, through Scripture, and through the teachings of Jesus Christ. But fear not, my brethren, for once you are saved, you will always be saved. Read the teachings of Martin Luther and find the truth. Escape from the road of eternal perdition, which you are sure to travel down if you are led by Man, and not God."

Dieter felt his ears go hot. It wasn't that a Protestant was preaching at the base of his church that angered him, but the fact that people were *listening* to him—Catholic faithful—nodding their heads. And this man was in the open, unafraid, speaking with sincerity and enthusiasm.

Who is this man, and where does he come from? Dieter wondered. *Are things so dire that people would listen to him, unafraid of retribution from Lord Werner and Archbishop Ernst? Is Bedburg losing its Catholic faith right under its nose?*

Without listening to the man any further, Dieter shuffled back up the hill and burst into the empty church. He sprinted toward the back of the room, passed the altar, and stormed down the hallway leading to the bishop's quarters.

He rapped at the door, hard, and a voice from the other side called out, "Hold."

Dieter shifted impatiently from one foot to the other. He could still hear the preacher's booming voice from outside.

After an agonizing moment, the voice said, "You may enter," and Dieter obliged.

Bishop Solomon was at the end of the room, rising from his bed and tightening his robe. The same distraught altar boy from the day before stormed by Dieter as the priest entered.

"We have a problem, my lord," Dieter said after the boy brushed by him. "There's a man outside, preaching—"

Bishop Solomon raised his hand. "Yes, yes, I know, my son." He clasped his hands behind his back and meandered over to his oak desk. He looked down at the table and sifted through a stack of parchments. "There's a Lutheran preaching in our courtyard."

Dieter nodded. "Who is he? Where did he come from?"

"Where? I don't know. Sister Salome tells me that he's a traveling pastor named Hanns Richter."

"What's he doing outside of *our* church, my lord?" Dieter spoke with a bit more flare than he'd intended.

The bishop slowly looked up from his table. "What do you think he's doing? He's undermining our faith, of course."

"Shouldn't he be stopped?"

Bishop Solomon nodded. He lifted a piece of parchment from the stack. "We are not to take action until *this* takes place. It's the archbishop's orders," he said, tapping the yellow paper with his fingers. He held out the parchment to Dieter, who mouthed the words as he read aloud.

It is with a joyous heart that I say, Bishop Solomon of Bedburg, that I will be sending a group of Jesuit priests to aid in your continued quest to rid Bedburg from the scourge of Martin Luther's and John Calvin's followers. As their numbers grow and their rebelliousness builds, I ask that you not partake in any ill-thought measures to reproach these sinners—either violent or peaceful—until my men have arrived.

Archbishop Ernst

"So he's sending us Jesuit missionaries . . ." Dieter's voice lowered.

Bishop Solomon nodded. "You read the same thing as I, did you not? The Jesuits are highly educated and persuasive. I fear what they might accomplish, and I fear that things will get worse before they get better."

Dieter handed the letter back to the bishop, scratching his head. "Why do you fear what they might accomplish, my lord? Is this not good news? We will have reinforcements to turn back the tides of rebellion."

Bishop Solomon sneered and waved a hand at Dieter. "Don't you see what this is?" he said. "I have worked years to quell any uprisings, nearly since the Cologne War first broke out. I came from Cologne to bring back the rightful faith. And I have succeeded, have I not?"

"You have," Dieter said, but was still confused.

"And now, at the first sign of trouble, the archbishop wishes to send *his* men into *my* domain—the place I've worked so hard to maintain. He wishes to take my glory and be the savior of Bedburg."

Dieter cocked his head and fumbled his words. "But . . . isn't it *God's* glory, Father? That is what you've always preached."

Solomon narrowed his eyes at the young priest. "You are young and naïve, my son. But it's no matter, there are other things we must attend to. Sister Salome tells me that you've had her keep an eye on that barbarous huntsman. Why is that? Is he a threat?"

"Georg Sieghart?" Dieter asked, taken aback by the quick change of subject. "I wanted to find out more about our congregation. There was no ill intent."

"Salome tells me that his family was killed by the Werewolf of Bedburg, and that he is here seeking revenge."

Dieter nodded.

"Well, then he is a dangerous man. Revenge is a dangerous motivator." The bishop began pacing around his table, and then wagged a finger toward Dieter. "I would like you to keep an eye on him a bit longer."

"Why, my lord?"

"To see if revenge is his true motive," Bishop Solomon said. "What if he holds deeper secrets? Do you not find it coincidental that these murders began reoccurring as he came into town?"

Dieter scratched the stubble on his chin. "I suppose. But how would we account for the murders that took place *before* he arrived?"

"Do we really know how long he's been here?" Solomon asked. "And why are we so sure there's only one murderer? What if our killer is conspiring with others? Maybe talk to that nosy investigator—he seems to always have an opinion on things."

Dieter bowed. "Very well, my lord. Is there anything else? I must prepare my sermon."

"One last thing," the bishop said. "It's come to my attention that a large group of men are going on a hunt following Mass—to bid autumn a farewell, and to 'take matters into their own hands,' as they see it."

"What matters, my lord?"

Bishop Solomon shook his head. "Don't you listen, boy? The same things we've been talking about—wolves, beasts, monsters! They want justice for those dead girls, and I don't blame them. So give them a powerful sermon, Father Nicolaus. Outshine that Lutheran mongrel and give our people something they can cheer for. It is your words that could sway the opinion of our congregation back in the right direction. Don't let me down, and don't let that pastor damn our faith's righteousness."

"Remember, my friends, that this monster killed two of our own—two of our beautiful faithful! I look in each of your faces and see courage. I see the same courage that Jesus showed in the face of utter diversity." Dieter paced back and forth on his platform. He made sure to stare at each person's face as he moved.

He was pleased that Sybil had returned, and she looked beautiful in a blue dress. He passed over her face the longest, then moved on to Investigator Franz, who lingered in the back of the church; to the barkeep Lars; to Georg Sieghart and his new patch-eyed friend; and to everyone else.

"Be the children of God that I know you can be. Salvation is nigh! Bring justice to our dead, and allow their souls peace in

Heaven. Show the might of your Catholic faith, and strike down the monsters who would do us harm." Dieter raised a finger in the air and stopped pacing, turning to face the congregation. "Don't rely on the false promises and lies of outsiders," he said, looking around the room for Pastor Hanns Richter. The Lutheran was absent.

"You are stalwart Christians, so remember to be resilient, obedient, and righteous in your resolve. Through your actions and remorse, and His teachings, you will repent and be saved. So go on this hunt with God's steely virtue in your heart, and don't slay this beast for your own namesake, but for God's glory!"

Dieter ended his sermon on a triumphant high note, and was pleased to hear a round of cheers from the room. He could tell the men were antsy and bloodthirsty. Nothing he said would have changed that, so instead of damning the hunt, he encouraged it, encouraged the killings, and thanked God for the people's bloodlust.

CHAPTER TWELVE

SYBIL

After Father Nicolaus' sermon, the congregation cleared from the church in a hurry. Every man leaving had dark grins on their faces, eager for the morning hunt. Sybil sat in a pew with her hands folded on her lap, waiting for the church to clear out.

A few people stayed—mainly the women giving confessions to Father Nicolaus, and those too young to hunt. One of them was Sybil's friend, Martin Achterberg. The altar boy was the first of three people to give penitence, and as he walked out of the confessional, Sybil stood from her pew.

Martin faced the ground, and as he passed by Sybil he looked up with big, tearful eyes. "Hello, Beele," he said, wiping his wet cheeks.

Sybil smiled warmly. "How are you holding up with everything, Martin?"

The boy remained silent for a long moment. Finally, he said, "I-I've got to go, Beele. It's nice to see you coming to church."

As the boy walked past her, Sybil turned to watch him leave the church, and started fidgeting inside a pocket of her dress. As she turned, Investigator Franz came from a corner of the room and stormed past her, toward Father Nicolaus. The investigator pushed past the next parishioner in line and started talking with the priest. Sybil furrowed her brow and crept forward, curious about what they were talking about.

Investigator Franz pointed a finger in the priest's chest. He seemed angry, or in a hurry, or both. Sybil sat in a pew next to the investigator and priest so she could listen to them talk.

". . . You need to tell me, priest. What did that boy just confess to?" the investigator asked in a low voice.

The priest raised his arms in surrender. "You know I can't do that, investigator. His confession is between him and God, and no one else. I can't, in good conscience, forsake that boy's trust."

Investigator Franz stamped his foot on the tiled floor, and kept waving his finger at Father Nicolaus. By his body language, Sybil could tell he was becoming increasingly frustrated.

"That's horseshit. I am a man of the law, priest. You need to tell me if he confessed to knowing a crime. I am trying to keep this town *safe*, goddammit!"

Father Nicolaus took a step back. "Please, Herr Franz, this is a house of God. Heed your words! You know that God, and God alone, is above the law. That boy's repentance is between him and God." The priest motioned to the elderly woman Heinrich had pushed away. "Now, please, I have confessions to take."

The investigator growled like an angry dog, spun around, and stomped down the aisle toward the stained-glass doors. When he reached Sybil, he stopped and towered over her. Sybil had her head bowed, as if in prayer, but as the investigator's shadow loomed over her, she slowly looked up.

"I must speak with you, Frau Griswold." Investigator Franz had his hands on his hips. "It will only take a moment."

Dieter saw what was happening and called out from the confessional. "Please, investigator, leave my congregation alone. The girl has done—"

Investigator Franz held up his palm and cut the priest off, without looking in his direction. "Just a few questions. Nothing more."

Sybil stood and folded her hands in front of her stomach. "Y-yes, my lord?" She glanced at the investigator's narrow nose and thin mustache, and her face burned.

"Your father denied the marriage between yourself and that altar boy who just walked by you, correct?"

"Who, Martin?" Sybil said.

"I saw you speak with him as he walked by. So you have *some* sort of relationship with him, correct?"

Sybil nodded sheepishly. "What are you getting at, if I may ask, my lord?"

"I'll ask the questions," the investigator snapped. He hunched over and put his hands on his knees, so that he was eye level with Sybil.

The investigator's bruised face was only inches from hers, and Sybil could feel his warm, stale breath on her cheeks. His dark eyes darted around her face, as if he were searching her soul, trying to find something. It took all of Sybil's nerves to keep from recoiling from the man.

"Despite the failed marriage," Heinrich said at last, "did you have *feelings* for Martin?"

"What do you—"

"Did you love him?"

Sybil finally did recoil from the man's gaze, and nearly tripped on herself as she took a step back. Her cheeks flushed.

"W-what? No! Martin is just a friend of mine."

Investigator Franz studied her for a long moment, and then stood to his full height. "Dorothea Gabler was your friend as well, correct?"

Sybil nodded.

"And she was a friend of Martin's, too?"

"Yes," Sybil said, "we were all friends."

"What was their relationship like? They were a bit younger than you—closer in age to each other—correct?"

Sybil's eyes went to the floor and she hesitated.

"Frau Griswold?" Heinrich probed.

Sybil's face shot up, and her eyebrows were scrunched. She narrowed her gaze at the investigator. "It was no secret that Dorothea and Martin had feelings for one another," she said. "I wanted them to be happy. I don't care about our difference in ages. And now poor Martin seems so sad! It's heartbreaking."

Sybil sniffled and wiped her nose with her forearm.

The investigator waited for a moment, and then reached into his tunic and came out with a piece of parchment and a quill. He wrote something in it, and then patted Sybil on the shoulder. "Thank you for your cooperation, Frau Griswold," he said, and then turned and took off at a brisk pace toward the exit of the church.

Just then, Father Nicolaus approached Sybil and put his hands gently on her arms. He shook his head. "What did that insufferable man say to you, my dear?"

"I-it's nothing, Father. Nothing important."

"Please, call me Dieter." The priest smiled and put his palm forward. "Come, will you walk with me?"

Sybil nodded, gave her best half-smile, and took the priest's hand. They sauntered down the aisle and through the stained-glass doors, out into a crisp morning full of bright, white clouds that stretched to the horizon. From the hill of the church, the day seemed so peaceful, despite the howling men that were headed toward the town's gates.

Dieter led Sybil to the western side of the church, where they came upon a luscious grove of flowers that lined the church wall.

Sybil couldn't help but smile, but it was a sad smile. She stared at the lilies and roses and poinsettias, their colors vibrant and luminous, and she faced the priest.

"Did you do all of this?"

Dieter nodded. "There's a vegetable garden on the other side of the church, too." Pride echoed in his voice. He watched Sybil lean in to the roses and smell them, but when she came away from them, her bottom lip was trembling.

Dieter frowned and said, "Do you not like them?"

Sybil shook her head. "N-no, it's not that. They're stunning. It's just that . . . it reminds me of my mother. My mother had rosebushes, and I loved them as a child. She died giving birth to my brother, Hugo, and my father let the roses die with her. He said that there was better use of the land . . ." Sybil's voice trailed off, and she sniffled again.

Dieter put a hand on her back. "I'm so sorry, Beele, I did not know. It's a shame that such beautiful things can bring back such painful memories."

Sybil faced the priest with red-rimmed eyes, but she was smiling. "Not painful memories . . . bittersweet ones. And as long as these flowers can add a little brightness to people during these dark times, that makes me happy."

Sybil started thinking about how Father Nicolaus had called her 'Beele,' her nickname that was only used by her friends and family. She started to blush, and then said, "Oh, I almost forgot! I have something for you." She grinned and rummaged through the front pocket of her dress. When she lifted her hand, she held an amulet. The amulet was a pair of wooden crosses, nestled side-by-side, hanging on a thin brown thread. She handed it to the priest, whose mouth was slightly agape. "I made it," she said, "from oak."

Dieter opened his mouth to say something, but no words came out. He gently took the necklace, clasped his hands around it, and brought it to his chest, over his heart.

"Do you like it?"

"It's the most precious gift I've ever received," he finally said. "Honestly."

Sybil smiled from ear to ear, and dimples formed on her cheeks. "It's to show that, even though people may have different beliefs and values, all Christians should be able to get along." She shrugged. "That's what I think, anyway."

"You are wise beyond your years, my dear. I love it. But why make this for me?"

Sybil shrugged. "I was hoping for a favor in return."

Dieter stared at the girl's fair face, and noticed that the innocence he'd come to love was replaced by a mischievous grin. "Wise . . . and cunning," he said. "Name it."

"I was hoping that you could teach me to read and write."

The priest hesitated. "What would your father think of that?"

"He doesn't need to know. You could teach me at the church, or somewhere else. It could be our secret."

Dieter grimaced. "I don't know, Bee—"

As if on cue, a booming voice from the front of the church reverberated through the hillside. "Sybil!" it called.

"Uh oh," Sybil said.

Peter Griswold rounded the corner of the church and growled. "What the hell are you doing with my daughter, priest?"

Dieter managed to clasp the amulet in his hands, behind his back, just before Peter noticed. "I was showing Sybil my gardens, Herr Griswold."

Peter's eyes narrowed. "I told you to stay away from her," he said, tugging at his dark beard. Then he faced Sybil and said, "And I told you the same, young lady. Let's go. We have a visitor, and you're going to help cook." He turned and stomped away.

Sybil took one last look at Dieter, and then started to leave.

Before she could get far, Dieter took her arm and leaned in close. "Yes," he whispered in her ear, "I'll do it. I'll teach you."

Sybil sat at the dining table with her brother, her father, and their guest, Pastor Hanns Richter. The man was as thin as a twig, with long brown hair and a beard that made him resemble Jesus Christ, which Sybil assumed was intentional. She glanced at her steaming bowl of potatoes and eggs, and then turned her gaze to the Lutheran pastor.

"You aren't to be seen at that church again, Sybil," Peter said, ripping off a chunk of bread from his plate. "Do you understand? I won't have you disobey me again."

Sybil looked back down at her plate and nodded meekly. "Yes, sir."

"Teenage angst," Pastor Richter said, and then eyed Peter. "It often leads to disobedience. If I were you—"

"And who are you, pastor? You're not my father," Sybil spat. She frowned at the holy man. "And isn't it dangerous to be seen with you?"

Peter paused with his bread just inches from his open mouth. He threw the bread down onto his plate, and said, "By God, did I not teach you manners, girl? Hanns is our *guest*, and my friend. You won't speak to him that way." He shook his head and pushed his plate away. "In fact, take your food and go to your room. You too, Hugo."

Sybil and Hugo began to protest, but Peter held up his palm and turned away from them. The two children slid off their chairs and disappeared into Sybil's room.

Inside, Sybil held her ear against the door, ignoring her bowl of food.

"You aren't supposed to eavesdrop, Beele. Father told you that already," Hugo said.

Sybil put her index finger up to her lips. "Shh," she said.

The doors in the house were paper thin, something Peter didn't realize.

Pastor Hanns Richter spoke first. "It's been four years since Archbishop Gebhard was deposed by Ernst, in Cologne. Ever since, our people have lived in fear, Peter. Once Ernst replaced Lord Adolf with the Catholic Lord Werner, here in Bedburg, I knew I'd have to take action. I'm sorry it's taken me this long to arrive.

"The battle rages, Peter, in every principality in Germany. We haven't lost. Even Queen Elizabeth of England has given our people financial support. The Catholics have Spain, and King Philip, however, and that is worrisome. But Philip is still embattled with the Dutch, which gives us an opportunity around Cologne. It's a small window, but it's there. All eyes are focused on this pivotal moment in history, Peter, and by God's strength, we will come out the victors."

"Amen," Peter said. "But what are you getting at, Hanns? Is

the fight coming here, to Bedburg?"

"I'm afraid there's a strong possibility that it is," Hanns said. "But I am here now, so we don't have to hide like rats in a cellar. Enough is enough. I will vocalize our faith, we will join our English allies, and we will take back our rightful outposts and cities."

"Tread lightly, my friend," Peter said. "It's still dangerous for us. Bedburg Castle is a garrison for Catholic soldiers. Lord Werner is no tyrant, but he will only be pushed so far. If our brothers and sisters come out of hiding now, I fear that it will result in terrible losses."

"Yes, but we must gain morale. We are in hiding, but we can't be for long. From Bavaria to Münster, Lutherans are fighting—in every corner of the Roman Empire. We've even gained alliance with the Calvinists in some regions. It's only a matter of time before the fight comes here. But I need your help, Peter."

Sybil heard her father sigh loudly.

"I am a simple farmer, Hanns—"

"You have influence with the Bedburg Protestants, my friend. They hold you in high regard."

"Even so, I'm no fighter. I don't wish to participate in violence. I am simply trying to live my life the best I can, for me and my children."

"So you would be overrun, living your life in fear for the rest of your days? That pains me to hear, Peter."

"I'm sorry," Peter said, sounding tired and defeated. "But there are people here who share your vision, Hanns. I can introduce you to them. Perhaps you can stir their emotions like you did in front of the church this morning."

"Your aid would be greatly appreciated, my friend," the pastor said. "That is all I can ask. If you could introduce me to these people, I would be indebted to you."

"I can introduce you tonight."

"Thank you. You are a good man, Peter Griswold."

Sybil leaned her back against the door and slid to the ground. She tucked her knees into her chest and thought, *What are you getting yourself into, father?*

CHAPTER THIRTEEN

HEINRICH

Heinrich felt a tingle run down his spine. His leads were starting to add up, and he felt hot on whatever trail he was headed down. Sybil Griswold had given the investigator more than she knew: She corroborated Martin Achterberg's story and confirmed that he and Dorothea Gabler had intimate feelings for one another.

The night before, Georg Sieghart had given Heinrich more information. Martin, though fourteen years of age, was Bishop Solomon's chief altar boy, and he often stayed long hours at the church, including the day of Dorothea's murder. Martin's mother had dropped the boy off and then left.

Heinrich played the newest timeline in his head. *After leaving Sybil Griswold's house, Dorothea went to Martin Achterberg's, hoping to meet with the boy. But Martin's father was the only person there.*

Heinrich tapped his chin. He let Sybil leave his sight, and then sped out of the church, trying to chase down Martin, who had hurried out after giving Father Nicolaus his confession.

Martin's confession is the key piece to this puzzle, Heinrich thought. *I can feel it.*

He pushed through the stained-glass doorway with both hands, and Georg Sieghart was waiting outside.

The hunter startled Heinrich. "Where are you going in such a rush, investigator? Are you not joining the rest of the men on the hunt?"

Heinrich rolled his eyes. "You barbarians have your fun," he said. "I have leads to follow." The investigator squinted and looked over Georg's shoulder, where a large man with a patch over his left eye was standing. Heinrich had seen the man sitting next to Georg during Father Nicolaus' sermon, but other than that, he'd never seen him before. The investigator gave Georg a curt nod, and then took off down the hill.

"Investigator!"

The voice came from behind Heinrich, as he reached the bottom of the hill. Frustrated and annoyed, Heinrich spun around and faced his guardsman, Tomas.

Heinrich sighed. "Not now, Tomas, I have matters that need taking care of."

"But sir, Lord Werner has summoned you."

The investigator grunted. "I said not *now*. The lord will have to wait."

Tomas readjusted the helmet on his head. "Where are you going? I'm supposed to accompany you until you go to the castle."

Heinrich cleared his throat and was about to say something. Then he paused and narrowed his eyes at the guard. "Fine then, come, come," he said, waving Tomas forward.

The two made their way through the winding dirt roads of Bedburg, and passed by the center marketplace. All the while, Heinrich's eyes darted around buildings and wagons and people. At the southern end of town, he finally noticed Martin Achterberg in the distance, hurrying toward the farmlands outside Bedburg's walls.

"Halt, boy!" Heinrich called out.

Martin's body went taut and he froze in his tracks. Then he decided to keep walking, as if he hadn't heard the voice calling his name.

"I said stop, boy, or I'll have you arrested!" Heinrich shouted.

The threat was enough to make Martin turn around. His face was red and his eyes were wide open.

Heinrich put his hands on his hips as he neared the boy. An unbearable stench caused him to gag, and he realized they were standing next to the town's leather tanner. "I have a few questions to ask you, Herr Achterberg, concerning Dorothea Gabler."

"I've told you everything I know, my lord," Martin said.

Heinrich frowned and looked down his nose at the boy, trying to seem as authoritative as possible. "I think you're lying," he said, "and I hate liars. At the very least, I think you're keeping things from me, which is also bad, if not worse."

The boy started trembling like a nervous wreck. "What do you mean, sir? I-I'm not keeping anything from you."

Heinrich crossed his hands over his chest and slowly started pacing in front of the boy. It was, of course, another tactic designed to scare Martin. "Yesterday, when I was at your estate and mentioned that Dorothea had come to your house the day of her murder, you seemed . . . *surprised*." With that last word, Heinrich stopped in his tracks and faced Martin.

The boy looked at the ground and started shaking his head profusely. "N-no, no, I wasn't surprised."

The investigator leaned forward and with one finger he lifted Martin's face by his chin, so they were looking eye to eye. "I said I don't like liars, Martin. You didn't know Dorothea had been by your house . . . because you were at the church, with Bishop Solomon."

Martin started fidgeting, turned his head away from Heinrich's hand, and opened his mouth.

"Think carefully about your next words, Martin," Heinrich said.

The boy kept shaking his head, and then his shoulders slumped and he sighed. "No . . . I didn't know she had come." He looked up at the investigator, and the rims of his eyes were wet. "Why would my parents keep that from me? How did you know I was with the bishop?"

"It's my job to know," Heinrich said. He bobbed his head from left to right, debating if he should clarify what he meant.

"And I have witnesses who place you at the church." The investigator coughed and cleared his throat, and then put his hands behind his back. "Your father, Karl, was the only one present at your house when Dorothea arrived." Martin started to open his mouth again, but Heinrich cut him off. "I know that because your mother took you to church."

Martin slowly nodded. "I guess so," he said with a meek voice.

Heinrich wagged a finger in Martin's face. "No, son, I *know* so." Then the investigator raised his voice and said, "And just what do you think your mother found upon her return to your estate?"

Martin shrugged and took a step back.

"I'll tell you, Martin. Your mother found your father and Dorothea *alone*." Then Heinirch said, "In *bed*, perhaps?" to test the boy's reaction.

The tears kept welling in Martin's eyes. "No! That's not—that *can't* be true!" he shouted, and started clenching his fists.

Heinrich took a step back, somewhat alarmed by the boy's sudden outburst. He stifled a smile because his claim had the effect he desired. Martin was rattled. He would say anything. And the fact that he had responded so angrily gave Heinrich all the firepower he needed. The investigator felt a tinge of remorse for picking on such a youngling, but that remorse quickly faded.

"The girl you loved betrayed you, Martin. You know, in your heart, that it's true."

Martin bent his knees, as if he were about to lunge at Heinrich.

Tomas took a step forward.

"Why are you doing this to me? Why can't you leave me alone!?" Martin screamed.

He's ready to explode, Heinrich thought.

"Tell me what you confessed to at the church!" Heinrich shouted, raising his gloved hands above his head.

"It's between me and God!"

"*Tell me!*"

People walking by started to look at the teenager and investigator yelling at each other.

Martin shut his eyes tight and clenched his jaw. His teeth clamped so hard together that Heinrich could hear them grind.

Martin growled, and then blurted out, "I think my mother did something bad!"

Ah hah! Heinrich immediately thought, pleased with himself. But then his mind whirled and he scrunched his brow. That is not what he had expected to hear. *His mother?* he thought.

Heinrich started to speak, but then stopped. "Thank you for your cooperation, Herr Achterberg."

Tears were dripping down Martin's cheeks, and his eyes were still shut. "Can I go now?" he growled through gritted teeth.

Heinrich thought for a moment, twirling his mustache. "No," he said at last, and then turned to Tomas. "Arrest the boy."

The soldier's eyebrows rose. He leaned in to whisper in Heinrich's ear. "For what, sir?"

"We'll figure that out later. Just do it," Heinrich whispered back.

Tomas shrugged and walked toward the boy.

"W-wait," Martin said, taking another step back. "What have I done? I've told you everything you wanted to know!"

"I know you did, son, and I thank you for that. You will be fine."

Heinrich turned away from the boy and leaned toward Tomas' ear again. "Take him to the jail, put him in the second room, and wait for me. I'll be there shortly."

As Heinrich walked away, he could hear Martin's sobs, until the regular noises of the town drowned them out. He left Bedburg through the southern gates and made his way to the Achterberg estate.

When he arrived, he knocked hard on the front door.

"Dammit, boy, what took you so long to get back?" called a voice from inside.

The door swung open and Heinrich stared at the face of Karl Achterberg. The farmer took on a horrified expression, as if he'd just seen Satan.

"Afternoon, Herr Achterberg," Heinrich said.

"Dammit all—what are you doing here? Haven't you hurt me and my family enough?" Karl asked. He was holding his bandaged hand.

"How is your hand doing?" Heinrich asked.

Karl spat on the ground. "Eat shit, investigator. Where is my son?"

Heinrich shook his head. "I'm not here for you, Karl," he said, ignoring the farmer's question. He looked past Karl and saw the man's wife sitting on a stool, knitting. "I'm here for her."

Karl crouched, took a wide stance, and made his hands into fists. "Not until I'm dead and buried," he said, clenching his jaw.

Heinrich backpedaled, reached behind his back, and swung his arm around. He aimed a pistol straight at Karl's forehead. "Easy there, farmer," he said calmly. "I am a man of the law, and your wife is under arrest."

All of the color drained from Karl's face as he stared down the barrel of Heinrich's gun. His fists went slack. "U-under what charges?" he stuttered.

"Murder."

"Bullshit."

Bertrude groaned and stood from her seat. After a moment, she waddled to the door. "It *is* bullshit," she said, "but could you stop being so melodramatic, Karl?"

Bertrude allowed herself to be taken into custody, without putting up an argument.

Heinrich followed the big woman all the way through Bedburg, toward the jailhouse at the northern end of town. Since Heinrich was alone and didn't trust her, he walked behind Bertrude and held his gun on her the entire way. Questioning eyes glanced in their direction, but, for the most part, people distanced themselves as the investigator and his suspect walked through the town.

During their long march, Bertrude asked again and again, "What have you done with Martin?"

Heinrich decided that Bertrude Achterberg was a strong woman. *Despite being so sullen, and having a broken family, she clearly loves her son.* Heinrich thought he might have even felt a bit of admiration for the woman.

"He's fine," Heinrich responded, again and again.

When they entered the dark, cold chambers of the jailhouse, they descended a flight of stairs. At the bottom, Heinrich gave his scarred punisher a nod. Ulrich took Bertrude into a cell.

The first room of the jail had four cells, one of which Bertrude occupied. Heinrich walked into the second room—which also had four cells—where Tomas was keeping watch over Martin. The boy was huddled in the corner of his cell, knees against his chest.

Heinrich leaned in to Tomas' ear. "Bring the boy to the cell adjacent to his mother's," he whispered. "Make sure he's quiet, and make sure she doesn't see him."

Tomas nodded.

Heinrich went back into the first room, and into Bertrude's cell. Ulrich had laid out a set of sharp tools on a small table, and a tin bucket in front of Bertrude. The woman sat on a steel table in the middle of the room, and her legs dangled above the floor. Heinrich placed the bucket at her feet, while Ulrich stood in the corner of the room, tapping his chin and playing with his torture devices.

Heinrich slowly took a parchment from his tunic, unraveled it, and placed it beside Bertrude.

"What in the hell is that?" she asked.

"A confession," Heinrich said.

"A confession for what?"

"For the murder of Dorothea Gabler."

Bertrude grunted and spat on the cold ground next to Heinrich's feet. "You're an evil man, investigator. I'll never sign that."

Heinrich left the cell and came back with another chair. He placed the chair in front of Bertrude's table, sat down, and crossed one leg over the other. "Practical? Yes. Truth-seeking? Absolutely. But evil? No, Frau Achterberg."

Bertrude kept staring at the investigator. Her frown caused her jowls to sag.

"I have all the evidence I need, Bertrude. I'm surprised, really, at your husband's willpower. I pulled every fingernail from his hand, and yet he still didn't scream your name. He must love you quite a lot."

"Karl is a fool," Bertrude hissed.

"Why is that?" Heinrich asked, tilting his head to the side.

Bertrude stayed silent.

After a long pause, Heinrich pointed at the bucket at Bertrude's feet. "You see that bucket?" he said, and cleared his throat. "Well, when it's filled with ice cold water, and your feet are dipped in, it's not so bad. Frigid, of course, but survivable. After a long enough time, however, your feet grow so cold that your entire body begins to shake, and then it starts to shut down. Your feet go numb, and before long, your toes are black. In order to keep you from dying, your feet will have to be removed."

Bertrude seemed unaffected. "And you say you're not evil?"

Heinrich stood from his chair and raised a finger toward the ceiling. "Or," he said, and started pacing, "we could place a rag over your face, and pour the cold water down your throat. You'll think you were drowning, but you'll live. Your lungs will burn so badly that you'll *wish* you were drowning." The investigator faced Bertrude and smiled. "Isn't it funny how your body could *burn* from something so cold?"

"Yes," Bertrude said dryly. "How funny." She put her hands on her big stomach and shrugged. "What is it you want from me, investigator?"

Heinrich frowned. "I know that Dorothea Gabler came to your estate the day of her murder. I know that your husband was the only person there, but you must have come home at some point, after leaving Martin at the church. The timeline fits—and God only knows what you witnessed upon arriving."

For the first time, Heinrich could see the fear start to creep into Bertrude's stone-cold face. Her expression changed. Her eyes went a little softer, her eyebrows slumped, and her lips started to quiver, ever so slightly.

"If it were *my* guess, I'd say you found your husband, together with a young, ripe, beautiful girl. Was he violating her? Or perhaps it was consensual?"

Bertrude scowled, and she shut her eyes. "Stop it," she demanded. "You don't know what you're talking about."

Heinrich began pacing again. "I wonder how that must have made you feel," he muttered. "I know I would be heartbroken. But your son . . . he was in love with the poor girl. He could *never* know what happened in your home, could he?" Heinrich's voice rose as he kept speaking. "No," he said, nearly shouting. "She had to disappear." He stopped pacing and faced Bertrude with a confused look. "Is that why your home is so broken—because your husband broke your trust? Because Karl broke your heart?"

Bertrude's eyes turned hard and steely. Her trembling lips turned into a straight line on her face, and her fear turned to anger. "I said stop it!" she screamed.

"Then tell me the truth, dammit! You or your husband killed that girl! Then you chopped up her body and hid her remains in the wild, to hide your guilt. You can save your soul, Bertrude! Confess and be forgiven in God's eyes!"

Bertrude clenched her teeth. She was on the verge of an outburst, Heinrich could tell, but she stayed quiet for a long time. She let out a long droning sound.

"*Yes*," Bertrude growled at last, "I found my husband with that Catholic whore. But I did not kill her! I only sent her away."

Heinrich pulled at his lip, and then his mustache. *But the Achterbergs are Catholic*, he thought. *And yet she calls Dorothea a Catholic whore . . .*

Heinrich said, "If you won't do it for your soul, or God, or your husband, then confess for your *son*, Bertrude. Confess for Martin's sake. Do you want your entire family in ruins?"

Bertrude began sobbing, and her anger faded away. "Don't talk about my son, you devil. N-not my son."

Heinrich nodded, knowing his evaluation was correct. *This woman cares for her son more than anything else. Martin was the catalyst for this entire affair, but it wasn't his fault. Bertrude will do anything to protect him.*

"Yes," Heinrich said, eager for a breakthrough. "Martin will be the son of an adulterous father and a murderous mother. He will be stigmatized for the rest of his life. So, tell me, before I dip your feet in the bucket, the *truth!*"

Bertrude's sobs turned into wails, and she started shaking. She put her head in her hands, and kept muttering, "Not my son, please . . . not my son."

After a long moment, she looked up with bleary eyes. "It . . . it isn't the truth."

"Ulrich, pour the water," Heinrich said. "I've had enough of this." He glanced back at the defeated woman and asked, "What will you do, Bertrude?"

The woman's shoulders slumped, her head sank, and she stared at the ground. She sniffed and wiped her nose and eyes, and muttered something under her breath, but Heinrich couldn't understand her.

"What was that?" he asked, leaning closer.

"I said I'll sign."

Heinrich let out a long sigh and put a hand on Bertrude's shoulder. Then he stood straight and turned to face Ulrich. He nodded to the torturer.

Ulrich pounded on the eastern wall of the cell, and within a few seconds Tomas strolled into the room, guiding Martin Achterberg by the shoulders. The boy was weeping.

When Bertrude looked up from the ground, she stared at her pained, shocked son, and she wailed.

"How could you, mother?" Martin asked. "How could you hurt Dorothea?"

"M-Martin, it isn't what you think, son," Bertrude stammered. She reached an arm toward the boy. "Please, come here, Martin."

But Martin had already left the room.

"Wait!" Bertrude's voice echoed in the cell. "It's not true, son! Please, come back!"

The last thing Bertrude heard from her son was the faint sound of feet, running up the stone staircase, and she wailed as unsettled dirt rained on her from the ceiling.

An hour after Bertrude signed the confession, Heinrich and Tomas arrived at Castle Bedburg.

The structure was a brick keep with four towers on each end, and two twisting spires near the front gate. Besides the town barracks, it was the largest structure in Bedburg. Heinrich couldn't be bothered with the majestic sight. He felt somewhat sour as he walked over the front bridge and through the gates, and he stamped his forehead with a handkerchief.

He strolled through the main foyer and found Lord Werner. Everyone knew Archbishop Ernst of Cologne was the real sovereign of the land, and Lord Werner was his puppet ruler in Bedburg.

Werner was a small man with a nervous twitch. Heinrich chuckled to himself as he approached the lord—Werner's large head didn't quite fit his small body, which made the phrase "puppet ruler" even more apropos, at least to the investigator.

"You summoned me, my lord?" Heinrich asked.

"Yes, some time ago," Werner said with a thin, annoyed voice. "How go the murder investigations?"

"I've just attained a signed confession for the murder of Dorothea Gabler, lord," Heinrich said proudly, straightening his back. "That is why I was tardy."

"And what about the other girl—the pretty one?"

Heinrich felt his lungs deflate. "Well, I haven't found the perpetrator in that case . . . yet."

Lord Werner stared at Heinrich with discontent, as if the investigator was nothing more than a useless, feeble-minded beggar. "What a shame," Werner said slowly.

After a moment of silence, Heinrich cleared his throat. "So, you sent for me . . ."

The lord squinted, and then his blank face lit up, and he pointed a finger in the air. "Ah, yes! It appears you will be traveling to Cologne."

Heinrich raised one eyebrow. "Excuse me, my lord? For what purpose?"

The small man scratched his forehead. "Archbishop Ernst wishes you to escort a group of Jesuit priests back here. That's what the letter says, anyway."

Heinrich pointed at his own chest. "Me . . . *escort*, my lord? Aren't there people more suited to the task?"

"That's what I said. But he asked for you personally."

"There are bandits and highwaymen on the road to Cologne."

Lord Werner shrugged. "Bring an entourage of soldiers. He asked for you *personally*, Heinrich."

The investigator rolled his eyes, away from the lord, so Werner could not see. "Very well," he said, "how long until I leave with this . . . *entourage*?"

"Three days time."

Heinrich pulled at his mustache and sputtered. "With all due respect, my lord, that doesn't give me enough time to bring our murderer to justice. It will be at least a week until a trial—"

"It's a shame, isn't it?" Werner interjected. He stared Heinrich straight in the eyes, as if challenging him. "At least you can leave knowing that your work on the case has been greatly appreciated by myself, and by the people of Bedburg." Then the lord smiled, as if to stick the blade a bit deeper in the proverbial wound.

Heinrich felt his body tense up, and his vision narrowed. He frowned, and he sighed. After a moment, through clenched teeth, he said, "Very well, my lord, I'll set to preparing."

"Good, good," Lord Werner said. He turned to leave the foyer, and noticed Heinrich was still standing in place. "That's all, Investigator Franz. You are dismissed."

All that work for nothing, Heinrich thought. *Stolen.*

As he left the castle, he swore he could feel smoke billowing from his ears.

CHAPTER FOURTEEN

GEORG

Georg was fueled with adrenaline as he left morning Mass. He and thirty men stomped through the misty roads of Bedburg, walking with their heads held high, taking up the width of the road. Merchants, peasants, and women alike stayed out of their way.

The hunt was meant to be a send-off for autumn, welcome winter, and quell the fear that permeated through the town.

We will find this beast, Georg thought, trying to stay optimistic. He followed behind Konrad von Brühl, who led the large group.

Most of the men carried firearms—arquebuses and muskets and pistols—but Georg had his recurve bow slung over his shoulder.

"You plan on killing anything with that?" Konrad asked, grinning and motioning to the hunter's bow. "It's a bit . . . outdated, wouldn't you say?"

Georg frowned at Konrad. "It's more accurate than your guns, and it's quieter. All you'll be doing is spooking the wolves."

"But a bow . . . on horseback?"

Georg stayed quiet. For someone who claimed to have once known him, Konrad clearly didn't understand how threatening Georg was with a sturdy bow in his hands.

He will soon see.

The group reached the southern end of town and then cut east, toward the largest stable in Bedburg. Everything had been prearranged—horses of all sizes packed the stalls. Georg picked a black, rowdy destrier named Alptraum, or Nightmare.

"She's quick, but unpredictable," the stableman told Georg. "Be careful with her, and bring her back in one piece, or I'll make sure *you* don't leave here in one piece."

Georg smiled at the man and nodded. He took the reins of Alptraum, hefted his boot on the stirrup, and hoisted himself on her back. The leather reins felt good in his callused hands. He ran his hands over her muscular neck and coarse mane, and then spurred the mare onward. Alptraum whinnied, and started trotting down the road.

Konrad was beside the hunter a moment later, bouncing on the back of his own brown-spotted steed. "That's a beastly mare you've got there," he said.

"It takes a beast to hunt a beast," Georg replied.

Konrad grinned, and the scar running down his face puffed outward.

The group was out of Bedburg and into the open countryside within minutes. One hundred and twenty hooves pounded the wet grass, and Georg could see the first signs of trees in the distance, about a mile east. The riders made their way over crops, up hillsides, and past houses and pastures.

A single rider came from the eastern trees, heading their direction. The scout made his way to Konrad and slowed his horse. "I've found a large den in the middle of the woods, Herr Brühl," the scout said, motioning over his shoulder. "There's a pack of wolves just waiting, unaware. I counted around twelve, not including cubs."

"Lead us there," Konrad said. He wheeled his horse toward his men and raised his right hand to the sky. "There are wolves in those trees, boys!" he shouted. "One of them could very well be our killer—maybe they all are. Be sure to see if they turn to men when they're killed."

A few of the men snickered, but most of the group kept quiet.

Their beliefs—while superstitious to some—were very real in their own minds. This hunt was no joking matter. The men were angry and scared from the deaths surrounding their town, and keen on protecting their families from further mourning. The German countryside had always been rife with wolves, but the last few years had seen those numbers multiply.

Konrad began laying out the plan. "The Peringsmaar Lake lies beyond those trees. If you've reached the lake, you've gone too far. My scout tells me the wolf den is in the middle of the woods, so it will be hard riding. We'll come at them from all sides, six horsemen per group, and cut off their escape. If they take off running, we'll give chase. Understood?"

Men grunted and nodded.

Georg took a look at the group of men. These were not the hardened, battle-tested soldiers he was used to riding with, but a group of peasants and townsfolk eager to prove themselves. *Konrad's plan is sound for laymen*, he thought, *but I'm no layman.*

He was a trained hunter and tracker. He *was* hardened and battle-tested. He'd killed much worse than wolves. Georg wanted to say something to Konrad, but didn't want to undermine the man's leadership and cause confusion, so he kept his thoughts to himself.

Surrounding the den with inexperienced men and firearms will create a chaotic crossfire. That's a danger I won't take part in. No, I think I'll work alone.

The scout relayed that the den was downhill from a butte, with a small cave nestled at the bottom of the hill. The five groups of men would meet at the top of the butte and set up formation like the points of a star. Konrad placed Georg at the head of five other riders, and Georg was supposed to take his group to the southwestern point of the star. All five groups would charge from the top of the butte and try to trap the wolves in a circle.

After the plan was set, the horsemen took off, first approaching the woods in two groups. As they reached the edge of the first trees, the two groups split off into their five parties. Georg could hear the nervous murmuring of his men as Alptraum trotted into the woods. Many of the men were unaccustomed to riding or hunting, especially through dense woods.

Georg crossed into the thick foliage of the alder trees and raised his right fist next to his head, ordering his men to stop talking. He pulled on the reins and halted Alptraum.

The men quieted and reined in their steeds behind the hunter. One man nearly fell from his horse.

"From here on, we're as silent as a group of deaf mutes," he whispered to his crew. He spurred Alptraum on and brought the mare to a steady gait, maneuvering through the thick alders.

Although it was almost winter, many of the trees still clung to life with branches full of dark green leaves. Georg could hear the constant chirping of insects and birds, the gentle pulsing of hooves on the forest floor. The forest was alive with hidden sounds of nature, and the sounds brought a smile to his face.

After a few minutes of slow moving around trees and fallen branches, Georg spotted one of the other groups in the distance. He realized his own crew was nearing the butte as they started to climb uphill.

The trees and undergrowth cleared a bit, and Georg reached the summit of the hill—the ridge of the butte. He looked over the ridge and noticed a steep decline, congested with dead leaves and dirt. The butte was shaped like a circle, as if a crater had landed in the middle of the woods. It was almost unnatural.

When it rained, the crater would fill like a pool, but it was a dry morning.

Some boulders at the deepest section of the slope were carved out, and the rock face created a small cave, just like the scout had warned.

Georg looked to his left and right and saw groups of men appearing through the trees, setting up their points of Konrad's star formation. Before long, the thirty men had the ridge surrounded.

A pack of wolves roamed around the bottom of the butte, in and around the cave. Cubs whelped and whined, and their parents stood guard over them. They appeared feral, hungry, and unaware of the men at the top of the hill.

Georg knew he'd be a fool to think that these beasts didn't know thirty men were staring down at them, ready to pounce. *Wolves have some of the keenest senses in nature,* Georg thought, shaking his head. *They will flee at the last moment, and create turmoil for these riders. Konrad's plan is flawed.*

For all the respect he gave the wolves, Georg was disappointed at their sizes. Not a single one looked over seventy pounds—most looked emaciated and gray, their fur clinging to their exposed ribs.

These are not the beasts I'm after.

At the top, northern point of the star, Konrad brought himself to the front of his group. He raised his hand high for everyone else to see. In his other hand, he cocked his arquebus.

"Weapons ready, boys," Georg whispered to his men. "On Konrad's mark, give them hellfire." He slung his bow from his back and grabbed an arrow from the quiver at his waist. He held the bow and arrow in his left hand, and Alptraum's reins in his right.

A harmony of sounds rang out as men around the hillside took out their guns, inspected them, loaded their gunpowder, and cocked their matchlocks.

Konrad's arm fell, and everyone spurred into action . . . everyone except Georg.

Men raised their weapons and shouted battle cries as their horses raced down the hill toward the wolves.

Georg's men streamed by him, but the hunter didn't follow. Instead, he wheeled his horse around and retreated the way he'd come. He circled around the southern end of the butte and back into the trees.

Rather than get tangled with the rest of the riders, he decided to find his own place—a place he knew the wolves would flee toward. He knew they would flee outwards, in all directions, splitting off from each other to elude their pursuers. He didn't want to get caught at the bottom of the hill with the rest of the hunters.

Georg had been on enough hunts to know where to be, and where not to be.

As he headed further south, away from the butte, he heard gunfire and shouts pierce the peaceful morning sky. The booming sounds ricocheted off the alder trees.

The hunt was on.

Alptraum cut around alder trees and leaped over high undergrowth. Georg ducked beneath low-hanging branches and gripped his bow. He steered the mare around a slanted hill and burst out of the trees at the southern ridge of the butte.

In front of him sat the Peringsmaar Lake—a wide, circular body of water—with its bank just a stone's throw away.

The cacophony of gunfire lit up the woods behind him.

Georg heard a rustling sound in the trees to his left. He craned his neck and lifted his bow to his chin.

Squeezing on Alptraum's haunches with his knees, he let go of the horse's reins, and Alptraum stopped in her tracks.

Two wolves vaulted from the trees and sprinted into the clearing, heading toward the bank of the lake. It was a mother and her cub.

Georg closed one eye and took aim, leading his bow in front of the mother wolf. As the wolves gained distance, Georg nocked his arrow and quickly released.

The mother wolf whelped and went tumbling. Georg's arrow protruded from her side.

The pup stopped to coddle its mother, confused.

Georg jumped from his horse and ran over to the felled wolf. He unsheathed a long knife and dropped his bow.

The cub sprinted off, back into the trees, and Georg kneeled beside the mother wolf. With a swift cut he put the animal out of its misery. Then he hoisted her on his shoulders, picked his bow up, and tied the wolf to the back of Alptraum's hind.

Georg was back on the hunt within less than a minute.

Alptraum galloped down the flat bank of the Peringsmaar, away from the commotion in the woods. After a minute of hard riding, Georg found a clearing in the trees and steered Alptraum in that direction.

The mare hurdled over a fallen tree trunk, and Georg found himself back in the dense copse of alders, ducking and weaving through the woods. Each steady gallop distanced Georg from the butte, and he headed further south, hoping to find more straggling wolves.

He heard a rustling over his shoulder, turned in his saddle, and lifted his bow. He saw a fellow rider in the trees, and Georg let his bowstring loosen. The rider quickly disappeared into the thick foliage, and Georg faced forward.

His eyes went wide and he ducked just in time to avoid being throttled by a neck-level tree limb.

Alptraum slowed her pace as the woodland became thicker and thicker with alders, making it almost impossible to travel through.

Georg's heart raced, and he surveyed his surroundings. He found a patch of trees less dense than the rest, and guided Alptraum in that direction.

He pulled on the reins, and Alptraum stopped in place. He took his bow from his back and drew a single arrow. He narrowed his vision and stared ahead, but could not see anything.

Then he heard a low growling.

Georg held his breath for a tense, silent moment, and slowly let Alptraum step forward.

A large, black wolf shot out from the underbrush, just ten paces in front of Georg. Alptraum whinnied, startled, and shot up on her hind legs, nearly throwing the hunter from her back. Georg gritted his teeth, kicked Alptraum in the side, and steadied the mare. He leaned forward in his saddle and Alptraum snorted and took chase.

This is not a wolf from the same pack, Georg thought. *It's too far removed from the others. No, this is a loner—a* big *loner.*

It was one of the largest wolves Georg had ever seen—easily one hundred and thirty pounds—and yet it moved effortlessly through the woods, gliding over fallen branches and around tight corners.

Georg spurred Alptraum over and over, but had trouble keeping pace with the wolf. Trees blurred by in all directions as Georg's steed barreled through the woods.

Alptraum jumped into a clearing and the sun glared into Georg's eyes. He winced, and tried to continue through the clearing. Before he could, Alptraum rose on her hind legs and wailed again, temporarily blinded by the sudden ray of sunlight. As his horse arched its back, Georg held tight to the reins and nearly fell from his saddle, again.

When he and Alptraum regained their composure, Georg saw the black wolf at the other end of the circular glade. The beast vanished back into the alder trees.

Before giving chase, something caught Georg's eye. He cocked his head to the left and noticed a small log cabin sitting in the back of the clearing. The wooden structure was nestled underneath a large tree, and looked decrepit and abandoned. Tree branches grew in and around the sides of the cabin, making it seem as though the structure was part of the forest itself, growing with Mother Nature.

Alptraum trotted slowly around the eerie house, and Georg glanced at the single window in the cabin. He tried to relocate the wolf's trail, but shook his head and squinted.

Georg did a double take and glanced back at the cabin, and swore he saw the face of a woman in the window, staring back at him.

He felt the hairs on the back of his neck stand on edge, and then he blinked hard.

When he opened his eyes, the window was empty.

These woods must be getting to me.

He cleared his throat, steadied his reins, and kicked Alptraum into a gallop, through the clearing and back in pursuit of the large, black wolf.

*   *   *

The sun waned and began its descent behind the horizon. Georg led his tired horse back to the southern end of Bedburg. One by one, other riders trickled in from the woods, including Konrad.

Georg noticed two dead wolves strapped to Konrad's brown-spotted steed.

Konrad glanced at Georg, and then nodded slowly as his eyes turned toward Alptraum and the three wolves slung over the horse's back.

"That's a big bastard you got there," Konrad said, gesturing to the large black wolf with a nod. "One of the biggest I've seen."

Georg patted the wolf's corpse and ran a hand through its fur. "Took me nearly an hour to catch him. He was an elusive one. Nearly tumbled off my horse, twice, trying to get him."

Konrad chuckled. "Well, you did better than anyone else." He hopped from his horse, handled his reins, and the two walked on foot toward the other huntsmen. "I suppose I should apologize for my words about your rickety old bow."

"How did the rest of the men fair?" Georg asked.

"Most of them weren't suited to the task," Konrad said with a shrug. "About half the boys came up empty-handed. But we caught fifteen in all."

"Not a bad day's work," Georg said. "Hopefully the people will feel safer."

"Do you think that black one could be our fearsome culprit?"

Georg scratched his head and said, "It's hard to say. He was alone, which is rare. But as you can see, he didn't transform into a man when he died."

Konrad chuckled. "A shame."

The two hunters reached the rest of the men. Most of them looked ragged and exhausted, with ambivalent looks of disappointment and pride on their faces.

"All right, boys," Konrad shouted. "A job well done today. Let's bring these beasts to the tanner. First round's on me for anyone who wants to join me at the tavern to celebrate."

A few of the men cheered, but most were too tired to say anything.

"See you there?" Konrad asked Georg.

"In a bit," Georg said. "I have some other things to do."

Konrad squinted. "I think your men would appreciate you showing up."

Georg frowned. "I said I'll be there." He turned and walked away, not bothering to mention that he'd left his ragged group of riders, which was why his hunt was so successful in the first place.

Georg led Alptraum through Bedburg, and the townsfolk gawked as they eyed the dead wolves on his horse's back. Some of the women smiled at him, and Georg smiled back, while others simply squinted at him.

On his way to the stables, Georg noticed Investigator Franz in the distance, walking with his guard.

"Georg," the investigator said with a nod. He took a look at Alptraum. "I see you had a successful hunt."

"Could have been better," Georg said. He yawned and stretched his arms. "What brings you this far down in the slums, investigator? Shouldn't you be with your noble friends?"

"I don't have any friends," Investigator Franz said, although he spoke with satisfaction rather than pity. "I'm headed to the Achterberg estate. I finally have a signed confession for the murder of Dorothea Gabler."

Georg's brow narrowed, and he tilted his head to the side. "You're saying this hunt was worthless? Who was the culprit?"

"Bertrude Achterberg."

Georg laughed. "That fat old lady? You must be joking. You really think she could be capable of such a grisly murder?"

"Anything is possible with the right tools, my good hunter. And either way, she signed the confession. Now I'm going to retrieve her husband, for adultery. Like to join me?"

"Sounds fun," Georg said sarcastically. Then he shrugged and started following the investigator. "It's been a busy day, eh?"

"Indeed, indeed," Investigator Franz said. He seemed strangely chipper, but Georg figured that was the effect that closing a case had on the strange lawman.

After a minute of walking in silence, Georg asked, "What about Josephine? You can find her killer now, right? Do you think she's still connected with Dorothea—"

"Alas," the investigator said, cutting Georg off, "I've been ordered by Lord Werner to travel to Cologne. I am to escort some priests back here. It's utterly ridiculous, but I'll be back soon. And then, you have my word, I will bring the whore's killer to justice."

Georg eyed the investigator with a frown.

Investigator Franz rolled his eyes. "I'll bring the *lady's* killer to justice," he said. "My mistake." He poked his head toward the wolves on Alptraum's rear. "What will you do with those?"

Georg glanced at the corpses. "I figure I'll sell the hides of the two smaller ones. The bigger one, though, I think I'll have him stuffed and mounted. He could be our *actual* killer, you know."

"I wouldn't be so sure." The investigator didn't elaborate, and the two men kept walking in silence.

Finally, Georg broke the peace and quiet. "I ran across a strange thing today, during the hunt."

Investigator Franz eyed the hunter.

"Remember how you said the woods might house the beast, as a base of sorts?"

"I do."

"Well," Georg said, spitting on the ground, "I came across a cottage in the woods. It was an old, broken-down thing. But the strangest part—and I might be going crazy—is that I swore I saw somebody inside, even though the place looked completely abandoned."

"Interesting," the investigator said.

"I think I'll go back sometime and see what's going on there."

"Unnecessary, Georg. We have our criminal. Leave the poor

hermits alone."

Georg shrugged. "Well . . . for peace of mind. Got to follow up any and all leads, right investigator?" He looked at Heinrich and winked.

A small smile crept on the investigator's face. "Whatever you say, my good hunter."

The trio reached the end of Bedburg's roads, and made their way to the hillside estate of the Achterberg family. When they reached the front door, Georg noticed that it was slightly ajar.

He shared a look with Heinrich, and they both furrowed their brows.

"Karl Achterberg, this is Investigator Heinrich Franz. I must speak with you."

The investigator motioned for Tomas, and the soldier nodded and stepped forward. He unsheathed his sword, nudged the door open, and then Heinrich and Georg came to his side.

Tomas' mouth dropped open.

"Dear God," Georg stammered.

Martin Acterberg stood at the end of the room with a bloody knife in his hand. He faced the men with a wild, crazed look in his eyes. "He stole my love from me," the boy said through clenched teeth.

Karl Achterberg was at the boy's feet, surrounded by a pool of his own blood.

PART II

The Devil's Instrument

CHAPTER FIFTEEN

DIETER

Father Dieter Nicolaus sat at a small table, hunched over a German translation of the New Testament. In one hand, he clutched the wooden amulet Sybil had given him, while his other hand traced over the text of the Gospels. The hearth next to his table was dark, the windows of his lodging were shuttered. A single flickering candle on his table was the only light in the cold room.

He eyed the amulet in his hand, feeling the rough edges of the two crosses, and smiled.

He heard a sound, and his gaze shot over to the front door of the room as it creaked opened.

Sybil's face poked into the doorway.

Dieter smiled again and waved his hand at the girl. "Come in, come in."

Sybil tiptoed into the room, quietly closed the door behind her, and crept across the length of the living room. She sat in a chair next to Dieter.

Dieter first noticed her clothes: a dark blue gown and woolen overcoat. But he frowned when he noticed her eyes darting around, a worried look on her face.

"What troubles you, my dear?"

"I'll admit," Sybil said, whispering, "I don't like meeting here." She cast her eyes downward, and Dieter followed them to the floorboards in the center of the room. The dried blood of

Karl Achterberg still stained the floor.

A week had passed since Bertrude Achterberg's confession and arrest, and Karl Achterberg's death at the hands of his son. The house had been vacant since. The events gave the room an eerie, ominous feel, especially in the dead of night.

Still, Dieter and Sybil had met at the house nearly every night since Karl's death and Martin's arrest. The priest taught the girl to read and write by poring through the Bible.

Dieter felt guilty for making Sybil uneasy. "It's the only place I could think of that's close enough to your estate so that we don't alert attention, my child." He placed a hand on her slender shoulder.

"Please, call me Beele, Father."

"Then call me Dieter."

Sybil's eyes were big and frightened when she faced him. "I know it's a good hideaway, being outside of town . . . but people *died* here. The werewolf lived in this house!"

Dieter gently squeezed Sybil's arm. "Don't believe everything you hear, Beele. I don't believe Bertrude Achterberg is capable of being the beast that everyone in Bedburg fears."

"But isn't this house cursed?" Sybil asked.

"Some might believe that, depending on their superstitions. But if we're seen sneaking out at night together, that could be a much worse omen for us. I would hate to see anything happen to you."

Sybil's gaze went back to the floor, and Dieter thought he saw her blushing.

"Besides," the priest continued, "this house will be blessed soon, and all will be forgiven and forgotten."

Sybil lifted her head. Dieter was smiling. "Do you really believe that," she asked. "What will happen to this house?"

"Well, the estate will go to the church. Bishop Solomon will absolve this place of past sins, and, if we're lucky, this place will become a house of worship."

"Hopefully after the blood is removed . . ."

Dieter's smile turned into a frown. He paused for a moment, said, "Come now," and moved his hand from Sybil's arm. "Let's continue where we left off," he said, and looked down at the Bible.

"All right, but I fear I don't have much time."

Dieter craned his neck to the side. "Does your father know you're here?"

"Of course not . . . but he left home earlier than usual. He might come back earlier, too."

Dieter nodded firmly. "Then let's get on with it." He looked far off, past Sybil, into the darkness behind her. "Tomorrow is an early start for me as well."

She must have noticed his distant stare. "What's tomorrow?"

Dieter sighed. He'd hoped to avoid dark topics with the girl he felt so dearly for. "Tomorrow is Bertrude Achterberg's execution, Beele. As a priest, I must speak to the people and the condemned before she is . . . well . . . it's going to be a gruesome affair. Please do not come, Beele. My heart would shatter."

Sybil stayed quiet for a long time. Then she startled Dieter by lunging and wrapping her arms around him. "That's horrible," she said.

She rested her head on the curve of Dieter's neck. He could feel tears running from her eyes down his shoulder, and her warm breath against his neck.

Dieter shuddered, felt his throat go tight, and the hairs on his neck stood on edge.

Sybil tilted her head back to look at his face. "Are you all right? Are you cold?"

Dieter shook his head fervently, but struggled to speak. He was not cold, but the opposite—his body tingled with fire. "N-no, no," he finally stammered.

Sybil ran a hand from the small of his back up toward his shoulder blades.

"P-please," Dieter said weakly.

Sybil ignored his protest and massaged his back for what

seemed like eons. "You'll be fine tomorrow," she said after finishing her massage. She moved her hand away from his back, but then leaned close to him and planted a wet kiss on the side of his cheek. "For good luck," she said, grinning.

Dieter's mind went dizzy and his cheeks turned cherry-red. He hurried to face his Bible, and flipped rapidly through the pages as if he were looking for a specific page.

Sybil chuckled.

"R-right," the priest said, trying to calm his racing heart. "Let's get on with it."

The next morning, a spitting rain woke the quiet town. Dieter stared at the stained-glass doors of the church, looking at his reflection in the windows. His eyes seemed sunken, the edges wrinkled by crow's feet. He sighed, knowing he looked nothing like an exuberant, youthful twenty-year-old.

He'd walked Sybil home the night before, gotten hardly any sleep, and spent hours praying, readying himself for this day. He was tired—physically and spiritually. His mind was conflicted and confined, both for the vitriol he was forced to preach to support his faith, and for the heartache he felt toward Sybil Griswold.

They were becoming close—too close for a Catholic priest and a beautiful young woman. But he couldn't stop his wandering mind, body, and soul. His years of training did little to prepare him for an *actual* encounter with such an alluring girl. The words he recited about resilience, chastity, obedience . . . they were just that. Words.

He tried to believe and live his life by those words, wholeheartedly, but they did nothing to prepare him for when he was in Sybil's presence.

"Father?"

Dieter shook his head, snapped into reality, and turned to face the somber nun, Sister Salome.

"The bishop would like to see you in his chambers."

Dieter nodded and then whisked past her, down the aisle. He hurried into the hallway and veered toward the bishop's oak doors.

The doors swung open, and Bishop Solomon stood in front of Dieter, hands clasped behind his back. His thin, white hair looked as though it could be plucked from his round head.

The bishop was frowning and studying Dieter's face. He groaned and said, "How are you doing, Father Nicolaus? You do not look well."

"I am fine, Your Grace. A bit tired, but that is all." Dieter took a moment to stare at the wrinkled face of his superior, and came to the same conclusion. The bishop did not look well—not sickly, but angry.

"And yourself, Your Grace?"

Bishop Solomon waved a hand in Dieter's face and shuffled into his room. He retreated to his oversized desk, and opted to sit on one of the edges of the desk, rather than his chair. "I am dismayed at losing my favorite altar boy. Martin Achterberg was a fine young man. It's a shame his mother was an instrument of the Devil. Martin had promise."

"An instrument of the Devil, Your Grace? Do you truly believe that?" Dieter immediately regretted speaking so fast and questioning the bishop's words.

The bishop shot Dieter a dismissive glance. "Someone who could commit such horrid atrocities? Truly, I do believe that, Dieter. Have you not seen the same confession that I have? It reads like a vile transcript from the lips of Satan himself."

Dieter stayed quiet for a moment, hoping to skirt the subject altogether. "What will become of the boy, Your Grace?"

"Martin?" The bishop groaned again and stood from his desk. He shuffled around to his chair and plopped onto it. His eyes seemed suddenly distant and unfocused. "Well, he *did* kill his father. Poor boy—his fate is clearly not an ecclesiastical matter. I assume he will suffer the trials and tribulations of the menial courts." He spoke with a bite in his tone, as if he didn't approve of the altar boy's providence, nor the competency of secular law.

"Anyway," he continued, shaking his head and waving his hand. "Are you ready for today, my son?"

"Ready?"

The bishop nodded. "In the few years you've been here, you haven't had to conduct a public ceremony of this nature. It can be quite trying on the spirit, but just know that God is always in your heart."

Dieter opened his mouth to speak, but then checked himself. He cocked his head and hoped he wouldn't regret what he was about to say.

"Is there something wrong?" Solomon asked.

"Well, Your Grace, it's just . . . when you speak of Him always being in my heart, I do have a question that is a bit removed from Bertrude and Martin Achterberg, if you don't mind."

The bishop raised his eyebrows, and his forehead wrinkled. "Speak freely, my son. What is it you wish to ask?"

Dieter found that he was fidgeting, and he tried to speak as delicately as possible. "I was wondering, Your Grace, how one as holy as yourself—filled with God's wisdom—could go so long to avoid any . . . *earthly* desires."

Bishop Solomon chuckled, unexpectedly. But to Dieter, it did not seem to be a happy chuckle. "Is it repentance you seek, Dieter?"

Dieter shook his head and felt his face redden. "N-no, Your Grace. These are just some of the things I ponder throughout my day."

The bishop cleared his throat. He leaned forward in his chair and folded his hands on the desk. "What are the three powers of the soul, my son?"

"Memory, intellect, and will," Dieter rattled off without thinking.

Bishop Solomon nodded. "You have always had the memory to learn, and the intellect to question, Dieter. That is good." He raised a finger. "But *willpower* . . . you must have the willpower, in your heart, to resist temptation. Eve was unable to, and look what happened to her." The bishop chuckled, despite himself. "Temptation is a hallmark of a pious man, Dieter. But perseverance and obedience are hallmarks of a *righteous* man. Do you understand?

"The evangelical counsels decree that we must endure voluntary poverty, perpetual chastity, and entire obedience. It is your entire obedience to Him that allows you to resist temptation and remain perpetually chaste. Your obedience will help lead you to salvation, my son. That is why God is both our Lord *and Savior,* is it not?"

In Dieter's eyes, the short speech came off as utterly contrived, scripted, and somewhat condescending. It was as if these were words the bishop told himself when he woke up each morning. Dieter wondered if the bishop had a single thought on the matter outside of Scripture.

Still, Dieter did not rebut. *It's best not to argue with my superior about the tenets of Christianity*, he decided. Dieter had his own ideas—these were the same tenets that he grew up studying, after all. He just wished the bishop had a more *human* oration to help him overcome his conflicted mind.

While Dieter remained quiet and contemplative, Bishop Solomon's eyes narrowed on the priest. "Now," he said, "when you question my belief that Bertrude Achterberg is an instrument of Satan, do not forget that she broke no less than *four* Commandments." His tone was darker than before.

"I can see your mind is elsewhere this morning, so I'll forgive your inane remarks," the bishop continued. He cleared his throat and shook his head. "Nonetheless, this shows that you are not ready for such a spiritually trying occasion. So I've decided, just now, that I will speak to the public congregation this morning, and to the condemned woman. You are relieved of your duty—so go get some rest."

Dieter's mouth dropped open. He was speechless, and before he could respond in any way, the bishop looked down at a stack of papers on his desk, and said, "Is there anything else you wish to ask me, my son?"

Dieter's shoulders slumped. "No, Your Grace."

"Then you're dismissed," Solomon said. The bishop looked up from his stack of papers. "And I think, in the future, that you should come to your own conclusions when regarding canonical tenets, especially when you learned those tenets as a *child.*"

Dieter stood on the raised platform alongside Bishop Solomon, Lord Werner, and an out-of-town magistrate whom Dieter had never seen before. Dieter glanced to his left, at Bishop Solomon, and felt a pang of anger. He felt guilty for the contempt he felt toward the bishop, but that guilt quickly dissipated. As usual, the dour bishop had belittled him, and Dieter had had enough.

He tells me he welcomes my questions, to speak freely, and then chastises me like a toddler when I ask them, the priest thought. *Questioning my teachings is supposed to be commendable, but how can I question them when I'm met with such patronizing responses?* Dieter shook his head. *Perhaps that's the last time I ask the bishop for his opinion.*

Dieter looked further down the line, to the magistrate. He was Baron Ludwig von Bergheim, a burgomaster and chief barrister for Bedburg and other nearby towns. He was a tall, serious-looking man with tight lips and a beaked nose. While Dieter, Bishop Solomon, and Lord Werner let the rain fall on their shoulders, the baron had a guard holding an umbrella over his head.

Dieter faced the crowd below the platform. The event was being held in the public square—usually the marketplace—and the crowd was quickly growing in number. No less than a hundred townsfolk had come to witness the day's event, even with the rain drenching them.

Executions were the most entertaining events that most folk witnessed in their monotonous lives, and Dieter recognized many of the faces in the crowd. He sighed and frowned when his eyes passed over Sybil's face toward the back of the congregation. She stood next to her father, and Peter had his thick arms wrapped across his chest.

A large wooden cross stood in the middle of the crowd, on a raised scaffold. The townsfolk made a circle around the cross and helped toss soggy kindling around it. A hooded executioner stood at one end of the platform.

Baron Bergheim stood forward and silenced the murmuring crowd. He produced and unraveled a scroll, and read off the charges that faced Bertrude Achterberg. He spoke sternly, enunciating every charge with a rolling finish—adultery, murder, blasphemy. Each new charge brought a loud hiss from the townsfolk.

After reading off the charges, the baron backed away, and Bishop Solomon walked forward to the edge of the platform. He raised his right hand high into the sky and, on cue, two guards started walking through the crowd. They came from the furthest end of the square, walking through at least eight rows of shouting townsfolk. Bertrude Achterberg shuffled along, in the middle of the two soldiers. Her tunic was filthy, her face distraught, and people threw lettuce, vegetables, and even rocks at her as she was led through the angry crowd.

Bertrude and the guards neared the wooden cross in the center of the square, and the woman fought back with every ounce of strength, squirming in the grasp of the guards. She wailed and writhed as she was led up the stairs and to the cross. Some of the people in the crowd started laughing at the spectacle.

The guards strapped her to the cross and bound her hands behind her back. People cheered as she screamed.

"Bertrude of the family Achterberg!" Bishop Solomon yelled. "I hold in my hand your signed confession!" He raised the parchment high over his head, and the crowd cheered even louder.

"This is a confession of a most loathsome nature, in which you knowingly carried out the evil deeds of Satan!"

The crowd booed and hissed.

The bishop's voice became a screech, piercing through the rain and the raucous horde of people. "You have been charged as a murderer and sorceress, wherein you used Satan's black magic to lure and devour an innocent girl! You've been charged as a succubus—a wretched adulterer—wherein you broke your Heavenly vows and forced your beguiling wit on the husband of another woman!"

If that was in the confession . . . I never saw it, Dieter thought, scratching his head.

"And, perhaps worst of all, you have been charged as a witch, a seductress who used your own son and indoctrinated him into your evil ways, forcing the innocent boy into murdering his own father!"

Of course, Dieter thought, nodding slowly. *The bishop's using his fancy for Martin to proclaim the boy's innocence, even during his own mother's execution. Perhaps this is why the bishop wanted to give the speech in the first place.*

"It isn't true! None of it is true!" Bertrude wailed. "I killed no one! I seduced no one!"

But the people weren't listening. The bloodthirst of the crowd was absolute and unrelenting. Nothing could sway the mass opinion that she was evil—a true instrument of the Devil.

"Repent, and let the power of Christ save your soul!" the bishop screamed. "You cannot save your body, but you can save your spirit! You can save the soul of your son! Do not bring your son with you into the depths of the abyss, witch!"

Bertrude would not give up. Her cries became inaudible, and she was racked with heaving sobs. Before long, the throng of watchers grew restless.

"Strip her, and show us the Witch's Mark! Show us the Mark of Satan!" Bishop Solomon announced.

The executioner walked up to Bertrude and tore off her filthy gown, exposing her large, naked body. He pointed to her collarbone, where a big black mark that looked like a mole—or a burn—was visible.

The crowd gasped, and their frenzy grew louder.

"Then let it be done," the bishop said, "and let your cursed ways die with your body and your soul."

Solomon nodded, and Ulrich the executioner produced a burning torch. The flames whistled and licked at the rainy sky, sending clouds of steam billowing into the air.

The executioner touched the corners of the kindling, and within moments the flames were at the feet of Bertrude. The woman cried out in agony and looked to the sky as the acrid smell of burning flesh met with the crisp rain.

As the fire engulfed her body and the cross, her bloodcurdling cries could be heard throughout Bedburg, ricocheting off buildings. As her skin blackened, her cries turned to wheezing gasps, and the echoes of her howling could still be heard. The crowd loved it. They cheered and hollered and clapped.

But Father Dieter Nicolaus bowed his head and turned away, before the ghastly image could become tattooed on his mind for eternity.

CHAPTER SIXTEEN

SYBIL

Sybil's eyes were clenched shut throughout the execution. As she gripped her father by the waist, tears trickled down her cheeks. Peter put his arm around her and brought her close. After the execution, he pushed her to arm's-length and she opened her eyes and stared at his stern face.

"That woman was evil, Beele. Her punishment was just. It's okay to cry, but know that her soul might be saved in the afterlife," Peter said.

Sybil shook her head and wiped the tears from her face. "That was awful, father! How can you say those things when you barely knew the woman?" She stole a glance to her side and saw the embers of Bertrude's corpse. She quickly regretted looking. The body was a crisp, blackened shell. "She was Martin's mother," Sybil muttered. "We knew the Achterbergs, and now that family is gone."

"That is why you must be careful in everything you do, Beele. We aren't safe in this town—do you see that now?"

"But the Achterbergs were Catholics! If *they* aren't safe here, who is?"

Peter stood to his full height and looked away from his daughter. Sybil followed his eyes. Two men approached. One of the men was the tall, lanky magistrate who had arbitrated the execution, Baron Ludwig von Bergheim. Beside him was a younger, handsome man who had twitchy eyes and a perpetual scowl on his face. The young man had fair hair and wore the linen regalia of a nobleman.

Peter bowed to the men as they approached, while Sybil stared back and forth from her father, to the nobles, and back to Peter again.

"Herr Peter Griswold," Baron Ludwig said, holding out his hand. Sybil expected her father to shake the man's hand, but was shocked when Peter bent and kissed his knuckle.

How does father know such esteemed men?

"Lord, it is my honor. That was a fine execution," Peter said.

Ludwig nodded. "May her wretched soul be damned." The baron looked down his beaked nose at Sybil. "Is this the girl?"

"It is," Peter said. "This is my daughter, Sybil. Beautiful, is she not?"

"Pretty, at best," the shorter man said. He had a rather high-pitched voice, and Sybil realized he was probably close to the same age as she was.

Peter eyed the noble boy with a frown, and then turned back to the baron. "Will you need a place to sup before the ball, my lord?"

If Sybil was confused before by the exchange, now she was absolutely flabbergasted. *What ball? What is going on?*

Baron Bergheim made a hoarse sound in his throat, somewhere between a cough and a chuckle, but from someone who clearly hadn't chuckled much in his life. "No, no, I'm sure Lord Werner will provide us with more . . . *adequate* means."

"Of course," Peter said, bowing his head. He gritted his teeth while he faced the ground. "My apologies."

"Then we will be off," Ludwig said. He turned to leave with the young man and waved nonchalantly at Peter and Sybil. Before he got too far, he shouted over his shoulder, "Make sure she is dressed appropriately, Herr Griswold. That garish gown simply won't do."

"Of course, my lord," Peter said. He crossed his arms over his chest as he and Sybil watched the two noblemen saunter away, into the parting crowd.

Peter ducked and barely avoided the clay mug as it flew over his head and smashed into the wall behind him. "Stop this nonsense, Beele!"

Sybil was already reaching for another plate. "You can't make me go, father! It's not fair!"

Although Sybil was angry that her father was forcing her to go to a ball, she was angrier that she'd miss her nightly meeting with Dieter.

"Johannes von Bergheim is a nobleman's son, Sybil. He has power and influence, and one day will inherit his father's entire wealth," Peter said, throwing up his arms. "It will be fun!"

"*Fun?*" Sybil screeched, as if her father had never uttered the word before. "They talked about me like I wasn't even there. I won't be seen in the presence of that boy for a single minute!"

Peter ran a hand through his hair and sighed. "Nobles weren't raised like us, dear. Wouldn't you like to be pampered for once? Wouldn't you like to own land and power—things that I can never give you? I may have some money, but that is nothing compared to what these people can provide. I'm trying to help our family, Beele."

"You can't force me to love someone," Sybil said. She put her hands on her hips and stuck out her chin.

Peter's mouth fell open and he was momentarily mute. "*Love?*" he said. "You think this is about *love?* Don't be naïve, girl, and stop thinking only about yourself. What about your brother? This is to help our family cement our legacy, for years to come."

As it was, Hugo was locked away in his room. Sybil imagined the nervous boy was hiding with his head between his legs, scared at the arguing between his father and his sister.

Legacy . . . years to come . . . Sybil's eyes opened wide. "Wait,

119

wait. Do you expect me to . . . *marry* that sod?"

Peter cleared his throat and looked away. "If all goes well . . ." he muttered and trailed off.

Sybil threw the clay plate in her hand and Peter dodged to the side, avoiding the object as it exploded into fragments behind him.

"I'll never do it!" Sybil said. She crossed her arms. "I could never love such a pig."

"You don't even know the man! Give him a chance, Beele."

"I've seen men like him before, father. He's the kind of man *you* warned me about. They're all the same, remember?"

Peter smiled stiffly and tried to take a different approach. "Wouldn't you like to be a lady of the court? Our family could have real influence—something that has never been possible! You could have your own handmaidens and servants, with fluffed pillows and silk sheets on your bed."

Sybil would not relent. She closed her eyes, arms still crossed, and breathed heavily.

Peter's smile turned into a snarl. "Stop being so selfish, girl!"

Sybil was about to open her mouth to continue fighting, but then Peter dashed in front of her and had a finger pointed at her face. "I'll hear no more of this," he growled. "You are my daughter and I am your father. This is bigger than yourself, and hopefully one day you will see that. If not, then I am ashamed to say I've raised you wrong."

Sybil tried to stay strong, but her bottom lip began to quiver and she could feel the tears start to build—a common occurrence in the recent days.

Peter must have regretted his sudden outburst, because he kneeled in front of her and grabbed her small hands with his one big hand. His voice softened. "Do this for your family, Beele. See what it's like. That's all I ask. You've told me that you're not a child anymore—that you're a woman. Well, then be strong and prove it."

*　　*　　*

Bedburg's nobility didn't host ballroom celebrations often, especially during winter. Only the rich and affluent—and their dates—were welcome. Most of the townsfolk lived quiet lives, were too poor to afford fine dresses and suits, and were too busy to partake in the frivolities of court life.

The official occasion was to celebrate the successful hunt from the day before. Lord Werner, not wanting to be outdone or appear uninformed, retroactively decided to host the event to show his support of the hunt—a hunt he'd never known was happening.

The ball was a means to quell the hysteria overtaking Bedburg, and to give the people a night of laughter, drink, and dance.

Sybil was certain she wouldn't partake in any laughing, drinking, or dancing. She wore the only fine thing owned by her father: a silk, purple gown that had belonged to her mother. A horse-drawn carriage picked her up from her estate and took her to Castle Bedburg. Other girls were in the carriage—daughters of lords and officials—and they all frowned, scoffed, and turned their noses at her.

Sybil longed to rip off her gown and flee to the Achterberg's cold, dark house, where she knew Dieter waited for her.

The carriage let Sybil and the other girls off at the front gates of the castle. She'd never been inside, or even *seen* the castle, and it was an imposing sight. Torches lit with dancing, colorful flames brightened a carpeted walkway. The noblewomen giggled as they passed by the blue, green, and yellow flames, and made their way to the castle's front doors.

Sybil stayed in the shadows of the noblewomen. She stared up at the spires and then turned and looked over her shoulder, at the carriage, and debated whether to quit the ball before it even started.

Before she could make up her mind, a high-pitched voice rang out. "Frau Griswold!"

Johannes von Bergheim stood in the large doorways of the castle. He wore a bright turquoise tunic with folded cuffs. His hair was oiled and slicked back. He smiled at Sybil with a snide look, as if to say, *No need to tell me how great I look, I already know.*

Sybil thought he looked ridiculous.

The nobleman walked up to Sybil and looked at her from head to toe, like she was a steak dinner that wasn't quite cooked right. He bobbed his head from side to side, and said, "I suppose that will do. Come." Then he took her arm in his and walked to the front of the castle.

Inside, Sybil could feel other girls staring and glaring at her. She assumed Johannes must have been somewhat of a prize, and that the girls were perplexed as to why his arm was entwined with a farm girl's arm. It must have been beyond their understanding, Sybil figured, as it was beyond her own.

Does father actually know these people?

"Don't worry, you'll get used to all the stares," Johannes said, apparently reading her mind. "It happens every time I attend court."

Sybil turned away from the nobleman and rolled her eyes. "Is that so, my lord?"

"Don't call me 'my lord.' I'm not a lord until my father croaks. Herr Bergheim will suffice."

Sybil nodded, and they continued to stroll past a few hallways and into a large ballroom. The ballroom was decorated with lights, flowers, a table of cakes and desserts, and a group of musicians.

Sybil couldn't believe how extravagant the entire affair looked. *Lord Werner must have gone bankrupt putting this together.*

In the center of the room was a wide, circular platform, shielded on all sides by a red curtain. Groups of well-dressed nobles mingled with each other in cliques of three or four. Lord Werner was in a corner of the room, dressed in a flowing gold robe that was ridiculously oversized for his small frame. He held the attention of six nobles and regaled them with a tale that seemed to require wild, lavish hand gestures.

Johannes led Sybil to a large table full of appetizers—shrimp, fruit, fine bread, cakes, wine, and other edibles Sybil didn't recognize. She felt awkward and out of place, and could still feel the eyes boring down on her from all sides.

She wondered, fleetingly, what she would become if she married this dud of a man. Then she shook the thought from her head and frowned as she imagined Dieter alone in that cold room with the bloodstained floorboards, waiting for her.

"Eat something," Johannes ordered, throwing a piece of shrimp in his mouth. "You could use it—you're thinner than a tree branch."

"I'm not too hungry, my lord—er, Herr Bergheim."

Johannes shrugged. "Fine. Want to dance?"

"I don't know how," Sybil said. "And . . . there's no music."

Johannes scoffed and shook his head. "You are pretty, girl, but your attitude is quite insufferable. I suppose that comes from being raised on a farm, with the animals."

Sybil felt her cheeks grow red with anger, and she turned away so Johannes couldn't see her scowl. As she turned, she faced a tall, elegant woman with a gown that pushed her breasts so far out that Sybil had to back into Johannes, lest she be smothered by the woman's bosom.

"I still don't see what father will gain from an alliance with your father, but I suppose there's a certain freshness to you . . ." Johannes trailed off as Sybil accidentally stepped on his foot. "Dammit, girl, watch where—" and then his eyes moved and he was looking at the tall noblewoman who had approached. He frowned and said, "Ah, Margreth . . . *you're* here."

The buxom noblewoman put her white-gloved hands on her hips. She flipped her long, brown hair to one side, revealing a small mole on her thin neck. Despite the noblewoman's extravagant gown and hair and physique, Sybil couldn't take her eyes away from the woman's breasts, which were at eye level.

Then the woman caught Sybil's stare and Sybil's cheeks went beet-red. "M-my apologies," she stammered, her eyes darting to the red curtain in the center of the room.

"Who's the child, Johannes?" the noblewoman asked in a

sultry voice.

Johannes motioned to Sybil, and then to the noblewoman. "Sybil Griswold, this is Margreth Baumgartner, the daughter of some lord here in town." Johannes craned his neck. "What is it your father does again, Margreth?"

Margreth frowned and crossed her arms under her ample chest. "Don't be an ass, boy."

Johannes smiled for the first time, and it wasn't a genuine or happy smile. "Ah, right, the daughter of the garrison commander." He leaned closer to Sybil and said, just loud enough for anyone nearby to hear, "She wants to marry me, but doesn't realize *my* father could buy *her* father's entire estate. That, and she's too old for me." The nobleman looked back at Margreth with a self-indulgent grin.

Somehow, Margreth managed to frown even more severely, and her lips took the shape of a horseshoe.

Sybil had to keep herself from giggling. *This is how the nobles talk to each other? With no respect . . . just . . . pretentiousness and scorn?*

She decided right then that her original assessment was correct: all nobles were the same. *If this foul banter is supposed to impress me . . . well . . . it's doing quite the opposite.*

"She's wanted my seed for years," Johannes continued. "But look at that face."

This time Margreth's mouth actually dropped open, and she looked astonished. "By God, Johannes, you really are such a little shit. Don't forget that one time you were so drunk we—"

Johannes raised his hand close to her face and looked away. "I *did* forget, Margreth. I was drunk."

Margreth was about to retort, but then a spoon tapped on a wineglass and everyone turned toward the noise. Lord Werner stood in the center of the room, next to the raised platform and red curtain.

The little lord waved his hands and took an exaggerated bow. "Thank you all for coming on such short notice. And let us all thank Baron Ludwig von Bergheim for his assistance in putting this ball together."

Eyes turned toward Johannes, since Ludwig—his father—wasn't present. Johannes' face held all the glib satisfaction of a toddler who'd taken his first successful shit without soiling himself.

Ah, so the magistrate put this on. All the staring eyes make sense now, but what is the baron's connection with Lord Werner . . . and with my father?

Lord Werner continued. "We are gathered tonight to celebrate the hunt from yesterday, and, more importantly, the work of a single huntsman. We believe he is responsible for finding . . . well, I'll just show you! Without further ado, let your hearts be warmed and your minds terrified! I give you, Georg Sieghart and the Werewolf of Bedburg!"

The red curtain plummeted to the ground. In the center of the stage stood the large hunter Sybil had seen before, as well as a huge, stuffed black wolf with fiery red eyes and excessively long claws. The wolf was made to look like it was lunging and snarling at a person.

The entire room of nobles gasped in unison. Sybil heard more than a few wineglasses shatter on the floor. One noblewoman even fainted, falling to the ground with a thud.

Sybil narrowed her eyes. *If this is the Werewolf of Bedburg . . . then why in the world did Bertrude Achterberg have to die? Are people so quick to forget that she was burned alive just this morning?*

"What a barbaric thing," Margreth said.

"It's just a wolf, Margreth. And if that's the Werewolf of Bedburg, then I'm the pope," Johannes said.

Margreth smirked. "I'm not talking about the wolf, little boy," she whispered as she leaned close to Johannes' ear. "That really is quite the *man*, though, isn't it?"

Sybil could see Johannes blush and stammer, but before he could say anything, Margreth Baumgartner was sashaying away, hips swaying from side to side.

"That bitch," Johannes said through gritted teeth. He turned to Sybil. "Don't become like her, girl. She's just angry she can't get what she wants all the time."

As if the same couldn't be said about any of you, Sybil thought, but she said, "As you wish, my lord."

"What did I tell you about—"

"My apologies, Herr Bergheim. I suppose I wasn't raised any better," Sybil said sweetly.

Johannes shrugged and nodded. "I suppose you're right."

The young nobleman suddenly stared at Sybil with a strange look. He motioned toward another table. "Come now, let's get some drink in you. I know there's got to be a vacant room *somewhere* in this ugly excuse for a castle."

Sybil felt a lump in her throat, and her heart started thumping. *A . . . vacant room?* A sheen of sweat started to soak her forehead, and her eyes darted around the ballroom. She caught the eyes of the menacing black wolf, which seemed to be staring into her soul.

The musicians started playing, people started dancing, and everything started moving fast and became overwhelming to Sybil all at once. Flustered, she refused to move to the wine table. Her feet were like bricks. "Uhh, ooh—"

"What in God's name are you trying to say?" Johannes asked, eyeing her with disgust. "You look like you're going to be sick. If you are, don't make a scene in here."

"My apologies, sir. G-give me a moment, please. It's nothing, really. I'll just be a moment."

"I'll come with you," Johannes said.

"No!" Sybil said, a bit too loudly. "I mean, d-don't bother, Herr Bergheim. You wouldn't want to be seen chasing after a girl like me, would you? It would seem presumptuous and pitiful, right?"

Johannes mulled that over. "Well, I suppose you're—"

Before he could finish his sentence, Sybil was sprinting out of the room, down the hallway. She reached the front gate of the castle and burst outside, her heart still reeling. She ran to the nearest carriage and jumped inside. A nobleman was kissing and groping a young woman, and the two giggled incessantly.

The nobleman stopped and grinned at Sybil. "I didn't think I'd get lucky *twice* tonight," he said, and Sybil yelped and leaped out of the carriage. Her gown caught on a hinge, tore, and she tripped and tumbled to the muddy ground.

She grabbed her torn dress by its hem and helped herself up. All around her were bright lights and bright colors and clothing and people she didn't recognize and her head and heart pounded and her eyes grew misty and she felt the urge to start bawling. She stumbled to another carriage, crawled in, and shouted to the coachman, "Please, get me out of here, sir!"

"Miss, are you all right? Where to, my lady?"

"Out! Please—just go south!"

CHAPTER SEVENTEEN

HEINRICH

On the day of Bertrude Achterberg's execution, Investigator Franz rode through the western gates of Cologne with Tomas and an entourage of five guards. He was still fuming at that damnable little man, Lord Werner, for not giving him his deserved recognition for arresting Bertrude a week earlier.

Gazing around, Heinrich noticed that Cologne hadn't changed much in the years since he'd last been. The city was still a sprawling metropolis with large stone walls to keep out intruders, and buildings and towers many times the size of any in Bedburg. The city was the capital of the region, and it housed more churches than any other city within fifty miles. The Rhine cut through its center, creating a seaside highway that made Cologne the main trading hub of western Germany.

Where Bedburg was rural and filled with uneducated peasants, Cologne was an enlightened, suburban city of scholars, royalty, and tradesfolk. The city was the the center of civility, and it held a great deal of power within the Holy Roman Empire.

Currently, Ernst of Bavaria was the elector and archbishop of Cologne, to the pleasure of Catholics—the majority—and to the chagrin of reformers. Politicians and wise men thought that Ernst was a placeholder and figurehead without much acumen or military power. But the pope supported him, and that gave Ernst immeasurable influence amongst the citizens.

Heinrich's meeting with the archbishop was delayed for a few hours while he waited in Cologne Castle. He sat in a plush foyer, annoyed at having to wait, and looked at the gold-plated columns and priceless paintings in the room.

Staring at a particular painting that depicted an age-old battlefield, Heinrich's thoughts began to wander. He thought of the political, religious, and military turmoil of recent years that made Cologne such a historically important city within the Empire.

Until recently, the city was a haven for Protestants. The bloody Cologne War, which ravaged the towns and peoples of both faiths over the past five years, changed all of that.

Even though it was widely believed that the war was coming to an end, Heinrich wasn't so sure.

Like so many wars, Cologne's began because of a woman. But while a woman was the root cause of the conflict, power was the obvious motive.

The city-state of Cologne was one of the seven electorates of the Holy Roman Empire. The leaders of the electorates, called the prince-electors, were responsible for choosing the emperor. Therefore, whichever religious faction controlled the greater portion of the seven electoral seats theoretically controlled the fate of the Empire itself.

Pope Gregory XIII did not favor this balance of power.

It was common knowledge that many electors, both Protestant and Catholic, were bribed to take office in order to control elections. Prior to the Cologne War, which began in 1583, Catholics controlled four seats, a majority. These electorates were the ecclesiastical states of Cologne, Trier, Mainz, and the seat of the Holy Roman Emperor, Rudolf II of Bohemia.

When Cologne's elector and archbishop, Count Salentin, died in 1577, the power of the Catholic Church was left hanging in the balance. Ernst of Bavaria was put up for election, but many Catholic leaders were skeptical of his ability to counter the growing Reformation. So the electorate chose a different Catholic, Count Gebhard Truchsess von Waldburg, to be Count Salentin's heir.

Catholics again controlled four of the seven electoral seats, but their celebration was short lived. Count Gebhard fell in love with a woman, Agnes von Mansfeld, who was a Protestant canoness. She held influence over the reformers, and quickly gained influence over Gebhard.

The church realized their dire mistake when Gebhard announced his conversion to Calvinism, a Protestant faction, in 1582. Archbishop Gebhard married Agnes in 1583 and pushed the Reformation on the city-state of Cologne.

Under his rule, Gebhard established parity for Calvinists in the archdiocese, and the pope demanded his immediate resignation. Gebhard would not uphold the law, which had been established thirty years prior during the Peace of Augsburg. The law stated that if a Catholic elector converted to Protestantism while on the seat, rather than forcing his subjects to convert, the ruler would resign from his position and be replaced by a Catholic.

Needless to say, Protestants didn't enjoy this law.

Instead of adhering to the Peace, Gebhard pushed Calvinism even further. His election made the electorate a Protestant majority. In 1583, Pope Gregory XIII deposed and excommunicated Gebhard, but the pope died two years later, and Gebhard continued ruling and converting the people of Cologne. Alongside Agnes, Gebhard sought to turn the Holy Roman Empire from an electorate, into a dynastic duchy. He wanted Protestant leaders to rule for generations to come.

Crisis erupted within the Empire. The church chose Ernst of Bavaria—the same man once refused for his apparent lack of ability—to be the new Catholic elector.

Thus, with two competing archbishops vying for the same seat, the Cologne War began. And with it came wanton destruction, pillaging, plundering, and economic disaster for the principality.

Heinrich shook his head and scoffed at the irony that these two "peaceful" sects would go to such destructive lengths for control.

Recently, after five years of chaos and ruin, Archbishop Ernst began to see things sway in favor of the Catholics. It was still obvious to Heinrich, though, that both Ernst and Gebhard were simply puppet-leaders bankrolled by higher powers that had vested interests in the outcome of the war.

On the Protestant side, those higher powers were Queen Elizabeth of England, Henry III of France, and the Dutch prince, Maurice of Nassau. For the Catholics, the pope sent Spanish troops, as well as Italian and Bavarian mercenaries. Together, both sides desecrated the countryside around Cologne. And now Heinrich was forced to walk into the belly of the beast to speak with Archbishop Ernst, a man he hadn't seen in quite some time.

"Lord?" a voice called out.

Heinrich snapped out of his reminiscence and looked up at a young, well-dressed courier standing before him.

"The archbishop will see you now," the man said with a bow.

Heinrich jumped up from his plush seat and followed the man down a hallway. Tomas began to follow, but Heinrich held out a hand to stay the soldier.

The courier led Heinrich down a marble-tiled corridor, to a large door protected by two spearmen. One of the guards opened the door, and the courier led Heinrich into the room. It was a vast, brightly-colored chamber with stained-glass windows built high on the walls. Curtains were pulled open and bright rays of sunlight splashed into the room, forming a rainbow of dancing colors on the floor.

"My lord, your guest, Heinrich Franz," the courier said. He disappeared back through the doorway.

"Ah, Investigator Franz, in the flesh," the archbishop said from the other end of the room. His back was turned, but then he spun around and faced Heinrich. He was a tall, stiff man with a pointed beard and short-cropped hair. He wore a lavish tunic, but looked more like a soldier than an archbishop.

"My lord," Heinrich said with a low bow.

"I trust your stay in Cologne has been well?"

"I've only just arrived, my lord." Heinrich walked to a small table that separated him from the archbishop, but continued to stand.

"I hope you'll stay for a while. I've been eagerly awaiting your arrival."

Heinrich shook his head. "I'm afraid not, my lord. There are pressing matters to take care of in Bedburg. A killer is still on the loose."

"I've heard," Ernst said. "But I've also heard that a woman has been tried and executed for the murders, just recently?"

If you've heard so much, then why am I here? Heinrich thought. "Yes," he said, "it's true that we've uncovered a witch in town, but I don't believe she's responsible for *all* the killings. I do believe she had some connection with the case, however."

Ernst smiled. "My tireless investigator," he said, folding his hands behind his back. "I'm assuming you wish to know why I've called you here, Herr Franz."

Heinrich nodded. "Not to question your decision, my lord, but I did find it strange for you to send me to 'escort' one of your priests back to Bedburg. I find that others may have been more suitable to the task."

Ernst offhandedly waved the investigator away. He pulled a chair from the small table, sat, and motioned for Heinrich to do the same. "Of course there are, Heinrich. I chose the word *escort* to keep your visit vague. After all, we do want to keep the truth of your employment under lock and key, correct?"

Heinrich sat and put his hands palm-down on the table. "Indeed, my lord. What is it you would have me do?"

"I will have you return with one of my finest priests and advisers. He is a Jesuit missionary named Balthasar Schreib, and he is to be my . . . *religious ear*, in Bedburg. I've noticed that Lord Werner and Bishop Solomon are inadequate converters, and Balthasar is not."

"As you wish, my lord."

"I also wanted to hear your side of things, in person, from a secular point of view. I have many ears and eyes in Bedburg, but none that I trust as much as yours."

Heinrich bowed his head and said, "You flatter me, my lord. Do you wish to know about the investigation?"

Ernst scrunched his nose. "No, no, nothing as mundane as that, Heinrich." Then he stared straight at the investigator with piercing, blue eyes. "I would like to know what you're doing partnering with Georg Sieghart the Savage, and what he's doing in Bedburg in the first place."

Heinrich twitched, just slightly, but the archbishop must have noticed, because he smiled and said, "Eyes and ears everywhere, my friend."

Heinrich coughed into his hand. "Firstly, my lord, I wouldn't say I'm *partnering* with him. I'm using him as a liaison with the locals, for reconnaissance during my investigation. He is a worthwhile tracker, and quite adept at gathering information."

"What do you know of his past, Franz?"

"I know he fought under the Duke of Parma, Alexander Farnese, against the Dutch. Then he defected, and his family was killed. I'm not sure about the order of those last two—"

"Georg Sieghart did not *defect* from the army, Heinrich. He was released. Do you know how he gained the name Sieghart the Savage?" The archbishop did not wait for a response. "He was a madman on and off the battlefield, and the same monster that you're searching for killed his family. He is a loose cannon, and if you're going to associate with him, be sure not to flap away any of our secrets. He is not a lawman, remember."

Heinrich nodded. "Of course, my lord. I would never betray any secrets or tell him anything of importance. He is a simple man."

"That may be true, but I have my eyes on him, and you'd be smart to do the same."

After a brief pause, Archbishop Ernst put his hands on the table and looked away from Heinrich. "What else can you tell me about the state of Bedburg? How do the conversions fair? The

Protestant rebellion?"

Heinrich sighed. "I fear you are right, that the Lutherans and Calvinists are growing stronger, and possibly joining forces to combat their common enemy, if you will. Recently, a pastor began preaching in town, right next to the town church. He has the ears of many disgruntled citizens, and he's been unfazed by any chastisement."

"That is disturbing indeed," Ernst said. He started pulling at his pointed beard. "That's one of the reasons I've ordered Balthasar to Bedburg. What about Lord Werner and Bishop Solomon—what can you tell me of them?"

Heinrich breathed heavily and shook his head. "If I am being honest, my lord, you were right about them as well. Lord Werner is a petty, fickle man. He is weak-willed, not emphatic at persecuting the Protestants, or even in his conversion efforts. He has trouble simply holding his position.

"Bishop Solomon, meanwhile, is the most ardent Catholic in town, but he is old, and the young man who might someday take his place is a conflicted priest in his own right."

The archbishop drummed his fingers on the table and nodded. "I've thought the same about Lord Werner," he said at last. "I should have never elected him. And Bishop Solomon, well, he's a radical without any real power." Ernst pointed at Heinrich. "There is something you need to know, Herr Franz. Pockets of Protestant rebels are forming all over the southern and northern regions of the principality, and I fear it is only a matter of time before Gebhard tries to retake the electoral seat. If—or when—he does, it will most likely begin with Bedburg. He will want to set up operations close to Cologne. We absolutely *cannot* allow the rebels to meet with any fringe sects that might be developing in and around Bedburg. If the Lutherans and Calvinists create communications with each other, that could be catastrophic."

Heinrich slowly nodded and twisted his mustache, confused as to what he was supposed to do about any of that.

The archbishop's face gained a sudden hardness, and his eyes narrowed on the investigator. "Don't forget why I sent you to Bedburg in the first place, Heinrich. Before I will give you what you want, you must give me what I *need*."

"Of course, my lord," Heinrich said. "I am trying to orchestrate my investigation as quickly as possible. I will stop the uprising by bringing the Werewolf of Bedburg to justice."

"Do that," Ernst said, "and I will give you your just reward."

The hardness vanished from the archbishop's face, and he clapped and smiled. "Enough of this talk, though. Are you sure you won't stay in Cologne for a bit? There's a new play in town, I believe penned by the playwright Thomas Kyd . . . *The Spanish Tragedy*, I believe it's called. Kyd is an English bastard, but it's quite an exquisite play! The Spanish Armada's defeat this year apparently brought a great inspiration to the arts."

Heinrich scratched one of his ears. "I am not a connoisseur of the arts, my lord. And I really should be getting back to Bedburg."

The archbishop frowned, and he looked somewhat offended. "Well, my tireless investigator, that is fine. But you will sup with me tonight, and in the morning you shall be introduced to Balthasar Schreib. Then you may return to your town."

The archbishop stood from his chair and slowly walked around the table. "Were your travels here uneventful?"

"Indeed," Heinrich said.

"That is good, but just be careful of bandits on the road back. It seems vagabonds are sprouting up everywhere these days."

"I appreciate your concern, my lord," Heinrich said with a bow.

Ernst chuckled. "My concern is with Balthasar, Heinrich. I don't want to lose my prized priest before he gets a chance to do his work."

CHAPTER EIGHTEEN

GEORG

Soon after the large black wolf was unveiled at the ball, all attention turned away from Georg. He had no qualms about that, as he felt out of place in the roomful of noblemen and women. They were dressed in their fineries, while he still wore his hunting furs and grimy clothes.

Not a single leader or noble offered him congratulations for bringing down the beast. Georg felt the wolf's display was a simple ploy by Lord Werner to arrange a celebration, and to stifle the hysteria that had shadowed over Bedburg.

He decided to sneak out of the ball early, and no one tried to stop him. As he exited the front gates of the castle, Georg breathed in the crisp night air and gave a great sigh of relief. Outside, Konrad von Brühl waited for him.

"You look like you could use a drink or three," Konrad said, nudging his chin toward Georg's tired face. The patch-wearing soldier and former comrade of Georg's was quickly becoming a close acquaintance—perhaps even a friend.

Georg pulled at his beard and nodded. "I'm not very fond of being the center of attention."

Konrad smiled. "You should have thought about that before you brought down the biggest wolf this town's ever seen." The man squinted with his one good eye. "I thought you wanted to be known for killing the Werewolf of Bedburg. Your reaction isn't exactly in line with your words, Georg."

Georg shrugged. "That thing in there is no werewolf. You and I both know that. And I want to kill the monster for what it's done, not for the accolades and rewards."

"This town has changed you, my friend."

Georg looked at the man's grizzled and scarred face. That was the first time Konrad had called him 'friend.' "Maybe it has," Georg said, "or maybe I just don't know what I'm doing here anymore. Could there really be a *werewolf* out there?"

As the two men strolled away from the gates, Konrad asked, "What do you mean?"

Georg scratched his scalp and shrugged. "Don't you feel there's something amiss in this town? What connection could Dorothea Gabler's, Josephine's, and Karl and Bertrude Achterberg's deaths all have with each other?"

Konrad said nothing for a moment. Then he cleared his throat and said, "Perhaps nothing. Maybe you're looking too much into it. That is a question the investigator must answer, Georg. It's not your job—you're a hunter."

His job or not, Georg couldn't let the thought go. Something wasn't right in Bedburg—he could feel it in his gut. Besides, Konrad didn't know that it partly *was* Georg's job to find out what he could, while Heinrich was away on business.

Why would Lord Werner send Heinrich away right after the investigator uncovered important clues and made an arrest? There's something Heinrich isn't telling me.

Konrad could see the slanted brows and scrunched face on Georg. It was the sign of a man in deep thought. "I wouldn't think too much of it," he said, placing a hand on Georg's shoulder. "Stay out of the politics of this town, Georg. Let's go drink ourselves into a stupor."

As Konrad finished his sentence, a loud commotion broke out from behind them. Georg spun on his heels and saw a girl in a purple dress tripping out of a carriage. She tumbled, sprawled on the muddy ground, and staggered to her feet. Then she jumped into another carriage and shouted something at the driver.

Konrad laughed. "Ah, young drunk girls . . . they are a shining light in this dark place. Makes me want to drown myself in liquor and find my own light."

Georg nodded, but was not laughing. He cocked his head to the side, thinking that he recognized the girl. "Go on without me, friend. I'll meet you at the tavern shortly."

Konrad opened his mouth to contest, but Georg was already jogging back toward the castle. Konrad shrugged and walked away—heading east—toward the tavern.

The carriage took off down the road and Georg was forced to jump out of its way. As it sped by, Georg saw the face of the girl in the window and was certain it was the Griswold girl. She had tears streaming down her face.

Georg sprinted after the carriage. He knew he couldn't keep up, but it headed toward the southern, destitute part of town, and a horse-drawn carriage in a place like that would be easy to track.

He followed the lines that the wheels made in the mud, past the cathedral, into the town square where Bertrude's execution had taken place that morning. The carriage barreled on toward the farmlands, but when it reached the southern edge of Bedburg, it veered to the right, in the opposite direction of the Griswold estate.

Georg kept after the carriage, jogged up a small hill, and then he fell to his belly as he looked over the lip of the hill. The carriage had stopped at the Achterberg's abandoned estate.

Sybil Griswold leaped out of the carriage and ran to the front door of the house. Georg's eyes went wide as the front door opened and Sybil went inside.

What are you getting yourself into, young lady?

Still at the summit of the hill, Georg craned his neck to the left, west, where he could see Peter Griswold's estate in the distance. Smoke billowed from a roof-vent, which told Georg that the house was occupied.

Georg couldn't identify who had greeted Sybil, and the hunter debated going down and crashing through the door to figure out what the girl was doing in a dead man's house. But the carriage was rounding back in his direction, and he decided on discreetness.

He stood and sprinted off the road, hiding in a bush as the carriage rolled by.

Then a realization came to him: He didn't need to go down to the Achterberg's house to know what was going on in there. He already had a good idea.

Instead, after the carriage passed him, he ran down the hill and headed in the other direction, toward the Griswold's estate.

Georg hid behind a copse of trees and peered at the house of Peter Griswold. It didn't take long before the doors opened. A hooded man walked outside and Georg immediately knew the man was hiding something—the man looked over his shoulders constantly, and his body language was skittish and fidgety.

The man wore a leather belt, and the moonlight gleamed and reflected off its surface. This was no expert of subterfuge.

Georg followed the man south, further away from the farmlands, and then east, toward a dark line of trees. Lit only by the murky moonlight, Georg realized they were headed toward the same woods where the hunt had taken place.

Georg followed the man through a long expanse of open-aired countryside, and he stayed back a ways, so as not to be seen.

After the man crossed into the dark trees, Georg felt his heart race. *This man has quite a pair on him to be venturing into the wolf-infested woods this late at night.*

The shadowy man cut further south, under thick branches and over ankle-high undergrowth, until he stopped, looked around as if he might be lost, and then finally continued on.

They came to a familiar clearing in the woods, and Georg hid behind a large birch tree.

At the back of the clearing was the same cabin that Georg had stumbled on during the hunt. It was dark and desolate, but the hooded man knocked on the door anyway—two hard knocks, followed by three soft knocks, and one more hard one.

The door swung open, and a long-haired silhouette greeted the hooded man. Even with the moonlight shining down on the clearing, it only created a shadow for the two, and Georg couldn't tell who the people were. The long-haired person had a frame that suggested it was a female.

The two shadows embraced—possibly kissing as they did. Then another lanky body appeared in the doorway, shook the hooded man's hand, and the three disappeared into the cabin.

Georg heard a rustling sound from behind, like someone had stepped on a brittle leaf. He snapped his head around and saw a small, dark form—also hooded—darting off away from him.

Georg growled and ran after the figure. *How could I let someone trail me* again? Georg thought, scowling. *I'm a damn fool! Too caught up in my own chase.*

The hunter pushed his way through the dense foliage and trees, forgoing any semblance of stealth. The figure was small and quick and hard to track, so Georg used his ears to keep pace—a skilled tracker's ears were just as useful as his eyes.

A few times he found himself within ten paces of the figure, trees whirling by on all sides, but then the person would dart off in some other direction.

Georg jumped over a fallen tree trunk, and the person cut left. *Bad move.*

As the trees grew scattered and scarcer, Georg knew they were headed toward the open countryside.

The hooded man burst through the edge of trees, sprinting at full speed toward Bedburg.

Georg was just moments behind, and when he reached the cool, open air of the country he nudged his bow from his shoulder and reached for an arrow.

"Halt!" he shouted, nocking his arrow. "Or I'll shoot you dead in the back!"

The figure hesitated, but decided it was in his best interest to stop. The cloaked figure was twenty paces away, back still facing Georg, and the hunter crept forward. His knuckles were white against the taut bowstring.

Georg walked within five paces and said, "Show yourself— and do it slowly, man, if you value your life."

The man turned, but was facing the ground.

"Unveil yourself."

The hood went down, and Georg almost accidentally let his arrow fly right into the person's neck. This was no man, but rather the nun who aided Father Nicolaus at the church.

Sister Salome had a solemn expression on her face.

"What in God's good name are you doing out here, and why the hell are you following me?" Georg asked after collecting himself.

"I was ordered to, Herr Sieghart," the woman said, her voice quivering.

Georg lowered his bow. "By whom?"

"Are you going to kill me?" Salome asked.

Georg shook his head, and Salome took a deep breath. "Who ordered you to follow me?" he asked again. "And what do they want with me?"

"Father Nicolaus, my lord. I believe Bishop Solomon ordered him to watch you."

"Why?" Georg slung his bow back over his shoulder. "What have I ever done to your precious congregation?"

Sister Salome shook her head. "It's not what you've done, my lord. You are a mystery to us, and the church likes to keep records of everyone who lives in town."

"Am I a threat to the bishop?"

"He isn't sure. That's why I followed you."

"And what did you see?"

"I'm . . . not sure," Salome said. Her eyes darted to the left and right.

"Was it you who followed me to the tavern some weeks back, and escaped into the night?"

The nun hesitated, and then slowly nodded. "Please, I wish you no harm. I'm simply following orders."

Georg sighed and shooed her away with a wave of his hand. "It's dangerous out here. Return to your church. If you're smart, you won't relay what you've seen here—whatever that may be. And if I see you following me again, I won't be as nice as I was tonight."

Sister Salome swallowed loudly, and her head bobbed up and down. When Georg said nothing more, she turned and ran toward Bedburg.

Georg shook his head as he watched the nun become smaller and smaller in the distance. "Stupid woman nearly got herself shot."

Georg made his way to the tavern and huffed as he sat down next to Konrad. He rubbed his temples.

Konrad patted him on the back. "You look even worse than before, if that's possible. What took you so long to get here?"

"Errands," Georg said. He sighed and put his hands on the table, motioning for the barkeep. "I found something strange tonight."

"What's that?" Konrad asked, taking a pull from his mug. The ale dripped down his chin and beard.

Georg didn't mention the nun. Georg believed Salome when she'd said she was just following orders. The church loved to keep tabs on everyone, and Bedburg was no different than any other town or city.

No, it was the cabin that stuck in his mind. He had so many questions: Who was inside? What was going on there? What purpose did the cabin serve?

Georg knew he would be venturing back into those dark woods some day, and the thought gave him a sharp chill down his spine.

"Something that might change everything," he said, mostly to himself. The vagueness in his voice caused Konrad to chuckle, but Georg decided not to expand on his words. He wanted to answer some of his own questions and tell Investigator Franz what he found, first. Though he thought he could trust his new acquaintance, he'd still only just met Konrad. Then he scratched his chin, realizing that he didn't know if he could trust the investigator, either.

The barkeep brought a mug of ale for Georg. The hunter tilted his head as the barkeep walked away.

"How ominous," Konrad said, smiling.

"That's not Lars," Georg said, motioning toward the barman with his chin. Lars was tall, with blond hair and a twinkle in his eye, whereas this man was shorter and had dark hair.

"Very perceptive of you, Georg."

"Where's Lars?"

Konrad shrugged. "No idea, but this man's ale is just as good as the other man's."

Georg nodded and massaged his temples again. *What a night*, he thought, closing his eyes. He grabbed his mug and took a long drink, wanting to forget—or at least understand—everything that had transpired.

CHAPTER NINETEEN

DIETER

A loud knock came from the door. Dieter stood from his chair. It was late. He snuffed out the candlelight and crept to the other side of the dark room. He slowly opened the door.

Sybil stood in the way, and a horse-drawn carriage was behind her, wheeling around to leave.

"Beele, I told you no one could know we were meeting here!" Dieter said with a frown. Then he noticed her tattered and mud-caked gown, her distraught face, and red-rimmed eyes. "Good God, what's happened? Are you hurt?" Dieter stood aside and made the sign of the cross over his chest.

Sybil stormed past the priest. Dieter followed her, and then she abruptly spun around and lunged at Dieter, embracing him. She nudged her damp face into his chest. "This has been the worst day of my life!" Her thin body shook from silent sobs. "I don't think I can trust my father ever again."

Dieter held Sybil out at arm's-length. "Slow down, Beele. Start from the beginning. What are you talking about?"

So she told him, starting with the image of Bertrude Achterberg's burnt body that flashed in her mind every time she closed her eyes, then how her father had forced her to go to a ball with the repulsive Johannes von Bergheim, and her eventual escape from the nobleman.

"That man was an utter snob and miscreant. You wouldn't

believe how these nobles speak to one another!"

Dieter sighed and led Sybil by the arm. He sat her down at the table. The candle's wick still smoked. He took a seat and pushed aside the open Bible. "I've known enough nobles to know how they act, my dear. Don't let them get the best of you."

"You don't understand," Sybil said. "My father expects me to *marry* this brute! Johannes tried to get me drunk without even knowing me for more than an hour. If my father finds out I ran away, he'll kill me."

Dieter's heart dropped to the pit of his stomach at the mention of marriage. He felt a lump in his throat. "I'm sure there's . . . *something* that can be done." He stared at the Bible sitting at the other end of the table, then back to Sybil. "Your father is only trying to do what's best for you, I'm sure."

"And how would he know what's best for me?" Sybil spat. She shook her head. "No, he's only trying to help himself. I'll never forgive that bastard!"

Dieter's eyes went wide. "Please, calm down, Beele. You mustn't say such things. He is your father, and he loves you. I'm sure this feeling will pass."

Sybil was still shaking her head, and she started fidgeting and biting her fingernails. "I don't think so." She stared back at Dieter and her eyes were bright and twinkling. "Don't you see, Dieter? This . . . feeling I have . . . I don't *want* it to pass."

Dieter leaned back, and his eyebrows jumped. "What do you mean?"

Sybil struggled to speak. Finally, she said, "What I'm feeling isn't about my father or that noble bastard. It's about *you.*"

Dieter was still confused, and his face showed it.

Sybil blushed and looked at the floor. Her voice cracked as she said, "I love you, Dieter. You're the only one who understands me, and who's been kind to me. I love *you*, Dieter Nicolaus. And I think you love me, too."

Dieter coughed and stuttered, unable to find his breath. His heart started to pound in his chest as he was caught thoroughly off-guard. All he managed to say in a small squeak was, "Y-you can't, Sybil."

"Why not?" Sybil asked, tilting her head.

"No, no, I mean, *I* can't. I am a man of God, Sybil. You are the daughter of a wealthy farmer. The notion is completely unheard of and out of line."

"So what? Is that supposed to mean that our hearts can't yearn for each other?"

Dieter still struggled to speak. He took a moment to calm his nerves. "We can't love each other, Beele. It is against everything I've been taught. We come from two completely different stations in life."

"Damn our stations in life!" Sybil shouted. Her voice grew angry, and she slammed a fist on the table. "Tell me, then. Tell me you don't love me, and I'll leave you alone right now—and forever."

Dieter's mind swirled, and he felt dizzy. He opened his mouth, but couldn't find the words—again, those pesky words. He turned to the Bible, ashamed, as if he'd failed, and slowly brought his gaze back to Sybil's muddied face.

Even under puffy red lids, her eyes looked like pools from a waterfall, waiting to wash him over. Even with her muddy face and makeup, her skin was like the moon—glowing and peaceful. Her hair was like a bright sunflower, waiting for its petals to be picked. Her rosy lips were like the lifeblood that coursed through every man's veins.

Dieter finally realized what he was feeling as he stared at her for a long while: He cared for Sybil more than anything he'd ever cared for. "I cannot," he said, bowing his head. "I would be lying if I said I did not love you, too."

Sybil's lips slowly curled into a smile. They locked eyes—hers, bright and lively; his, dark and tired. They leaned closer, until their faces were just inches apart, and they could feel one another's quick breaths. The Bible sat open beneath their chins, like it was living and breathing and staring up at them.

Dieter closed the Bible.

Sybil pushed forward and kissed Dieter hard on the mouth. She grabbed the side of his head and held his face as her soft lips perused around Dieter's tongue and mouth.

Dieter could hear Sybil's heart beating, and he imagined she could hear his, too.

Then he shook his head and forced his lips away from hers, rearing his head back. He groaned and whispered, "We can't." But Sybil's face was too sweet, her eyes too piercing, her lips too inviting. Dieter knew that words would do nothing to save him. He was trapped between his love for Sybil Griswold, and his love for God.

And Sybil Griswold won.

They embraced in another furious kiss and stood from the table. Dieter wrapped his arms around Sybil and felt every part of her body.

They clumsily stumbled to the bed at the other side of the room, their bodies still entangled.

They found the bed and Dieter gently laid Sybil down on her back and grappled with her dress straps. Sybil wrestled Dieter's robe off.

For a long moment Dieter took in Sybil's naked body, while she took in his, and then Dieter leaned on top of her, and they locked together.

A few minutes later, they were breathing and huffing loudly, their moment of passion and lust subsiding. They both chuckled. Dieter turned to his side and gazed at Sybil's body once more. A sheen of sweat had enveloped her. Her small breasts perked toward him. Her wide hips were smooth, like an untouched, snowy mountain slope. Her sunflower hair was tangled and wet against her neck and forehead.

Dieter tried to tell himself that what had just happened was a moment of depraved lust—a lapse in judgment—but he knew that wasn't true.

Sybil was right: Dieter loved her. There was no way he could reconcile any differently. He'd given into temptation and abandoned his vow of perpetual chastity. But, even though he tried, he couldn't feel guilty. In fact, he felt relieved in a way— renewed and invigorated.

Dieter never expected the satisfaction he felt in that moment could, when he least expected, turn to guilt. And that it would come down on him tenfold and threaten to tear down the walls of his morality.

Lying in a dead man's bed, they slept in each other's arms.

In the early morning, Dieter opened his eyes and was blinded by a piercing light coming from the single window in the house. He clenched his eyes shut, and then they shot open wide. He rushed into action, not knowing how long he'd been asleep.

He threw on his robe, almost tripped on the cuffs, and went out into the chilly morning, leaving Sybil to rest soundly.

No one was waiting outside to crucify him, or even notice him.

He left the Achterberg estate and traveled through the poor section of town, through the marketplace where it was busy and he'd be less noticed, and up toward his church on the hill.

The Lutheran pastor, Hanns Richter, was giving a loud sermon to a group of listeners at the base of the hill. The pastor's group was larger than ever before—easily twenty strong. Dieter paid the man no attention and hurried past him.

He opened the doors of the church.

Bishop Solomon was at the pulpit, preaching to a full congregation. Dieter stood in the doorway, dumbfounded, and all eyes turned back toward him.

The bishop narrowed his eyes at Dieter, but continued his sermon, swinging his arms about wildly as he decried the Protestant heretics.

Dieter's face turned bright red, and he made himself as small as he could. He sat down in the back, near the doorway, next to Georg Sieghart. The hunter smelled of mud and sweat, and his friend Konrad sat next to him. Dieter sighed and gave a slight nod to Herr Sieghart. The hunter simply stared back at him with a deep frown. His eyes seemed to be studying Dieter, and the priest looked away uncomfortably.

He heard the bishop's words, but couldn't listen to them. His mind was jumbled, and countless thoughts went through his head.

He looked around at the quiet congregation. *Do they know that I'm as much a sinner as all of them?*

The bishop ended his sermon with a prayer, and then everyone bowed their heads and clasped their hands. Dieter was the only one with his head still up, surveying the churchgoers. He didn't pray with the rest of the folk, and he finally felt a pang of guilt.

After the prayer, Bishop Solomon excused the room, and the churchgoers stood and shuffled their way out.

Georg Sieghart did not. As Dieter tried to stand and leave, the hunter grabbed his arm.

"I need to make a confession, *Father*," Georg said.

Is that spite in his voice? Disapproval? Dieter wondered. The priest tried to squirm away, but the hunter was too strong. "Now is not a very good time, sir."

"It's as good a time as any, priest. I need to make a confession, *now*, and I believe it's in your best interest."

Dieter tilted his head. He sighed, and after a pause he nodded. "Very well, let's go."

They made their way to the confessional, and Georg started off in the regular way. "Bless me, Father, for I have sinned."

"How long has it been since your last confession, my son?"

"A week."

"And what is the nature of your sin, my son."

Georg's voice lowered an octave. "I know a man who's been dishonest to the people who trust him most."

Dieter glanced through the small holes in the cage. Georg was staring right at him. "What does this man's deceit have to do with your sin?" Dieter asked.

"Well, if I were an honest man, I would bring his sins to the ears of the public, and to those above him. If I were a better man, I'd tell everyone of his dishonesty."

Dieter swallowed loudly and felt a bit unnerved. "What has this man done that is so wrong?"

"He is a holy man, Father, and I suspect he's given into temptation and broken his vows. I think he's fallen in love with someone besides God."

"You say, 'I think,' my son. What do you *know*?"

Georg cleared his throat. "I know my instincts, and I know what I've seen—a holy man who has fallen in love with a young lady. Why, just last night I found myself following this young lady to a place where she should not have been."

"And where was that?" Dieter asked, closing his eyes.

"A dead man's house."

Dieter sighed. He felt a chill sweat building on his forehead. "What is it you want, Herr Sieghart?"

The hunter kept staring at him through the cage. "I need to know a few things, Father. If you can help me with these things, I'm sure my drunken mind will forget whatever it thought it saw last night."

Dieter's voice turned suddenly hard and vicious. "You may *think* you know what you saw, huntsman, but you don't know a thing. I won't be threatened by the likes of you."

Georg shrugged. "I guess I'll just have to see if Bishop Solomon thinks my words hold any weight," he said calmly. "But you might be right. What do I know?"

The hunter stood.

Once Georg was out of the confessional, Dieter closed his eyes and massaged his temples. "Wait," he finally called out.

The hunter turned and sat back down.

"What is it you want to know? I won't have that girl be hurt, Herr Sieghart."

"I don't want that either, priest." Georg paused and leaned closer to Dieter. Then he whispered, "I want to know where her father is going each night. I followed him, too, so don't deny it. Just tell me what secrets he keeps. I know she must confide in you—I see you two getting chummy every time I come to Mass."

"I don't know what you're talking about," Dieter said, bowing his head. *Give me strength, God.*

"Very well," Georg said. He started to rise again.

"What is it you would have me say?" Dieter asked, panic in his voice. "I cannot betray her family."

Georg banged on the cage with an open palm and Dieter leaped back. "Yes, you can!" Georg growled. "What do you owe them? I don't care about the girl, fool, I just care about her father. So tell me, dammit, what is he doing sneaking off into the woods every night?"

Dieter crossed himself and moaned. "He's . . ." Dieter trailed off. His mouth was dry, and he felt faint. "He goes to a cabin in the woods, southeast of Bedburg."

"I know that," Georg said, impatiently tapping his fingers on his knee. "What does he *do* at the cabin?"

"I believe he meets with other people—with Protestants. The pastor at the bottom of the hill, Hanns Richter, I think he's one of them."

Georg smiled wryly. "Shameful, Father Nicolaus. You know of secret Protestant meetings and you don't alarm your own bishop, or the law?"

"It's for Sybil's safety."

"Who are the other people he meets? Who makes up this secret faction of Protestants?"

Dieter shrugged. "Honestly, I don't know. As God as my witness, that's the truth. Peter Griswold and Hanns Richter are the only two I've heard of, and Sybil doesn't know either, so don't go harassing her." Dieter looked through the holes and locked eyes with Georg.

After a long moment of silence, Georg turned away with a dark smile on his face. "Very well, Father. Say five Hail Mary's and your sins shall be absolved."

Dieter clenched his jaw. "Are we done here?"

"Not quite," Georg said, facing the priest again. "There's one other thing I'd have you help me with."

"What?" Dieter asked through gritted teeth.

"You can read, correct?" Without waiting for an answer, Georg continued. "It's my understanding that the church keeps records of every citizen in Bedburg—*detailed* records. I would like to look over some of those records."

"Absolutely not. Those records are only for church officials and lawmen."

"I'm sure we can make an exception. Besides, as your little nun must have already told you, I'm working with Heinrich Franz, and he's a lawman."

Dieter was taken aback at the mention of Sister Salome. *How does this man know so much? Maybe Bishop Solomon's warning to keep an eye on Georg Sieghart was valid after all . . .*

"Who would you like to learn about?" Dieter said in a low voice.

"I'd like to learn more about the Achterbergs and the Griswolds . . . and about Investigator Franz."

Dieter scratched his scalp. "Why do you want to investigate your own partner?"

Georg stared at Dieter through the small holes in the confessional. "You let me worry about the 'why,' Father."

CHAPTER TWENTY

SYBIL

Sybil awoke with the sun beaming through a single window, showering her body in warmth. She stretched her arms, groaned, and turned over in her bed with a smile. Opening her eyes, she saw the imprint of Dieter next to her, but the bed was empty. She ran to the window and peeked up at the sky, and a sense of dread fell over her.

The sun was far too high. *Why didn't Dieter wake me?* Her worry turned to panic as she realized what oversleeping might entail.

Father . . .

She threw on her muddy gown and burst out of the house. It was the sunniest day of winter, but the air was still cool and biting as Sybil made her way home.

She wondered what kind of chastising her father would give her, but then another thought came to her mind: *What if he doesn't find out?*

She'd never deceived her father, but she felt like a new woman after the night before. For once, she felt independent. *Besides, father lies to me all the time.* She smiled, and felt a strange sensation through her body. Her heart was light in her chest, and she already missed Dieter. Even though she had no one else to compare him to, she felt that he'd been a kind lover.

As she continued down the winding path that led from the Achterberg estate to the Griswold's, her elated mind cleared a bit. *No,* she thought, *I won't deceive father. He'll just have to understand. I'll make him understand. I don't care about titles or land or any of that. I want Dieter—I want a kind man—not a brute like Johannes von Bergheim. I don't care what that little imp has to offer. If father truly loves me, he will understand that and come around.*

The road bounded up a green hill and she saw her house in the distance. White smoke billowed from the roof. She smiled again. Everything seemed normal.

As she drew closer, she stopped smiling. A carriage was near their fields. Sybil's father was standing outside, talking to a tall, stiff man.

It was Ludwig von Bergheim.

The baron paid no attention to Sybil as she approached the field. His conversation with Peter ended, and he walked by Sybil and scowled at her as he stepped into his carriage.

As the baron's carriage whisked him away, Peter watched with his thick arms crossed over his chest. He frowned at his daughter and said, "There's no point trying to explain yourself, Beele. The baron has told me everything."

Sybil clasped her hands in front of her ruined dress and stared at the ground. "Are you angry with me?"

Peter sighed. "I'm disappointed, Beele. Those nobles are our best chance at becoming a reputable family, and you're throwing it away . . . what, on a whim? I never knew you to be so vain." Peter's shoulders slumped as he shook his head and walked back toward the house.

"I don't love Johannes von Bergheim, father, and I never will," Sybil called out. She felt a stab of guilt, but her confidence was still riding high, and she knew she might not get another chance to speak plainly with her father.

Peter turned and had a sad expression on his face.

"I love Father Nicolaus," Sybil said, her voice firm.

Peter squinted and trudged toward Sybil. She backpedaled, startled. Peter looked like he was about to snarl, and he leaned in close to her. "That man is a *priest*, Beele, and not even a priest of our faction. Are you trying to ruin his life, too? He can offer you nothing! If your infatuation with him is ever discovered, he can bring this family down in an instant!" He put his hands on his hips. "Hugo tells me that you've been disappearing at night—"

"No different than you!"

Peter's anger disappeared like snow in summer. He looked as though he was about to try and defend his actions, but then he sighed and said, "I may not be able to stop you, Beele, but I've at least smoothed things over with Baron Bergheim. His son was too embarrassed and angry at your little display to show his face, but the baron has agreed to give you one more chance to make things work with his son."

Sybil stomped her foot on the ground. She realized she was clenching and unclenching her fists. "Make *what* work? What makes you think I won't do the same thing next time I see Johannes?"

"Because you won't be staying at this house if you do." Peter didn't speak with the authority of a demanding father, but with the tiredness of someone who had exhausted all options.

"Fine!" Sybil shouted.

"I won't support you any longer if you won't help support our family," Peter added. "Johannes will come after he's had his pride healed. Luckily, the baron says he has a short memory."

Sybil was all spit and vinegar. "Disown me then, father! Kick me out! If you won't accept my decisions, then I don't need you." She crossed her thin arms and looked away, closing her eyes.

"And where will you go, Beele?"

Sybil opened her mouth, but Peter's eyes looked through her. She followed his eyes and turned. In the distance, another carriage was approaching.

Peter groaned and walked past Sybil. "Let's see what other damage control I have to do."

The carriage stopped a few paces from the fields, and a tall, voluptuous woman stepped out. She wore a lavish dress, had her hands on her hips, and looked around her surroundings disapprovingly.

"Lady Margreth Baumgartner," the coachman introduced, "would like a word with your daughter, farmer."

The noblewoman strutted past Peter and stared down her thin nose at Sybil.

"So *you're* the little girl who's trying to make a big splash at court," the woman said.

"I-I'm not trying to do anything," Sybil said with a shrug. "We met last night, my lady. Don't you remember?"

"How could I remember something so plain?"

Sybil frowned.

Margreth pointed at Sybil's forehead and said, "Don't lie to me, you little whore! I see what you're trying to do with Johannes."

"Hey!" Peter shouted, stepping between his daughter and Margreth. "No one calls my girl a whore, do you understand me?"

Margreth took a step back and nearly tripped over herself. She gasped, and her mouth dropped open. "Stay out of this, old man. Do you have any idea who I am?"

"I don't care if you're the daughter of the Holy Roman Emperor himself," Peter said.

Margreth's face grew even more shocked. "My father will seize your house, you cur!"

Peter nudged his stubbed hand in her direction. "Back down, woman, and be civil when you're on my land."

Margreth ran her hands down her hips, smoothing her dress.

When Peter saw that she'd regained her composure, he said, "Now, who in the hell are you?"

The noblewoman crossed her arms over her breasts. "I'm Margreth Baumgartner, you simpleton. My father is Commander Arnold Baumgartner of the Bedburg garrison. Are you really so foolish?"

Peter shrugged. "Simpleton, foolish . . . I've been called worse. What is it you want with my daughter, Frau Baumgartner. What did she do to you?"

"She invaded my ball," Margreth said, pointing her chin up to the sky, as if the celebration from the night before had been held in her honor.

"She was invited by Baron Bergheim, and the arrangement between Beele and Johannes was set up by the baron and I. So if you have any qualms, direct them at me."

"She's trying to steal my man's heart!" Margreth screeched. "And I won't allow her! I won't see her at another ball, do you hear me?" Then she squinted and looked at Peter from head to toe. "You named your daughter Beele?" She grinned cruelly. "I suppose that makes sense."

Peter crossed his arms over his chest and craned his neck. He stayed quiet for a moment and then said, "I think I'm going to have to ask you to leave, Frau Baumgartner."

"Why is that, farmer?"

"Because you're an insufferable bitch, and I have crops to till."

Margreth's eyes bulged like they were going to pop out of her skull, and her lungs deflated. Sybil couldn't help but chuckle.

"Y-you . . . barbaric *cretin*!" Margreth screamed.

"Still not the worst thing I've been called, my lady. Not even the worst thing I've been called *today*, if I'm honest." Peter shrugged. "With that big, educated brain of yours, you could use some practice at throwing insults."

Margreth huffed and puffed and her head looked like it was about to explode. "You won't get away with this, you vile reprobate!"

"That's a bit better," Peter said.

The noblewoman stumbled on her heels and nearly tipped over as she turned around. She stomped away toward her carriage, and when she reached it she spun around and thrust a thin finger at Sybil. "Just remember, you little peasant," she yelled, "I won't leave this godforsaken town until I have Johannes' hand!" She spat on the ground and climbed into her carriage.

"How unladylike," Peter muttered. He waved innocently to the noblewoman as she rode off in a hot fury.

After Margreth was gone, Sybil eyed the ground, fell silent, and then meekly said, "Thank you."

Peter frowned and cursed under his breath. "I don't know what you did, Beele, but we could be in big trouble. We can't afford to be on the wrong side of the nobility."

Could this day possibly be worse than yesterday? Sybil thought, and then shrugged. *At least yesterday I ended the night in Dieter's arms.*

"What will we do?" Sybil asked.

Peter turned and walked away from his daughter, toward the front door of the house. "I'll think of something," he said, over his shoulder. "I need to talk to some people."

CHAPTER TWENTY-ONE

HEINRICH

Heinrich left Cologne on horseback, through the city's western gate. Archbishop Ernst had convinced him to stay longer than he'd planned, but his stay had still been limited to less than a week. He was eager to return to business in Bedburg. His entourage had grown—besides Tomas and the five guards, three Jesuit missionaries also accompanied him.

Two of the missionaries were quiet and somber, and Heinrich never learned their names. The third was a talkative, stout man with a round face, named Balthasar Schreib. Although he was the archbishop's chief religious representative, the man wore the indistinct robes of a simple monk. Besides the walking stick slung over his back, the Jesuit lacked even the most basic material possessions.

To Heinrich, Balthasar seemed to be a very pious—albeit annoying—man in his late twenties. The investigator wondered how the man had risen to such a high station at such a young age.

Heinrich bounced on the back of his steed as it trotted up a hilly roadway, and he stared up at the sunny, midday sky. He hadn't noticed that Balthasar had come up alongside him, until the priest spoke.

"A beautiful day," Balthasar said, smiling.

Heinrich grunted and nodded. He eyed the priest and asked, "Why does the archbishop place so much trust in you?"

Balthasar shrugged. "I suppose it's because I have a powerful network of priests that travel the area. They give the archbishop much to think about."

Heinrich twirled his mustache. "So you're the reason he knows of the Protestant army's whereabouts?"

"They're not an army, Herr Franz. They're a rabble of lost souls. They don't understand that they have already lost, and that Martin Luther and John Calvin will be forgotten in a matter of years."

Heinrich shook his head. "You might not be so sure of that after you see Bedburg."

"I will turn the unbelievers to our true Christian faith, in Bedburg, just as I have done in Cologne. Their heresy will not stand."

Heinrich shifted in his saddle. Despite his young appearance, Balthasar was full of confidence and vigor. "How will you do that? Through treachery and manipulation?"

If his intention was to offend or bait the priest, Heinrich's words fell flat. The Jesuit stayed quiet for a moment, and then looked away from Heinrich, toward the surrounding countryside. "No, Herr Franz. I will teach them with forgiveness and understanding. I will show them the error of their ways, and they will listen. The pope is our voice, and anyone else is just an imposter." Balthasar faced Heinrich with a sly look. "I'm getting the feeling you are not a pious man, investigator. You seem very sure of yourself, but you sound conflicted."

"Isn't every man conflicted?" Heinrich asked. "I'm confident in my abilities as a man of the law, and in that I am not conflicted. I'm just a seeker of the truth." He cleared his throat and continued. "But no, I am not convinced that God is everywhere."

"Perhaps we can change that."

"I doubt it," Heinrich said, smiling. "You won't have enough time during this trip, and once we're in Bedburg I'll be too busy to listen to your preaching."

Balthasar sighed and said, "You are a strange case, my lord. I'll give you that. But I am no preacher. I teach through logic and understanding."

Heinrich slowed his horse and frowned. Either this man was utterly naïve, or utterly cunning. Either way, his disposition was too optimistic for the investigator's liking. He wanted to get under the priest's skin, to see who he *really* was. "Okay, Herr Schreib, answer me this: If you were never taught what to believe, whether by the pope, or Luther, or Calvin . . ." he trailed off and narrowed his eyes on the missionary, "then how would you know who to love or hate?"

Balthasar cleared his throat. "That is where your truth becomes fiction, investigator. It is not a matter of love or hate. I live through God's tenets, and He lives through me. As a minister, I speak to Him, and He gives me signs, and loves me, as He loves everyone."

Heinrich felt that the priest didn't answer his question, but he wasn't sure how to turn Balthasar's words against him.

Their steeds reached the top of a hill, and from its apex they were given a glorious, clear sight of the countryside. Even in winter, trees dotted the horizon, grass grew in thick tufts, and puffy clouds moved through the sky. "You just said it's not a matter of love or hate," Heinrich said. "Aren't you contradicting yourself there, when you say He loves you?"

They began to descend the hill after taking in the sight for a short moment.

"Yes, not in the same terms as when *you* say 'love' or 'hate,' investigator. I was *born* with God in my heart. That will never change. In fact, everyone was born with God in his or her heart. It's just a matter of finding Him."

Heinrich grunted and spat on the grass. "Bah," he said, "you were born a suckling pup, just like the rest of us. You're no better or mightier than any other man, Herr Schreib. I don't doubt you're a good man, but that comes from being kind and honest, not because God willed it. *That* will never change."

Balthasar made a clucking sound with his tongue. "If I am a good man, it is because I follow Christ's and God's teachings. They give my spirit salvation. I am a sinner, Heinrich, as with the rest of Man. But God has given me a holy path to redemption, and I gladly follow it."

As they descended the hill, Balthasar spread his hands to the land before them. He took a deep breath, and when he exhaled he had a smile on his face. "Tell me, son, how do you explain the air we breathe? Or the water we drink? How do you explain the sun in the sky, which gives us life and warmth, and the moon beside it, giving us peace and quiet? How are we able to learn so much, build such magnificent structures, and converse with each other, unlike any other beast? It is our *souls* that separate us from animals, investigator, and if you believe Man is responsible for the countless miracles bestowed upon us, without His righteousness, then you are more foolish and lost than I first believed."

Heinrich felt his ears turn hot. He clenched his teeth and tightened his grip on his reins. After a quiet moment, he said, "We are able to do these things because we *learn*, through trial and error. God didn't plant or sow my crops—"

"But He gave you a bountiful harvest," Balthasar said, pointing to the sky.

"The sun did that!" Heinrich said. He was growing impatient and frustrated with the calm priest. *This man believes too much. He thinks men are good . . . and that is naïve, foolhardy . . . and dangerous.*

Balthasar still smiled. "And He *gave* you the sun. Don't you see? That is what we mean when we say He is everywhere and anywhere. God is within all of us, like I said. Is it just up to you to find Him, and I can help in that search."

The minutes dragged on, and despite the quiet contemplation and sound of hooves on grass, Heinrich grew more agitated. Eager not to lose an argument, he cleared his throat and said, "So how do you explain all the warring and killing and hatred in life, priest? Why would God allow such things?"

Balthasar was shaking his head before Heinrich even finished. "Ah, the typical approach of a jaded, disheartened man. Men are sinners, investigator. They wage these battles for material things: wealth, land, title—"

"They wage them in God's name!"

"It's a farce, Herr Franz! They may claim whatever they want, but these men haven't actually *found* Jesus or God. They are lying to themselves. They'll have to eventually atone for their sins and actions, or they'll burn in Hell." Balthasar scratched his chin and stared off into the trees in the distance. Then he tilted his head and gazed into Heinrich's eyes. His face took on a sudden hardness that Heinrich hadn't seen yet.

"Heaven is not for everyone, investigator. Especially not the vain, greedy, or depraved. That being said, anyone can be forgiven."

Heinrich frowned. "Even the murderers, rapists, and liars?"

"Anyone."

Heinrich turned away from the priest and chuckled. "I think not. It is my job to give the wrongdoers a carriage ride straight to their maker, to be judged."

"There is much loathing in your heart, my lord. What does that say about you, as a man? You say I am kind and honest because I was born and raised that way." Balthasar frowned. "Well, weren't you, too, before being driven by the same things that other men are driven by?"

Heinrich cocked his head and furrowed his brow. "What are you talking about?"

"I believe you can be a good man, like you once were, Heinrich. But you've let hatred sully your spirit, and your pride won't allow God into your heart."

The group reached the bottom of another hill, and Heinrich looked over his shoulder. The guards and other missionaries had backed off, obviously not wanting to be involved in the debate.

Heinrich leaned close to Balthasar and jabbed a finger in his chest. "Listen to me, priest. I only hate those who would harm or corrupt the ones I love. I am a harbinger of the law, not of retribution."

The priest scratched his forehead and shrugged. "Weren't you raised by a religious mother, Heinrich? A woman who advocated for the rights of other women, and who pampered your older brother? Did she not wish for a daughter, to continue her legacy, but got you instead? Did God corrupt your mother, then, for not giving you the love you deserved? Is that why you hate Him so, or why you hate and fear women?"

Heinrich felt an anger swell within his chest. It was a heavy anger, such that he hadn't felt in years, and his head cocked back in surprise. "Where in the hell did you gather all of that, priest? That's nonsense." Spittle flew from his mouth, onto Balthasar's robe. "You know nothing about me."

"I know what the archbishop has told me about you, Heinrich. I was his religious ear, remember?" Balthasar's happy, positive demeanor had suddenly vanished, and was replaced by a grim look. This was not the smiling "man of the cloth" Heinrich thought he was—this was a manipulator full of fire and brimstone.

If this man can't win with his silver tongue, he'll win with his forked one.

"Don't forget," the priest continued in a low voice, "that our archives in the church are vast, and our records go far, far into the past."

Heinrich found himself yelling, with his arms flying about wildly. "Quiet yourself! I said you know nothing of me, priest!"

Balthasar frowned. "I know that when you were young, your older brother drowned, and your father and mother blamed you, and then your father left your family."

"I'm warning you, hellion," Heinrich spat. "My father fled because he accidentally killed his friend. He was a coward, and he would not own up to his crime!"

The priest shrugged and raised his hands in surrender. His grim expression was once again changed to indifference and calmness. "Very well, very well, my apologies," he said as the group reached the top of another hill. "But before I finish, let me pose you the same question you opened with." The priest cleared his throat. "How would you know who to love and hate, if it weren't for the things you know and learned growing up as a boy? I learned how to love because of God. You learned how to hate because you lacked faith. I believe you know these things because you feel the love and hatred in your heart and soul, where God resides. These things tear at you night and day, but I have news, my friend . . . if you let God in, he can ease your suffering. But only if you allow him to."

Heinrich stared forward, fuming, and Balthasar grabbed his reins and pulled his horse away from the investigator. Heinrich tried to block out the priest's words, but his mind raced and he knew he wouldn't be getting much sleep that night.

The same thought kept playing in his mind, over and over: *It was God who* brought *my suffering, you fool. He cannot* save *me from it.*

"My lord!" a voice called, but Heinrich was still lost in his thoughts. "My lord!"

Heinrich heard hooves from behind and snapped back to reality. He turned in his saddle. Tomas was galloping toward him, one hand holding the reins of his steed, the other gripping an arquebus. He pointed the gun in Heinrich's direction.

The investigator's eyes grew, and he spun forward.

Five riders approached from the bottom of the hill, screaming toward the group with mad looks in their eyes. They were dressed in ragged clothes, with filthy faces and dirty beards. The missionaries retreated, while Tomas and the five guards rode over the lip of the hill to make their presence known.

Heinrich pulled on his reins and his horse went on its hind legs and reared loudly, pushing the investigator back on his saddle. He reached to the back of his trousers, fumbled with his arquebus, and felt the gun fall to the ground.

Shit.

The bandits were just as the archbishop had warned—hungry and desperate. Heinrich figured they'd probably only seen him and Balthasar at first, at the top of the hill. But as the six guards swept by the investigator, guns drawn and arms raised, the bandits scattered in all directions, but kept coming.

Guns shot off and bullets flew. Smoke filled the sky.

Heinrich's horse panicked and started circling, and the investigator searched the ground for his dropped weapon.

One of the bandits went down with a scream, while one of Heinrich's guards fell silently from his horse, clutching his neck.

A lone bandit came up from the side of the hill, flanking the group, and headed straight for Heinrich. The investigator's mouth gaped. He could see the man's yellow teeth.

The bandit aimed his gun at Heinrich.

A shadow flew by.

Balthasar had placed himself between the marauder and the investigator.

The gun fired.

Balthasar's horse whinnied and sent the priest flying to the ground. The horse collapsed on him, and Balthasar cried out in pain.

Heinrich jumped from his steed and rolled awkwardly in the grass. He crawled on his hands and knees toward his gun, and he came up with the weapon, holding it in both hands.

The bandit dismounted and pulled a knife from his belt. He ambled toward Balthasar, who was trapped under his own horse.

Heinrich still felt dizzy and disoriented. He leaped past his horse and staggered toward the bandit, whose attention was on Balthasar.

The priest grimaced and struggled to free his crushed leg from under the steed, but to no avail.

The bandit was on top of Balthasar, with his knife, pulling his arm back to strike.

Heinrich walked up behind the bandit, pointed his gun, and blew off the back of the man's head. Balthasar and his horse were showered with brains and bits of skull. The bandit crumbled to the ground with his knife still poised in the air.

Balthasar had a terrified look on his blood-spattered face. Heinrich breathed heavily and fell to his hands and knees, beside the priest and dead marauder.

Three of the bandits lay dead on the bloody hillside, as well as two of Heinrich's guards. The other two bandits fled, spurring their horses downhill and toward the trees on the horizon. Tomas and his remaining troop gave up the chase and circled back, heading toward Heinrich and Balthasar. One of the other two Jesuits trembled and pissed himself.

"Are you injured, my lord?" Tomas asked, jumping from his saddle. Heinrich was unable to speak, due to the adrenaline, so he simply shook his head.

With the help of the other three guards, Tomas helped lift Balthasar's dead horse, freeing the priest's leg, and then he helped the priest to his feet. Balthasar winced and reached for the staff slung over his back. He leaned on it and then wiped the bandit's blood from his face. His leg was clearly broken, and Heinrich assumed he'd walk with a limp for the rest of his life.

Still panting, Heinrich faced Balthasar. "So, priest . . . did God save your life right then?"

Balthasar frowned and clutched at his leg. He stared at Heinrich. "I don't know, investigator . . . did He save yours?"

CHAPTER TWENTY-TWO

GEORG

Georg finished his ale, belched loudly, and pulled at his beard to wipe away the drops that missed his mouth. The barkeep set down another mug in front of him.

"Much appreciated, Lars," Georg said.

The blond man smiled. "Anything for the hero of Bedburg," he said, and walked off to tend to other patrons.

Georg's eyes locked onto a pair of wide hips strutting away from him. They belonged to a dark-haired beauty, Lars' newest hire.

The hunter's eyes bulged and he faced Konrad, to his right. Despite the dark hair, the woman reminded him of Josephine. It reminded him how quickly someone could be replaced and forgotten. He knew the likelihood of finding Josephine's true killer was slim, and the sense of urgency in finding the killer was fading more and more every day.

In a pious town like this, who cares about the death of a single woman with a questionable profession? Only me.

"That woman could make a Moor blush," Georg said, drawing a hearty laugh from Konrad. He wasn't talking about the girl with the black hair, though he kept that to himself.

"How does it feel to be a hero?" Konrad asked, looking away from the woman.

Georg leaned forward on the table and looked down at his

mug. "I'm no hero."

"True." Konrad finished his ale, slammed the mug down on the table, and asked Lars for another.

Georg looked around the tavern. *It's midnight, and loud men still tell their stories and strike drunken deals with people who will never remember the deals tomorrow. Perhaps the hysteria is truly gone.* He inhaled deeply. "I did miss this place," he said.

"You missed the smell of piss and vomit?" Konrad said.

Georg glanced at him from the corner of his eye. "I missed the warmth of the fire, the whispers flying from table to table. I tell you, following shady figures in the middle of the night is no way to spend a winter evening."

"I wouldn't know," Konrad said. He lifted his mug to his mouth. "You said you had something to tell me, about that investigator? Is he one of the shady figures you speak of?"

"He talks big, but I think he's harmless enough. I saw him get slammed to the ground in here, a few days before you showed up." Georg tilted his head back and forth. "He's a strange one, though. I've seen him without his gloves on—he wears a wedding ring, but has never been married. He lives here, but has no permanent place of residence in Bedburg. It's all very odd."

"Sounds like a slippery fellow."

Georg nodded. "The church records are supposed to be all-telling . . . I think he's been hired by outside forces that allow him to keep secrets, even from the church. It's like he answers to no one here."

"Didn't he just travel to Cologne? That could be the place to look."

The tavern door swung open, and a thin man ambled in. Georg glanced at the man, and then did a double take. "Ah," he said, "speak of the Devil." He motioned for Investigator Franz to join him.

"Hey, lawman!" Lars called from the other end of the bar, "I don't want your trouble in here!"

Heinrich waved the man off. "I'm not here for trouble, I

assure you. I've seen enough of that today." He walked up to Georg and put a hand on his shoulder.

The investigator's eyes seemed far away, like something was troubling him.

"Investigator Franz," Georg said, "this is my friend, Konrad von Brühl. Konrad, Investigator Heinrich Franz."

Konrad frowned. "I've seen the man," he said, and then turned back to his mug.

Investigator Franz stared at Konrad's purple scar that went from cheek to chin, and the patch covering his left eye, and then faced Georg. "Friend?" he said. "I thought I was your friend."

"You don't have any friends, remember?" Georg said flatly. He patted the stool next to him, and Heinrich plopped down on the seat. Lars brought the investigator a beer, grunted, and wandered off.

"How was your holiday?" Georg asked.

"It seemed long," the investigator said, and then sighed.

After a bit of silent drinking, Georg leaned close to the investigator's ear and whispered, "I've gathered some . . . titillating news since you've been gone."

"*Titillating?*" Heinrich said, "where did a soldier learn *that* word?"

Georg ignored him. "Remember the Achterbergs?"

"You mean the family whose matron I had burned as a witch, whose patriarch was murdered, and whose son rots in jail for the murder? No, please, remind me."

Georg frowned and grunted. "You don't have to be an ass."

Heinrich waved off the hunter. "I've had a long day. Had to blow a man's head off this afternoon while saving a *priest*, of all people."

Georg leaned back in his stool. "Not so harmless after all," he said, drawing a chuckle from Konrad. "Anyway, I learned that the Achterbergs were ex-reformers. They were Protestants less than three years ago."

"I'm assuming you gathered that from Father Nicolaus and the church records?"

Georg nodded.

The investigator finished his ale. "Well, I assumed as much when I heard Bertrude Achterberg call Dorothea Gabler a Catholic whore."

Georg cocked an eyebrow. "Why didn't you tell me that? Could have saved me some legwork."

"We aren't partners," Heinrich said with a shrug. He looked at Georg's grimy beard. "And I thought it didn't matter."

Georg crossed his arms over his wide chest. He reached for his mug, drained half of it, and said, "Fine, then I won't tell you what else I learned." Then he turned away from the investigator.

Heinrich rolled his eyes. "I apologize," he said, putting his hand on Georg's shoulder. "For such a big man, you have a surprisingly thin skin. But, please, do tell."

Georg leaned in conspiratorially. He looked over both his shoulders, and his voice was barely more than a whisper. "That cabin that I found during the hunt . . . I wasn't just imagining things. I tracked a man going there a few days back, and saw a woman at the door. Not a ghost, but a flesh-and-blood woman."

Heinrich began nodding.

"And guess who the man was," Georg said excitedly. "Peter Griswold."

The investigator's head shot up from its slumped position, and his weary eyes lit up. "So that's where he goes at night . . ."

Georg nodded and clapped his hands, drawing a few offended eyes from around the tavern. "He goes just about every other night. I don't know who the woman is, but I wanted to wait for you to return before barging in. I wouldn't have the right questions."

Heinrich slapped Georg on the shoulder and smiled. "Nice work, my good hunter. Maybe we can be partners after all. Were you seen?"

171

Georg opened his mouth, hesitated, and winced. "Not . . . by them," he began, "but I was followed, and it turned out to be that damn nun from the church! I gave her a good scare, so we won't have to worry about her anymore."

Heinrich scrunched his face. "Why would the church be keeping an eye on you?"

Georg shrugged. "That's a good question. See, you always have the good questions."

The investigator tapped his mug of beer and started twirling his mustache. "What would the bishop want with you?" he asked under his breath. Then he shook his head. "It doesn't matter. Would you like to go find out who our mystery woman is?"

Georg looked at Heinrich, then his mug, then back to Heinrich. "Right now? This late at night?"

Investigator Franz smiled. "Precisely the best time, my good hunter."

"But I'm drunk."

The investigator was already standing from his seat. "And you won't be tomorrow night?"

Konrad begged to join them in the woods, but Heinrich and Georg left him at the tavern to drown himself in ale. As Georg was leaving, he watched Konrad strike up a conversation with the black-haired woman, and the woman promptly slapped him across the face.

Georg smiled. "He's a good man, you know," he told Heinrich as they took off down the road. The night was cold and crisp, and all the townspeople were either asleep, or at the tavern. "He was a comrade of mine when I fought for Alexander Farnese."

"The Duke of Parma?" Heinrich asked.

Georg nodded.

"Well, I'm sure he's a good man, but I don't know him. Also, you need to stop flapping your tongue when you get drink in you. Our partnership is confidential."

The hunter coughed and waved his hands. "I was whispering. There's no way he was listening. Did you see how drunk he was?"

The investigator rolled his eyes. "Just tell me your news in private next time."

They made their way south, to the edge of town, and then cut east toward the Griswold estate. The house was dark, and no smoke came from its chimney. At the current hour, everyone was likely asleep.

They ran past the house and broke out into the open countryside. Before long, they came to the woods, sauntered past the first rows of trees, and Georg took the lead. He led them gingerly through foliage that grew thicker and thicker the deeper they went. He swung at low-hanging branches and cleared the way for Heinrich. A few times, he heard the investigator spitting leaves out of his mouth and cursing.

"Aren't you afraid of wolves preying on us in here?" the investigator whispered.

Georg craned his neck and whispered over his shoulder, "Are you kidding me? I killed the Werewolf of Bedburg. They wouldn't dare."

They crept through the woods until they came to the clearing. It had taken them an hour to penetrate the woods. The moon was hidden beneath gray clouds and treetop canopies, and in the darkness the decrepit cabin was nearly impossible to see.

But Georg knew where to look, and he crouched and led Heinrich forward.

At the front door, Georg breathed heavily and then knocked: twice hard, thrice soft, and then once more hard.

Heinrich eyed the hunter with a questioning look.

They heard movement coming from inside, and Heinrich drew his arquebus.

A voice was speaking before the door even opened. "Back already—" the voice started, but trailed off as the woman in the doorway saw the two unfamiliar faces of Georg and Heinrich. She tried to slam the door shut, but Georg's foot was in the hinge, and he held out a big hand and shoved the door back. The woman yelped and retreated into the house.

Georg and Heinrich dashed forward.

The woman reached for a pitchfork in the corner of the room.

Heinrich pointed his gun in her face, and she froze.

That was the first time Georg got a good look at the woman: She was middle-aged, with lines on her face, and gray-black curls that swept to her shoulders. Despite the stone-cold look in her eyes, she still held the beauty of a younger woman.

Staring down the barrel of Heinrich's arquebus, her brows curved toward her nose. "Who the hell are you?"

"We'll ask the questions," Heinrich said. "Put down the fork."

She hesitated, but finally lowered the tool and let it clink to the ground.

Georg took a gander around the house. It was quaint, small, with a hearth at one end, a small bed, a stove, and a round table in the center of the room.

"Who are *you*?" Heinrich asked, tucking his gun back in his trousers. "What is your name?"

"I'm . . . Katharina. Katharina Trompen."

The investigator leaned his head to one side. "Are you sure? Georg, does she sound sure to you?"

"Sure don't," said the hunter, who was staring into the flames of the hearth.

The woman put her hands on her hips. "I'm as sure as I'm sure it's night outside."

"What's your relationship with Peter Stubbe?"

"Peter . . . Stubbe?"

Heinrich rolled and cracked his wrist, and then nodded. "Peter Griswold. What's your relationship with him?"

Katharina took a step toward the table, ran a hand over the wood, and stared at the investigator. "Are you going to kill me? You still haven't told me who you are, though I guess the big one is Georg."

The hunter chuckled.

"No," Heinrich said, "we aren't going to kill or harm you. My name is Investigator Franz, this is my associate, and now that we're all acquainted will you tell me what I want to know?"

Katharina cleared her throat. "Would you gentlemen like some food? I have freshly baked bread—"

"Quit stalling, woman."

"I am a widower, investigator. All right? It isn't something I'd like everyone to know. I'm sure you understand."

"I do," Georg chimed in, and then he walked to the table and took a seat.

Heinrich gave the hunter a disapproving look. "And Peter Griswold?"

"He is my friend and . . . my caretaker."

"Caretaker?"

"I don't leave the house very much, if you can imagine." Katharina swept her hands out at her meager cabin, while also alluding to the fact that she lived in a forest. "So, yes, Peter comes to me and gives me food and other things I need. Is that a crime?"

"How long have you known Herr Griswold?" the investigator asked, stroking his chin. He started pacing around the table, and then his face lit up. "And why are you hiding from Bedburg?"

Katharina took a seat across from Georg. "I've known Peter for years. And I'm not *hiding*, investigator. I'm just living. It's really none of your concern."

"But it is," Heinrich said. He clasped his hands behind his back as he paced, and then pointed a finger toward the ceiling. "There are lots of strange things happening in and around Bedburg, and when we see an eerie, secret cabin in the woods, it gives us reason for alarm."

Katharina sighed, and she ruffled her gray-black locks. "I don't like my affairs to be noticed by the church, if you must know. If they found out I've not been paying taxes, they would take my home. I'd rather not go through the trouble, and, as it is, I'm not causing anyone any problems."

"She makes a point," Georg said.

Heinrich stopped in place and nodded. "We appreciate your candor, Frau Trompen. Now, before we're on our way, let me ask you another question: What do you know of the Protestant rebellion?"

Georg stomped on the ground, taken aback. Any word about the Protestants was news to him. *What did you find out in Cologne, you sneaky bastard?*

Katharina looked at her feet, and then back to the investigator. "I don't have a clue what you're talking about."

Heinrich nodded, slowly, and the seconds dragged on excruciatingly. "Very well," he finally said, smiling. "Thank you for your time. Georg, let's go."

Georg stood, nodded to the woman, and then followed Heinrich outside.

Katharina Trompen stood in the doorway, watching them leave. "Come back any time, boys, and you'll see I have nothing to hide," she called out, and then disappeared into her cabin.

"Why didn't you arrest her for evading her taxes?" Georg asked when they were back in the midst of the trees.

"I want to watch her," Heinrich said. "We might need her later."

Georg shrugged. "Well, she seems like a nice enough woman."

"Nice enough, yes. But she's also lying to us, my good hunter."

"How do you know—" Georg began to say, but then shook his head. "Never mind . . . *it's your job to know.*"

CHAPTER TWENTY-THREE

DIETER

In the early morning, Father Nicolaus gave a somber sermon to his congregation. He spoke about the trials and tribulations of having a crisis of faith, and how to stay obedient and resilient to God.

Dieter was lethargic, and could tell the congregation knew. Tired words and stutters replaced his usual enthusiasm, and he frowned at the churchgoers after giving his sermon.

Sybil was absent from the crowd, as she had been for half a week. *Perhaps she's finally heeding her father's words.*

Investigator Franz stood in the back of the room, the first appearance he'd made since returning from Cologne. Next to him stood a bald man with a round head whom Dieter didn't recognize.

After leading the congregation through a prayer, Mass was dismissed, and people shuffled out quietly.

As the church emptied, Investigator Franz walked up to the pulpit, with his bald acquaintance behind him. The man wore priestly robes and limped with the aid of a wooden staff.

"Father Nicolaus," Heinrich said as he approached, "I give you Vicar Balthasar Schreib, a Jesuit deputy from Cologne. He speaks on behalf of Archbishop Ernst."

"This is the man you were sent to retrieve?" Dieter asked. He glanced at Balthasar and stayed quiet, before finally bowing to the priest. "Please excuse my rudeness. Welcome, brother."

Vicar Balthasar smiled and bowed. "Thank you, brother. I've been sent to aid in your conversion of the Protestants. Investigator Franz and I have just returned from a discussion with Lord Werner."

"I'm not much for politics," Dieter said, "but I hope things went well."

Investigator Franz started backpedaling. "My work here is finished, so I'll leave you to it."

Once Heinrich had left, Balthasar said, "I was hoping for an audience with your bishop, if that's possible."

Dieter nodded. "Indeed. Please, follow me."

Before stepping away from the pulpit, a loud voice from outside caught the attention of both priests. Balthasar looked at Dieter for an explanation, and the younger priest sighed. "That would be Pastor Hanns Richter, a rather vocal preacher of the Lutheran faith. He's been sermonizing outside of our church for some time now. He's liked by the public, and is the only man with the gall to speak openly about the values of Martin Luther."

Balthasar sniffed and frowned. "A heretical act that must be stopped," he said, "lest he draw the whole town to his burdensome beliefs."

Dieter nodded. He led Vicar Balthasar down the back hallway, passing Sister Salome as they walked. The vicar bowed to the nun, and Salome bowed even lower, as a sign of respect.

Dieter rapped on Bishop Solomon's door. He was called in, and Dieter introduced Balthasar. Solomon excused Dieter, and the priest left the room.

Back in the nave, Sister Salome was sweeping the dust from around the pews. Father Nicolaus went to the pulpit and went on his hands and knees in front of a statue of Christ. He clasped his hands in front of his face.

Dear God, he said to himself, *I beg You to show me a sign— show me what to do. I've not seen Sybil in three days and nights, and I fear I've lost her, or worse, that she's given up on me. I preach about chastity, obedience, and resilience, but You know I've failed in this. I am lost, Lord, and I seek*

Your guidance.

Send me a sign, Father. I love that girl, and cannot hide my feelings much longer. My heart aches. I know I've failed You, Lord, but please don't rebuke Your humble servant. Send me back on the path of righteousness, so that I may serve You with my entire heart, once again. Amen.

"Father Nicolaus?"

Dieter went to his feet and turned. He smiled.

Sybil stood in the doorway of the church.

The priest looked skyward, said a silent word of thanks, and rushed over to Sybil. She looked distraught and lost, just as he felt. She was holding something under her dress.

"My dear," Dieter said, resting his hands on Sybil's shoulders. "Come, let us go to the gardens."

As they walked outside, Dieter craned his neck and noticed Sister Salome standing, broom in hand, watching as they retreated outside. They went to the flower cloister on the east wall of the church, and Dieter produced his wooden cross amulet from beneath his robes. He smiled and said, "I still wear your gift everyday, Beele."

Sybil faced the ground.

Dieter frowned and tried to meet her eyes. "What's wrong? My heart leaps at seeing you—are you not happy to see me?"

Sybil stared up into the priest's tired eyes. "I don't regret what happened three nights ago, Dieter. I hope you don't, too."

Dieter stuttered, but then closed his mouth.

"I've been absent because my father has insisted I give Johannes von Bergheim another chance at meeting with me. I've been in his company for the past two nights, and I don't know how much longer I can stand it."

Dieter furrowed his brow and squinted. "Has he harmed you?"

Sybil shook her head.

"I will speak with your father."

"No!" Sybil said, eyes opening wide. She looked around, aware that she'd shouted the word. "No, please don't. I told him I love

179

you, but he can't know about . . . what we did. No one can, like you said. But I came to say I miss you, and to give you this." She produced a thin booklet from the folds of her dress.

Dieter took the booklet. "What is this?"

"I want you to teach me to read that next. I stole it from my father's chambers."

Dieter opened the leather-bound cover of the booklet. The pages were old and weathered. "You know stealing is unacceptable, Beele." He turned to the first page and read a few lines. Then his mouth dropped open. His eyes darted around, and he slammed the booklet shut. With a hushed tone, he said, "What is the meaning of this, Sybil? This is Martin Luther's *Ninety-Five Theses*! I can't be seen with this! Do you know what would happen if you were caught reading this?"

Sybil put her hands together and leaned closer to the priest. "Please, Dieter, do this for me. I want to learn more, and I know you must be curious as well."

"Beele . . ."

"Just consider it," Sybil said. She looked over her shoulder, and then to the roses and lilies. "It's a winter miracle that they're still in bloom," she said, smiling.

Dieter said nothing as he stared at the leather-bound book.

"I must go before my father finds out I've been here," Sybil said.

Dieter sighed, but before he could say anything else, Sybil rushed into his arms and embraced him, and leaned her head into his chest. After a long hug, she scampered off down the hill, passing by Pastor Richter.

Dieter stood in the doorway of the church, hands on his hips, staring down at the Lutheran preacher. His mind raced. *This girl will be the death of me*, he thought. But he didn't care. He still loved her.

"Ah, Father Nicolaus, there you are. Will you join us?"

Dieter turned around. Vicar Balthasar was limping down the aisle with Bishop Solomon behind him.

"Join you in what?"

"In doing the Lord's work," Balthasar said with a wry smile. His round, jovial face looked odd and serious. "And not just the *Lord's* work, but also Lord Werner's."

Confused, Dieter scratched the stubble on his chin. Instead of asking the vicar to clarify, he followed Balthasar and the bishop and headed out of the church, and then downhill. They came to Pastor Richter, who had a group of ten or so townsfolk listening to his fiery sermon.

Three armed soldiers appeared from the shadows of nearby buildings. The pastor stopped speaking when he saw spears being brandished. The group listening to him silently dispersed.

Pastor Richter stepped down from his overturned fruit crate, and the soldiers kicked the crate away.

The vicar, bishop, and priest surrounded him.

Vicar Balthasar stood with his arms crossed over his chest, a smug smile on his face. "Pastor Hanns Richter," he said.

"What do you want?" the pastor asked, frowning. He stared at the spearheads pointed in his direction.

The vicar cleared his throat. "With the power vested in me by Lord Werner of Bedburg, Archbishop Ernst of Cologne above him, Pope Sixtus above him, and God above all, I hereby place you under arrest. You are to be placed in Bedburg's jailhouse, until you are tried."

All of the pastor's congregation could hear Balthasar's loud voice.

"What is the meaning of this?" the pastor asked. "I am a peaceful speaker. Under what charges am I being tried?"

"Heresy."

A shadowy twilight overtook Bedburg, and Dieter sat on a pew in his dark church, surrounded by his own thoughts. He placed his hands on his knees and stared at the weeping statue of Christ's crucifixion. Over the last two years, since arriving in Bedburg, he'd prayed to the statue nearly every day. He'd been sent by Archbishop Ernst to help Solomon run the church. He never expected that running the church would be so vexing.

Since his stay, he'd accomplished many things: He'd helped sway opinion back to the Catholic faith; he'd grown gardens and flowers, and gave people a renewed hope; he'd preached unforgettable sermons, heard the confessions of hundreds, helped the needy and poor.

He'd fallen in love.

Now, for the first time in his life, Dieter wasn't sure if the statue of Christ held the same meaning it once had. He doubted his true destiny in life.

Perhaps this is what God wants, he thought, *for me to doubt His word, so that I could find my path back into His loving arms.* For the first time, God didn't have the answers that Dieter sought.

Outside, snow started falling. A cold wind swept ice and fluff against the church's doors and walls.

Inside, it was cool and silent. Dieter felt a sickness in his stomach. The few candles that lit the hall flickered, and Dieter shivered and wrapped his cassock tight around his body.

He was alone, wallowing in self-pity, but he knew it didn't have to be that way. He could immerse himself. It was blasphemy to read the manuscript Sybil had given him, *But maybe Martin Luther's diatribe is the sign I'm looking for. Perhaps that's what God is trying to show me.*

After praying for the third time that day, Dieter stood from the pew and shuffled down the hallway. He opened the door to his small, quaint chamber. The room had only a bed and a table, for reading and writing. It was more like a jail cell than a room.

He lit the candle on the table. He sat down, sighed, and produced the manuscript from under his robe. He set the booklet on the table, stared at it, and then ran a hand over its rough, leather cover. *To think, that such a small document could hold so much power, and cause so much change in the world. To many, the words in this manuscript hold more power than any length of steel.*

With a heavy heart and soul, Dieter's eyes hovered over the leather-bound manuscript of the *Ninety-Five Theses*. Then he took a deep breath, opened the cover, and began reading.

CHAPTER TWENTY-FOUR

SYBIL

Sybil sat in a massive stateroom with her hands on her lap. She peered around the mansion—one of Baron Bergheim's private estates—at the high ceilings, carved columns, and beautiful paintings on the walls. Ludwig von Bergheim had one of the largest houses in Bedburg, and it was only his vacation home.

Three housemaids entered and left the room at various intervals, bringing tables for wine and food and other accoutrements. Other than the maids, the house was left entirely to Sybil and Johannes von Bergheim for the night.

Sybil wore a modest green gown that highlighted her fair skin and hair. She'd taken a carriage from her estate, offered by Baron Bergheim. As she sat, tense and uncomfortable, she still wondered what the baron could possibly want with an arranged marriage between his noble son and a farmer's daughter.

In front of her luxurious chair was a red, Persian rug, and beyond that a large hearth was built into the wall. The hearth crackled with flames. Johannes von Bergheim stood on the Persian rug, dressed in an exquisite tunic, looking every part the nobleman.

Johannes crossed his arms, staring at Sybil through narrow eyes, and then he tapped his chin. He snapped his fingers, and a servant girl shyly entered the room. "Bring us food and wine," he ordered. The girl scampered off, leaving Sybil and Johannes alone.

"My father is happy how things have been getting on since our embarrassing . . . *mishap*. You even look halfway decent for a change." Johannes stared at Sybil with a sideways glance. "You don't have the classical beauty of Margreth, but there is some appeal in your common appearance." The nobleman smiled. "You're an every-day girl, and though your wardrobe decisions are hideous, they somehow accentuate your prettiness." He spoke as if Sybil wasn't sitting right in front of him.

Sybil eyed the ground. "Thank you, my lord."

"Your breasts could be bigger," Johannes said with a shrug. "Margreth does have some big ones, does she not?" He snickered. "Perhaps yours will grow in. You're still young."

Sybil's face turned red.

Lord Johannes took a seat across from Sybil, next to the fire, and put one leg over his knee. The fire behind him caused his shadow to loom across the entire room. He stared at Sybil, who looked at everything except the nobleman—the patterns on the Persian rug; a painting above the fireplace; her own feet—and then a side door opened. Two servant girls appeared, one holding plates of food, the other with a carafe and a bottle of wine.

The food plates were filled with boiled quail eggs, snails from France, caviar, fine cheeses, and other delicacies. After placing the food and wine on the table, the servant girls bowed and started to leave.

"Wait, Hilde, come back," Johannes said, snapping his fingers. The girl who'd brought the wine stopped in her tracks and faced the young lord. She was a bigger girl, but no older than twenty. She looked scared as she stood next to Johannes.

"Yes, my lord?"

"Show Sybil what a voluptuous woman looks like," Johannes said.

Hilde's scrunched her forehead. "E-excuse me, lord?"

"Come on," Johannes said, "lower your dress and show Sybil your breasts. Show her what she has to look forward to."

Sybil's heart sank for the scared girl. She sat forward in her chair and said, "Really, my lord, that's not necess—"

"Quiet," Johannes said in a dark tone. He looked back at Hilde, whose eyes were beginning to tear up. "Well," he said, "do you want me to tell my father you've been disobedient?"

The servant girl's eyes took on a distant stare as she quietly slid the top of her dress from her body.

Lord Johannes giggled, and he grabbed and squeezed at the girl's exposed breasts. "Ah!" he said, "that's good, Hilde. A *real* woman. Now go on and leave my sight." Johannes slapped the girl's ass as she hurried out of the room.

Sybil felt disgusted, and she lost any appetite she may have had. *How can this spoiled brat get away with so much, without any consequence?* Sybil shook her head. *That girl was petrified.*

"I can tell you don't approve of my actions," Johannes said, studying Sybil's face. "But Hilde is *my* servant, and I can do as I please with her." With a calmness that suggested he didn't give the event a single thought, the nobleman said, "I can't wait to leave this place." He gazed around at the countless paintings on the walls, and sighed. "Bedburg is such an ugly town." He stood from his chair and walked over to the food table and picked up a slice of cheese.

He moved to the wine table and blocked Sybil's sight with his body. She heard him pour two glasses of something, and then he handed one of the glasses to her.

"I'm really not thirsty, my lord," Sybil said.

"You will drink," Johannes commanded. He shoved the wineglass in Sybil's face, and then took a sip from his own glass. "As I was saying," he said, walking back to his seat, "I belong with my friends and colleagues. The people here are boring and uncultured. And then there's that dreaded witch, Margreth." The lord shook his head. "And you, I suppose. But you must know that you will not be my only woman once we are married. A man like me deserves more."

A man like you deserves a sword down his throat, Sybil thought. A quiet anger swept over her, and she took a sip of wine to hide her discomfort.

"It's a nobleman's job to spread his seed to as many women as possible," Johannes said confidently, as if he actually believed his words. "Because babies die far too frequently, and I need one to stay alive." He smiled cruelly.

"You would father bastard children . . . knowingly?" Sybil asked, shocked. She instantly regretted speaking out.

Johannes frowned and narrowed his eyes. He looked like he was about to spit on Sybil, or on the rug. "Watch yourself, girl. You have no place judging me. I would see that my family's legacy continues on. You wouldn't understand that, though. You're just a commoner."

Sybil took another, longer gulp of wine, and before long she felt her cheeks getting warm and rosy.

"Are you a virgin?" Johannes asked abruptly. "I mean, you must be, the way you ran out on me the other night. You were like a scared lamb." He chuckled. "Any other girl would *pay* to have me. I mean, just look at how Margreth groveled at my feet."

Sybil's body stiffened, her neck tightening. A thin sheen of sweat formed on her upper lip. *You mistake groveling with patronizing, you intolerable ass.* She looked at her wineglass. *I'll need to watch my drinking, lest I speak my mind and really make a mess of things.*

"Well?" Johannes asked, raising one eyebrow.

"Y-yes, my lord. I am a virgin."

Johannes clapped his hands and smiled. "Good. When we move from here I suspect that your father will help supply Bergheim with pigs. As a bonus, I'll get a wife who's as pure as first snow in winter. Perhaps this isn't such a terrible deal after all."

Sybil stumbled over the words. "Excuse me, my lord. When we *move?*"

Johannes drained his wine and stood to pour some more, but then paused. "Of course. You didn't expect we'd stay in this cesspool of a town, did you? No, you'll live in one of our mansions in Bergheim. Or perhaps we'll move to Cologne . . .

187

some place with a learned, civilized people."

"What about my father? What will he do? What will *we* do?"

Johannes stopped mid-pour and faced Sybil. "I could care less what he does," he said. "But as for you and me, what do you think we'll do? Are you really that shallow? We'll do what married people do, girl. You'll father my children, I'll have heirs, and I'll join parliament and take care of matters you wouldn't understand. My father is getting old, and I will take his position someday. Being a married man—even to someone such as yourself—will give me more clout in office."

"But what if I don't want to be your housewife," Sybil said, raising her voice. She looked down at her wine cup. *Dammit*, she thought, angry at herself for speaking so bluntly.

Johannes stayed calm. "What you want is of no concern to me. Everything's already been arranged by our fathers."

Sybil had the urge to throw her cup on the Persian rug. But before she could get any angrier, her mind started to get fuzzy, and she became suddenly drowsy. It started off as a dull headache, but quickly grew worse and worse.

"Are you feeling all right?" Johannes asked.

Sybil's vision started to blur around the edges of her eyes, and she knew something was wrong. She'd been drunk before, although not often, but this was something different. Something diabolical was afoot, creeping up through her body. Her tight muscles began to relax, and she heard her cup drop to the ground with a clang. She stared up at Johannes with a confused look, tried to say something, but couldn't be sure if any words came.

"That took longer than expected," Johannes muttered to himself. He ambled toward her, and stared into her listless eyes. He grabbed her shoulders and had a dark smile on his face.

Then he said something, but Sybil couldn't understand his words. All she could see was his cruel grin, and then her eyes were facing the floor, which was rushing up to meet her, and she slipped into darkness.

CHAPTER TWENTY-FIVE

HEINRICH

Peter Griswold awoke with a start, lying in a pool of his own sweat. His heart raced. Something was wrong. It was the middle of the night, but he could feel it—something was wrong.

The door to his room opened with a creak, and he jumped to his feet. His son, Hugo, stood in the doorway with a frightened look on his face.

"Father, did you hear that?" the boy asked.

Disoriented, Peter threw on a robe to cover his nakedness, and then he ran and embraced his son. He didn't know what Hugo was talking about, and he couldn't remember if he'd been in the midst of a nightmare when he awoke.

"What is it, son? Go back to sleep," he urged.

Hugo whimpered and shook his head. "I'm scared," he said. "I heard something." He held a stuffed doll tight against his chest. Sybil had made the doll for him, and it resembled a horse.

Clank.

The noise came from outside. "Stay here," Peter said. He wrapped his robe tight, but struggled with his one hand.

Still sweating, Peter left his room. He crept to the front of the house and held his ear against the door.

Ting.

This time it sounded like someone had kicked a bucket. "Dammit," a voice cursed.

Peter ran back to his room and reached under his bed. He pulled out a long rifle and a few bullets. Hugo was huddled in a corner of the room, wide-eyed, knees pulled up against his chest.

Peter hadn't used a gun in years. He grasped the gun in his knees and loaded it with his one good hand. He ran back to the front of the house and took a deep breath.

He slowly pushed the door open and walked out into the fields, barefoot. Even though it wasn't snowing anymore, the night was crisp, and white clumps of soft snow had settled over his crops.

He moved slowly—like a wolf stalking his prey—to the side of the house, where he'd heard the noises coming from.

He raised the rifle and nestled the butt of the gun against his right shoulder. The gun quivered against his shoulder because he couldn't grip the barrel to aim properly.

He thought his eyes played tricks on him, and he blinked hard. The moon was hidden above a blanket of clouds, and he stared into pitch-blackness. He edged closer to his two barns—one that housed pigs and cows, the other with horses and slaves—and squinted into the shadowy alcoves of the structures. He didn't see any shapes, and the animals and thralls slept soundly.

Breathing deep, he mustered the willpower to speak. "Show yourself!" he called out, "or I'll shoot you dead!"

His bare feet were turning numb from the snow, and he stopped moving. He aimed his gun in all directions, unsure of where to point the muzzle.

He heard a rustling, back behind the barns.

Peter took off sprinting toward the noise. He rounded the side of the barn where the pigs and cows were sheltered. He reached the back of the barn and spotted a silhouette.

The figure was on four legs. Its back was turned to Peter, and a hood covered its face. Peter slowly shuffled toward it.

Abruptly, the figure stood on two legs and took off running, away from the barn and into the darkness.

"Damn you!" Peter shouted. He aimed his gun at the figure's back, which became smaller and smaller as it ran into the night.

Peter's hand trembled, and he put his finger on the trigger.

He breathed heavily, but couldn't rally the courage to shoot. Within moments the figure had disappeared into the darkness. Peter sighed loudly and let his rifle fall to his side. He groaned, and then his eyes followed the footprints in the snow.

Whoever—or whatever—had been snooping around his estate was headed back toward Bedburg.

It was morning, and Heinrich Franz hurried away from Castle Bedburg, toward the church. It was a gray, gloomy morning. Townsfolk shoveled snow out of the roads so that they could guide their carts to the marketplace. Heinrich passed a few people he recognized and nodded to them, but few of them returned his nods. The gray clouds and snowy roads made the town seem despondent.

As he kept walking, Heinrich realized that the weather might not have been why people seemed to be avoiding him. He'd become somewhat of a nuisance in the quiet town—always questioning people and causing a ruckus—and while he was in Cologne, his absence had probably been a welcome sight.

It seemed that anyone who talked to the investigator ended up in trouble, so most people wanted nothing to do with him. It was a bad omen for Investigator Franz to be seen at your door.

He knew his reputation, but shrugged away the thoughts. *It's not my job to make friends,* he reminded himself.

He reached the church just before morning Mass, and entered through the stained-glass doors. Father Dieter Nicolaus and Sister Salome were speaking to each other next to the pulpit at the end of the room.

"Investigator Franz," Father Nicolaus said in a flat tone as Heinrich approached. "To what do we owe this pleasure?"

Heinrich chuckled. "No need to feign kindness with me, Father. I know you hate me."

"I don't hate you," the priest said, "I am a man of God. But

I'm also not feigning kindness."

"Nonsense," Heinrich said. "Even God hates me." He saw Sister Salome's mouth open wide, and he waved his hand. "That's neither here nor there. I require the aid of one of you."

Father Nicolaus sighed and nodded to Sister Salome. "I'll help him, but could you prepare my sermon for me? It should be sitting in my chambers."

The nun bowed her head and shuffled out of the room, toward the back hallway.

Father Nicolaus put his hands on his hips. "What is it you need?"

"Records," Heinrich said, reaching into his tunic and presenting the priest with a roll of parchment, "and knowledge. I figured the best place to look for those two things would be the church."

"Our records are not for public viewing."

"I'm on official business," Heinrich replied. He handed the roll of parchment forward.

Father Nicolaus scratched his head as he read the document, and then he shrugged and turned, waving for Heinrich to follow him. "I guess you've come to the right place."

They walked down the hallway, passed the chambers of the priests, nun, and bishop, and came to a small stairwell at the end of the hall. The stairs spiraled down for two flights to a dark, damp room. A torch was perched at the bottom of the stairs, and Father Nicolaus lit it, illuminating the room. They walked to the other end of the chamber, to a closed door.

Father Nicolaus placed the torch on a holder on the wall, and then opened the door. "We don't allow lit flames in the records room," he explained.

"Probably for the best," Heinrich said.

The room was dusty and had high ceilings, and columns that held up the roof. Rows and rows of bookshelves were set against every wall. Though the place was dark, a few windows near the top of the ceiling allowed murky light to shine in, and it didn't take long for Heinrich's eyes to adjust.

"The church's records room holds information on the history of Bedburg, including anyone who's ever moved or lived here in the last seven centuries," Father Nicolaus said. "What are you looking for?"

"Records on the history of the Griswold family."

Father Nicolaus raised his eyebrows, and Heinrich could tell that his muscles tightened. "Peter Griswold's family?"

"Is there another Griswold family in Bedburg? I'll need records on his son and daughter as well, whom I'm aware you know quite well."

"I don't know them well," the priest snapped, but his body language and the speed to which he responded betrayed his words.

"It isn't good to lie in a holy place, Father," Heinrich said with a wry smile.

The priest walked to a shelf deep in the room, as if he'd pinpointed the location without needing to think about it. He shuffled through some papers, muttering to himself, then pulled several yellow, crumpled pieces of parchment from the shelf.

"Here is the information we have on the Griswolds, investigator. Can you read? Would you like assistance?"

Heinrich narrowed his eyes at the priest and frowned. He snatched the papers away and said, "I can read, but I'll need some privacy."

"Might I ask what you're inquiring about? Maybe I can help."

"You're too eager for your own good, priest. Just give me privacy."

Father Nicolaus stood upright. "I'll be on the other side of the room. I'm sure you'll understand that we don't allow anyone to read the records in solitude. It's a matter of protecting the documents and making sure they aren't . . . *modified*."

Heinrich nodded and shooed the priest away with a wave of his hand. He leaned over the first page and started reading. The page told of the first generation of Griswolds to arrive in Bedburg, namely Peter Griswold's father.

It didn't take long for Heinrich to have a good understanding of the family.

Peter Griswold's father, Ubel, was a Rhenish settler. He'd lived in a rural town called Epprath, near Cologne, before coming to Bedburg.

The family has never been too far from Bedburg . . .

Ubel died young, of unknown causes. So did his wife. Before dying, Ubel's wife birthed two children: a son and a daughter. When he was old enough, Peter moved to Bedburg with his new wife, Helena, and his sister. Peter became an influential pig farmer in Bedburg.

Peter had two children with Helena: Sybil, his daughter, and Hugo, his son. Helena died giving birth to her son. Shortly after Helena's death, Peter's sister went missing. She vanished, and was thought to have either died during a cold winter, or to have fled the electorate of Cologne, for unknown reasons. She hadn't been heard of since.

Heinrich kept scanning the pages. His brow perked up when he came to a particular side note: Peter and his family were Catholic converts, and the church believed they still practiced Lutheranism, to this day.

Heinrich squinted as he stared at the side note. The ink was certainly much fresher than the ink on the rest of the pages, like it had been a recent update.

Other pages showed the Griswold's yearly tax yield, what they grew and how much of it, and other statistics that Heinrich shuffled into his memory, but had little use of at the moment.

When Heinrich placed the records back on the shelf, he couldn't help but smirk, though he tried to hide it from Father Nicolaus. He knew he'd just learned valuable information, and was inching closer to the truth he desired.

*   *   *

Heinrich took a horse to the southern farmlands, to the Griswold estate. It was midday, and the sun's rays finally peeked through the gray clouds.

To his surprise, a carriage loomed next to the estate. The tall, stiff baron, Ludwig von Bergheim, was speaking with Peter outside the farmer's house.

Heinrich spurred his horse and got within earshot of the two. Peter sighed as he watched Heinrich approach.

"I'm not entertaining guests tonight, investigator," Peter called out.

"I'm afraid you are, Herr Griswold." Heinrich dismounted and led his horse toward the baron and the farmer.

Baron Bergheim turned and stared down his narrow nose at Heinrich, and gave the investigator a slight sneer. Then he turned back to Peter and said, "As I was saying, the girl drank quite a bit, but she should feel better soon."

"And you're certain of the other thing?" Peter asked, glancing at the investigator.

Ludwig nodded. "My son told me as much. If you'd like, I could send a doctor to check on her."

Peter frowned and slowly nodded. "That would be fine."

Heinrich stared at the two, trying to make sense of their conversation. It had become public news that the magistrate of Bergheim and the wealthy farmer had been brokering a marriage arrangement between their children. Ludwig's words seemed to confirm that notion.

"Very well," Baron Bergheim said, nodding to Peter. He spun on his heels, waltzed past Heinrich, and stepped gingerly into his carriage, which wheeled around and took off down the road.

"You shouldn't have heard any of that," Peter said to Heinrich once the baron had left.

Heinrich waved at the farmer. "Nonsense," he said, making a motion of zipping his mouth shut. "Your secret's safe with me."

Peter scoffed.

Heinrich smiled.

"What is it you want, investigator? My daughter is in a bad way, and I must tend to her."

"I won't keep you long," Heinrich said. He clasped his hands behind his back. "I trust the marriage between Sybil and Johannes von Bergheim is going swimmingly?"

Peter began to say something, but then he closed his mouth and looked away.

Heinrich gave him a pointed look, as if to accuse him of something that hadn't even happened yet.

Peter faced Heinrich. "Rather than pester my family," he said, "perhaps you could look into the crazed noblewoman who threatened my daughter, and arrest her."

Heinrich reached into his tunic, pulled out a quill and parchment, and scribbled something down. "Crazed . . . noblewoman," he said as he wrote. "And her name was—"

"Margreth Baumgartner."

"Ah, the daughter of the garrison commander, Arnold Baumgartner? I'll look into it." Heinrich gave his best fake smile.

Peter rolled his eyes and crossed his arms over his burly chest. He tilted his head and narrowed his eyes on the investigator, like he'd just thought of something. "You know, I saw someone creeping around my barns last night. You wouldn't happen to know anything about that, would you, Herr Franz?"

Heinrich scrunched his brow. "Not a clue. But I could look into that as well, if you'd like." Then his eyes turned cold and his demeanor changed. "However, that brings us to other, more serious matters, Herr Griswold."

"What might that be?"

"I've noticed in my . . ." Heinrich waved his hand in the air, trying to find the right word. "In my . . . *inquisition*, some odd anomalies about your estate." Heinrich cleared his throat. "I'm wondering if you could explain some things to me. Firstly, would you agree that you are one of the richest farmers in Bedburg?"

Peter bobbed his head from side to side. "I've worked hard to provide for my family, yes."

Heinrich twiddled his wispy mustache with two fingers. "Then why does it seem that you live so frugally, Herr Griswold? Why, it's as if you had no money at all."

"I like to save my wealth, for when things get dire."

Heinrich began to pace in front of Peter. Anyone who knew the investigator knew that that was a bad sign. He was thinking, or at least pretending like he was. "Understandable," he said, pointing a finger skyward. "But you're supposed to have some of the most bountiful fields in the region, with the plumpest pigs."

"Is that a question, Herr Franz? What are you asking?"

Heinrich stopped pacing and stared straight at Peter with his cold, gray eyes. "Where does it all go? Even from here, it seems that you have barely enough to live on."

Peter flinched. It was a subtle change in his expression, but something the investigator was trained to notice. Heinrich had seen that change of face hundreds of times, and it always came when someone was cornered. It meant Peter was about to make an excuse, or he was about to tell a lie.

"If you're going to arrest me for something, investigator, then do it. Otherwise, we're done here."

"No, we're not," Heinrich said flatly. "If I wanted to arrest you, I wouldn't have come alone. I just want to know what you're doing feeding and funding the Protestant rebellion. That could be considered treason, you know." The way he said it, so matter-of-fact, sounded like Heinrich was chastising a child.

Peter nearly choked. "I don't know what you're talking about, Herr Franz. *What* rebellion?"

"You can play dumb with me, Peter, but you aren't very good at it. You're a smarter man than you look, so don't take me for a fool. If you won't answer me that, then answer me something else—"

"I have a daughter to take care of," Peter said, and then he turned and began to walk away.

"What is your relationship with Katharina Trompen?" Heinrich called out.

Peter stopped in his tracks, two steps from his doorway, and his shoulders stiffened.

"Yes, Peter, I know of your secret rendezvous with that woman in the woods. What is she to you? She says you're her caretaker, but I don't believe that. Is she a widow? A lover?"

Peter turned and faced Heinrich. His jaw was set and his teeth were clenched. "Why are you talking to her?"

"I'm doing what any good investigator would do, Peter. I'm investigating. So, either talk to me, or find your lover in a difficult situation. The choice is yours."

Peter thrust a finger in Heinrich's direction. "She's not my lover!" he shouted.

"I know she isn't," Heinrich said calmly. "She's your sister. The same sister who's been missing for years."

Peter's jaw loosened and the color drained from his face. His shoulders slumped and he took on a look of defeat, as if all the fight in him had washed away in an instant.

"She . . . told you that?"

Heinrich crossed his arms over his chest. "No, Peter . . . you just did."

"What are you going to do to her?"

Heinrich shrugged and turned away from the farmer. "I don't know," he said, "but I would tread lightly, Herr Griswold." He walked and hoisted himself back on his horse. Before riding away, he called out and said, "Oh, and I'll be sure to look into that issue you're having with Margreth Baumgartner. Have a nice day, Herr Griswold!"

CHAPTER TWENTY-SIX

GEORG

Georg Sieghart sat in his usual spot at the bar, alone. His listless eyes perused the patrons and women of the tavern while he put back mug after mug of ale. Either Lars or the new barkeep, named Cristoff, had hired two more ladies since the night before. Their names were starting to blur in Georg's mind. None of the new women had the same fiery attitude that Josephine had possessed, but they all reminded Georg of the lost girl.

Josephine had opened doors in Georg's mind that he'd tried to keep closed. She reminded him of his deceased wife, Agnes Donnelly. Both of the women had been redheaded beauties of Irish descent, with radiant personalities. The memories of both women were tragic ones for Georg, and he couldn't find solace anywhere except at the bottom of a bottle.

He hadn't been hunting in days. He hadn't done anything of use in days. His funds were running out. His beard grew in unkempt patches.

He took a swig from his mug and realized it was empty. He called Cristoff over and ordered a new one. The dark-haired barman stared at him for a moment, then he shrugged and slid a mug in Georg's direction.

Maybe it's time I leave this place, Georg thought, pitying himself. Then he shook his head and decided, *No, I must find Agnes' killer. I mean Josephine's . . . I must find Josephine's killer, with or without that damn investigator's help*. He slammed his fist on the table and nearly fell from his stool. Keeping his balance with an outstretched hand, his dreary eyes made it to the back of the bar, to the staircase that led up to the bedrooms.

Konrad von Brühl stumbled his way down the stairs, with a stupid grin plastered on his face. Behind him, a dark-haired girl followed and readjusted her corset.

Konrad came up beside Georg and slapped him on the back. He took a seat next to the hunter and ordered a drink.

"How was she?" Georg asked.

"Aellin? Just as good as she was last night, and just as good as she will be tomorrow," Konrad said, still grinning.

Georg grunted.

Konrad looked his friend up and down. "You look in a bad way, Georg . . . again. You can barely keep your eyes open. Why don't you take a break?"

"No . . . non . . . nonsense," Georg said, struggling to tackle one word at a time. "I'm tip-top."

Konrad pulled at his beard and said, "You know Josephine isn't coming back, Georg. What are you waiting for here?"

Georg growled and suddenly shoved Konrad. It was a misguided, weak shove, and Konrad easily took a step back and allowed Georg to go plummeting off his chair. The hunter fell to the ground with a thud, and people in the tavern laughed in his direction.

"Screw you all!" Georg said as he wobbled to his feet. He still held his mug, and he waved it around like it was a sword, showering ale around the tavern.

The door to the tavern swung open, and Investigator Franz entered. He saw Georg flailing about wildly, and he muttered something to himself. Then he walked to Georg, grabbed him by the arm, and helped him to his stool. "Jesus, Georg," he said, shaking his head.

Georg spun around to face his imaginary attacker. Then his face lit up when he realized who it was. "Ah! Heinrich! My friend without any friends."

"Can you take care of him?" Konrad asked. "I'm tired of keeping watch on the poor sap."

"And I'm tired of serving him," Cristoff shouted from the other end of the bar. "He's been here all day, and I'm sick of getting showered by booze."

Investigator Franz nodded and led Georg by the arm, out of the tavern. The big hunter stumbled into a table as he was helped to the exit. The people at the table gave him nasty looks.

"Come on, you big fool," Investigator Franz said, "we have better things to be doing. I'll take you to the inn first."

"No, no, no," Georg muttered. Once they were outside, he closed his eyes. "I'm not as drunk . . . I'm as . . . I'm not as seemly drunk as I am."

Despite his protests, the investigator took Georg to the nearby inn. He struggled to keep the hunter upright as he made his way to a sofa. He turned to the innkeeper, Claus, and said, "Get this man some coffee. He needs to sober up in a hurry."

"Right away, my lord," the old man said, and he scurried off into another room.

Heinrich rested Georg on the sofa, and the hunter was snoring before his head even touched the headrest. Claus came back into the room with a pot of coffee, and handed it to Heinrich. The investigator woke Georg and forced the hot stuff down his throat.

"I guess I'll have to do this one alone," Heinrich muttered to himself, sighing. He ran a hand through his hair.

"N-no, you won't."

Heinrich turned and, to his surprise, Georg was sitting upright with the pot of coffee in his hand.

"This stuff has a . . . strong effect on me," Georg explained.

Heinrich pulled at his mustache. "Well, that's some welcome news, my good hunter."

*　　*　　*

An hour later, Georg seemed like he was ready to join the world of the living again. He groaned and grunted as he stood from the sofa, and he thanked Claus for the coffee. Then he joined Heinrich outside in the cold. The moon was at its peak, and the wind bit at his face, sobering him up even more. He kept his arms beneath his massive wool coat.

"So, what is this mission you need me for?" he asked.

"We need to go back to Katharina Trompen's cabin, and I'm afraid I'd get lost in the woods without you."

Georg snorted and said, "Bah, why don't you leave that woman alone? Is it so necessary to bother everyone you meet?"

Heinrich shrugged. "If I'm doing my job correctly, then yes. And besides, she's more important than we originally thought."

"I'm guessing you found a *clue* today?"

"Precisely, my good hunter. Multiple clues, in fact. That woman is not a poor, widowed tax-evader. She's Peter Griswold's sister." The investigator said it as if it were the most diabolical thing, being Peter Griswold's sister.

Georg grunted and said, "So? We've all had sisters at one point." Then he looked to the moon and thought that over. "Well . . . I haven't had a sister. But what's your point?"

Heinrich looked at Georg as though he were a toddler. "Peter Griswold is using his wealth and means to aid the Protestants. Now . . . why would he meet with his sister, in the dead of night?"

The investigator paused for a moment to let Georg think, but the hunter was still a bit drunk.

"To give her food?"

Heinrich sighed and shook his head. "No! Peter can't be seen interacting with the Lutherans, because it would ruin his good name. But if he has someone to pass the intelligence to . . . someone who no one knows exists . . ." he trailed off.

After a brief pause, Georg's eyes went wide. "Like his sister!"

Heinrich smiled and nodded.

"So she's his, uh . . ." Georg snapped his fingers, looking for the word.

"Liaison."

Georg clapped his hands and pointed at Heinrich with a smile.

The investigator slapped the hunter on the shoulder. "It's time we see what this family is really up to."

Less than two hours later, with the moon waning, Georg and Investigator Franz were watching Katharina's cabin from a distance. From the tree they hid behind, they had a clear vision into the single window of the house.

A soft, orange glow illuminated the inside of the cabin. Every few minutes, Georg and Heinrich could make out the silhouettes of people passing by the window.

"If only we could get closer," Heinrich whispered.

"We'd be spotted, investigator. Sometimes you have to just be patient."

Heinrich frowned at the hunter, but they waited.

And waited.

An hour later, the door opened.

Georg was sleeping with his head and back against the trunk of the tree. Heinrich kicked him in the side. Startled, the big man awoke, and wiped drool from his beard.

Heinrich held a single finger up to his mouth, gesturing for the hunter to stay quiet.

The first man to step out of the cabin had the stout body type of Peter Griswold. He turned his back to Georg and Heinrich as he stepped outside, and two other people joined him.

The first was clearly Katharina Trompen. Peter embraced her and kissed her on the cheek.

The other figure was tall and lanky, but he was standing in the doorway and was silhouetted by the orange glow from inside the cabin.

Then he stepped out into the night and gave Peter a handshake, and his blond hair was unmistakable.

"Is that . . ." Georg started, but trailed off.

"Lars," Heinrich said, nodding.

Georg grunted. "I was just starting to like him, too."

Instead of leaving the cabin, the barkeep stayed, and only Peter left the area. The farmer looked over his shoulder and then headed back into the woods, toward Bedburg.

Lars towered over Katharina, and then he embraced the woman and kissed her on the lips, while grabbing her backside with his hands.

Both Georg and Heinrich raised their eyebrows and looked at each other.

"What should we do?" Georg asked. "Follow Peter?"

Heinrich shook his head. "Let's see what plays out here."

Georg chuckled. "I'm pretty sure we know what's going to play out here, Heinrich. It doesn't take an investigator to know that."

"No, dammit, I mean *after.*"

So they continued waiting, and it didn't take long for their patience to pay off.

The moon was descending over the canopies of the woods when the door opened, and Katharina Trompen exited the cabin and stepped out into the wilderness. She shut the door.

Lars was nowhere to be seen—presumably still in the cabin.

"Shall we go speak with Lars?" Georg whispered.

Heinrich shook his head. They both watched as Katharina took an unexpected route out of the clearing. Rather than heading west, toward civilization and Bedburg, she headed north, toward the other end of the woods.

"Where's she headed?" Georg asked, as if Heinrich knew all the answers.

"Let's find out."

They followed her from a fair distance, through the thick undergrowth and wild birch trees. A couple times they feared they'd lost her in the darkness, but Georg, even in his current state, managed to find signs of her travel—broken twigs and stomped earth—and put them on the right track.

Katharina made her way north and east, out of the woods and to the western bank of the Peringsmaar Lake. She kept heading north, staying just outside of the woods.

Georg and Heinrich followed her for another hour as she meandered her way around the lake. As the Peringsmaar's western coast curved northeast, Katharina kept with the shore.

Then she came to a steep hill, on the northern end of the lake.

Georg and Heinrich struggled to keep pace with the woman, but they eventually reached the top of the hill as Katharina was heading down the other side.

Georg held his arm out in front of Heinrich as they reached the apex of the hill, and they both stopped. The hunter surveyed the landscape—green and void of trees, except for a small copse of birches in the distance.

"Good vantage point," Georg whispered, gesturing to the trees.

They both crawled to the trees, and then Georg brushed aside some branches and crouched. He peered through the branches, and his eyes went wide.

The southern end of the hill tapered off into a valley with a wide gorge. The trees in the valley had been cleared. In their place were tents—many, many tents. Campfires burned and people loitered around them. The breeze from the Peringsmaar Lake swept away the scent of the campfires, while the high walls of the valley kept the smoke from the woods. Altogether, the camp was hidden from prying eyes, unless you were looking from the top of a hill, like Georg and Heinrich were.

"Shit," Georg said. "That's . . ."

Heinrich took a deep breath. "That's an army."

CHAPTER TWENTY-SEVEN

DIETER

Dieter rolled around in his small bed, unable to sleep. His anxious mind had him tossing and turning all night. Finally, during the darkest hours of night, he sat up and breathed heavily. Beads of sweat dotted his upper lip. He stood from his bed and took two short steps to where his black cassock hung from his door. He stared at the robe, and then moved past it, to a brown, hooded tunic.

Dieter wrapped himself in the brown tunic and sat down at his small table. He lit a candle and penned a letter. After writing the letter, he folded the paper and poured hot wax to seal it. He tapped his chin, and then took Sybil's amulet from his neck and pressed the two crosses into the wax, embossing the letter.

He stuffed the letter into his tunic, put his amulet back on his neck, and crept out of his chambers. He walked down the dark hallway, into the nave, and left the church. When he was outside, in the cold, empty night, he pulled the hood of his tunic over his head.

I'll only find peace if I can find answers, he decided. He'd spent the better part of the night reading over the *Ninety-Five Theses* in his small chamber, in secret. For years, he'd been taught to hate the document, but now he threw his ignorance to the wind.

Through indoctrination and constant pressure, Dieter had been trained to believe that Martin Luther's diatribe was sacrilegious, heretical, and an act against God. But after reading

Luther's carefully penned manuscript, Dieter started to question his own ignorance.

This was not an unholy, hellbent man. Martin Luther was an opponent to oppression. He was a scholar with, quite frankly, some valid points—ninety-five of them, in fact.

The document caused Dieter's crisis of faith to become exponentially more dire.

The young priest could think of only one man who was similar to Martin Luther—one man who had the strength of will to publicly stand up to those he believed were oppressing and manipulating the people.

Dieter made his way north, up a long hill and across the Erft River, into the part of town he visited the least: the district of the gentry and aristocrats. Here, the nobility held their extravagant balls and parties and lived as though they were in an alternate reality, completely unaware—or uncaring—of the struggles of the rest of Bedburg.

Castle Bedburg was in the northern district of town, as were the courts, the garrison, and the jailhouse.

Dieter sought the latter.

The priest looked over his shoulder time and time again, paranoid of anyone following him. It was so late at night that he didn't see a single soul on the road. It was eerily quiet.

He made his way to the jailhouse, which was nestled away from civilization, and away from prying eyes.

Two guards stood at the gates of the monolithic, gray structure. They lowered their spears at the hooded man who approached.

"Gentlemen," Dieter said with a bow.

"The jail isn't for visiting," one of the guards said. "What's your business here so late at night?"

Dieter produced the letter from his tunic and handed it to the guard. "I come on behalf of Bishop Solomon, the religious counsel to Lord Werner."

The guard snatched the letter and eyed Dieter. He unsealed it, read it, and looked at Dieter suspiciously. "Again, why do you come so late?"

"It's a matter of discretion, sir."

"This letter says you want to speak to the Protestant captive. Why?"

"Again, my lord," Dieter said with a smile and a slight bow, "a matter of discretion. It's a religious matter."

The guard glanced at his comrade, who shrugged. After a long moment of silent inspection, with the jailer watching Dieter, he finally sighed, opened the gate, and handed Dieter his forged letter. "Talk to Ulrich at the bottom of the stairs."

"Many thanks, my lords," Dieter said, nodding.

When he entered the jail, he shivered. It was colder inside the dank place than it was outside in the winter chill. Even the torches on the wall did nothing to warm his bones.

Dieter walked gingerly down the narrow corridor, to a set of concrete stairs. At the bottom of the staircase was a wide room, with two jail cells on either side. A man with a badly scarred face sat at the end of the room, with another door behind him. He made no move to stand as Dieter walked toward him.

"My name is Father Dieter Nicolaus, and I'm here on business for Bishop Solomon, to see your prisoner, Hanns Richter." Dieter handed the scarred man the letter.

"The Protestant?" Ulrich asked, frowning.

"Indeed."

"Through this door, last cell on the right," the man said, without looking at the letter. "Have your way with the bastard, but be quick. You have ten minutes."

Dieter nodded to Ulrich, opened the door, and walked by him. The next room was exactly as the first, with two jail cells on either side. Dieter walked to the second cell on the right and peered in. A man with a long beard sat in the middle of the cell, legs crossed, eyes closed. Rather than being huddled in a corner, or wallowing in misery, the man seemed at peace, as if meditating.

"Pastor Hanns Richter," Dieter whispered. The man didn't open his eyes, so Dieter repeated himself, louder.

The pastor's eyes finally shot open. He squinted at Dieter, and Dieter felt that the pastor looked right through him.

"I'm Father Nicolaus, from the church."

"I know who you are. You're one of the men responsible for putting me in here." The man had a raspy, worn out voice. He also had bruises around his eyes, a cut on his forehead, and welts on his arms.

Dieter shook his head. "N-no, I had no idea. I was not respons—"

"I forgive you," Pastor Richter interjected. Despite the strong likelihood that he'd never see another sunrise, the pastor seemed strangely calm. "I've made my peace with God."

"I'm glad."

"You shouldn't be. I don't forgive you for my own sake, but for God's. You are simply a man doing Man's will—not His. You Catholics must learn that penance is the only path toward forgiveness in His eyes, for the vitriol and hate you spew against my people."

Dieter scratched his head. "You preached with the same vehemence against *my* people."

Hanns shook his head and uncrossed his legs. He stood, slowly, and walked to the bars of the cell. "I spoke against the idolatries of Catholics. I spoke against your leader, who believes he speaks for God." The pastor coughed. "Any man who thinks he has that much power, who thinks they are a direct voice to God, is surely foolish. You cannot *buy* yourself out of eternal damnation, priest. But you will never understand that." The pastor turned his back to Dieter.

"I think I do understand," Dieter said.

The pastor stopped. "Excuse me?"

Dieter leaned forward and spoke in a low voice. "I think I'm beginning to understand your cause. I've read Martin Luther's work."

"Have you?" Pastor Richter asked, facing Dieter with a furrowed brow. "Why? Don't you believe the Werewolf of

Bedburg is the work of Protestant devilry?"

Dieter shook his head. "I don't know what to believe anymore, and that's why I'm here. I don't wish to speak about the werewolf, Herr Richter. I believe he's as much a fabrication of my faith as he is yours. I wish to speak about the tenets of Martin Luther."

Pastor Richter pulled at his long beard. "Do you now?" he said, and then chuckled. "An open-minded Catholic. Now I've seen everything. What is it you wish to discuss?"

Dieter gripped the cold bars. "Your leader was a man, just like the pope . . . but he was firmly against indulgences and pardons. You spoke for him, in public, with danger all around you. Why?"

"Simple," Hanns said. "We've been oppressed for too long, by your pope. Yes, Martin Luther was a man, but he didn't have the impudence to believe that he was the sole messenger of God. People should hear the truth." The pastor began pacing in his cell. "Pope Sixtus appoints his nephews as cardinals, without them showing a hint of merit. He sells positions of power to his friends. His acts of nepotism and simony cannot stand. Your church is powerful, and yet your pope believes he collects taxes in God's name. His actions are egregious and greedy." The pastor faced Dieter and cocked his head. "This can't be new to you, can it?"

Dieter shook his head. "I've been trained to ignore it all, but I can't do that any longer. What can I do to help you?"

Pastor Richter paused, and then broke into a deep laugh. "Help?" he said, coughing. "You have no power here, priest. I will die in this cell, or at the end of a rope. But my people will not forget my cause. They will come for retribution—not out of vengeance, but out of love. Your bishop, Solomon, is ridiculed behind his back. The people do not respect him here."

"I'm aware," Dieter said. "I hardly respect him any more, either."

"What are you saying?"

Dieter sighed. He wasn't sure what he was saying, and his words were coming out faster and looser than he'd planned. He

CORY BARCLAY

decided to speak from his heart, before his mind could get the better of him. "I wish for a *sign*. I wish for something or someone to show me which path to follow."

"Only God can decide that, Father Nicolaus. You will either find a sign through tragedy, or through epiphany. I cannot help you in that." The pastor frowned and began pacing again. "Besides, like I said, I'm stuck in here."

"When do you go to trial?"

Hanns smiled. "You're naïve, priest. Do you really think your bishop and lord will take me to trial? They'll torture me for any information I might have, and then kill me out of sight from the public. They'll try to tarnish my reputation and make me forgotten. But they will fail."

"Torture you for information? What kind of information do you speak of?"

"Nice try, Father Nicolaus," the pastor said, still smiling. "I'm not convinced if you're talking to me out of guilt, or if you've been sent by the bishop to harass me. I think our time here is done."

As if on cue, the door of the room opened, and Ulrich showed his scarred face. "Your time's up, priest. You need to be on your way."

Dieter raised a finger to the man. "Just one more moment—"

"No," Hanns Richter said. "The punisher is right. It's time for you to go home, Father Nicolaus. You don't belong here."

Dieter had a renewed energy at Mass the next morning. He was dismayed that Sybil wasn't in the congregation, but he spoke with an enthusiasm that he hadn't felt in some time.

Still, he was worried that Bishop Solomon would find out about the forged letter. He felt that the sins and lies he'd been committing were leading him toward some kind of self-discovery.

He just didn't know if what he'd discover was a bad thing, or a good thing.

As the congregation emptied out of the church, Dieter decided he'd go visit Sybil, to see how she was doing.

Hopefully she still wants to see me.

Before he could get the chance to leave the church, however, Bishop Solomon approached him. "Father Nicolaus," the old man said, hobbling his way from the back hallway.

Dieter felt a pang of panic rush through his body. "Yes, Your Grace?"

"We are to meet with Lord Werner and Vicar Balthasar at Bedburg Castle."

"We?" Dieter said, a bit confused.

"Yes, you will come with me, to support my endeavor. But I want you to stay quiet unless spoken to. Understand?" The bishop seemed frazzled, and his thin white hair was ragged and unkempt. As he walked out of the church, Dieter followed him. A carriage sat in front of the church, waiting for the bishop and priest.

Once they were in the carriage and on their way to the castle, Dieter asked, "What, if I may ask, is the reason for our meeting with the lord and the vicar, Your Grace?"

"We're going to find out what to do with that damnable pastor, my son."

Bishop Solomon and Vicar Balthasar stood side by side, facing the diminutive Lord Werner. Dieter stood behind the bishop, with his hands folded in front of him, and one of Balthasar's Jesuit missionaries stood behind the vicar.

In the lord's room, Werner's young son ran around ceaselessly, causing a commotion. Vicar Balthasar smiled and waved to the boy. The child was simple, and hardly ever made public appearances. He was clearly an embarrassment to Lord Werner. Some say the boy was God-touched and mad. But since arriving in Bedburg, Vicar Balthasar had taken to the boy, and was teaching him the word of Christ.

In fact, since arriving, the Jesuit had made short work of turning the tide of conversions in the Catholic's favor. He was friendly and authoritative, and the people liked him.

Vicar Balthasar took a "top-down" method of conversion, first dealing with the nobility. He believed that, in order to get the townsfolk involved, one had to begin with the leadership.

Bishop Solomon hated the man, of course. He hated Balthasar's charisma, and he feared that Balthasar was trying to uncover everything he'd worked so hard to veil over the years. Solomon believed Balthasar was trying to usurp power, and that he had Archbishop Ernst's approval to do it.

In Dieter's eyes, Vicar Balthasar was doing just that. He had the ear of Lord Werner—more than the bishop ever seemed to have had.

"Since this is a matter of tolerance and religion," Lord Werner began, "I would like both of your opinions on Pastor Hanns Richter. What should be done with him?"

Solomon cleared his throat. It was customary to allow the eldest counsel the first opportunity to speak, and Vicar Balthasar made no move to steal that tradition from the bishop.

"If I may, my lord," Solomon began, "I believe the man is a nuisance to Bedburg, a travesty to the bishopric, and a wart on your good name. He is a hate-fueled, blasphemous bigot, and he must be silenced. We cannot allow such a person free reign in Bedburg, as he aims to denounce the word of Christ and God." The bishop nodded, seemingly proud of himself for delivering such a succinct oration.

Dieter raised his eyebrows. *Well, he made his position clear in a hurry.*

Vicar Balthasar stayed quiet and calm.

Lord Werner said, "What are you implying, Solomon?"

The bishop stretched his arms out wide, like he was trying to steal all the air from the room. "In order to defeat and silence the Protestant rebels, I believe he should be made an example of. We should publicly denounce the pastor's claims, and he should be summarily executed for all to see. That is the best way to quell the rebellion, my lord."

A long silence followed, and Lord Werner tapped his chin.

"What if it doesn't?"

All heads turned to see who'd spoken out of turn.

"Excuse me?" Lord Werner asked, cocking his head.

"Yes, excuse me?" Bishop Solomon said, pursing his lips and scowling.

Dieter stepped forward. "What if his death doesn't quell the rebellion, my lord? Is scaring the public really in our best interest? What if his death does the opposite and stokes the flames, or makes Herr Richter some kind of martyr? We saw the size of the crowds the man was preaching to. Is publicly killing him the best way to silence the Protestants, or will it only serve to bolster their arguments and claims?"

Bishop Solomon gasped, and he had a befuddled look on his face.

Vicar Balthasar simply smirked.

Lord Werner's brows went high on his forehead.

It was Vicar Balthasar who spoke next. "I'm inclined to agree with the young priest."

"Why is that?" Lord Werner asked, facing the vicar.

"Because God is merciful, not vengeful. What better way to show God's mercy than to act with tolerance? Protestant or not, Pastor Hanns Richter is a man of God, and many of the townsfolk listen to him. It might do us a disservice if we were to kill their only outlet to God, no matter how wrong his views might be, my lord. I believe I can sway his people to our *just* path—without the need for death."

Bishop Solomon shook his hands furiously. "And *I'm* inclined to think that you might be a Protestant yourself, vicar, after hearing you speak in such a baffling manner!" The bishop's face was bright red as he turned from Balthasar to Lord Werner. "My lord, you can't really believe—"

Lord Werner stuck his palm out toward the bishop, and the old man was left stammering, with his mouth hanging open. Then Werner turned to the vicar and asked, "What would you recommend?"

"I believe," Balthasar said, clearing his throat, "if we are to act in good faith and tolerance—that we do not execute Hanns Richter. Showing him kindness and mercy will in turn reflect nicely with the peasantry. The Catholics will seem like the bigger people—turning the other cheek, if you will. If we do that, then we simply allow him to fade away. He will never have the same power in Bedburg that he once had, I assure you, my lord."

Bishop Solomon shook his head over and over. "A-are you *actually* implying that we just . . . that we just . . . let him *go*? Have you gone mad, vicar? What were you even sent here for? Has Cologne rotted your brain?" The bishop's speeches were much less succinct when they weren't prepared or practiced.

"Bishop, please," Lord Werner said.

Vicar Balthasar faced the angry bishop, calmly, and nodded. "I'm not implying it, Your Grace. I'm *saying* it. I believe we should move for the immediate release and banishment of Pastor Hanns Richter."

"But you were the man who *arrested* him, dammit!" Solomon screeched. He faced Lord Werner and said, "My lord, you can't actually believe this to be a good idea?"

The little lord was tapping his chin, apparently deep in thought. Dieter could see the cogs turning in his mind.

"You would come across as a peaceful lord, and would regain the favor of the peasantry," Balthasar said, putting more of his ideas in Lord Werner's head.

This man is good, Dieter thought. *He took my words, which sparked a controversy, and is using them as a breaking point between himself and the bishop.* Dieter chuckled beneath his breath. *Pastor Richter said I have no power here. Let this prove him wrong.*

"You would come across as weak!" Solomon rebutted.

215

"All right, all right," Lord Werner said, putting his palms forward again to silence the raging bishop. "I am inclined to agree with Vicar Balthasar and Father Nicolaus."

And just like that, the power that Bishop Solomon had enjoyed for so many years in Bedburg practically vanished, in an instant, right before his eyes. Dieter knew that Solomon would no longer be the religious voice that Lord Werner turned to. *Whenever Lord Werner wishes for advice, he'll think of this moment in time, as precedence. There's a new voice in town, and it comes from the mouth of a stout, limping Jesuit—it comes from an outsider.*

"My lord," Solomon begged, "please reconsider. Hanns Richter is a nuisance and a tyrant. He will spell the downfall of the Catholic faith in Bedburg! And Vicar Balthasar is colluding with him!"

Lord Werner chuckled. "Bishop, you're being quite melodramatic, don't you think? My mind is made up. We'll keep the pastor in jail to try and gain information from him. A week from now, he'll be released, pardoned, and removed from Bedburg. Hopefully his influence goes away with him." The lord turned to the vicar. "I hope you're right about this, Herr Schreib, or God help us."

"His influence *would die* with him, my lord, if you only said the words!" Solomon protested. But his words fell on deaf ears.

With a flick of his wrist, Lord Werner dismissed everyone from the room.

Outside the lord's room, Bishop Solomon fumed. Vicar Bathasar looked smug, and he gave Dieter a nod, before limping away with his staff clacking on the tiled floor.

The bishop's cheeks looked like two red-hot tomatoes. He faced Dieter, and with all the venom and spite he could muster, he hissed, "That's the last time I allow you to undermine me, boy. *Et consummata sunt.*"

You are finished.

CHAPTER TWENTY-EIGHT

SYBIL

Sybil heard voices as she drifted in and out of consciousness.

". . . And you're sure?" said one voice. It sounded like her father's.

"Yes. She is no longer chaste." A long pause, and then Sybil slipped back into darkness.

When she awoke, it was the afternoon. A splitting headache rippled through her head, down her back. She felt sore all over her body, especially around her thighs. She blinked a few times and then wiped the muck from her eyes. Sitting up, she held her head in her hands and groaned. She had no idea how long she'd been asleep, and was surprised to find herself in her own bed.

"Father?" she called out.

Peter barged into the room within seconds. "Beele, my dear, you're awake!"

"Where's Hugo," Sybil asked. She wasn't sure why that was the first question that came to mind.

"He's asleep in my room. I wanted to let you rest." Peter walked over to his daughter and put a hand on her forehead. "You're still warm, but it seems your fever broke."

"Fever? How long have I been asleep?" Sybil could hear her head throbbing in her ears, and she couldn't think clearly.

"Baron Bergheim returned you late last morning. You slept all day and night. He said that you'd been drinking with his son."

Peter's voice sounded on edge. "What's the last thing you remember, Sybil?"

She tried to think. After a long silence, she said, "I remember being at Baron Bergheim's mansion with his son . . ." she trailed off. "The last thing I recall is Johannes saying, 'That took longer than expected.'" She blinked and started massaging her temples.

Peter closed his eyes and sighed. "Do you remember what you did with Lord Johannes?"

Sybil shook her head. "I remember drinking a bit of wine, but that's it."

A hard knock came from the front door of the house. Peter stood from Sybil's bed, cursed under his breath, and called out, "Who is it?"

"It's Father Nicolaus, sir. Please, let me in. I must see Sybil."

"I'm growing tired of all these visitors, priest," Peter said through the closed door. "You'll have to come back—Sybil is unwell."

"N-no, father, please," Sybil said, "let him in. I want to speak with him." She hadn't seen Dieter in nearly a week, since their passionate stay at the Achterberg's estate.

Peter groaned, but after a moment of staring at his bedridden daughter, he relented. "Fine. But when you're feeling better, you must get ready."

"Ready?"

Peter swiped his forehead with the back of his forearm. "Yes, ready to leave with Lords Ludwig and Johannes. Do you not remember the arrangement?"

Sybil narrowed her eyes at her father. "Who were you talking to while I was sleeping? I heard voices."

Peter's eyes looked around the room, and he scratched the back of his neck. "That was a . . . a physician, sent by Lord Ludwig."

"And what did he tell you, father?" Sybil said, growing increasingly suspicious. Her father seemed anxious and skittish. Thoughts of the night with Johannes started to flood through her mind as her head became less hazy. She scowled at the thought of Lord Johannes' face.

"Well . . . Lord Bergheim told me that . . . that your relationship with Johannes had been . . . consummated, Beele. The physician confirmed it."

An image flashed through Sybil's mind. She remembered the wineglass falling from her hand, and the sound it made as it hit the ground. Her eyes were suddenly wet, and her lips trembled.

Peter opened his mouth, and then closed it. He hesitated, and then he left the room and went to open the front door.

Anything but this, Sybil thought, touching her legs and thighs.

Dieter popped his head into the room. He had a warm smile on his face. He rushed over to Sybil and embraced her. As he looked at her face at arm's-length, his smile disappeared.

"Beele, are you all right? What's wrong? What happened?"

"Beele?" Peter said, coming to stand next to Dieter. "Only her friends and family call her that."

Dieter glanced at Peter, and then turned back to Sybil. "I know that."

"Father," Beele said, sniffling, "please give us privacy."

Peter sighed, crossed his arms over his chest, and then slowly nodded and ambled out of the room. He closed the door behind him.

"I missed you so much," Dieter whispered to Sybil. "When you didn't show up for today's Mass, I grew worried."

"I've been sick," Sybil said, and then tried her best to smile. "But I've missed you, too."

There was a lull in the conversation as the two just stared at each other. Sybil seemed on the verge of tears, and she finally said, "Oh, Dieter, I'm so sorry. I am to move with Lord Johannes, and to become his bride."

Dieter shook his head furiously. "That can't be. I won't let that happen."

"There's nothing you can do," Sybil said. "It's already been decided."

Dieter closed his eyes, and then he ran a hand through Sybil's damp hair. When he opened his eyes, he was on the verge of tears, just like Sybil.

Sybil leaned forward and touched her forehead to Dieter's. "There's something else," she whispered. "But you must promise to keep it a secret from my father."

Dieter wiped his eyes with the back of his sleeve. "Of course, you can tell me anything."

Sybil opened her mouth to speak, but said nothing. She stammered, blinked a few times, and then decided to just blurt it out. "My cycle is very late."

The priest looked confused as he craned his neck. Then he took on a look of revelation, and his eyes opened wide. "You mean . . ."

Sybil nodded, half-smiling. "I believe I'm with child."

"My God!" Dieter shouted, much too loud. He frowned, then smiled, and then seemed like he didn't know *what* to do with his mouth. He stood from the bed, and his eyes took on a distant look. As he stared through Sybil, his lips slowly turned into a straight line. "The sign . . ." he muttered.

"What? What sign?"

"Through tragedy or epiphany," Dieter said, still with a faraway look in his eyes. After a long moment, he shook his head. "I'm sorry, Beele. I must go do something. It will benefit both of us!" Dieter sounded ecstatic and nervous, like Sybil had never seen him before.

"I'll find a way to stop that damn noble brat," he said.

"W-wait, Dieter, there's something else."

But Dieter was already halfway to the door, bubbling excitedly. He was nearly skipping and hopping. "Hold that thought, Beele! I'll return shortly. Everything will be fine!"

Peter was standing on the other side of the door with his arms over his chest. He grunted as Dieter nearly bumped into him. The priest nodded to Peter and said, "Herr Griswold," and then rushed out of the house.

Once he was gone, Sybil broke down and started bawling. She brought her knees to her chest and put her head in her hands as the tears flowed. She felt weak, like she'd betrayed Dieter's trust.

Peter walked into the room and watched his daughter weep. "So, you couldn't tell him about your escapades with Johannes?"

Sybil shook her head, and lifted it from her knees. "It's not that, father. You don't understand."

"I think I understand quite perfectly," he said, frowning. "What I don't understand, is how you could know so soon that you're pregnant. And why would a priest be happy about that?"

"You were eavesdropping?" Sybil shouted, smudging her tears on her red face.

"We can both play that game, Beele." Peter cocked his head. "But why are you so sad? Shouldn't this be a joyous occasion?"

Sybil shook her head. "I said you don't understand."

Peter pointed a finger toward the roof. "Ah, your humors are unbalanced. Right. I saw this with your mother."

Sybil was shaking her head profusely. "Oh, stop it!" More tears dripped down her face. "Don't you get it? What Baron Bergheim and the physician told you? Are you that blind?"

Peter tilted his head as he walked to the side of her bed. "Make me understand, Beele. I can't stand to see you like this."

"I . . ." Sybil began, but couldn't continue.

Peter leaned closer to his daughter and nudged his chin forward, trying to coax the words from her. "You . . ."

"I was violated!" Sybil shouted at last, able to see clearly for the first time since she'd woken. She saw past the embarrassment and the guilt and the shame. "That bastard you would have me *marry*, father! He defiled me!"

PART III

The Werewolf of Bedburg

CHAPTER TWENTY-NINE

HEINRICH

1589 — Bedburg, Electorate of Cologne

A week passed in relative quiet, bringing strong snowfall and a new year. People stayed huddled in their homes, hoping that their autumn yields would outlast the cold winter.

Investigator Heinrich Franz stood in the opulent throne room of Lord Werner. Rays of sunlight gushed in through the stained-glass windows, brightening the room with colors of green, purple, and yellow.

"We must fortify the town, my lord," Heinrich urged.

The small lord was flustered and red-faced. "Don't you think I know that, Herr Franz?" He thrust a thin finger in Heinrich's direction. "As much as I've tried to keep things calm, your drunk, loud-mouthed friend has been scaring the townsfolk all week!"

Dammit, Georg, Heinrich thought. He massaged his temples and said, "Then why don't you do anything?"

Lord Werner grabbed a piece of paper from his desk and shoved it in Heinrich's face. "Do you know what this is?"

Heinrich stepped back to focus on the writing, but Lord Werner snatched the paper away before Heinrich could read it.

"This is a letter I received two days ago from Archbishop Ernst. He's sending an army from Cologne, to aid us. He doesn't want us to make any actions against the Protestants until the army arrives. There's nothing I can do." The lord threw up his arms and looked dejected.

Heinrich cleared his throat. "With all due respect, my lord, we have a whole garrison of Spanish and Catholic mercenaries. Shouldn't we at least create a barrier around the town? We wouldn't be making an action against the Protestants, and we must defend ourselves in case we're attacked. Spring is coming fast, and I fear the Protestants have been waiting for just that time to strike, once the snow has thawed."

Lord Werner tapped his chin. "Even though they're less than ten miles from Bedburg, I can't circumvent the archbishop's orders."

Heinrich looked to the floor and shook his head. *What a weak, pitiful man.*

"And besides," Werner continued, "I want something from you. The Protestants are none of your concern."

The Protestants are my only *concern at this point, you fool.* Heinrich played with his mustache. "What would you have me do?"

"I want you to do what you've been tasked to do, investigator. Find the Werewolf of Bedburg, and bring faith back to our people. Otherwise, I fear, we're lost."

Heinrich ran a hand through his dark hair, frustrated. "My lord, that won't mitigate the threat of the Calvinists and Lutherans. The entire town believes Georg Sieghart killed the beast. You had a ball to honor his name and celebrate him as a hero!"

Lord Werner spat on the green and yellow colored tiles, and said, "I know what I did, Heinrich. But do you really think that wolf was responsible for those grisly murders? Come now . . . first it was an overweight woman, and now an overweight wolf?"

"That's what people believe, my lord."

Lord Werner frantically spun his hands in circles. "I want you to find me a more suitable candidate, Herr Franz—one that looks and plays the part. You and I both know that no creature, acting alone, could have killed those two girls in such gruesome ways."

Heinrich agreed, but it didn't change his opinion. If the search for the werewolf stalled, it would be merely a hiccup. But if the

Protestants besieged the town, it could be the end of them all—and the end of Catholicism in Cologne. "My lord," Heinrich said, softly, "there won't *be* an investigation if the Calvinists take Bedburg."

But the little lord seemed unnerved and confused about his priorities. He wanted to look good to his people, but didn't realize that he might lose his lordship before he had that opportunity.

He needs a suspect that will frighten the Protestants, Heinrich thought. Then his eyes opened wide. *Or, maybe he just needs a suspect that will scare the Catholics into action . . .*

Heinrich twirled his mustache and hummed. *If that is the case, then I might be underestimating this devious little man. Fear brings out the savage in everyone, and maybe Werner is just trying to capitalize on that fear.*

After a moment of tense silence, Lord Werner said, "I'll focus on defending the city, Herr Franz, and you focus on your job." He walked back to his large table and slammed the letter from Archbishop Ernst on the desk. With a wave of his hand, and without looking up at Heinrich, he said, "We're done here."

Toward the end of 1588, the Protestant, former archbishop, Gebhard Truchsess, formally relinquished his title as the elector of Cologne. He retired to a city called Strassburg.

The Calvinist reformer had fought for five long years, razed many cities and won many battles, but the Cologne War between himself and Ernst grew tiresome. The stalemate between the two archbishops was crumbling on the Protestant side. The Catholics went on a bloody rampage to reacquire their lost strongholds and towns.

Most people thought the vicious war was nearing its end.

But, even though Gebhard retired from war, he handed over his army to some formidable allies: Count Adolf von Neuenahr, the able-minded former lord of Bedburg, who had been replaced by Lord Werner; and the brilliant soldier-general, Martin Schenck.

Adolf provided the funds, and Martin Schenck provided the

army. But now Martin Schenck was busy fighting in the Dutch province of Nijmegen, trying to salvage the last strongholds of Cologne's Protestants.

The Catholics rejoiced because the top military mind of Gebhard's reformers was away, and the Protestant army was splintered. But the rest of the armies were left in the capable hands of Count Adolf, who had the support of Gebhard's brother, Karl Truchsess, among others.

Even without Martin Schenck, Count Adolf had a powerful force, and Heinrich was certain it was Adolf who knocked on Bedburg's door in a last ditch effort to snatch his former lordship from Werner.

On the other hand, Archbishop Ernst had the military support of the Spanish army of Flanders, led by the indomitable general, Alexander Farnese. Ernst's older brother, Ferdinand, also aided in Ernst's Counter-Reformation.

Ernst hailed from the Bavarian House of Wittelsbach, which had been a German royal dynasty for over four hundred years. His claim to the Cologne Electorate was strong.

Heinrich guessed it would be Ernst's brother, Ferdinand, who came to the aid of Bedburg, since Alexander Farnese was currently in the Netherlands on a different campaign.

Either way, whoever came, Bedburg was slated to become the pivotal fight for the Calvinist Protestants' hopes of Reformation.

Arnold Baumgartner, the commander of the Bedburg garrison, went about preemptively fortifying the town as he prepared for Archbishop Ernst's army to arrive with help. He decided he didn't need Lord Werner's permission to protect Bedburg.

On the same day that preparations began, Pastor Hanns Richter was unceremoniously released from prison. It was a baffling event, and a crowd of townsfolk settled around the jailhouse to witness his release. Many believed the Protestant pastor would be assassinated right upon his release.

With his arms folded over his chest, Heinrich watched as the pastor was unchained and pushed out of the jailhouse. Hanns stumbled a bit, and people booed and jeered at him. Heinrich furrowed his brow when he noticed the pastor and Father Nicolaus share a look, and the pastor gave a slight nod to the young priest.

Interesting, Heinrich thought, scratching his head. He didn't know what to make of the nod between the Catholic and the Protestant.

Pastor Richter made it through the vicious crowd and was immediately exiled from Bedburg. He would give no more sermons from his overturned fruit crate—not while Catholics still held power.

The pastor was given a horse. He headed north, away from Bedburg. Heinrich watched the pastor leave, toward the woods and valleys, where the investigator was certain the Calvinist army was preparing for battle.

That night, the reinforcements from Cologne arrived. Thousands of soldiers poured into Bedburg, led by Archbishop Ernst's older brother, Ferdinand of Bavaria. The people of Bedburg appeared from their homes and watched in awe as the army paraded into town.

Ferdinand was a tall, bearded man. The general met with Lord Werner and Commander Baumgartner in the garrison, which overflowed with soldiers.

Though all eyes were turned toward the garrison, and the army that congregated within, Heinrich was busy at the tavern. He sat with Georg Sieghart and Konrad von Brühl, and they were getting their last drinks of the night.

"You're actually going to fight for Ferdinand?" Heinrich asked Georg.

The big hunter belched loudly and nodded.

Heinrich was bewildered. "The same army that released you from service for being too . . . savage? What has Bedburg ever done for you? You owe them nothing."

Georg squinted at the investigator. "Who told you I was released from service? I left on my own volition."

"Never mind that," Heinrich said with a wave of his hand. "Why are you fighting?"

"I'm no coward, investigator. Konrad is fighting as well. Isn't that right?" Georg turned to Konrad, who adjusted his eye-patch and nodded.

"Maybe we'll be in the same regiment," Georg said, smiling. He turned in his seat and faced Heinrich. "I'm fighting for the way of Catholic life. You should understand that."

"You aren't even Catholic!"

A few patrons in the tavern looked at Heinrich with suspicious eyes.

"Jesus, quiet yourself! Of course I'm Catholic. Are you saying you won't fight?" Georg scowled as he looked over his shoulder.

Heinrich frowned and stared down into his empty mug. "I have other things to attend to. My investigation is still ongoing."

"Bah," Georg said, but he might as well have called Heinrich a coward. "You won't have an investigation if the Protestants take the town. This battle is for our very survival. Your investigation can wait."

"According to Lord Werner, the investigation *can't* wait."

"Screw Lord Weasel," Georg grumbled. He drained the rest of his ale and stood from his seat. He stretched his arms and groaned. "In any case, gentlemen, if we never meet again . . . have a good life."

The hunter smiled and left the tavern. Konrad grunted to Heinrich and followed the hunter, and Heinrich was left alone to ponder his future, which he knew involved more ale.

Next morning, all eyes were still on the garrison, which made it all the more shocking when another person turned up dead in the city.

It was Margreth Baumgartner, the daughter of the garrison commander. She'd been murdered, and people wept openly in the streets.

She was found in the southern, poor district of town, ironically next to where all the beggars stayed. Her corpse was hanging and swinging from the gable of the tanner's workshop. She had a slashed throat, as well as numerous other gashes and bruises. She'd been drained of most her blood, which seeped down her curvy body and pooled at her feet. She hanged in front of the tanner's door, about four feet off the ground. She was naked, and her eyes were open and bulging, giving her a surprised, frightened look.

"Such a tragedy!" peasants said. They hugged each other and consoled one another.

"She was so beautiful and young! How could this happen?" cried others.

There was no doubt in Heinrich's mind that Margreth's murder would be a declaration of war for her father, Arnold. Maybe the death of his daughter would even blind his strategic mind. Perhaps he would be inconsolable—that was probably just what the Protestants wanted.

Georg stood next to the investigator. Both of them shook their heads and had their arms folded over their chests.

"Maybe Lord Weasel was right," Georg muttered. "Maybe the investigation can't wait."

Heinrich shrugged.

"I have a question, though." Georg pointed to the top of the peaked roof, where the rope around Margreth's neck was tied off. "How did the werewolf manage to get so high up?"

Heinrich frowned at the hunter. "I don't know if this is a time for comedy, Georg. Arnold Baumgartner will be seeing red because of this."

"I know, I know." They stayed quiet for a moment, and then Georg said, "Do you think it was the Protestants? Maybe there are spies in Bedburg."

Heinrich shrugged again.

Another long silence, then Georg continued, saying, "I heard she was quite a bitch. A pretty one, though. Everyone at the ball the other week seemed to be ogling her."

"Have some decency," Heinrich said. "This could be the beginning of a terrible thing. I mean, who cares about a murdered girl, or a fat witch, or a prostitute."

Georg's eyes bored into the investigator when Heinrich said the word "prostitute."

"My apologies," Heinrich said with a sigh. "But . . . a noblewoman? Imagine what kind of storm that's going to bring. A woman of such high class, found in the slums of Bedburg."

"I guess you were right when you said that no one was safe," Georg said. "Anyone can be a victim."

Heinrich was right about the storm, too.

A new wave of hysteria swept over Bedburg, stronger than it had ever been before.

CHAPTER THIRTY

GEORG

That afternoon, Arnold Baumgartner issued a huge monetary reward for anyone with information on his daughter's killer. In his dazed state, the commander wanted to do many things. He wanted to round up all the beggars in the southern district of Bedburg, to question them on what they might have seen the night before. He wanted to attack the Protestants outright. He wanted to go on another hunt. All three ideas were denied by Lord Werner—rounding up the beggars was too time consuming; attacking the Protestants was preemptive and foolhardy; another hunt was too dangerous, as they'd be near enemy lines.

General Ferdinand took over the garrison's forces and went about setting up defenses around the northern and eastern borders of Bedburg. Wooden palisades were quickly erected, makeshift gates were created to stop people from coming into Bedburg, and guards were stationed at those gates. The commanders were afraid of spies infiltrating the town—if they hadn't already.

It was a sunny day, and the winter snow was melting fast. Citizens and soldiers alike expected the Protestants to attack at any time.

"Do you think they have spies in town?" Georg asked his friend Konrad, referring to the Calvinists. "Surely they know what kind of defenses we have, and that reinforcements from Cologne have arrived."

"Even with the added regiment, it's only a matter of time before they strike," Konrad said. "They must be waiting on reinforcements of their own. There are groups of Protestants littered throughout the principality. If they all converge on us together, Bedburg could be in trouble."

The two soldiers stood on the northeastern side of town, near the jail where Hanns Richter had been released. They stared at the palisades and into the dark woods in the distance. "How do you know there are other groups of rebels out there?" Georg asked.

"Because I've been a soldier all my life, Georg."

Georg stared at the soldier's purple scar that ran down the right side of his face. "What do you think about Margreth's death?" he asked.

Konrad shrugged. "Releasing the pastor might have been a diversion tactic to kill the commander's daughter on the other side of town. But I'm not sure. All I know is that the killer must be in Bedburg."

Georg sighed and looked to his right. Soldiers were staking the wooden palisades into the ground, and stone walls were being cemented together behind the spiked poles. Georg pointed at the ramparts. "Do you think those walls will stand?"

"Maybe against footsoldiers and archers. But you said you saw cannons when you discovered the camp. Those walls won't hold against cannons."

"You have little faith in our fortifications, my friend. We've been fending off the Calvinists and Lutherans for years."

Konrad chuckled. "And you have too *much* faith in the town's defenses. The Protestants are desperate to reclaim what they believe is theirs. This battle could be very different than any before it." The big soldier adjusted his eye-patch and scratched his scalp. "Not to mention our western and southern borders are exposed. If they attack those sides, we're screwed."

"Maybe we should warn Ferdinand," Georg said, pulling at his beard. "Although I'm sure he knows. Ferdinand has a fine military mind. You should know that as well as I, after our experience fighting under him." He glanced over at Konrad.

"You're right. He's a strong commander," Konrad said, nodding.

Georg looked back to the walls being built. His mind started to race as he kept pulling on his beard. Before he could say anything else, Konrad put a hand on his shoulder.

"I nearly forgot," Konrad said. "Remember when you said there were some strange things about that investigator?"

"Heinrich? Well . . . yes, I do. But we were drinking. I haven't thought any more on it since then."

"Well I have," Konrad said. He grinned beneath his bushy beard. "I found something you might want to see."

Georg's eyebrows went high on his forehead.

"It will be easier if I just show you."

Georg nodded and said, "Good. I'm tired of watching this wall being built."

Konrad turned and motioned for Georg to follow. They headed away from the eastern border, toward Castle Bedburg, down a curved road. After a few bends in the road, they came to the castle. At least fifty soldiers were stationed in front of it, looking stoic and tense. Konrad grabbed Georg's arm and nudged his head away from the castle.

They walked further south, down a hill and past the jailhouse. They rounded the monolithic, gray structure, and came to the back of the building. Konrad stopped in his tracks and held his arm in front of Georg.

"What am I looking at?" Georg asked, staring at the bland, stone wall.

Konrad pointed at a reclining section of the jailhouse, near the ground-level of the building. The stones that made up the section looked decrepit, while the rest of the building looked strong and sturdy. The bottom of the wall looked like it was about to crumble apart.

"You told me the investigator was hard to track," Konrad said. "I think I found out why." He pointed at the dilapidated section of the jailhouse and walked closer to it. When he came to the wall, he crouched and peeked back over his shoulders.

Georg followed him. On close inspection, it wasn't that the wall was about to fall apart—it already had. Georg noticed a small crevice in the wall that sunk down into the earth. It was like a sinkhole, or a cave that went straight down. At the mouth of the crevice was a ladder that leaned against the cave and reached down to the darkness below.

"This, my friend, is a secret tunnel. I discovered it the other day," Konrad said with a smile. "Two nights ago, I found that it goes all the way underground, beneath the jailhouse, and leads right underneath Castle Bedburg. There's another ladder at the end of the tunnel that reaches into the basement of the castle."

Georg scratched his head. "It must have taken years to dig this," he muttered, and then turned to Konrad. "You think Investigator Franz is using this tunnel to go in and out of the castle?"

Konrad nodded.

"What makes you think that?" Georg asked. "He's a man of the law. He can go anywhere he pleases. Why would he need to travel in secrecy?"

"I don't know, but I took after your own instincts and followed him. I saw him use it, Georg." Konrad put his hands on his hips. "Think about it . . . the jailhouse is one of the places he frequents the most. It only makes sense that he would use the building he knows best as his secret road and means of travel."

Georg squinted at Konrad. "And what do you think he has to hide?" He couldn't help but grow suspicious. *How could no one know about a secret tunnel this close to the castle?*

"I was hoping we could find that out together."

"Right now?" Georg asked, his voice raising in pitch.

"Why not?" Konrad said with a shrug. "We might not be alive tomorrow. Aren't you the least bit curious?"

Georg had to admit that his interest was piqued. *What could Heinrich be using this tunnel for? Trafficking? Travel? Secret rendezvous?* With a shrug, the hunter grabbed the ladder—it felt new and smooth in his hands—and he started climbing down into the cave.

Whoever worked on this tunnel put in a lot of time and effort, Georg thought as he descended. The mouth of the cave widened, and as he went deeper into the earth it became darker and darker, with only a glimpse of light shining in from above. Before long, he reached the gravelly ground, which he assumed was at the basement level of the jailhouse.

Konrad followed Georg down the ladder. When they were both on sturdy ground, he looked to the left of the ladder and found a torch on the wall. Georg eyed him curiously.

"I put this here the other night," Konrad assured. He lit the torch.

Georg crept forward. He put his hand on the smooth, rocky wall. "This is definitely man-made," he said, "and took a lot of time to build." The wall was sculpted with grooves that acted as a sponge to keep water from seeping in from above.

Then Georg heard the click.

The hunter closed his eyes and sighed heavily. His shoulders slumped. After a moment of silence, he said, "Who sent you?"

"No one sent me."

Georg slowly turned around and faced Konrad, who held the torch in one hand and an arquebus in the other. The gun was pointed at Georg's chest. The patch-eyed man was ten paces away, at the opening of the tunnel. Sunlight showered his body, and the torch's flames created a dim aura around him.

"Bullshit," Georg said. He appeared calm, but in his mind everything turned red with rage.

Konrad shrugged and had a cruel grin on his face, which was accentuated by the flickering torchlight. "Okay, the archbishop *hired* me to keep an eye on you, but I would have done it for free. I was already on my way to find you."

"And you lured me down this tunnel . . . for what? Does it even lead anywhere? Did Investigator Franz even use it?"

"How the hell should I know? You really are quite the dolt, Georg."

The hunter narrowed his eyes on Konrad and held his arms out to his sides. "That might be true. But I know we never served together in the army, as you claimed we had."

"How do you know?" Konrad said. "You're a madman, remember?" His grin grew wider.

"Because I never served under Ferdinand of Bavaria. I've never even met him. I fought in Alexander Farnese's army."

Konrad hesitated for a moment, and then chuckled. "Well . . . you got me. I suppose I'll concede that to you, Georg—we never fought together."

Georg took a step forward, and Konrad raised his gun so its sight was level with Georg's eyes. "Not a step further, bastard."

"What did I do to you, Konrad? What is it you want? Money?"

Konrad frowned. "No, you cur, I told you money does not concern me. You really don't remember me, do you? You must be crazier than I thought."

Georg shook his head and shrugged. "Besides the patch over your eye, I'm afraid you're quite forgettable."

Konrad growled and clenched his jaw. He brought his hand that held the torch up to his face. He slid his eye-patch away and revealed a perfectly normal eye. "How about now?" he said, as if unveiling some groundbreaking epiphany.

Georg's face lit up and he pointed repeatedly at Konrad and seemed like he was about to exclaim something, but then he took on a somber look and shook his head. "Nope. Still nothing."

Konrad spat on the ground. He couldn't hide the frustration on his face, and his smile twisted into a sneer. The purple scar on his cheek seemed to pulse.

Georg knew he was getting the better of the man's emotions, but thought, *Maybe it's not in my best interest to taunt a man who's holding a gun to my chest.*

"How about Donnelly . . . does that name sound familiar?"

Georg swung his arms out wide, trying not to pay attention.

"Your eye-patch is fake, this tunnel is a ruse, we never met before a few weeks ago . . . are you even from Brühl?" The hunter shook his head and put his hands on his hips, but then whatever Konrad had just said registered in his mind. "Wait," he said, "did you say Donnelly?"

Konrad nodded.

Georg pulled at his beard. "Konrad . . . Donnelly." He paused and his eyes focused on the gun pointed at his face. "Like . . . my wife?"

Konrad sighed. "Yes, goddammit!" he shouted, and spittle flew from his mouth. His anger intensified. "Agnes goddamn Donnelly."

Georg's eyes narrowed, and the rage started to seep back into his mind. Although Josephine had reminded him of his wife, he hadn't heard Agnes' name spoken out loud in years. "How the hell do you know my wife?"

Konrad looked like he was going to slap his own forehead. He shook his head and said, "You really are dense . . ." he trailed off, and sighed. "She was my sister, you fool! You are my brother-in-law!"

Georg pulled at his beard some more, trying to rack his brain. All the memories of the past were blurry. He'd worked years to forget those times. "That's impossible," he said, "she never mentioned your name once."

Konrad looked to the ground and shuffled his feet. "She was ashamed of me for leaving our family to go to war, rather than helping our parents. But she was still my sister, and I always loved her." He paused, and then his voice became dark. "And you killed her."

Georg's face turned hot, and he shook his head furiously. "You're delusional. I would never harm Agnes."

"Your wife, and your unborn child. Why do you think they call you Sieghart the Savage? You're a madman, Georg! You were responsible for your own family's death—for my sister's death! I am here for vengeance. You weren't there to protect them. I

237

don't care how they died—her *husband* was not there to protect her!" A few tears rolled down Konrad's scarred cheek.

Georg gnashed his teeth so hard that he felt they would break. Through a clenched jaw he said, "I was at war."

"You've been at war your entire life."

Something in Georg's mind snapped, and words became muddled in his mind. He couldn't hear Konrad speaking—no one had the right to speak of his dead wife and son.

He roared and dug deep, pushing off the ground with both of his legs. He rushed toward Konrad and closed the gap with one long stride. His mind broke and went berserk.

He let the savage out of its cage.

Konrad Donnelly squeezed the trigger of his gun.

The bullet whipped from the arquebus and planted itself in Georg's left shoulder. The hunter's entire left side, from hip to shoulder, went immediately numb, and the bullet caused his body to jerk back.

But the momentum of Georg carried him, and the big hunter crashed into the stout soldier with a bone-crushing thud.

The torch flew from Konrad's hand and bounced against the wall behind him. His arquebus fell to the ground.

The stout man struggled to wrestle Georg, trying to stay on his feet. They both grimaced and circled each other with their arms on each other's shoulders.

Georg bared his sharp yellow teeth and snapped at Konrad like a wolf. Spit and phlegm flew from his mouth, onto Konrad's beard and face. Though he could only feel his right arm, he felt no pain—only an unbridled rage.

Still circling and grabbing at each other, Konrad put his left leg behind Georg's right foot, and squeezed hard on Georg's shoulder. Blood spurted from the wound and oozed around Konrad's hand.

Georg screamed.

Konrad pushed with all his weight, and Georg tripped over the man's foot and fell to the ground, on his back. A cloud of dirt billowed into the air around him.

Konrad went low and straddled Georg's chest. He swung hard and punched Georg in the face.

Georg growled like an animal, even as his nose broke and his eyes became bloodied and bruised.

Georg felt his strength start to leave him as Konrad kept raining punches down on his face.

Then the hunter bucked his chest, causing Konrad to become unbalanced. Georg reached out with his good hand and punched Konrad in the stomach. The air flew from Konrad's lungs, and he let out a wheezing cough and grabbed his stomach.

Georg took the moment to twist his body and push with all his strength. Konrad was stout and strong, but Georg was still bigger, and with his right arm he managed to writhe in the dirt and get his legs on top of Konrad's.

Georg spun on top of Konrad and straddled him. With his left arm dangling, Georg let out a vicious snarl and brought his huge right hand around Konrad's thick throat. He squeezed as hard as he could.

Konrad's face started turning purple, and he used both hands to reach up and throttle Georg's neck.

They became locked in a strangle hold.

Georg felt his good hand start to weaken, and the color on Konrad's face returned.

The hunter tried smothering Konrad by leaning forward and pressing down on his mouth and nose, but then Konrad suddenly let go of Georg's neck.

Georg watched Konrad reach for something in the dirt.

Konrad snatched the arquebus from the ground, and he hoisted the gun.

Georg's eyes went wide.

Konrad swung the butt of the gun around his body, trying to smash it into Georg's head.

The hunter ducked low, putting his head on Konrad's chest, and the gun whizzed over him. Konrad held onto the barrel of the weapon and brought it back for another swing.

Georg growled. Air was coming in ragged gasps, and he used

the only weapon he had at his disposal. He ducked beneath the swinging gun and lunged downwards, baring his teeth. He brought his face to Konrad's neck and clamped down as hard as he could, with his jaw.

Konrad shrieked and blood gushed from the wound as Georg tore the flesh from his neck.

The hunter clenched down even harder and felt the tendons and skin rip in his mouth. Blood dribbled down his chin. With his mouth as a vice, he ripped backwards and tore Konrad's throat out.

The blood bubbled, and Konrad's screams became a raspy gurgle. The soldier grabbed at his torn throat, and his body started to spasm and twist and the blood pooled around his neck. Both of his eyes turned glossy, and then murky, and then gray.

He stared into Georg's eyes with an odd look, and then his writhing stopped.

Georg sat over him and huffed as the blood dripped from his mouth, face, and beard. He spat out bits of flesh and then heard a noise from above. His eyes shot upward, to the opening of the crevice, and he squinted as he stared at the blinding sun.

A silhouette stood at the top of the ladder. "Oh my God!" the voice screamed. "The nightmares are true! The legend is true! The Devil is here in Bedburg!"

Georg narrowed his eyes to adjust to the light.

Sister Salome had a hand covering her open mouth. She shrieked and took off running.

Georg looked down. He was crouched on all fours, over Konrad's dead body, with blood pouring down his beard and chin and pooling at Konrad's head, and he realized at that moment that he looked more like a monster than he ever thought possible.

CHAPTER THIRTY-ONE

DIETER

As Pastor Hanns Richter left the jailhouse that morning, he gave Dieter a slight nod, as if he knew the priest had spoken on his behalf. The pastor shuffled through the throng of angry bystanders, ducking from thrown vegetables and rocks.

"Sinner! Liar! You sold us false promises!" the peasants cried out.

The pastor's long walk from the jailhouse was meant to be a public display of embarrassment and shame. The same mob that Hanns had created had become incensed and unreasonable.

They feel betrayed . . . but for no good reason, Dieter thought. He knew Bishop Solomon had filled the peoples' heads with his own rhetoric. It didn't matter that Pastor Richter had been released— he had betrayed them by being arrested in the first place.

"How much did you pay for your freedom, heretic?" one peasant screamed as Hanns walked by. "Are you too scared to die for the same beliefs you preach?"

Within a week, Hanns had gone from being a figure of defiance in the face of the Catholics, to a figure of deception. Now the people wanted blood. The Calvinist army was on Bedburg's doorstep, and the town was on the verge of war, again, for the first time in years.

The people blamed Pastor Hanns Richter for all of it.

The pastor's idea of a "new hope" had turned into a tide of

hatred, which Dieter assumed was spearheaded by Bishop Solomon.

"It seems your idea was worthwhile." Vicar Balthasar had come to stand beside Dieter. He leaned on his staff, watching as Pastor Richter was led out of the city. "It's interesting how public opinion of the man has swayed so quickly."

Dieter glanced at the vicar. *Perhaps Bishop Solomon isn't the man to blame for the public unrest after all.* "I didn't expect that," Dieter said. He knew there was a silver lining to the pastor's departure, however. *He might be leaving with his dignity shot and his tail between his legs, but at least he's leaving with his head still on his shoulders.*

"He gave the people something they could believe in," Balthasar said, "but ultimately it was a promise which he could not deliver." The vicar started nodding. "I believe his time here will fade into obscurity."

"I suppose," Dieter said, disappointment in his voice.

Vicar Balthasar turned to him. "Wasn't that our goal? You kept the man alive. You should be proud of that. Your bloodthirsty bishop would have had it any other way." He trailed off, but kept his eyes on Dieter, who refused to make eye contact with the man. "If there's one bit of advice I could give," Balthasar continued, "it would be to watch out for Solomon. Overshadowing your superior is a dangerous move. You might have saved your conscience by saving Hanns Richter's life, but you probably gained a new enemy . . . and a powerful one."

Dieter's head slumped, and he left the crowd and retreated back to his church.

Bishop Solomon was absent, as was Sister Salome. Dieter was surprised, though, to find a single man sitting in the pew closest to the altar.

It was Peter Griswold.

"Herr Griswold," Dieter said, taken aback. "This is quite shocking. What brings you here?"

Peter looked up at Dieter. His eyes were puffy and his face was wet. His lower lip trembled, and he said, "I wish to make a confession, priest."

Dieter wrinkled his nose. "You aren't of this denomination, Herr Griswold. What could I possibly do for you? Why not speak with Pastor Richter—he was just released, and he's your friend, is he not?" He turned and started to walk away, but as he looked up at the statue of Christ's crucifixion, a pang of guilt ran through him.

"I beg you," Peter called out, "hear me. This has nothing to do with Catholics or Protestants, Father Nicolaus. This has to do with my daughter."

A chill ran down Dieter's spine, and he almost tripped over his own feet. He swallowed, and slowly turned his head. Staring at Peter, he realized this was the first time he'd ever seen the stoic man so deflated. It was also the first time Peter had called Dieter by his Catholic title. It softened Dieter's demeanor.

He sighed and gestured for Peter to follow him to the confessional. Once inside the booth, he asked Peter what happened.

"I've failed my family. I made a terrible mistake, and I'm afraid I cannot be forgiven for it. I'm afraid I'll burn in Hell."

Dieter said, "If you were a Catholic you'd know that *anyone* can be forgiven in the eyes of God. So, tell me, what happened—and start from the beginning."

Peter shook his head. "The one I love most was harmed. I was blinded by my own selfishness and greed."

Dieter said nothing, but his muscles tightened.

Peter sniffed and continued. "I know you know my daughter. Sybil fancies you, and I've seen the way you two look at each other. I can't, in good conscience, allow such a union to take place. I'm sure you know that . . ." he trailed off to gather himself, coughed, and cleared his throat. "But I . . . I made her do things against her wishes, and now I fear she'll never forgive me." He wiped his nose with his sleeve. "I made her accompany a young nobleman, even though she hated him. She's become his bride-to-be, and is set to leave town with him."

Inside, Dieter bristled, but outside, he stayed calm. "What happened, Peter?"

Peter stuttered and struggled to speak. Then his sniffling became sobbing—the sobbing of a grown man, and a loving father. Dieter realized that this was a man who truly had his daughter's well-being at heart, but he'd made mistakes along the way. Like any parent, he wished for the best, but had to learn from his blunders.

Just how grave was this mistake?

"Sybil confided in me this morning that . . . that she'd . . . that she'd been defiled by that *damn* nobleman." He punched the nub of his left arm into the open palm of his right. "My little girl was hurt, and there was nothing I could do to help her." Peter pulled his knees close, put his head on them, and wept.

Dieter froze and felt his stomach drop. He suddenly felt the urge to vomit. Thoughts raced through his mind, but in no clear fashion. *Why didn't she tell me? How could you let this happen, you bastard of a father? What will that mean for our future?*

His eyes went wide. *Whose child is growing in Sybil's womb?*

A final thought brought him back to reality and back to his training as a Catholic priest.

Forgiveness.

He felt it hard to fight back the tears, but Dieter looked through the cage of the confessional and stared at the downtrodden father of Sybil Griswold. "It will be all right, Peter. You will be forgiven, and you will make it through this—and so will Sybil." As he spoke, he felt as though the words were coming from far off—like from a spirit, removed from his body.

Dieter wasn't sure if he believed his own words, and after he dismissed Peter he sat in the confessional for nearly an hour, staring at the spot where Peter had been sitting, trying to wrap his head around this new knowledge.

*　　*　　*

Dieter left the church dazed, with his knees wobbling. It was late afternoon, the sun beat down on his face, but his eyes were wide with shock. He felt lost, and he couldn't think or walk straight. He wandered from the church, like a ghost, and headed north. Now it made sense to Dieter why Sybil had been crying when she told him she was pregnant. That wasn't the whole story.

How could I be so blind? I was so ecstatic that I didn't even stay to listen to her. His shoulders slumped. *I don't deserve her. I am no man.*

His self-pity continued for what seemed like an eternity. He found himself at the northern edge of town, watching the soldiers as they staked the palisades in the ground.

Then his anger quickly shifted from himself, to his creator. He stared up at the sky and the puffy clouds and thought, *How could You let this happen, Lord? This is how You treat Your innocent children? You led me to believe that this was a sign of triumph and celebration, but You fooled me. Tragedy was the catalyst for this sign.*

He walked out of the town, through the northern gate. With all the commotion and preparation going on around him, no one even noticed as he walked through the gate like an animated cadaver.

He kept heading north, away from Bedburg and closer to the trees in the distance.

He damned himself, he damned Peter, and he damned God. His normal thoughts of forgiveness were replaced by dark, spiteful thoughts—thoughts he'd never had before, thoughts that he'd kept stifled and locked away. He felt as though innocence had drifted from his soul—innocence he couldn't get back—and it had only taken a single confession. The person Dieter damned the most for hurting the woman he loved was Johannes von Bergheim.

Dieter knew what had to be done. He ventured three miles outside of Bedburg, into the woods, toward his destiny. He'd received a sign, and it was clearer than a river in springtime.

As he trudged through the rolling countryside, he felt a presence following him, but he didn't even bother to turn around.

He made it to the trees, struggled a bit through the brush and undergrowth, and came to a clearing.

Pastor Hanns Richter was waiting for him, sitting on a tree stump.

Hanns tilted his head as he watched Dieter approach, like he could read the many emotions on Dieter's face—agony, sadness, pain. "Are you regretting your decision to help me, Father Nicolaus?" Hanns asked, scratching his head.

"My life is doomed," he said drearily, "but no, I don't regret helping you."

Hanns massaged his chin. "You control your fate, Dieter. You're only doomed if you allow yourself to be."

"I thought God controlled my fate."

Hanns smiled. "Sometimes you have to take control. Would you still like to go through with this? I must be leaving shortly."

Dieter nodded. "Are your people going to attack Bedburg?"

"I can't be certain. But if John Calvin and Martin Luther's words are to be remembered, we have to take back our towns. We can't survive on the fringes, Dieter, and I can't allow my faith to disappear without a fight. The pope must hear our cries."

"Even if you die?"

"If that's God's will, so be it. Whether in life or death, our words *will* be heard. That is my calling." Hanns paused. "And what is yours, Dieter?"

"Well, I'm here," Dieter said with a shrug. "I imagine my superiors won't be too thrilled when they learn you didn't 'fade into obscurity,' as they hoped you would."

The pastor chuckled. "I suppose not. Maybe it's a sign that your time in Bedburg is coming to an end."

"Maybe so." Dieter rubbed the back of his neck and said, "Let's get on with it, shall we?"

"We shall," Hanns said, nodding. He cleared his throat and paused for a moment. Then he said, "The Holy Spirit dwells within us and empowers us, Dieter Nicolaus. We must all come to understand that. The orthodox religion of Catholicism is not devoted completely to Jesus. Do you understand those words?"

"I do."

"If you are to be saved and born again," he continued, "then you must obey the Holy Spirit's calling at all times. You cannot rely on the papacy. Your fate is your responsibility. If you disobey God, He may exempt you from Heaven, without any guarantee of absolution. Do you understand?"

Dieter nodded.

Pastor Richter rattled off a few more formal statements, and then he motioned for Dieter to follow him.

He led the priest through a clearing, to a small pond in the woods that was about three feet deep. Dieter stripped off his robe and undergarments and walked into the water. The coldness stung him to his bones, and he shivered. As his body tingled, he closed his eyes, held his breath, and allowed the Holy Spirit to consume him.

Hanns put his hand on Dieter's head and submerged him in the water. "With this Holy Baptism," the pastor said, "you must work through daily contrition and repentance to cast aside your old ways. A new man will arise and walk before God, in righteousness and purity. If you live in sin after this baptism, you will lose your grace. So rise," Hanns said, lifting Dieter's head from the pond, "and be born again, Dieter Nicolaus, a servant of God and Jesus Christ."

Dieter exhaled deeply and shook his head, spraying water from his hair and face. He opened his eyes and felt an immediate wave of relief wash through his body, as though the simple pond had cleared his conscience completely.

He was no longer a clergyman of the Catholic faith.

And though the conversion itself was important to him, the freedom it gave him meant even more.

*   *   *

Before parting ways, Dieter and Hanns ambled through the woods, side by side, and the sun began to fall.

"I assume you won't join our cause?" Hanns asked.

Dieter turned to face the pastor. "No. I'm not a warrior, and I have to find the one I love."

"Tread carefully, brother. There are many more dangers in Bedburg for you now, lurking around every corner."

Dieter scrunched his brow. "What do you mean?"

"There are things in Bedburg that are happening right under your nose . . . things that you and the Catholic people are unaware of. The werewolf you seek, for instance—do you not see what it is?"

Dieter shrugged and ran a hand through his wet hair. "I assume you're going to say it's a bogeyman story to scare children? But if that's the case, what about the *actual* deaths that have been committed in the beast's name?"

Hanns shook his head and stopped walking. He put both his hands on Dieter's shoulders. "Listen to me, brother. The werewolf is not a bogeyman story. It is a story used to scare Protestants."

Dieter chuckled. "I think you have that backwards, my friend. If the werewolf is a means to scare Protestants, then why have all the victims been Catholic?"

Hanns sighed and frowned. "Then you are clueless," he muttered. "I don't have long to explain, but the victims in Bedburg have been the *illusion* of being Catholic, Dieter. Any reformer knows the truth, as terrible as it sounds, that the ploy has been *created* by the Catholics."

"You aren't making any sense," Dieter said, feeling suddenly confused. "What on earth are you talking about?"

"The people of Bedburg believe that a Protestant devil is killing Catholics, correct?"

Dieter nodded.

"This is to scare Catholics into action," Hanns said, pausing. "But what if I told you that all the people who've died were not actually Catholics."

"Then what were they?"

"Protestants. Bishop Solomon and Archbishop Ernst know this—even Lord Werner is probably privy to this information. But the public has no idea." The pastor breathed in and kept his grip on Dieter's shoulders.

Dieter felt baffled and lost.

"Let me put it this way," Hanns continued. "How do you get Catholics to fear and kill Protestants?"

"By saying a hellbent beast has been summoned by the Protestants . . . to kill Catholics," Dieter said. He'd heard it before.

Hanns nodded. "Right. But the Lutherans and Calvinists know the truth, which is one of the reasons we're revolting in the first place. The people who have been killed have been Protestants, Dieter, not Catholics." The pastor raised his index finger. "Josephine, the harlot who regularly went to Mass? She was a Protestant spy, and would give us information about your church. While she worked, she listened to what the drunk soldiers told her and relayed that information to our armies."

Dieter's head started to spin. "I don't believe that."

Hanns raised another finger—his middle finger. "The Achterberg family?" he said. "They were Calvinist reformers. They placed their own son in the hands of Bishop Solomon. He was an altar boy, yes, but he also gave us pertinent information that only he could find out from Solomon. I feel terrible for the boy, for what he's been through—losing his family and being in the hands of that vile man—and he's still sitting in a jail cell somewhere, if he's not already dead."

The pastor raised a third finger and said, "Peter Griswold? He's a friend of mine. He helps fund our cause. When Karl Achterberg wanted to wed his son to Sybil Griswold, the marriage wasn't denied because the families *hated* each other . . . it was denied because Karl had to keep the *illusion* that his family was Catholic, whereas Peter has always been suspected of being a

Protestant. If those two families joined together, it would have been highly suspicious and would reek of collusion."

Dieter shook his head and shrugged the pastor's hand from his shoulder. "That all sounds like quite a reach, Hanns."

Hanns shrugged. "It's the truth, Dieter. Josephine and the Achterbergs were spies, and they were silenced. The Catholic townsfolk don't know that, of course, but every damn fighting Protestant knows who those people were. I don't know how, but the Catholics must have discovered the agents in their midst, and now they're picking us off one by one. Even with what you said on my behalf, I have no idea why they allowed me to live."

Hanns paused to let Dieter mull the words over, and the pastor stroked his chin. "The one person I hadn't been able to place my finger on was the most recent victim, Margreth Baumgartner. She's been the only person murdered who was *actually* a Catholic, as far as I can tell. But I think I'm starting to understand." Hanns put his hands on his hips and faced the foliage at his feet. "It's like I said—how do you scare the Catholics into action? No one cares about a dead prostitute, or a young girl . . . but by killing a Catholic noblewoman and deifying her, and blaming the Protestant devil . . . it's all very brilliant on the archbishop's part. Your town is in such a frenzy now that they'll do anything to exact their revenge against us."

As he thought aloud, Hanns started pacing. "The noblewoman's death is one action we did not anticipate—we didn't think the Catholics would actually have the gall to kill one of their own, let alone the daughter of a prominent military commander. In short, Dieter, I suppose you're right . . . the Werewolf of Bedburg is a bogeyman, but not as far removed from the truth as you'd think. You must be careful in Bedburg, brother. If anyone finds out what I've told you, your life—and the lives of those you love—will be in terrible jeopardy."

Dieter didn't have the words to speak. He opened his mouth a few times, but stayed silent each time. His mind whirled. *If what Hanns is saying is true . . . then the conspiracy in Bedburg goes far deeper than I ever thought possible. Could it reach all the way to the archbishop of Cologne—or above that . . . to Pope Sixtus himself?*

It was overwhelming, but, as disturbing as it was, Dieter wasn't too surprised. He shook his head and looked the pastor in the eyes. There was a sense of tiredness and sadness in Pastor Richter's brown eyes.

They said their farewells, embraced, and Hanns turned and headed east, futher into the woods.

Dieter felt a weight on his conscience, but he couldn't tell what it stemmed from. It was a nagging suspicion . . . that as he watched the pastor disappear into the woods, he couldn't help but feel as though that was the last time he'd ever see Hanns Richter.

When he thought back on the pastor's words and warnings, he shook his head. *No,* he decided. *Hanns Richter is telling the truth. And that means two things: I have to get Sybil, and we need to get the hell out of Bedburg.*

CHAPTER THIRTY-TWO

SYBIL

After Sybil had recalled what happened with Johannes von Bergheim, and told her father, Peter had left their home in a drowsy stupor. Sybil didn't ask where he was going. Instead, she spent the time resting, until Hugo shyly crept into her room about an hour later. He still clutched the horse-doll she'd made him.

"Are you all right, Beele?" Hugo asked.

Sybil gave her little brother a hug.

Hugo said, "I love you," and it was almost enough to make Sybil cry, but she held the tears back. She had done enough weeping, she decided, and wouldn't allow herself to feel abused any longer.

I will be like a stone wall, strong and impenetrable.

"I know," she whispered in Hugo's ear, "I love you too."

"What's going to happen to us?"

Sybil stared into the boy's big, round eyes. He was small for his age, but seemed to be growing recently at a rate Sybil hadn't seen before. She smiled. "What do you mean? We're going to be fine." She stood up from her bed and ran her hand through Hugo's shaggy hair.

"Do you promise?"

"I do."

"But what about Johannes? He's going to take you away from us. I'll never see you again," Hugo said. His big eyes seemed to shrink.

"That's not true," Sybil said. "Not if I have anything to say about it."

"But what can you do? You're just a girl."

The words stung Sybil. As innocent as they sounded, they caused her to stutter and pause. She steeled herself and clenched her jaw. "I am just as strong as any man, Hue. Don't forget that."

Hugo nodded and fiddled with his doll. "I know . . . but other people might not. Will I see you again after you leave?"

"I'm not going anywhere."

Hugo looked up at her. "You promise?"

"I promise," Sybil said, smiling. *That's two promises in two minutes*, she thought. *I hope I can make good on them.*

The boy jumped in Sybil's arms and they embraced again.

"I have to run an errand, Hue, but I'll be back soon." Hugo opened his mouth, but before he could say anything, Sybil said, "I promise."

Hugo smiled and ran out of the room.

Sybil watched her brother leave, and then exhaled heavily and smoothed her dress.

Night fell on Bedburg, and the town bustled with activity. Last minute preparations to fortify the southern and western walls of the town were being finished, and soldiers paraded the streets, fully dressed and battle-ready. It was a much different atmosphere than most of the townsfolk were used to.

Sybil made her way through the curving roads, heading south and west. Her eyes darted around in all directions. She felt paranoid about being followed. The whole city was on edge.

At the Achterberg estate, Sybil grabbed the *Ninety-Five Theses* from behind the wall of the hearth. After Dieter had kept it in his chambers at the church for one night, he decided to hide the book at the Achterberg's, away from prying eyes.

Sybil sat at the small table and lit the candle. The flame

brought immediate warmth and light to the dark room. Sybil opened the manuscript. As she read, time flew by. The purple horizon turned a darker shade as time passed, until the sky was black and littered with stars.

Every so often, she poked her head up from the book and peered out of the single window of the house, wondering where Dieter was. They'd made no plans of meeting that night, but Sybil had hoped Dieter would show up anyway.

The fleeting minutes turned into long hours, and there was still no sign of Dieter. Sybil's paranoia grew worse. She feared that her father might have left the house and, in his haze, done something awful. She feared that God had taken Dieter from her. She feared that someone might have found out about their torrid relationship. She feared anything and everything—whatever could go wrong, would. She sighed deeply and shook her head. *He is stubborn, but my father is not a bad man; God would never take Dieter from me; no one knows of our relationship.* She had an answer for every silly thought in her head, and she smiled.

Sybil hoped that someday her father would give her his blessing. Peter must have seen the way she looked at Dieter, and he could not deny their relationship forever. Sybil knew Peter must have felt an insurmountable shame after forcing her through the horrible tirade with Johannes.

A creaking sound stole her from her thoughts. She shifted in her seat and stared at the front door. She smiled as the door slowly opened, and then she stood and said, "It's about time. You took long enough." Her smile faded as she stared at the two shadowy figures standing in the doorway.

After hearing Peter's confession regarding Sybil and Johannes, and after meeting with Pastor Richter, Dieter still felt uneasy. On one hand, his spirit was rejuvenated from meeting with the pastor. But on the other hand, Hanns' words unnerved him.

He left the woods and headed back toward Bedburg in a

hurry. He wanted to check on Sybil, to make sure she was safe. When he realized that the town's northern gate was well guarded, he headed toward the western entrance instead. The western gate had a weaker military presence, but to be safe he stayed outside of the town's walls.

The detour around the walls of Bedburg cost him over an hour of time. At one point he had to hide behind a copse of trees as a scouting party from Bedburg made their rounds near him. He eventually reached the fields to the south of town, and stood between Peter Griswold's estate to the east, and Karl Achterberg's to the west.

Where will she be?

He looked in both directions, over and over. The sky was pitch black, and he couldn't afford to waste more time by choosing the wrong house to go to.

He decided to head to the Achterberg estate. He figured Sybil might have gone there to calm her nerves and separate herself from her father.

Dieter made it to the hill that led to the Achterberg house, and then broke into a sprint, unable to contain his excitement. He had so much to tell Sybil.

He almost tripped on his robe as he reached the front door.

He burst through the door without knocking, and as the door swung open he said, "Beele, are you here? We must gather our things and leave this place immediately! I've learned a terrible—"

He stepped through the doorway and saw Sybil sitting at the table at the other end of the room, her hands tightly clasped on her lap.

"Dieter!" she yelled.

He heard a sharp crack and his eyes lost focus. His entire body went numb, and the floor rushed to meet his face. He put his hands out instinctively and caught his fall. On his knees and hands, he blinked a few times and saw blood dripping onto the floor. He groaned and crumpled to his stomach.

As Dieter rolled onto his back, the last thing he saw before losing consciousness was a golden cross dangling over his head.

*　　　*　　　*

When Dieter awoke, his hands were bound. He sat next to Sybil, at the table, and the *Ninety-Five Theses* was open in front of him. His vision started off blurry, until he blinked away tears.

Two figures stood at the other end of the room.

It took him a long moment to regain focus.

Bishop Solomon and Vicar Balthasar stared at him from the doorway. The vicar was leaning on his walking staff. The top end of the staff was crusted with blood.

"I'm so sorry," Sybil said to Dieter. Her hands were also bound.

"Quiet, you wretch," Bishop Solomon ordered. He was hunched over, and his hands were clasped behind his back. He started pacing the room and clicking his tongue.

"I'm disappointed in you, Father Nicolaus," Vicar Balthasar said. "I truly believed you to be an honest man of the cloth, and not a traitor to your own people."

Dieter frowned and tried to stand. His knees knocked together, and Vicar Balthasar ran the length of the room in an instant and held his staff out toward Dieter's throat. All signs of his limp were gone.

Dieter stared at the round-faced priest, sat back down, and said, "I've betrayed no one."

Bishop Solomon was shaking his head. "You've betrayed God. I have the evidence to prove it."

"You won't get away with this, Solomon," Dieter growled.

The bishop shrugged. "Of course I will. When I said you were finished, did you think I was bluffing? Tsk, tsk, Dieter." The bishop's sagging face tightened, and his eyes narrowed. "Stand up. Both of you."

Dieter wobbled as he stood, and his head brimmed with a sharp pain. Sybil leaned toward him to help him to his feet.

Vicar Balthasar walked around the captives and prodded them in the back with his staff. "I never took you for such an exquisite student of subterfuge and manipulation," he said, and then sighed. "What's done is done, I suppose." The vicar cleared his throat and raised his voice. "With the power vested in me under Archbishop Ernst of Cologne, Pope Sixtus above him, and God above him, I hereby place you under arrest, Dieter Nicolaus, for various crimes."

Dieter noticed that Lord Werner's name was not mentioned in the vicar's formal decree. He craned his neck to try and watch Balthasar read off the charges.

"Firstly, for reading a heretical text." The vicar nudged his chin toward the *Ninety-Five Theses*. "Secondly, for staying in this house, a property of the Catholic church, without proper title or taxation. Thirdly, for treason, by abetting the Protestant rebels and supplying them with pertinent information about Bedburg's defenses." The vicar yawned and sounded bored. "Fourthly, for corrupting this young woman into your blasphemous faith, against your vows of perpetual chastity. And finally—and worst of all—for disavowing God from your heart."

Vicar Balthasar prodded Dieter one more time with his staff, and then turned away. "You lied to us about Pastor Hanns Richter, Herr Nicolaus. Your clever manipulation surely knows no bounds."

"What are you talking about?" Dieter asked.

"You talked us into releasing the man, in the name of mercy, so that he might go away forever. Well, scouts have told me they've seen him fraternizing with the Calvinist army, possibly leading their religious sect on the front lines. That isn't quite 'fading into obscurity,' is it?"

Dieter spat on the floor. "You know those charges against me are untrue. Would you, vicar—a minister of the faith—truly bring me up on such falsities?"

Balthasar shrugged. "I see no untruth in those claims. You brought all of this upon yourself." He turned to Sybil and poked her in the back with his staff, and she let out a startled yelp. "And as for you, Sybil Griswold, I place you under arrest for aiding in treason against your people, for reading a heretical text, and for witchcraft and sorcery, where you stole a once-good priest away from the salvation of God."

Sybil's eyes sparkled, but she kept the tears away.

Dieter grew angry—angrier than Sybil had ever seen—and she watched him snap and growl at the vicar and bishop.

Balthasar forced Dieter and Sybil to walk forward, while Solomon went outside and brought a carriage around. It had been hidden up the hill, away from the house.

Before they boarded the carriage, Bishop Solomon leaned close to them and said, "May your souls be damned to Hell for eternity."

As the carriage bumped and rattled over the road, Sybil whispered to Dieter, "What will they do to us?"

They were inside the coach. Sybil felt scared, and her hands trembled. Solomon sat next to the driver of the carriage, outside, while Vicar Balthasar sat opposite Sybil and Dieter, in the coach.

Balthasar studied Sybil and Dieter's faces. He frequently tapped the bottom of his staff on the ground, but he never took his eyes away from the former priest and his lover.

Dieter met eyes with the vicar and said, "They mean to kill us, Beele." There was a hint of venom in his voice. He continued matching stares with Balthasar.

Sybil faced Dieter, and then turned to the vicar and raised her eyebrows.

Vicar Balthasar nodded. "Given the severity of your multiple crimes, that does sound like an apt outcome. Treason alone carries that sentence."

"You must try us first, under the rules of law," Sybil said. She tried to loosen her wrist-bindings by squirming in her seat, but failed.

Before Balthasar could confirm or deny his intent, Dieter said, "We were found guilty the minute these two stepped onto the

Achterberg's estate, Beele. We won't see a fair trial."

Vicar Balthasar raised his hands up, as if surrendering. "I am just doing as the law requires. I arrested you in the archbishop's name, but he is not here. Bishop Solomon controls your fate . . . and after your fiasco in front of Lord Werner, I doubt that the bishop feels very forgiving."

Dieter looked away from the vicar and turned to the curtained window to his right.

"Who do you think could have done this to us?" Sybil asked Dieter. She didn't bother to conceal her words from Balthasar.

"Georg Sieghart," Dieter said without hesitation. He sighed and stared at the rolling countryside outside the window. "He knew of us, and I should have known that the drunk blabbermouth would never keep his word. I'm sorry for not listening to you, Beele. Your father came to me this morning. He was a wreck and gave me a tearful confession."

When Dieter turned to face Sybil, his head was shaking. His lips trembled as he struggled to speak. Finally, he said, "He told me what Johannes von Bergheim did to you. I'm so sorry I couldn't do anything—I've failed you."

Sybil gritted her teeth. "You were never charged with my safety or well-being, Dieter. I'm not a child."

The carriage rolled into Bedburg under the cover of darkness, right through the middle of town. They made it to the jailhouse. Sybil and Dieter were both hooded as they stepped out of the carriage. They were led down the stairs of a place that smelled like a moldy cellar.

At the bottom of the steps, their hoods were removed.

Heinrich Franz sat in a chair at the end of the hall, reading over a piece of paper. As Sybil and Dieter were escorted around the investigator, Heinrich gazed up and had a perplexed look on his face, one that showed he didn't understand why the priest and the farmer's daughter were there.

They walked into the second room, where Ulrich the punisher stood with a key in his hand. He grinned, causing the scar on his face to become disfigured, and then he opened a gate.

Sybil and Dieter were thrown into the cold cell together. Across from them, in another cell, a prisoner sat huddled in a shadowy corner, whimpering, with his knees drawn up to his chest.

CHAPTER THIRTY-THREE

HEINRICH

Heinrich was livid. "You should have consulted me before arresting those two, dammit." He spoke to the vicar and bishop. "It's my job to find and arrest the criminals in Bedburg, not yours!" He pounded his gloved hand against his palm as he walked back and forth in the jailhouse hall.

"I guess we did your job for you," Vicar Balthasar said. "You should be thanking us."

Bishop Solomon grinned slightly. "Please, investigator, does your vanity and pride always have to get the better of you? Must you always be the hero who saves the damsel and arrests the unlawful?" Bishop Solomon's grin turned into a frown, and his voice turned steely. "In case you haven't noticed, that strategy hasn't been working."

What is going on here? Heinrich thought, looking back and forth from Bishop Solomon's gray face, to Vicar Balthasar's round, cherubic one. *Just the other day these two seemed ready to rip each other apart, and now they seem like they're . . . friends.*

Heinrich took a deep breath and thrust a finger in Solomon's direction. "I have an ongoing investigation, Your Grace. These arrests make everything messy. Your prerogative should be aimed at your parishioners, while mine is aimed at the criminals. If we stay out of each other's way, things go smoothly—but not like this."

The bishop chuckled and eyed Balthasar, who stayed quiet in the corner of the hall, leaning against his walking staff. "We gathered intelligence, Herr Franz," Solomon began, "and had to act quickly. In your line of work, I'm sure you understand the value of acting expeditiously."

Heinrich studied the old bishop's wrinkled face and wry smile. *So smug*, he thought, shaking his head. *He thinks he can do anything he likes. He thinks he owns this town . . .*

Heinrich's heart quickened, and he stopped pacing in order to calm himself. "Under what charges did you arrest them?"

Vicar Balthasar reached into his robe, pulled out a roll of parchment, and handed it to the investigator. "Take your pick."

Heinrich grabbed the parchment and read over the charges. When he was done, he eyed the vicar and bishop and said, in a low tone, "It's still my authority to execute arrests."

Vicar Balthasar shook his head and said, "You're causing a ruckus for no reason, investigator. I get my authority from a higher power than the laws of man. I get my authority from Archbishop Ernst."

Heinrich felt his blood boil. "So do I! You know that!" he blurted, and immediately regretted his outburst.

Bishop Solomon eyed Heinrich and Balthasar suspiciously. Before Solomon could open his mouth, Heinrich added, "There is no higher power than the law."

The hall became stuffy and quiet. The investigator had overstepped his bounds, and he knew it. Claiming the laws of man superior to the laws of God could be considered heretical, and he'd just said it in front of the two most powerful clerics in Bedburg.

Bishop Solomon's mouth fell open, but Balthasar Schreib had other concerns. "What, exactly, is the archbishop giving you, Herr Franz, for what you're doing here in Bedburg? How much land and wealth are you getting from this? A new title, perhaps? And you still believe your 'laws' are greater than God's glory?" The Jesuit missionary leaned on his staff and raised his brow.

Heinrich stammered, trying to formulate a response. Before he could utter another word, the door at the top of the staircase shot open and crashed against the wall, shaking the entire jailhouse.

Tomas came running down the stairs. "My lord!" he shouted as he bumbled down the stairs. He stopped abruptly when he saw the bishop and vicar. With a bow he said, "Your Graces," and then turned to Heinrich. "My lord, the Protestants have begun their siege. Their general is Count Adolf, and he's attacking the eastern walls."

Bishop Solomon gasped and made the sign of the cross over his heart. "Lord have mercy on us all," he said, turning to Vicar Balthasar. "I believe that is our cue. Let us fortify ourselves in the church—I have provisions enough for us."

The vicar tapped his staff on the floor and narrowed his eyes on the old bishop. He cleared his throat and said, "My brother, while you fortify yourself with food and provisions, I will fortify our army's morale. It is my *duty* to do as much. You'd be well not to forget the sins of gluttony and sloth."

The bishop scowled at Balthasar's condescension, but before he could respond, more footsteps could be heard coming down the stairs.

Georg Sieghart walked into the hall, looking dazed. Heinrich looked at him from head to toe. His tunic and beard and chin were all caked in dark brown blood, and his face was splattered with red. His eyes were wild, as though he'd seen a phantom.

The vicar and bishop both gasped at the hunter's appearance.

"I found him wandering aimlessly around town, my lord," Tomas told Heinrich.

"Good God," Heinrich said, "it looks like you were rolling around with a butchered pig. What happened to you?"

Georg said nothing. He stared at the investigator with a blank look.

"Where's your *friend* . . . Konrad?" Heinrich said with more than a little spite.

"He's gone," Georg said.

Heinrich stared into the man's crazed eyes, but decided not to push the subject. Just by looking into Georg's eyes, he could tell that Konrad was likely dead. It was a shame, because Heinrich enjoyed the hunter's company, but he'd have to do away with him eventually. Georg was a menace to others, and to himself.

But right now there are more pressing matters.

Another long silence plagued the stuffy room, until Vicar Balthasar said, "I'm going to meet with General Ferdinand." He limped toward the stairs, his staff cracking against the stone floor.

Georg cocked his head toward Balthasar. "With a limp like that? I'll join you."

Heinrich waved at the hunter. "No, Georg, I need you for another matter. I'm going to arrest the murderer of Margreth Baumgartner, and I'd like your assistance."

"What about me, my lord?" Tomas asked.

"You may accompany us, Tomas."

Bishop Solomon said, "You've already found her killer, in a single day? Who is it?"

Heinrich frowned at the bishop. "None of your concern, Your Grace. Lord Werner pressured me to find the killer, and I believe I have. But please, go hole yourself up in your precious church." His eyes narrowed. "We wouldn't want anything . . . *bad* to befall our beloved bishop."

Bishop Solomon wrinkled his nose and waddled toward the investigator. He jabbed a finger in Heinrich's chest and said, "So you know . . . for all intents and purposes, Sybil Griswold and Dieter Nicolaus were killed in the initial attack by the Calvinists. Spread that to the public, if you must. Do you understand?"

The investigator stayed quiet, and just stared at the hunched old man.

The bishop snarled and bared his teeth at Heinrich, leaned close, and whispered, "If you wish to say otherwise, I'll be sure Lord Werner strips you of any title and rank, and *you'll* be the one rotting in a jail cell."

If Heinrich felt threatened, he didn't show it. He remained

stoic, and Solomon scowled and shuffled toward the stairs with Vicar Balthasar behind him.

"Sybil Griswold and Dieter Nicolaus?" Georg said.

Heinrich nodded. "The bishop and vicar arrested them. I didn't know about it."

Georg stormed past Heinrich, into the next room, and found Sybil and Dieter huddled together in the back of a cell.

At seeing Georg, Dieter jumped up and charged the bars. He gripped them tight, his knuckles turned white, and he said, "You're a dishonorable man."

Georg stared at Dieter with a solemn expression, but said nothing.

"Come on, my good hunter, we have things to do," Heinrich said from the other room.

The hunter sauntered back into the room and said, "No, I'm afraid I can't help you."

"What are you talking about? I'll get lost in the woods without you. We have to arrest Peter Griswold before he has a chance to escape Bedburg."

Georg shrugged. "I doubt he will be going anywhere, investigator—not while the Protestants are attacking. You know where to find him." The hunter pointed his chin toward his left arm. "This arm stopped working, so I can't even use a bow. I've also decided to help the Catholics ward off the Calvinists."

Heinrich's jaw dropped. "You've gone mad, Georg. You just said you can't use a bow, so what good would you be in a battle? And why would you fight? What allegiance do you owe these people?"

"I've lived without a purpose for too long, Heinrich. It's time I start helping, rather than hurting. Besides, what allegiance do I owe *you*?"

"We're partners! You'd rather help by *killing people*? What sort of logic is that?"

Georg shook his head. "You said it yourself, investigator. We aren't partners. I was simply your lee...lee-ay— "

"Liaison."

Georg sighed. "I'm going to follow General Ferdinand into battle, to protect this city. I won't feel like a coward any longer. And even with this lousy arm . . . I'd love for you to try and stop me."

Heinrich's ears went hot, and he could feel the veins in his neck pulsating. Rather than throwing a fit, he simply gestured to the hunter's blood-soaked clothes. "Whatever this is from . . . it's surely rattled your small brain."

"I suppose the savage hasn't been removed from my heart, investigator."

Tomas turned toward Heinrich and stiffened his posture. "I would like to accompany him, my lord," the soldier said, saluting.

Heinrich looked down his nose at the wiry guard. "No, Tomas, I don't think so."

"B-but, lord, my duty is to protect the town. I am a soldier of Bedburg."

"Your *duty* is to remain by my side, goddammit." Heinrich felt like shoving the soldier, but instead he just balled his hands into fists. "So you will gather three of your best scouts and meet me at the southern gate. Do you understand?"

Tomas' shoulders slumped, and he nodded slowly.

The three men walked toward the stairs, to part ways.

Before he reached the stairs, however, Heinrich turned and caught the attention of the quiet torturer, who stood vigilant at the end of the hall. "Ulrich," he said, "keep an eye on those cells. And make sure you don't kill them."

Ulrich grinned cruelly, and the scar on his face twisted as he smiled.

Just before dawn, in the darkest hours of night, the Calvinist Protestants staged their first assault on Bedburg's eastern walls.

CORY BARCLAY

At the same time, Heinrich Franz was crouched behind a wheelbarrow, near the southern gate, staring up at the guards patrolling the ramparts. Tomas was behind him, with three scouts.

At first, Heinrich had tried to simply waltz out of town, but the guards had stopped him. "It's too dangerous out there, my lord," one guard had told him. "No one is to leave or enter the city—even you. The Calvinists are in the eastern hills and woods, and it's only a matter of time before they converge southward."

Heinrich had cursed at the guard, but relented. He came up with a new plan, and he'd only need a few precious seconds to execute it.

"Scout . . . whatever your name is," he whispered to one of the soldiers. "You're going to be our decoy. See that bell?" Heinrich pointed away from the two guards who watched the gate, to a brass bell a few feet away from them. The bell served as the guards' alarm system.

The scout nodded to Heinrich.

"Throw a rock at it," the investigator said.

"A rock, my lord?" the scout asked, tilting his head a bit.

"Yes, a rock, an arrow, anything! Just make sure the bell rings out. When the guards go to check on it, we'll simply walk through the gate."

"What if the gate's locked?" Tomas asked.

"I'm sure it is," Heinrich said. His eyes moved to a small room on the ground level, beneath the ramparts, which led up to the guard-post. "The lever to lift the gate is in that room, which is why scout number two over here is going to lift it as we move. You might be caught, but I'll see that you aren't reprimanded."

The second scout looked skeptical.

Heinrich rolled his eyes. "I'm a lawman, dammit."

After reassuring their confidence, Heinrich put the plan into action. It was a simple one, even though the guards were on high alert.

The first scout crawled and headed straight toward the foot of the ramparts, while the other scout went left. Heinrich, Tomas,

267

and the third scout rose from their crouched positions and came out from behind the wheelbarrow.

Ting!

The guards on the wall jumped into action as the bell rattled and rang. They left their post, and as they did, the gate started to slowly rise.

Heinrich and his two followers strolled through the gate. The investigator could hear yelling from the ramparts, and yelling from one of his men. Only one of the decoy scouts made it outside, and Heinrich wasn't sure if it was the one who had rung the bell, or the one who had lifted the gate. It didn't matter.

The four of them ran through the countryside and headed toward Peter Griswold's estate.

When they reached the farmhouse, Heinrich noticed it was dark, which he'd expected.

"To the woods," he said.

They jogged their way toward the woods, with Heinrich trying to retrace his steps. They zigzagged south and then cut east over a crop of fields, up and down rolling hills. All of the men had guns brandished the entire time, in case they caught the eye of any Protestant scouting parties.

Heinrich felt alive in the darkness, with the crisp wind biting at his face and blowing in his hair and mustache.

Within half an hour, they'd traveled the two miles to the edge of the woods. Heinrich stopped and tried to calculate where they were, and where they would enter the trees. He needed to be certain, lest he get his envoy lost, which could have dire consequences once dawn broke the horizon and he was sitting near enemy lines.

He eventually shrugged and picked a spot that looked as good as any. The men wrestled with the trees and branches and foliage as they made their way through the woods in a methodical manner. The investigator found traces of footsteps—something he was thankful Georg had taught him to look out for—and he followed the steps until they finally came to the clearing.

Heinrich recognized the clearing, and he let out a sigh of relief. He crouched behind a large tree—the same one that he and Georg had originally hid behind—and squinted to find the cabin in the back of the clearing.

A candle flickered in the house, illuminating the single window.

Heinrich saw a glimpse of shadows in the cabin, and he smiled. "There will likely be at least three people in there—maybe more. Our target is a man who's missing his left hand. Don't kill that man. If there's a woman, don't kill her, either. I want them subdued, but not dead."

"What about anyone else inside?" Tomas asked.

Heinrich shrugged. "I don't care. Do what you will."

Without wasting any more time, Heinrich silently counted off and prepared to charge. He breathed in deep, clicked back the hammer of his handgun, and whispered, "Let's go."

The men split away from the tree and into the clearing.

Halfway through their charge, everything went wrong. The cabin door opened, and four people stepped out. As quiet as Heinrich and his men were, it was impossible to keep the footfall of four men silent in the woods.

All four people in front of the cabin turned in their direction.

Shouting erupted, and the four silhouettes took off running north, into the trees.

Heinrich bit down and ran toward the first, nearest man. Tomas and one of his scouts ran beside him. With their cover blown, everyone broke into full sprint.

Heinrich couldn't recognize the people he chased after. The four silhouettes split off in four different directions when they reached the trees.

Heinrich knew that time was a pressing issue—he was getting closer and closer to the Protestant encampment the further he went into the woods. He tried to run faster.

A large man jumped out from one of the trees as Heinrich passed, startling the investigator. The man swung a long knife overhead, and Heinrich's eyes went wide. He managed to lower his head, instinctively, and the knife passed right over him.

Hearing a grunt from behind, he turned his neck. The knife had caught the scout running behind Heinrich, slashing his throat. The scout fell, then Tomas appeared and shot the assailant in the head.

Heinrich pressed on. The trees whizzed by on both sides, eventually thinning out a bit. He heard Tomas running to catch up behind him, while the other scout was lost somewhere in the woods, chasing after one of the silhouettes.

Heinrich squinted and thought he noticed a man through the branches, running for his life, who had a stump where his hand should be.

The investigator jumped over undergrowth and then something caught his foot and he tripped and went sprawling forward. He gasped as he fell toward the ground.

Another man appeared from behind a tree and shot at the investigator. If Heinrich hadn't been falling, the bullet would have hit him square in the chest, but as it was, the bullet lodged itself in the tree behind him. Embers and bark chips cascaded onto Heinrich's back.

The investigator rolled to his side, groaning, and brought himself to his knees. He grabbed his gun, which he'd dropped as he fell.

Heinrich heard a scream and looked up.

Lars was charging at him. The barkeep had thrown away his gun after his shot missed, and now held a dagger high above his head.

The lanky man chopped down and grunted.

Without thinking, Heinrich lifted his gun.

Clang!—metal on metal rang out.

Lars clenched his jaw, pulled back, and hacked down again.

Heinrich tried to stand, but as he parried with the muzzle of his gun he was knocked back to the ground onto his back.

Lars looked up—away from Heinrich—with a confused expression on his face.

Heinrich coughed, and a shadow leaped over him. He blinked,

and Tomas was standing in front of him with a sword in his hands.

The soldier lunged forward and skewered the barkeep in the chest. The tip of his steel stuck out of Lars' back, and Lars coughed blood and crumbled to the ground. Tomas unhinged his sword from the barkeep's body, whose eyes were still wide with surprise as he died.

Heinrich panted and crawled on his hands and knees until he righted himself. He ran past Lars and Tomas, but could see no sign of Peter or the fourth runaway. His eyes searched around the forest as he tried to conjure any semblance of Georg's tracking expertise . . .

And he heard a rustling to his right.

The investigator jumped into action, but realized as he ran that he'd dropped his gun when Lars had tried to kill him. He swiped wood chips from his eyes and felt warm blood running down his cheek.

He came hurtling out of the trees and found himself at the bank of the Peringsmaar Lake. He stared at a face that looked back at him.

It was Peter Griswold, trying to run on the soggy, rocky sand. He was bigger than Heinrich, and slower, so the investigator quickly gained ground on the farmer.

Heinrich clenched his jaw as he drew within five steps of the farmer. He looked down at the man's boots, then lunged.

He caught Peter by the leg of his pants, pulled down, and went crashing onto the rocks.

Peter's left boot went flying from his foot, and he too went tumbling to the ground.

The farmer growled at Heinrich and they writhed and struggled against the sharp stones. Pain shot into Heinrich's back as a rock jutted into him. He howled.

Suddenly Peter's right hand was around Heinrich's throat, and he tried to straddle the investigator. He struggled to hold a strong grip with his one good hand, so he brought his left arm down, smashing his stump into Heinrich's face. Cartilage crunched and

Heinrich could feel blood gushing from his nose.

Peter reached back to smash him again.

Heinrich jabbed his knee into Peter's groin. The big farmer went down in a heap, grabbing his crotch and rolling to his side.

Heinrich scooted away from Peter and went to his knees. He snagged a large rock from the ground and jumped on Peter, rolling him onto his back. Heinrich's mind flashed with rage and everything got dizzy around him.

He found himself lifting the stone in the air, ready to shatter it on Peter's face, and all he could see was the farmer's eyes—shocked and horrified.

"I've got her!" a shout echoed from somewhere in the woods.

Heinrich spit blood on Peter and lifted the rock, then . . .

"I surrender!" Peter shouted, raising his hand and his stump into the air.

Heinrich's senses came whooshing back to him and he managed to steer the rock and smash it on another stone just inches from Peter's face.

Peter gasped. "Just don't hurt my sister, please!"

Heinrich huffed and tried to gather his breath. He rolled off Peter's stomach and fell to his back, heaving. Blood dripped into his mouth, nose, and eyes.

Tomas appeared from the trees, Katharina Trompen's body slung over his shoulder.

CHAPTER THIRTY-FOUR

GEORG

The sun burst through the clouds and signaled a new day in Bedburg. Despite the murders and scared townsfolk, the prior months had been relatively peaceful. But now that peace was shattered.

Smoke and screams filled the sky.

Count Adolf von Neuenahr, Calvinist commander of the Protestant forces, had besieged Bedburg throughout the night. He blasted the stone walls with dozens of cannons that were set up high on a hillside to the northeast of town.

Still, Adolf had not sent any foot-soldiers to charge the town. The defining battle of the Cologne War was being decided by a violent onslaught of cannons and catapults.

As morning came, Count Adolf ceased his assault.

Georg stood on the eastern ramparts of Bedburg. He stepped over a dead body and looked over the side of the wall. He shielded his eyes from the sun with his hand, and surveyed the wreckage in the countryside.

Adolf had split his regiment into three separate companies. One company was on the eastern hillside, guiding the artillery; another, below the hillside, hidden by trees; and the third company was a bit further south, in the deeper part of the woods.

Georg looked at the crumbling infrastructure of Bedburg's walls. *It's only a matter of time before he sends soldiers to charge this shoddy excuse for a barrier.*

The town wasn't prepared for such a violent attack. Their walls were small and weak. Their army was big enough, but scattered around different entrances of the city. Their palisades were made of cheap wood. People feared a rear attack from the western and southern parts of town.

All of these factors made the battle seem hopeless, and it looked as though Bedburg was doomed to be handed over to the Protestants.

"What do you see?"

Georg turned and watched as a tall man with a pointed beard and mustache walked in his direction. The man had the air of a leader, and Georg gave him a salute.

"Well, sir, if I may speak plainly—"

"Please do."

Georg pointed out toward the horizon. "Their artillery is protected by the company beneath the hill, but I think their southern battalion is lingering too far from their encampment. They're lost in the woods."

The man stroked his beard and nodded. "A fine observation. What do you suggest?"

Georg bobbed his head from left to right, thinking. "If it were up to me, I'd round up a fast group on horseback and attack that lingering company. I'd go through the woods to the south, out of their sight, and then head north along the Peringsmaar's embankment. Attack them with a hit-and-run to keep the men honest, so they can't diverge too far from their camp. That way, at least in my mind, we'd keep them from spreading and flanking the southern and western gates."

The tall man said, "And could you lead such a group?"

Georg stammered. He was still crusted in blood from the night before. He looked menacing, and did *not* have the air of a leader about him. "Me?" he asked, pointing at his own chest. "You don't even know me, sir."

"You're Georg Sieghart—'The Savage,' as they call you—are you not?"

274

Georg looked at the man with a sideways glance. "How do you know that?"

"Duke Farnese has told me about your endeavors on the field of battle. He told me to look for you—that you'd be here. You seem to have a mind for strategy, and you certainly look the part of a savage, if you don't mind me saying." The man gestured at Georg's bloody garb.

"Not at all," Georg said, smiling. *So this is Ferdinand of Bavaria,* he thought. *Older brother of Archbishop Ernst, and one of our greatest generals.*

Georg had never met the man, but he'd heard of Ferdinand's many successes in battle. He looked at the general in a new light, and could see the steely eyes of a hardened commander—and the stalwart face of someone who was used to having things go his way. Besides a collared gable around his neck, he wasn't adorned in flashy armor or special accoutrements. He looked like most other soldiers, except maybe a bit older, with just a wisp of dark hair on his otherwise bald head. It was his face that showed his experience and stature.

"How many men would you need to head up that southern side? I figure you could at least *scare* the bastards." Ferdinand smiled. "It shouldn't be too hard given your current appearance."

Georg chuckled and faced the ground.

"I have a mind to set Commander Baumgartner against the two center companies," Ferdinand said. "It would be nice to have a flanking group to keep that southern company busy and away from Baumgartner's sides."

Georg thought for a moment, and then looked below at the soldiers on the battlefield. There were hundreds of men in the woods, and the battle would be a guerrilla fight—dangerous at best, suicide at worst.

Ferdinand seemed to notice the doubt in Georg's eyes. "I wouldn't ask you to stay on the field, Herr Sieghart. A toe-to-toe fight with those folks would be foolish. Just a quick skirmish—either you scare them into following you, or you scare them back to their main regiment."

"I could do it with a hundred smart men," Georg said with confidence in his voice.

"Done," Ferdinand said. "That company has at least double that . . . are you sure you just need a hundred? You seem to be missing the use of your left arm."

Georg looked down at his arm. It dangled uselessly at his side.

"You should get that bullet wound checked out, before it festers."

"I can do it with a hundred men," Georg repeated.

Ferdinand threw up his arms. "Very well—I can't argue with that. I'll put you in charge. Wait for an hour, until that company is having their morning meal, and then I'll order Commander Baumgartner to strike. Be ready to do the same." The general strolled away without another word.

"As you wish, my lord," Georg whispered under his breath, but Ferdinand was already too far to hear.

And just like that, Georg had become a commander in General Ferdinand's army.

I'm assuming he gave me my position out of necessity, rather than merit, Georg thought. As he doubted himself, he wondered how many able-minded commanders the Bavarian general actually had at his disposal.

Does the Bedburg garrison—with its Catholic soldiers and Spanish mercenaries and reinforcements from Cologne—actually have the manpower to defeat these bastards?

He stared at the faces of the young men he would lead, and he couldn't help but feel guilty. *My plan was so hasty . . . what if it doesn't work? Many of these men will never see another sunset. In fact, there's a chance none of us will.*

He hadn't led a raiding party in years, and he hadn't been referred to as "Sieghart the Savage" in just as long.

He shook his head and pushed the thoughts of doubt from his mind. He wouldn't back down from this challenge. He would make General Ferdinand proud, to the best of his abilities.

I will not be a coward any longer.

The sun rose higher in the sky, and the hour spent gathering the soldiers passed quickly. He had a hundred men at the southern wall, mounted and ready to go. They were a hodgepodge of a group—each man had a patchwork of armor and weapons. Georg would not be leading a highly trained and cohesive unit, like he was used to.

He had sixty arquebusiers and forty pikemen. He assumed many of his men were Spanish mercenaries—not because of what they wore or how they looked, but because they were more interested in the spoils of war than the actual outcome.

That's probably why they agreed to go on this mission in the first place.

After the hour expired, Georg led his group out of the southern gate. The walls of the town hid them, and they made a wide circle to get to the eastern woods. They galloped around the woods and came to the embankment of the Peringsmaar Lake.

His plan was to surprise the southern Protestant company, hit them quick, and then flee, hoping to draw them away from their main army. He expected artillery fire to start soon after they hit the Protestants, and he prayed that his group's horses were fit and fast.

As he made it to the southern bank of the Peringsmaar, Georg gave a signal. His horse broke into a full gallop, with a hundred other horses doing the same. They barreled over small dunes and rocks as they trudged up the coastline.

In the distance, Georg saw men on horseback. He immediately knew something was wrong. They weren't part of the southern company—they were too far from their main army.

That's a scouting party, he thought.

There were twenty men, and Georg hoisted his gun in the air. "Route them!" he shouted to his men. They broke off into a ragged 'V' formation. "Don't let them escape—they'll warn the larger company!"

Georg knew that if even one of these men managed to make it to the southern encampment, his entire preemptive strike was blown.

The Calvinist horsemen, seeing Georg's approaching force, wheeled around, trying to flee up the coastline. The scouts turned in their saddles and shot at Georg's party.

Georg closed in on one of the fleeing men and aimed his gun. He waited for his steed to settle, bounced up on his saddle, then—as his rear fell back on his horse—leveled his gun and fired.

The man went down with a scream and toppled off his horse.

Bullets whipped by Georg's face. He holstered his gun and unsheathed his sword from his belt. He squeezed tight to his horse with his knees, unable to hold the reins with his left hand. A less-experienced rider would have fallen in seconds.

Georg brought himself alongside another fleeing scout, and could see the man's scared, blue eyes. He was no more than eighteen years of age.

Georg slashed at the young man's back. He gave a primal scream and lifted his bloody sword in the air as the man fell from his horse.

One of Georg's men flew by and leaned forward in his saddle. He stopped abruptly as a bullet found his neck, and he went flying backwards, off his horse. His steed kept moving.

Georg rode beside another enemy. This one had an arquebus, and the man aimed his gun at Georg's face.

The hunter's eyes went wide as he ducked low in his saddle.

The scout's gun erupted in smoke. The bullet whizzed by Georg's shoulder, combining with the noises around him to create a piercing ringing in his ears.

Georg leaned forward and stabbed, sticking the man beneath the ribs. He didn't wait to see if the man lived or not. As he rode past the wounded man, he realized he was running out of real estate on the bank of the lake. They were coming to a hill—the same hill he and Heinrich had originally climbed when they first spotted the Protestant army.

Georg scanned the battlefield: A few of the Protestants were ditching their horses and jumping into the woods. Then more of the horsemen followed.

"Shit," Georg said under his breath. *We don't have enough time to stop them all.*

As he kept scanning the field, he saw something and cursed. He noticed black dots on the hillside—a group of infantrymen were charging down and screaming. A red banner was erected somewhere in the middle of the group.

This was the southern company that Georg had been looking for. Now the enemy had the higher ground, and they poured over the hillside in alarming numbers.

Georg tried to keep himself from panicking, but his heart felt like it was going to leap from his chest. His horse kept charging forward, but many of his men were too scared to follow.

The men at the top of the hill crouched into a long line and leveled their guns.

Then they fired on Georg's group, as a single unit. The rest of their scouts retreated behind their line.

Smoke drifted into the sky, and horses and soldiers fell all around him, in unison.

Georg's horse whinnied and reared up on its hind legs. He gazed over his shoulder, at his men, and the situation looked dire.

Georg's steed was hit in the stomach while it was on its back legs, and it started to topple to the ground.

The hunter pitched over his saddle, falling to the rocky ground. He moaned and rolled onto his back, spitting out sand. He crawled to his feet and shouted with a raspy voice, "Fall back! Retreat!"

Another round of gunfire shot off and, a moment later, another round of soldiers screamed as they fell. One of the men was staring at Georg and was about to say something until the side of his head suddenly exploded.

Georg took the reins of the dead man's horse and leaped onto the saddle. He wheeled the steed around and kicked it in the side.

He and his remaining soldiers headed south.

The Protestants did not pursue.

As the wary, demoralized group made their way back to Bedburg in defeat, Georg realized he'd lost sixteen arquebusiers and thirteen pikemen—nearly a third of his force—in a matter of seconds.

He cursed himself. He'd failed his general, and he knew the rest of the Catholic army would suffer because of his misjudgment.

CHAPTER THIRTY-FIVE

DIETER

In a dark cellar of Bedburg's jailhouse, Dieter and Sybil listened to cannon-fire striking the walls of the town. The rumbling shook the foundation of the jail, and dust rained down from the ceiling, covering Dieter and Sybil in a sheet of dirt.

The explosions and yelling above-ground seemed to go on for hours. Dieter had no idea if it was night or day, or if Bedburg still belonged to the Catholics. He figured that a Protestant soldier might come down the stairs at any moment, either to kill him and Sybil, or to release them. He hoped it might be Pastor Hanns Richter who would come to their rescue.

Sybil kept staring out from the bars, to the cell across from them. A small figure stayed hunched in the shadowy corners of the chamber.

Sybil became agitated when she overheard Investigator Franz's plan to arrest her father for the murder of Margreth Baumgartner. "I know my father and the investigator disliked each other, but there's no way Investigator Franz could ever do such a thing. It's all false!"

Dieter didn't put much faith in the lawman's integrity. He also knew that a father would go to any length to protect his child— even if it meant killing. But why go after Margreth, and not Johannes? It made no sense to him.

Dieter remembered Peter's confession. *It was Johannes who caused his family so much grief. Margreth was just a noisy nuisance.*

Dieter's head started to ache, and he couldn't think about Peter or Heinrich or Johannes or Margreth any longer. He put his hand on Sybil's shoulder and said, "I'm going to marry you when we get out of this, Beele." He noticed that the girl was still focused elsewhere. "I'm going to take care of your—of *our*—child."

"How are you going to do that? And what makes you think we'll get out of here?" Sybil asked coldly.

Dieter was baffled, but he smiled nonetheless. "I converted to your faith," he whispered. His smile quickly faded as he registered the second half of Sybil's question. *How in God's name can I talk of marriage and children when we're sitting in this frigid cell?*

They hadn't been given any food, and they'd been in custody for hours. They were starving, parched, and a big lump was starting to form on the back of Dieter's head. It was tender and painful to touch, but he didn't complain. For Sybil's sake, he tried to stay positive.

Every once in a while, Ulrich would amble by them and smile with a dark look on his face. He wouldn't say anything, but his presence was enough to make Dieter shiver.

When the small figure in the shadows of the other cell started sobbing quietly, Sybil's eyes turned soft. She squinted, as if she recognized the face.

Finally, the prisoner lifted his head for a split moment, to wipe away his tears.

"M-Martin?" Sybil said with a shocked look.

The prisoner's head perked up, and the person crawled out of the shadows and into the dim light. His face was grimy and scruffy, and though he was still just an adolescent, he looked more like a man than a boy.

"Beele?" said a small voice. It was indeed Martin Achterberg—Bishop Solomon's former altar boy; murderer of his own father; the boy who Sybil had been arranged to marry, years ago.

Judging by his filthy face and tunic, it looked like Martin hadn't been let out of his cell in months.

"My God, it *is* you!" Sybil exclaimed.

"Quiet in there, bitch!" Ulrich shouted from across the hall.

Sybil looked back through the bars and whispered, "How long have you been in here, Martin?"

"I've lost track of time," Martin said, shrugging. "No one will tell me anything, and I haven't eaten in days, I think. Why don't they just kill me?"

Dieter frowned, suspecting that he knew the answer. He'd seen Martin leave Bishop Solomon's chambers numerous times, at the strangest hours. He tried not to imagine what sort of horrors took place in those chambers.

Solomon is waiting to use the boy for something, Dieter told himself. *Maybe as a false witness in a trial . . . maybe as a personal servant.* He shuddered at the thought.

Sybil spoke with Martin at length, in low whispers. The scruffy adolescent was fifteen now—at least by his own estimation. He said Bishop Solomon would come visit him every so often, but would never give Martin a definitive answer regarding his future. The way Martin explained it, Dieter felt the bishop was just toying with the boy, which caused the former priest to fume.

Dieter's heart felt heavy. He'd found so much hate in the recent days—with Georg Sieghart's betrayal, the malice of Bishop Solomon, Johannes von Bergheim's terrible deeds. It was becoming harder and harder to forgive and forget.

At one point, much to Dieter's chagrin, Sybil and Martin started talking about Karl Achterberg's murder. It was hard for Dieter to listen to, but he couldn't stop himself.

"You don't understand, Beele," Martin began. "Yes, I hated my father. He stole Dorothea from me. But that wasn't all."

"What do you mean?" Sybil asked.

Martin struggled to get the words out. He paused for a moment to gather himself, and with a voice that was on the verge of tears, he said, "You have no idea how terrible it was to be in the care of the bishop. The things he did to me . . . the things he made me do to him. I was miserable, but I had to relay whatever information I could back to my father. He made me a spy for his own twisted goals. He never cared about me. My father forced me into that arrangement, Beele, just like he tried to force me into marrying you . . ." Martin's eyes went wide and he grabbed the bars of his cell. "I-I didn't mean for it to sound like that," he exclaimed.

Sybil frowned. "It's fine, Martin, I . . . I understand what it's like to be forced into something against your will. My father did the same to me, just recently."

Martin hesitated. "I'm sorry, Beele. It seems we come from the same stock." He tried to smile, but then his face became hard and distant. "I couldn't stand it any longer. I could put up with the bishop's impulses, but when my father stole Dorothea from me . . . my love . . . that was the end. I'm not insane, Beele, you have to know that."

"I know Martin. I think you're stronger than you know."

Martin smiled, probably for the first time in months. As he did, Ulrich walked into the room. The punisher smacked the bars of Sybil's cell with the handle of a knife. The bars rattled and Sybil flew away from them with a yelp.

"I told you to shut up!" Ulrich said, pointing the butt of the knife toward Sybil. When all was quiet, he added, "You have visitors," and disappeared back into the other room.

Time seemed to slow as Dieter watched two figures enter the hall. Behind Bishop Solomon a smaller person followed. Dieter squinted to see who it was.

Sister Salome stepped forward.

What is she doing here?

"As I mentioned earlier," Solomon said, walking up to Sybil and Dieter's cell. "You undermined me for the last time, Father Nicolaus, and in front of Lord Werner no less. I have all the evidence I need to put you in the ground. But before I do, I feel obligated to let you know where my evidence stemmed from."

Dieter was baffled. *No,* he thought, *it can't be.*

Sister Salome stepped forward shyly. Her hands were clasped

in front of her, and she faced the ground, as usual.

"Tell him what you know, Salome," Solomon urged.

The nun stared at Dieter for a long moment, as if studying his face. Her hands shook, her eyes were barely open, but she seemed to look at Dieter as though she pitied him. She cleared her throat. "I . . . I found a copy of that damnable book, the *Ninety-Five Theses*, when I was preparing your sermon the other day, Father." There was a dark tone in her voice that Dieter didn't recognize. It didn't sound like the quiet, trustworthy nun he'd always known.

"I witnessed you stealing away into the woods after Pastor Richter was released and banished. I saw your visit with the Protestant blasphemer!" Her voice rose, and she was on the verge of hysterics. "I saw your baptism in the pond." Her shaking hands trembled even more. "How could you do that, Father? How could you betray your own people? Your eyes, they . . ." she trailed off and then turned her gaze to Sybil, who was sitting against the back wall of the cell. "Your eyes were blinded by this . . . by this . . . *succubus!*"

The nun's words turned into screeches, and Dieter saw the real Salome for the first time. She was unable to control her rage. Dieter looked into those angry eyes and saw something, and that's when he put the pieces together and realized why she felt scorned and betrayed.

It's jealousy, he thought, resting his forehead against the cold bars. The mild-mannered, plain woman who always kept to the fringes—invisible and undistinguished—and always had her eyes looking at the floor . . . Dieter finally saw the burning pain behind those lucid eyes. *It's not anger or evil in her heart that brought her to do this to me.* Dieter shook his head. *On the contrary—like any other person in the world, she just wants to feel loved and recognized. I . . . failed at that.*

Even though she went behind my back, I can't think of a person who deserves my forgiveness more.

A sudden surge of pain shot through his stomach, rose into his heart, and he felt that uncontrollable fury again. He frowned, and thought, *No . . . it isn't my life I care about.* Locked in his inner turmoil, Dieter glanced at Sybil, who wore a confused expression on her face. He had remained silent for quite a while, and it seemed as though everyone in the room was waiting for his response. *You hurt Sybil, Sister Salome. You put my love in harm's way, and that is unacceptable. That is something I cannot forgive.*

Dieter shook his head and turned away from the nun.

"Look at me, Father! Look at me!" Salome screamed.

Dieter would not.

Salome started bawling, and she put her head in her hands. Then she ran from the room.

Dieter felt no pity for the woman. He felt . . . empty. Soulless.

Bishop Solomon chuckled. "Now that you know the truth, Dieter, can you find peace with God? Do you see what you've done to that poor woman, and to my congregation?"

Dieter narrowed his eyes on the bishop. "You're a sad, petty man, Solomon," he spat. "You are no man of God. You live in decadence, surrounded by corruption, fueled by pride." The former priest walked up to the bars and grabbed them, trying to stick his head as far through the empty space as he could. "You are a disgrace to Catholics," he said in an angry whisper. "I may die, but my soul will be exempt from pain and agony. I will find salvation. I *will* see God's glorious face. You, however, will wallow in your pitiful life, forced to live in seclusion, with hate in your heart—devoid of love or forgiveness."

Dieter's knuckles turned white as he gripped the bars of the cell and cleared his throat. "I forgive you, bishop, but I *pity* you even more. When you are judged, you will burn in Hell for your constant sins and abuses." Dieter released his hands from the bars and threw them in the air. "So do your worst to me. But know that I will leave this earth as a Christian, with my head held high. You cannot break me, Solomon. You can break my body and my bones, but you will never break my spirit or my soul."

Bishop Solomon's smile disappeared. His face turned from smug and proud, to shocked and horrified, and he became as white as a ghost. His temper got the best of him, and he snarled at

Dieter. He banged on the bars of the jail cell with his old, frail hands. The bars barely rattled.

Dieter just laughed.

"Punisher!" Solomon shouted. "Get in here!"

When the scarred man entered the room, the bishop screamed and pointed his finger at Dieter. "He says he cannot be broken, good sir. I want you to prove him wrong! Find out what he knows about the Calvinist army."

Ulrich nodded, and then smiled at Dieter and Sybil with his gap-filled grin.

The bishop turned to leave, and his robe billowed in the air.

"Have a blessed life, Your Grace!" Dieter shouted to the old man, who cursed and shook his fists in the air as he made his way to the stairs.

"What would you have me do with them after I get your information, Your Grace?" Ulrich asked before Solomon was gone.

Solomon growled. "Kill them! I want no evidence that these heretics ever existed, or ever stepped foot in my church!"

"No!" Martin cried from the other cell.

The bishop spun on his heels and pointed at the boy. His voice softened. "Don't worry, Martin. You'll be back in my care shortly."

Martin started sobbing, and he crawled back to the shadowy corner of his cell.

Ulrich stepped away for a moment, and came back with a whetstone and a cruel-looking dagger. As he sharpened the blade in front of Dieter, he smiled. "It's about time I had some fun."

CHAPTER THIRTY-SIX

SYBIL

Sybil tried to keep from trembling as she watched Ulrich prepare his barbaric tools. He had knives and pliers and scissors of various sizes and shapes splayed on a table in the center of the hallway. He gingerly ran his hand over a pair of pliers, and then moved to a rusty set of scissors. He stroked his chin, and then moved his hand back to the pliers.

Ulrich seemed to relish in his preparation. He was like an actor in a play, setting the gruesome scene to come. Sybil could tell that, for whatever reason, this man genuinely enjoyed inflicting pain on others.

Martin was a wreck. He wept and tried to hide his face in his knees.

Sybil tried to calm him down. "It's going to be okay, Martin. Everything will be fine—just look away."

"Yes," Ulrich said while sharpening his tools, "everything will be fine." He grinned.

"You don't have to do this, Ulrich," Dieter said.

"I know I don't, priest. But I want to." Ulrich stared at Dieter with a blank look. He shrugged. "Besides, orders are orders. You heard the bishop."

"I know there's a good man beneath all that hate. Please, I'll tell you whatever you want to know," Dieter pleaded. His voice quivered.

"I know you will," Ulrich said, lifting the pliers and inspecting them. "But that wouldn't be very enjoyable."

When he was done perusing his wares, he sighed and let out a deep breath. He left the room for a moment, and came back with a small chair, which he placed in front of the table. "I doubt you have much to tell me, anyway," he said to Dieter.

"Then why are you doing this?"

Ulrich crossed his arms over his chest, didn't bother to respond, and looked back and forth between Sybil and Dieter. "Now . . . who's going to go first?"

"I will," Dieter said without hesitation.

Ulrich chuckled. "It's not that simple, priest." He pointed his pliers at Dieter, and then at Sybil, and then back to Dieter. He repeated this for some time, while counting silently to himself. After a minute of tense anticipation, the damp air in the room seemed to thicken.

Finally, his hand slowed, and it ended on Sybil. With a last-second motion, he pointed the pliers at Dieter. "You're a lucky man, priest," Ulrich said, showing his gap-riddled smile.

The torturer opened the cell with a key, and Sybil ran up to him. Ulrich easily shoved her to the back of the cell, and then reached and grabbed Dieter's wrists.

Dieter struggled for a moment, but he was too weak and malnourished. He was dragged from the cell. Martin yelped, but Sybil held back her emotions, refusing to let out so much as a whimper.

I won't give this savage the satisfaction of seeing me suffer, she thought. She sat at the back of the cell in painful silence.

Ulrich pushed Dieter down onto the chair, and then strapped his left hand behind his back. He took Dieter's right hand and slammed it on the table, and then wrapped his wrist with a rope.

Dieter wiggled his fingers and moved his hand, but that was all the mobility he could muster.

Ulrich took the pliers and tapped them on the table. "What do you know about the Protestant army?" he asked. He seemed bored, as if his questions had been rehearsed.

"God as my witness, I know nothing of their plans. I simply met with the pastor to—"

Dieter let out a bloodcurdling scream as Ulrich twisted his thumbnail out of its socket and tore it from his hand.

As Dieter howled, Sybil covered her ears and clenched her eyes shut. Martin started babbling to himself.

Ulrich pressed down on the tender flesh and blood dribbled around the wound.

Dieter gnashed his teeth.

"If you bite down too hard," Ulrich said, "you'll break your lovely smile. I've seen it happen. Just let it out." He kept squeezing Dieter's thumb, and Dieter groaned.

Ulrich picked up the pliers again. "Are the Calvinists bringing reinforcements? Why are they only attacking the town with cannons?"

Dieter's eyes blinked. He blurted out, "Because they plan on starving Bedburg!"

Ulrich tapped his bloody pliers against the scar on his cheek. "Hm," he said, and then shook his head. "You're lying. Bedburg could last weeks, and the Protestants don't have that kind of time to waste." He stretched Dieter's index finger, clamped the pliers down, and ripped off the nail.

Dieter coughed. Blood started to drip down his forearm and pool on the table.

"Try again, priest. Why are the Protestants only using cannons, rather than using soldiers?"

"Because it's working!" Dieter shouted. He began heaving.

Ulrich chuckled. "How would you know? You've been in here since the siege began." With that, he ripped the nail from Dieter's middle finger. "This is going to get a lot worse before it gets better. Why don't you think before you say whatever first comes to your head?"

With every nail that Ulrich pulled, Dieter became more reserved. Besides the initial shock, the pain began to numb his senses.

From upstairs, there was the familiar sound of the jailhouse door opening. Footsteps pounded down the stairs.

Dieter looked away from his hand and grimaced.

"Look at your hand, priest, or I'll pluck your eyeballs from your skull."

The warning was enough for Dieter to turn back and stare at his bloody hand, unblinking.

"Stay strong," Sybil called from inside the cell.

Ulrich looked over his shoulder "If you don't stay quiet, I'll switch you out with your lover, right now."

"How are things going here?" asked a voice from behind the torturer.

Dieter tried to look at the person behind Ulrich, but his eyes were blurred with sweat, and he couldn't recognize the figure.

Ulrich growled and said, "Get out of here. Can't you see I'm busy working?"

"And a fine job you're doing, punisher, but you're going to want to see this."

Ulrich sighed, put his hand on Dieter's shoulder, and stood to his full height. He tossed the pliers onto the table and turned around. "What the hell is—"

There was a loud thump. Ulrich's body went stiff, and then the torturer wobbled in place. He fell over and crashed into the table, scattering his instruments onto the stone floor. Because his hand was roped to the table, Dieter went with it and fell on his side.

Dieter grunted, then furrowed his brow and squinted.

Georg Sieghart stood over Ulrich's body. He held the pommel of a sword in his hand. The hunter bent down and shuffled around in Ulrich's tunic, until he found a set of keys. He flipped his sword around and cut away Dieter's bindings. He grabbed the cloth that Ulrich's tools had been set on, and wrapped it around Dieter's hand. Then he helped the weary priest to his feet.

Dieter gasped and looked at Georg, confused. He clutched his hand.

Georg moved to the jail cell and used key after key, until one of them clicked and the gate opened. He glanced at Dieter and said, "Am I still a dishonorable man?"

Sybil jumped out from the cell and leaped into Dieter's arms, helping him to stay standing.

Dieter wheezed and said, "I-I'm sorry, Herr Sieghart. I owe you an apology, and my life."

"So soon?"

Dieter nodded. "I've learned that it wasn't you who publicized our secret."

"You're damn right it wasn't." Georg sighed and kicked Ulrich's unconscious body in the leg. "Let's get going. I have no idea how long this big bastard will stay sleeping."

"Wait!" Sybil cried. She ran over to Martin's cell. The boy was still distraught, and was still talking to himself. "We have to release him . . . please, I beg of you."

Georg peered into the cage, and then he turned to Sybil with a look of disbelief on his face. "You realize that's the same kid who butchered his father right before my eyes, don't you, my lady?"

"I know. But he's not that boy anymore." She put her hands together, like she was praying. "Please."

"You're right, he's not that boy," Georg said. "He's a murderer. I've seen it."

"I'll take responsibility for the boy," Dieter said. "Just please give Beele the key."

Georg hesitated, and then sighed and finally handed the keys to Sybil. She unlocked the gate. Martin was barefoot, and more than a little skittish, but Sybil helped him out of the cell.

"You people need to leave Bedburg right away. We're losing the battle for the city," Georg said.

"Where will we go?" Dieter asked.

Georg ran a hand through his beard. Flakes of crusted blood fell to the ground. He reached into his tunic and came out with a few pieces of silver. "Take this money—it should be enough to get you passage from the Dutch shore. Go to London. People will accept you there—Queen Elizabeth is a Protestant sympathizer." Georg used his hand to gesture directions. "Head west out of Bedburg, and keep going west. Don't stop or look back until you reach Amsterdam, or the sea. Take a ship from there—it shouldn't be too difficult."

"We can't accept your money, Georg," Dieter said.

"Like hell you can't." Georg put his one good hand on his hip. "Now is not the time to act prideful, Father. Just take it and leave. Try and stay hidden as you travel through the countryside. Take the woods if you must, but stay away from the roads."

Dieter looked to the ground, and his body seemed to deflate. "Thank you, Herr Sieghart." He suddenly reached out and embraced the hunter, who looked baffled, to say the least.

Dieter pulled back once Georg gave no sign of returning the embrace. "Why are you helping us?" he asked.

Georg shrugged and scratched his head. "I'm not sure. I guess I might . . . sort of . . . *like* you people." He frowned. "I suppose I might see something in you two that I once shared with someone, a long time ago. Get out of this cesspool and make a life for yourselves."

Dieter and Sybil both smiled at the hunter. Dieter asked, "Where will you go?"

"I have a few errands to take care of."

Georg didn't elaborate, so Dieter simply nodded to him. Then he took Sybil's hand, and Martin's, and the trio ran past Georg and headed for the stairs. When he was at the bottom of the stairs, Dieter turned and said, "By the way, Herr Sieghart. I overheard you talking with Heinrich and the clerics earlier . . . and I know you're wrong."

Georg furrowed his brow. "About what?"

"You're not a coward, or a savage. In fact, you might be guilty of being a good man."

Georg smiled at the priest, and then Dieter disappeared up the stairwell.

CHAPTER THIRTY-SEVEN

HEINRICH

Heinrich and Tomas arrived at the jailhouse with Peter Griswold and Katharina Trompen. The place was in disarray. Ulrich was sitting on a chair, hunched over and nursing a nasty lesion on his forehead. His tools were scattered on the ground.

Heinrich took one look at the torturer and then surveyed the rest of the hall. Dieter Nicolaus' and Sybil Griswold's cell was open, and they were gone, as was Martin Achterberg. Heinrich cursed under his breath. He had wanted to use Martin as a witness against Peter, since he knew the Achterbergs hated the Griswolds. Now he would need to force a confession out of Peter, unless Martin was found. And since Sybil was also gone, he couldn't threaten the farmer with Sybil's well-being.

Unless Peter never learns that she escaped . . .

Heinrich kept Katharina and Peter upstairs, in the care of Tomas, while he asked Ulrich, "Why are your tools on the ground? Who ordered you to use them?"

"Bishop Solomon came in with that ugly nun. The priest really pissed off the bishop. Solomon wanted me to squeeze information out of the priest and then kill him and the girl."

"I'm assuming you didn't?"

"Didn't get the chance."

Solomon really believes he can take the law into his own hands, Heinrich thought, shaking his head. *Only I can do that.*

Heinrich looked at the floor and noticed dried spots of blood around the turned-over table. "Who helped them escape?"

Ulrich groaned as he massaged his tender, bruised forehead. He shrugged. "It happened so fast. I'm not sure. As you can see, someone bumped my head pretty good."

"You'll live," Heinrich said. He twirled his wispy mustache. After a brief moment of silent contemplation, he thought he had a good idea of who rescued the priest and the girl. It didn't matter right then, though. He had to move quickly.

"Pick up your tools and put them away," Heinrich ordered. "The table, too."

Ulrich nodded, slowly rose from his chair, and went about retrieving his pliers and scissors and knives.

"Tomas, bring down the prisoners," Heinrich shouted once Ulrich's table and utensils were stowed away. The soldier came down the stairs with Peter and Katharina in front of him. The captives' hands were bound behind their backs.

Heinrich pointed to the cell where Sybil and Dieter had been. "Put Herr Griswold in that cell." Then he motioned to the door at the end of the hall, which led to another room of jail cells. "Put the woman in that room."

Tomas nodded, pushing Peter into the cell and slamming the gate shut. He took Katharina to the end of the hall, then disappeared into the next room.

"I, uh, don't have my keys," Ulrich said, feeling around his tunic. "They must have taken them."

Heinrich sighed and frowned. "Get creative," he told Ulrich. Then he walked to the end of the hall and went into the next room, where Tomas was closing the gate on Katharina. He took a step toward the soldier and grabbed him by the arm. "I want you to retrieve Peter's son from his estate," he whispered. "He's young, so it should be simple. Bring him here."

"Yes, my lord," Tomas said, saluting. He left the room.

"I'll deal with you in a bit," Heinrich told Katharina. The gray-haired woman stayed quiet and pursed her lips.

As Heinrich watched her for a moment, a thought came to him. He pondered it while continuing to gaze at her for nearly ten more minutes. Finally, he returned to the room where Peter was jailed.

Staring at the man through the bars, Heinrich sighed. He took Ulrich's chair, set it in front of Peter's cell, and sat down.

"Where's my daughter and son? I want guarantees that they'll be safe," Peter said. He looked exhausted.

"It's too late for that, Peter. I can't guarantee those things." Heinrich stretched his arms out wide. "I don't know how to say this easily . . . but your daughter and Father Dieter Nicolaus were killed in the initial Protestant attack."

Peter's face remained stoic and blank. "I don't believe you."

"My men identified their bodies before we came to your sister's house."

Peter tried to stay strong for a long while, but his lips finally started to quiver. His narrow eyes grew wide and looked suddenly soft and dejected. "I failed her," he said. "I pushed her right into that bastard's arms, and now I'll never be able to tell her I'm sorry. Please, tell me you're lying. Tell me she's alive."

"Which bastard would that be?" Heinrich asked as he pulled a piece of parchment from his tunic.

"Johannes von Bergheim."

Heinrich raised an eyebrow. "And now your own people have killed her," he said, referring to the Protestants. He felt a slight pang of guilt—*The things I do to uncover the truth*—but it quickly subsided.

Peter studied Heinrich's face as the investigator scribbled on the parchment. He cocked his head and said, "I still don't believe you. For a man who claims to seek the truth, you aren't a very good liar, Herr Franz."

"Believe what you will," Heinrich said, shrugging. "But if you want a different fate for your son, you will cooperate."

"Hugo?"

Heinrich nodded. "Your son is probably alone and scared at

your estate, as we speak. We have you, Peter, and if you cooperate, I will promise that Hugo will be safe. Your time in Bedburg is finished, but your legacy doesn't have to end here."

Peter sat down against the back wall of the cell. "Katharina?"

"She told me everything. I know you were abetting, feeding, and funding the Calvinists. You're much more significant to their army than I originally realized." He ran a hand through his hair and sighed. "Even though you might not be a violent person."

"Katharina would never say such things."

"I was surprised, too, that she spoke so easily. Maybe she's just tired of all this madness."

Peter leaned against the wall and scratched the back of his head with the grainy stone. "What is it you're charging me with, exactly?"

"Well, treason, of course. And the murder of Margreth Baumgartner—you're the only person I've found who had a motive to kill the noblewoman."

"You know I did no such thing," Peter growled. "She was just a silly girl."

"It doesn't matter, Peter. How do you think Arnold Baumgartner will react at trial? That 'silly girl' was the daughter of our garrison commander . . . a man fighting for our city's survival, as we speak. Do you really think the word of a traitor will outweigh the testimony of such an esteemed leader? He will be seeking vengeance, and he will get it."

Peter spat on the ground. "You're a dog."

Heinrich ignored the farmer and raised both hands, palms facing up. "Or, on the other hand, you could save your sister and son by confessing to the multiple crimes you're charged with. Why not save the ones who you hold most dear? Would you really let your own kin suffer for *your* transgressions?"

Peter shook his head and shouted, "I killed no one, dammit!"

Heinrich responded by raising his voice, too. "Don't be so blind, Peter! You practically slept with the enemy!" He stood from his chair and grabbed the cell's bars. He was seething—a rare moment of discomposure for the investigator—but he quickly calmed himself.

Peter paused, a smile slowly forming on his face. "And what if the Calvinists take your city, Heinrich? What then, when you have no trial to conduct?"

"I suppose this will all have been for naught. But I wouldn't count on that so soon, for your family's sake. A lot can happen between now and Bedburg's fall . . ." Heinrich trailed off and watched as Peter's wry smile turned into a disheartened frown.

Peter stayed silent for a moment, and then cleared his throat. "If you can promise me the safety of my son and sister, what would you have me say?"

Heinrich nodded firmly, feeling like he was finally getting somewhere. He rolled the cuffs of his sleeves to his elbows, and sat back down. "I'd have you confess to killing Margreth Baumgartner. Your motive was to eliminate her from interfering with the marriage between your daughter and Johannes von Bergheim. We both know, Peter, that sooner or later, with her clout, she would have gotten what she wanted. If that happened, she'd have Johannes, and your daughter would still be the daughter of a farmer—without prospects or title."

Peter sighed and ran his head up and down the wall again, massaging himself. "Is that all?"

"Admit to assisting the Calvinist forces, with your sister as your liaison."

Peter's brows went high on his forehead, and he said, "Is that everything?"

Heinrich coughed and said, somewhat under his breath, "And confess to murdering Josephine Donovan."

Peter chuckled. "Josey? She was a friend of mine—"

"It will help cover up loose ends," Heinrich admitted. He blinked a few times and said, "She was also a player in your scheme. Lars was, too."

Peter tilted his head. "What happened to Lars?"

"He died when you were running from me and my men.

Don't worry, though, he tried his damnedest to kill me."

The farmer's shoulders slumped. He shook his head. "Katharina will be devastated."

"Yes I know. They were lovers."

Peter glanced at the walls of the cell. "As far as Josephine—not even you could spin *that* story, Heinrich."

"Don't worry about that, Peter, I'll make it work. Perhaps she denied your advances."

"She was a prostitute!"

Heinrich pretended to yawn. "Trust me, Peter."

Peter seemed to snap, and his calm demeanor turned biting and loud. "What will you say to God, you monster—"

"I doubt I'll ever meet Him."

"You think you can just lump all of these murders under my name?"

Heinrich bobbed his head from left to right, as if thinking. Then he nodded.

Before the investigator could open his mouth to say anything, Peter hissed and said, "Wait, don't tell me—you're a seeker of the truth." He let out a rumbling laugh, and it echoed through the hall.

They both went silent, staring at each other for some time. Eventually, the door upstairs opened. A ray of sunlight lit the dark room. Tomas came down the steps guiding Hugo Griswold by the shoulders. Heinrich motioned for Tomas to bring Hugo in front of Peter's cell.

Peter jumped to his feet.

"See," Heinrich said, presenting Hugo as if the boy was a prize. "Unharmed, as I promised." He grabbed Hugo's shoulders with his spindly hands.

Peter rushed to the front of the cell. "Get your hands off him," he yelled, then faced his son. "Hugo, did the soldier hurt you, my boy?"

Hugo had his horse doll in his hands. He looked back at Tomas, then to his father. He shook his head. "What's going on, father? Why are you in there? And where's Beele?"

Peter's hand started shaking. "I'm so sorry, son. I promise that everything will be okay." He turned back to Heinrich and stared into the investigator's eyes with a look of pure hatred. His eyes were so intense that Heinrich felt unnerved for a moment.

Heinrich cleared his throat and said to Tomas, "Take the boy into a different room."

"To a jail cell?" Tomas asked.

Peter growled. "Why you basta—"

"No," Heinrich said, "just to a different room."

Tomas nodded and led the boy away.

Peter tried to stick his head through the cell's bars, to watch his son go. "I love you, Hue!" he shouted.

Then the boy was gone. The door slammed shut.

Heinrich watched Peter stew with rage. Then, without much hesitation, Peter blurted out the words that Heinrich had been waiting to hear. "Fine," he said, "I'll do it. Just don't hurt my son."

Heinrich bowed his head. "You know this won't be pleasant, Herr Griswold . . . don't you?"

Peter squinted. "Do you want me to change my mind?"

"I'm just warning you."

Peter half-smiled. "How gallant of you." He shook his head. "Just get on with it, coward."

Heinrich nodded and walked toward the stairs. Before he reached the bottom of the steps, he turned around and pulled at his mustache. "For your cooperation, Herr Griswold, I'll give you one last truth, for your peace of mind."

Peter looked at the investigator expectantly.

"You were right. I am a shoddy liar. Your daughter is still alive . . . I think." The investigator bowed to his prisoner, then disappeared up the stairs.

Peter Griswold closed his eyes, breathed out, and smiled.

*　　　*　　　*

Outside the jailhouse, the normally quiet town of Bedburg was in a state of upheaval. People ran in all directions. Smoke filled the sky, billowing from the eastern gates. Several buildings lay in ruins.

It was enough to make Heinrich dizzy. Until then, he hadn't seen the full extent of the chaos and the sight of it was disorienting and shocking.

He stumbled by a few soldiers, staring up at the bitter, black sky. He made his way to Bedburg Castle, where Lord Werner was huddled away in the confines of his safe-room, surrounded by an envoy of guards.

The little lord seemed terrified at everything happening around him. Seated in an oversized chair, he seemed flustered at the investigator's arrival, tapping his hands on his knees.

Heinrich told Werner that he'd finally obtained a confession for the murders of Margreth Baumgartner and Josephine Donovan.

"Oh, like you obtained the confession from the 'witch,' Bertrude Achterberg? Do you have any idea how that farce made me look?" Lord Werner whined.

Heinrich scratched his neck and tried to ignore the annoying little man. "I'll have a public trial prepared."

Lord Werner mumbled inaudibly, and then said, "Who cares about that at a time like this?"

Heinrich sighed. "You were the one who wanted me to continue my investigation, my lord."

Waving off Heinrich, Werner asked him to report on the battle outside. But Heinrich had no news, emphasizing that he'd been chasing shadows in the night and questioning suspects for many hours.

Lord Werner screeched. "I want you to go to the front lines and get me a report, dammit!" he yelled, obviously unimpressed by the investigator's endeavors.

Heinrich scoffed, staring down at the shivering little man. Ignoring the lord's order, he decided he had one more thing he needed to accomplish before his investigation was complete.

*   *   *

Heinrich found Georg Sieghart near the eastern wall. The soldier-turned-hunter-turned-soldier was at the helm of a group of young men, directing their crossbow volleys at the enemy line, far beyond the gates.

"Are you hitting anything?" Heinrich asked, walking up to the hunter. He put his hand over his eyes to shield them from the sun, and looked over the ramparts. Bodies lay scattered on the plains, torn apart by cannon blasts.

Georg shrugged. "I doubt it. Just trying to keep them at bay. General's orders."

Heinrich smiled. "Ah, so you're a commander now? How quickly you move up the ranks, my good hunter."

"I didn't ask for it."

Heinrich slapped the big man on the back and smiled.

"Did you hear the news?" Georg asked.

Heinrich furrowed his brows.

"There's been a report that more Catholic reinforcements are en route, coming from behind the Protestants. We may be able to trap them." Georg said. Though ecstatic, he looked on the verge of exhaustion, his adrenaline somehow keeping him upright. "It's a miracle, Heinrich. We might be saved!"

Heinrich smiled. *I suppose that's a report, but I'll let Werner sweat a little more.* He stared at Georg, who kept yelling and ordering and cursing at the soldiers. Heinrich thought, *I'll miss this man.*

He put his hand back on Georg's shoulder and said, "Georg, it's done."

Georg looked at him with a blank stare.

"I've got the confession we've been searching for—for Margreth's death, and . . . for Josephine's. My case here is finished."

"That's great news, Heinrich. I'm happy for you, but I'm a bit busy here." Even though Georg was shouting at his men and throwing his hands in the air, his face had a subtle look of relief.

Heinrich sighed and said, "I know it was you, Georg."

Georg's hands froze in midair. He squinted at Heinrich. "What was that?"

"I know you helped free Dieter and Sybil. And I have an itching suspicion that you're responsible for Konrad von Brühl's disappearance."

Georg shook his blood-caked beard. "Prove it," he said. Then his face turned angry. "What are you going to do, Heinrich? Arrest me?"

The investigator shook his head.

Georg narrowed his eyes. "Then why are you telling me this? Justice truly is blind, eh?"

"Indeed it is, my good hunter."

"You didn't answer me, Heinrich. Why are you here? Shouldn't you be interrogating some poor sap in a damp, dark jail cell?"

"I'm here as a warning."

"About what?"

"There is going to be a trial, Georg, and I expect it will be bigger than any we've had in this town before. I'm trying to tell you that, in the coming weeks, things are likely to get very . . . *bizarre*. You need to leave Bedburg, Georg, as soon as you can. Are you listening to me?"

Georg was directing more men to the ramparts, while sending off others to tend to wounded soldiers on the battlefield just over the walls. Without facing Heinrich, he nodded. "Why do I need to leave? I'm just starting to like it here."

Heinrich hesitated and said, "Just trust me," then started to walk away.

"Why?" Georg called out. When the investigator turned around, Georg added, "Why should I trust you?"

Heinrich twirled his mustache and thought for a moment. "Because you're my friend," he said, smiling.

Heinrich turned to leave again, but when he got about ten paces away, Georg called out: "You don't have any friends!

Remember?"

Heinrich held up his gloved hand and waved to Georg, but kept walking away. "Very true, my good hunter!"

"Say, investigator!" Georg called out again. "Did you ever figure out who the real Werewolf of Bedburg was?"

Heinrich sighed and turned one last time. Pinching his mustache, he shrugged. "Who knows? Perhaps there never was one at all." He raised his hand and gestured at Georg's blood-caked face and tunic, his disheveled beard and hair, his paralyzed, bullet-riddled arm. Then he motioned to his own purple, bloated nose, which had been broken by Peter Griswold the night before.

Heinrich couldn't help but chuckle. "Perhaps we all are, my good hunter!"

CHAPTER THIRTY-EIGHT

GEORG

The incoming reports were true. Reinforcements came within hours of the field scouts' reconnaissance, to aid the defending Catholics. Georg stood at the top of the ramparts of the eastern wall, looking over the hills and woods. On the horizon, he saw bright yellow banners embroidered with a blue fleur-de-lis, approaching from the rear of the Calvinist forces.

Alexander Farnese, the Duke of Parma and Governor of the Spanish Netherlands, had been successful in his Dutch campaigns. He had arrived at Bedburg, to the surprise of every one except General Ferdinand. Farnese was already a war hero for his campaigns against the Dutch, and he'd come to further his reputation.

With Farnese's army coming from the north and east, the Calvinists were all but trapped between the two forces: Ferdinand's defenders at Bedburg, and Alexander's regiments behind the rebels.

After his failed skirmish the night before, Georg had been very hard on himself. He took to drinking, as usual, until General Ferdinand approached him. Even after Georg gave a slurred apology for his failure, Ferdinand told him that the hunter's defeat came at a massive price to the Calvinists. Though the individual outcome might have been a failure, as a whole, Georg's mission was a success. His quick strike had left the bulk of Count Adolf's army vulnerable and unbalanced.

Toward the start of the morning, Adolf suffered heavy losses against Arnold Baumgartner's main force.

Georg still felt guilty for leading countless men to their deaths, but his courageous charge had not been a complete loss.

Still somewhat drunk, he'd gone to the jailhouse and rescued Sybil, Dieter, and Martin. He'd hoped he could at least do *some* good by breaking them out.

Afterward, Georg returned to his general. "What would you have me do, my lord?" he asked.

"Have a short memory, soldier. Don't let your losses demoralize the men," General Ferdinand answered. He pointed to Georg's disheveled, drunken appearance. "And don't let them see you this way." He turned to leave, adding, "You still have over sixty men at your disposal. Get back on those ramparts and make use of them."

Georg went to the inn. He asked Claus for a pot of coffee, which sobered him up quite nicely.

With Ferdinand's encouraging words giving him renewed vigor, for the next two hours Captain Georg Sieghart commanded and directed crossbowmen from atop the wall, raining hell on the enemy.

When reports came of Alexander Farnese's imminent arrival, the Calvinists went into a panic. Count Adolf foolishly forced many of his men to charge Bedburg's walls, in a last ditch effort to raze the town and steal it from the Catholics.

Georg and his sixty men were ready. Hundreds of Protestant soldiers were shot down and lay dead and dying, splayed on the bloody plains of Bedburg's countryside. Their moans drifted with the wind—in all directions—to the ears of soldiers on both sides of the battlefield. Crows circled the fields, preparing for a feast.

As Alexander Farnese's army became visible in the distance, the men on Bedburg's ramparts pumped their fists toward the sky and cheered.

Georg was relieved, but not cheering. He was puzzled why Count Adolf would direct his army to such desperation—charging the walls—rather than spare countless deaths by just surrendering.

Then he remembered seeing a man on the Calvinist's front lines, minutes before Adolf's order to charge. The man had shouted, "We will not be forgotten! Praise God!" then rushed the walls with a group of like-minded soldiers behind him.

Georg's eyes drifted just down the hill, to the body of that suicidal Protestant, now dead on the battlefield alongside his men. On closer inspection Georg realized it was someone he knew: the recently released pastor, Hanns Richter.

When Count Adolf's orders went largely unheard, it was Pastor Richter who gave the men the morale and zeal to make a final stand. And now he lay dead on the battlefield—surrounded by countless others—sure to be forgotten. It was Georg's crossbowmen who had struck him down.

With Pastor Richter dead, Count Adolf's army lost all order and cohesion. The surge came to a screeching halt, and the Protestants who still lived threw down their weapons. With their spiritual leader dead, all hopes of victory were gone.

If he's remembered at all, Georg thought, *he'll surely be remembered as a martyr to his people.*

Somehow, Count Adolf von Neuenahr managed to escape General Farnese's approaching army. General Ferdinand and Commander Baumgartner weren't thrilled with that, so they sent a troop to scour the countryside for the fleeing general.

But whether Adolf was caught or not, the siege of Bedburg was over. The Catholics had prevailed. They took many prisoners, but some of the adrenaline-fueled mercenaries still had a bloodlust that needed to be sated. They went about the battlefield, butchering Protestants and putting others out of their moaning misery.

Such were the horrors of warfare and Georg could do nothing about it. For every two prisoners the Catholics took, a third was slaughtered.

Men became relegated to beasts—savage and barbaric—to the dismay of the many gallant soldiers who showed restraint.

Georg was one of those gallant soldiers. He wanted no part in the angry, bloodthirsty killings. He remembered his talk with Heinrich, his multiple confessions with Father Nicolaus, his killing of Konrad.

His savage heart had been fed. Moral depravity no longer coursed through his veins. He looked at his rough, right hand, turned it over a few times, and hoped that he would never have to kill again. Then, shifting his gaze to his useless left hand, he realized he'd probably never be able to anyway—which was fine since he felt like he'd finally found his true purpose, or at least a spiritual reckoning of sorts.

Maybe now I can stop being a soldier and actually focus on my faith. He wanted to find God more than anything else. Perhaps the battle would serve as the conduit.

It's time to rebuild my God-forsaken life and start anew, just as Father Nicolaus is hopefully doing. That is . . . if he made it out of the city alive.

As the battle concluded, the sun began to wane. Georg found himself face-to-face with General Ferdinand.

"You fought well," Ferdinand said. "And you led even better. What do you say in joining my regiment as a regular lieutenant, Herr Sieghart? I could use you."

Georg looked down at his hand, and then to the general. "With all due respect, my lord, I'm tired of being used. I'm afraid I've seen enough blood for a lifetime." He gestured to his dangling left arm. "Besides, I doubt I'd be much use with this ruined arm of mine."

"I'm asking for your mind, Georg, not your body."

Georg shrugged and smiled. "I'm flattered, but I'm still going to have to decline your honorable offer. I'm sorry, my lord."

Ferdinand sighed. "Very well. It's a shame to lose someone who actually knows what they're doing."

Georg didn't think of himself like that. Even though he felt he'd found a new lease on life, he still felt lost. If he had known what he was doing, he would have never led his men into a deadly ambush. If he had known what he was doing, he would have never befriended Heinrich Franz or Konrad von Brühl. "Tell that to the families of the men I got killed last night, my lord," Georg said, shaking his head.

Ferdinand placed a hand on Georg's shoulder. The general tried to smile, but failed. "I want you to report your casualties and opinion of the battle to Lord Werner, before you leave," he said, and then started to walk away.

"Lord Werner will have my report by sundown, my lord."

"Take your time, Herr Sieghart. You've earned it."

CHAPTER THIRTY-NINE

DIETER

Dieter, Sybil, and Martin stepped out of the jailhouse into what could have been a scene from Hell. Shielding their faces and squinting as their eyes adjusted to the blaring sunlight, they silently surveyed the utter chaos before them.

The city was in total turmoil. People darting from building to building, dazed soldiers meandering aimlessly, shouts and screams and other unidentifiable noises bombarding them from all directions.

A woman was crouched over a man, weeping—her tears dripping onto his bloody, soulless face. Dieter witnessed a gang of homeless children breaking into a vacant mansion.

At the foot of the hill below the church, men stacked corpses, the pile growing at an alarming rate. Families surrounded the mountain of bodies, some waiting for news that their husband, or father, or son had been killed; others searched through the gray, blank faces of the dead on their own

It was as if the Devil had visited Bedburg overnight—and didn't plan to leave anytime soon.

"Good God," Dieter said, watching the turmoil. He still wore his ragged priest's cassock, and people ran up to him and cried hysterically, begging for his blessing, asking why God had done this and demanding answers that he couldn't give. He was weary and famished and overwhelmed. He made the sign of the cross with his bloody, bandaged hand, and looked at Sybil.

She was frowning at him. "We can't be seen out here," she said.

Dieter nodded. He felt helpless. *I can do nothing for these people.* He was baffled as to how religions could cause such pandemonium and catastrophe. He could only imagine how the Protestant side of things looked, but couldn't dwell on that for too long.

From the jailhouse, the trio waited for a lull in the action, then they ran into an abandoned house nearby.

Dieter felt a tugging and noticed Sybil pulling at the bandage on his hand. "This will get infected," she said, unwrapping the cloth. Finding a pot of cold water, she used it to clean Dieter's hand.

"They're just fingernails, Beele. They'll grow back," Dieter assured her with a crooked smile.

"Don't try to be a hero."

Dieter winced. It was as if the girl he'd known in the previous months had suddenly grown into a woman, overnight. Her face had a hardness he didn't recognize, and her words came out short and choppy.

"Martin, try and find us some food," Sybil ordered.

The boy perked up and ran off. He returned a minute later with a stale slice of bread. He gave it to Sybil, and she handed it to Dieter, who frowned.

"You should eat it," he said, "or we should split it."

"None of us have eaten for days, but you look the worse for wear," she said.

They waited in the house for nearly an hour, resting and gathering their wits. Dieter sat on the floor, his back against a wall. He closed his eyes and almost immediately fell asleep.

He awoke to the sound of cheers.

"How long was I asleep?" he asked. It was still light outside.

"Something's changed," Sybil said. She poked her head outside the house. "People are hugging each other."

"Maybe we've won," Dieter said. He quickly realized "we"

meant the Catholics, who he was no longer affiliated with. It was a strange thing for him, being caught in the middle of two beliefs. He was recognized around Bedburg as the church's preacher. If anyone realized he had betrayed that faith and become a Protestant . . .

Georg was right—we need to get out of here. "I suppose now is our chance," he said.

They left the house and prowled through the streets, trying to stay out of sight. Dieter had no idea who might have seen them enter the jailhouse as prisoners. *It won't do us any good to be seen outside of the jail.*

They stuck to the shadows, eventually making their way to the west side of town, where it wasn't quite as chaotic. They hurried past a stable and the town's tannery toward the western gate.

We'll still need to get through the guards somehow, Dieter thought.

Before he had that opportunity, fate caught him. The cacophony from the northern district of town had become a faint echo. It was eerily quiet as they neared the western walls. Dieter looked over his shoulder, then stopped dead in his tracks. He held his hand out in front of Sybil. His eyes narrowed.

Sybil furrowed her brow, looking confused. "What is it?" she asked. Then she followed his eyes and let out a small yelp.

Johannes von Bergheim stood no less than thirty feet from them, hiding in a shadow behind a building. The nobleman looked frightened. He was doubled over, panting, as if he'd just fled from someone.

It came as no surprise to Dieter that Johannes would be so far removed from the battle that raged on the other side of town.

"There's no time for this," Sybil pleaded. "Please, Dieter, let's just go." She put a hand on his shoulder and tried to pull him away.

But Dieter stayed still as a stone.

He didn't hear her words, and he couldn't feel her touch. It was as if Dieter's soul was in the sky, looking down, unable to control his body.

And Dieter's body was already storming toward the nobleman.

Whatever sense of forgiveness and mercy and repentance Dieter had ever felt . . . vanished. The qualities that had made him a caring and loving person were replaced by thoughts of toxic rage and violence.

As he laid eyes on the bastard who'd harmed Sybil, everything outside of Dieter's senses—the smell of smoke, the sounds of screams and cheers, the taste of blood—fell away.

"Johannes von Bergheim, you coward!" he called out as he neared the young man.

Johannes turned and had a look of utter confusion on his face, which quickly turned into a look of utter disbelief. It seemed as though he pointed at Dieter, but his finger seemed to loom past the former priest, and was aimed at Sybil. "What are you doing with my woman, priest?" Johannes called out in his high-pitched voice.

"She's no one's property, you filthy troll."

Johannes smirked.

Dieter's blood boiled even hotter.

"You can have her, priest. She's a lying whore, anyway." His gaze fell on Sybil. "You lied to me, you bitch! You weren't even a virgin!"

Clenching his fists, Dieter felt warm blood trickle down his bandaged hand. He glanced over his shoulder—the western gates were just forty paces away—their freedom so close. There were no guards at the post—they could simply walk out of Bedburg and be free.

"But that child is still mine," Johannes said.

Sybil gritted her teeth.

"What, you're shocked? The physician who attended you told my father you were pregnant. The baby in your womb is still my heir . . . it's just too bad you won't be there to see him grow." Johannes turned his gaze back to Dieter. "You can keep the whore," he goaded, "but that baby is mine. And with it, her father's beloved pig farm."

Dieter's legs moved like the wings of a hummingbird. Within seconds he closed the gap between himself and his target.

Johannes' self-indulgent smirk faded as he realized what was happening. His eyes went wide. He fumbled in his belt for his sword, and unsheathed it as Dieter closed in.

Dieter clenched his jaw and gnashed his teeth, charging Johannes with fists flying. He thought of everything that had derailed him from his glorious path of righteousness.

It would have been easy for Dieter to turn the other cheek, to forget all that had transpired in Bedburg. It would have been easy for him to just start anew—a new life, a new beginning. Hate, he'd been taught long ago as a boy, was one of the worst sins.

But he was no longer that boy. In fact, he was no longer even the same man he'd been just one night ago. And at that moment, he no longer felt God's calling or His loving embrace. The hate in his heart had taken over the once-treasured values he'd preached.

Johannes, sword in hand, crouched for impact, his blade pointed forward so that Dieter might skewer himself. But the nobleman didn't expect Dieter to charge with such force, the former priest lunging forward while still five paces out.

Swiping the sword away with his bandaged hand, Dieter used his weight to tackle Johannes to the ground.

"Help!" Johannes cried as he tumbled and twisted in the mud.

Dieter growled like a man possessed. He tried to strangle Johannes as they rolled around on the ground. Blood trickled down his arm and smeared onto Johannes' face. The former priest grabbed at the nobleman's collar.

Johannes kept Dieter at arm's-length by pushing at Dieter's face, trying to wrench his eyes. Then he did the only thing he could think of and bit down on Dieter's bandaged hand as hard as he could.

Dieter cried out. His instincts told him to recoil, but his body kept pushing.

As Johannes tried pushing Dieter away, he fumbled for something at his waist, grabbing a small dagger from his belt.

"Dieter!" Sybil cried out.

Johannes stabbed Dieter, gashing him across the thigh.

The former priest pushed on without so much as a wince—so powerful was the adrenaline in his veins. As the dagger pressed into his leg, pain seared through his body. He looked up for a quick second and noticed three men running in his direction from a nearby building.

They wore leather shirts, had swords drawn, and were less than fifty feet away and closing in fast.

"Run, Sybil! Go!" Dieter shouted.

Sybil was frozen in place. Her gaze shifted from Dieter, to the three charging men, to Martin, and then to the gate. After a still moment, Martin tugged at her dress. She looked one more time at Dieter.

She felt tears pooling—tears that she'd promised herself never to show again. Then she grabbed Martin's hand and pulled him away, sprinting toward the western wall.

The men were less than forty feet from Dieter and Johannes.

Dieter grabbed Johannes' hand that held the dagger, and kept it from striking again.

The men were less than thirty feet from Dieter and Johannes.

Dieter felt his leg go weak. His hand bled profusely, but he still held onto Johannes' hand.

"I'll kill you, you filthy bastard!" Johannes screeched.

Dieter felt something dangling from his neck.

The men were less than twenty feet from Dieter and Johannes.

Dieter pulled at his neck and snagged the amulet that Sybil had given him. He yanked the wooden cross pendant from its band, the same pendant that signified peace and love and unity between all religions and people.

It was the first time Dieter had removed the amulet since Sybil had given it to him.

Johannes' eyes grew big and terrified. His hand that held his dagger remained immobile.

Dieter drove the amulet down as hard as he could.

The men were less than ten feet from Dieter and Johannes.

Dieter cried and screamed as he punched the cross into Johannes' forehead.

The first blow broke the skin, and blood spattered.

The second thrust pierced Johannes' skull, and the nobleman's eyes went wild.

The third strike drove into Johannes' brain, and the amulet broke off into shards. One of the crosses protruded from Johannes' forehead.

The nobleman's three guards arrived, circled around Dieter, and the former priest closed his eyes, content to let his life slip away.

A silver flash split the sky and Dieter heard steel ring out against steel. His eyes shot open.

Georg Sieghart stood over Dieter, his sword locked with one of the three guards' swords.

"Get the hell out of here, priest!" Georg screamed. He kicked hard with his right leg and caught the guard in the chest. The man went flying backwards.

Dieter stammered.

"You've done your work, now run!" Georg's face was cringing.

Dieter stood and tried to run, but his bleeding leg almost caused him to fall. He limped toward the gate, and as he reached the wall he looked over his shoulder and saw Georg Sieghart whirling his blade around in a circle.

The big hunter stepped away from Johannes' body and twirled his sword in his hand. The three soldiers swept out and surrounded him.

The last thing Dieter saw before he disappeared behind the gate was Georg Sieghart smiling, goading the guards to attack him. Then, with their swords pointed toward the heavens, the three men descended on the hunter.

CHAPTER FORTY

SYBIL

Sybil stood outside of the western gates, holding Martin's hand. She stared ahead, into a smoking city filled with political lies, religious strife, and death—a city on the brink of disaster. She looked over her shoulder, to a wide expanse of grassy hills and green woods in the distance, behind her—a countryside that signaled freedom.

As much as Sybil detested Bedburg, she couldn't turn away. She would put herself through all the strife and death and lies again, as long as Dieter was by her side.

And so she waited.

The sun was beginning to set on a fiery pink horizon, causing the woods in the distance to draw great shadows on the land. She knew she had to leave soon, if she was going to give herself any chance of escaping the region.

But she still waited. She was frozen, and couldn't convince herself to move.

Sybil looked at Martin. He fidgeted and bit his lip nervously. "Beele," he said, "do you think it's time?"

Sybil stayed quiet. *What's the point of leaving here if I don't have my love and family with me?* Even though she knew Martin was right, she couldn't bring herself to act.

She stared at the dark woods behind her and wondered how safe she and Martin would be alone, at the mercy of the wilderness. *Anyone we might run into could recognize us as fugitives. Or worse, if vagabonds found us at night—a young woman and young man— what sort of depraved thoughts might they harbor?* Sybil shook her head and sighed. *Georg told us to go west, but I've never been outside of Bedburg in my life. I have no idea where to go.* Her own thoughts started to make her anxious and helpless. She felt her body begin to sweat. She tried to stay strong, but her paranoia was causing her to panic.

"Beele?" Martin said, as if he could see the turmoil playing out in her head.

"I heard you, Martin. Just give him one more minute, please."

Martin hesitated, and then he scratched his scruffy beard. "There were three soldiers, Beele, headed right—"

"You don't need to remind me." Her head sank. "I know . . . you're right. I'm sorry."

Sybil took one last look through the gate and then turned to leave. As she stared at the hills and trees and plains ahead of her, another thought crossed her mind: *How will we survive out here? We have no food, and I've never hunted a day in my life. Foraging will only get us so far . . . and this is a place without roads or trails.* Her feeling of helplessness turned into one of ineptitude, and her shoulders slumped.

She turned one last time to say farewell to the town she'd known her entire life. Thin plumes of smoke still wafted from the ramparts and buildings. *Had I known the Protestants were capable of such destruction, maybe I'd never have followed father's ways in the first place.* She immediately regretted thinking that. *Aren't the Catholics just the same? They're both fighting for the same God, just in the name of different men. It seems so . . . meaningless.*

Sybil knew that politics and money and power had just as much to do with the bloody Cologne War as religion did.

She felt someone pull on her arm and was shaken from her thoughts. Martin's eyes were gazing at something toward Bedburg.

Sybil turned around. Her heart fluttered.

Dieter Nicolaus was limping toward them as fast as his feet would take him. He clenched his left thigh as he ran, his cassock spattered with dark blood.

Sybil put her hands to her mouth. *How could he possibly be alive, God? Did you do this?* She smiled and her eyes lit up. She didn't care why he was there. Celestial intervention or not, all that mattered was that he was. She ran toward him, and the biting wind caused her tears to flow—the first tears she'd cried since she'd made her promise never to cry again. But these were far different tears.

She opened her arms and they embraced. Passionately. She whispered into his ear, "It's a miracle. God has smiled upon us."

Dieter chuckled. "Either Him or Georg Sieghart."

Sybil cocked her head to the side.

"I'll explain later," he said. "We must go."

"But you're hurt." She ran a hand down his leg.

Dieter winced, but didn't recoil. He tore the bottom cuff of his robe, ripping off a piece of the holy cloth to use as a tourniquet around his thigh. Then he gave Sybil a small smile. "All better."

She grabbed his hand, and Martin's shoulder, and the trio set off into the country.

As night fell, Dieter explained that Georg had come to his rescue. "Twice in one day," he said.

"What happened to him?" Martin asked.

Dieter shook his head and looked to the ground. "I didn't see . . . but it didn't look good. I feel ashamed for leaving him behind."

Sybil put a hand on his shoulder. "He wanted you safe, Dieter. Otherwise he wouldn't have helped you. He knew what he was getting himself into, my love. You can't blame yourself."

Dieter nodded but stayed silent.

"Remember," Sybil added, "he wanted us to start our life anew. We'll live the life he never could, in his name and honor."

"Amen," Dieter said.

They pushed on over the hills and into the woods, until the

canopies of the trees concealed the moonlight. They'd traveled several hours and felt far enough away to elude capture from any patrolmen.

Dieter started to gather wood for a fire, and when Sybil gave him a curious look he said, "I may be a man of the cloth, but I've learned a thing or two in my day."

Sybil grinned and leaned close to him. They kissed.

Dieter sparked a fire by knocking stones together. Then the three of them gathered close and retreated to their own thoughts.

It was Martin who broke the long silence when he asked, "What will you guys miss most about Bedburg?"

Dieter threw a stick in the fire and scratched his neck. He looked up at the dark branches overhead, thinking. Then he turned to Martin and said, "My gardens."

Martin and Dieter both faced Sybil. She had a sad look in her eyes. "My brother," she said, drawing her knees to her chest. "I wish I could see my brother and father again. I'll never know what became of them, and I promised my brother . . ." she trailed off as her voice cracked.

Dieter rested his hand on her knee. "One day, Beele, we'll find your brother. I can't say what might have happened to Peter, he was an ally of the Protestants . . . but I promise we'll find your brother."

"I could go my whole life without hearing or giving another promise," Sybil said, shaking her head.

Another stiff silence fell over the group as they watched the flames flicker and crackle.

"I never knew my parents," Dieter said after a lengthy moment of introspection. "My foster family raised me as a good and right Catholic, but I never felt the true love that a blood-parent might give. I wish I could understand, Beele. But it's simply too dangerous for us to return to Bedburg right now. I can't afford to lose you again."

Sybil nodded, wrapped her arms around her shins, and placed her chin on her knees. "My father was awful to you," she said.

Dieter half-smiled. "*That* I can understand."

Sybil kept thinking. She felt so small, like she was trapped in a wide-open world, and she didn't understand it. *I'm a fugitive and a bastard child now . . . without a home, without land, and without a family. Will I be a beggar for the rest of my days? Will people pity my child? Will I even live to see my child's face?*

Pressing her hand to her stomach, she felt a small bump.

Dieter looked at her as if he understood just what she was thinking. "We'll make it through this, Beele. I prom—"

Sybil put her finger on his lips. "Don't say it," she said.

Dieter nodded. "Well, I will help support your child, if you'll allow me to."

Sybil wrinkled her brow. "If I allow you? I love you."

Dieter looked at his bloody robe, then opened his right fist. His eyes widened. He hadn't noticed that his hand had been clenched shut the entire time.

In it was one of the crosses from the amulet that Sybil had given him.

"What happened to the other cross?" Sybil asked, touching the amulet and running her hands over the rough side, where it was ripped and splintered.

"I thought that Johannes needed it more than I did."

Sybil cocked her head to the side, confused, and was ready to ask questions, but Dieter spoke first. "Look at me," he said, still staring at the cross in his hand. "I've become the thing I've always tried to escape from. Hate has filled my heart, Beele." He looked at Sybil, and his eyes were wet. "I've let God out of my soul, and I'm surely not the same man you fell in love with. I know that. I am . . . I've become . . . a monster."

Sybil clasped her hand over Dieter's, both feeling the wooden cross underneath. She stared deep into his eyes and watched the orange flames throw shadows on his fair face. She smiled and said, "No, Dieter, you're wrong. What you did in Bedburg was the most heroic thing I've ever seen. You didn't become a monster, my love. On the contrary . . . you became my savior."

CHAPTER FORTY-ONE

Archbishop Ernst arrived from Cologne the day after the Protestant army was defeated. He hadn't been to Bedburg in over a year, and his arrival was lauded by the townsfolk. They waited with bated breath for the prince-elector to make his grand entrance.

Ernst had received word that his older brother, Ferdinand, as well as Alexander Farnese, were the heroes of the battle. Arnold Baumgartner was also given praise. What the townsfolk didn't know, however, was that Ernst hadn't come to Bedburg because of the victory over the Calvinists and Lutherans, but because he'd learned that the Werewolf of Bedburg was in custody.

Both Lord Werner and Bishop Solomon brooded in the shadows as Archbishop Ernst and his entourage sauntered through the city on horseback. They feared that the archbishop had come to take credit for the victory over Count Adolf. Neither lord nor bishop accepted that Bedburg would have likely been doomed without Ernst's reinforcements.

What maddened Bishop Solomon even more than the triumphant victory parade was watching Vicar Balthasar Schreib join along the archbishop's side. Just as Solomon had predicted, Ernst was seizing all the religious power and influence in Bedburg.

That damn vicar, with his noble ideals and pitiable limp, thought Solomon as he watched the cherubic-faced Jesuit pass by. *I'm a fool for agreeing to help him.*

What the bishop hadn't considered, was that while he was protected from harm in his church, Balthasar had joined the front lines of the Catholic forces, to offer morale and support and prayers. Solomon didn't realize that he'd dug his own grave, and that his actions had made Balthasar the more likeable religious figure in Bedburg.

Balthasar the Newcomer was a breath of fresh air to the people, whereas Solomon the Ancient was a bitter old man who lacked enthusiasm and zeal.

As the parade swept through the streets of Bedburg, it became clear that the Electorate of Cologne remained safely in the hands of the Catholics. Four of the seven electoral seats of the Holy Roman Empire still belonged to the Catholics—and, more importantly, to Pope Sixtus.

Still, Bishop Solomon believed that the Cologne War would have a lasting effect in and outside of Germany. Queen Elizabeth of England would certainly be furious with the outcome. Henry III of France had been assassinated by a Catholic fanatic a month prior to Peter's trial, but his brother-in-law, Henry IV, was believed to support the Protestants as well.

The Reformation was far from over.

After congratulating the generals, and before meeting with any other lords or officials, Archbishop Ernst met with Investigator Heinrich Franz. He congratulated the investigator for uncovering the Protestant conspiracy in Bedburg.

"A job well done, Heinrich. Your estates in the southern Cologne principality are solidified and well deserved," the tall archbishop said to the investigator. "Your houses are under regency until you see fit."

Investigator Franz bowed to his liege and said, "I thank you, my lord, but I believe everything is not as it should be."

Ernst raised one eyebrow. "Can this wait? I have many people to meet with. Why don't you celebrate your position." The archbishop cleared his throat. "You . . . do have the right man in custody, correct?"

Heinrich nodded. "Oh, yes, yes, we certainly do. My words can wait until after the confessor's trial, my lord."

Heinrich bowed again to the archbishop, and then they parted ways. Heinrich headed toward his old stomping grounds: the jailhouse.

Before Archbishop Ernst's arrival in Bedburg, Johannes von Bergheim's body was found by a group of beggars. Though it was strange that his body was inside the town, it came as no surprise to many that he'd been killed so far from where the real battle raged. The young noble's reputation preceded him.

What interested the nobility was *how* he had been killed—a wooden cross lodged in his forehead.

Priests and holy people felt that his death, and the murder weapon, alluded to some kind of sign or statement from God. And though there was speculation, no one ever really knew what that sign or statement meant.

After Johannes' grisly murder, Baron Ludwig von Bergheim returned to Bedburg to see his son's killer brought to justice. Commander Arnold Baumgartner, one of the heroes of the siege on Bedburg, joined the baron in wanting to see his daughter, Margreth, avenged.

Despite his celebrated victory, Arnold Baumgartner never recovered from his daughter's death. He moved from Bedburg and lived a life distant from civilization. There were rumors— though never confirmed—that, in despair, he hanged himself.

In contrast, Baron Bergheim seemed very cold and unaffected by the death of his son. He continued making controversial and lucrative trades, each one increasing his wealth and success.

The baron purportedly said it was a shame that he would never get to do trade with Peter Griswold, because the farmer offered so much in the way of pigs and cattle.

The real reason Baron Bergheim was disappointed in Peter's outcome, however, was that the farmer could have helped to bolster the baron's coffers. Now, that would never come to pass.

*   *   *

Heinrich Franz visited his premier prisoner, Peter Griswold, to inform him of the recent news around town.

"Archbishop Ernst and his nobles have arrived in Bedburg," he told the farmer.

Peter chuckled. "I will be the most celebrated monster to ever live."

"At least you can find the comedy in tragedy."

Peter's smile faded. "You're a true bastard, investigator."

"So you've told me," Heinrich said. He paused. Looking up, he searched the cracks in the jailhouse ceiling. "A strange thing was discovered after our victory yesterday."

"Why should I care?"

Heinrich shrugged. "Johannes von Bergheim was found murdered."

Peter wrinkled his nose.

"He was found with a wooden cross lodged in his skull."

Peter smiled. He had seen his daughter secretly sculpting that amulet for many days, and he'd wondered what his daughter had done with it. He kept that bit of information to himself.

"What a shame," Peter said, his smile remaining.

Heinrich laughed. "I agree with you. I'd say it was justifiable—a sublime act of justice. No girl should have to go through what your daughter went through."

Peter clenched his jaw. "Don't speak of my daughter."

Heinrich leaned close to the bars of the cell, his pale face lit up against the shadows of the room. "My only wonder is . . . who could have done such a gruesome thing?" He trailed off and narrowed his eyes. "We'll surely have to send a patrol after the killers, whoever they—"

"It was me," Peter claimed. "I confess to killing that boy." His face took on a look of sheer panic at Heinrich's implication.

The investigator put his hands on his hips and tilted his head. "Now, now, Peter. That timeline doesn't add up, does it? You were in prison when Johannes was killed."

Peter balled his hand into a fist and pounded on the bars, clouding the room with dust. He stared at the investigator's cold, gray eyes. He knew who was likely responsible for Johannes' death. Looking at Heinrich's eyes, he could tell the investigator also knew.

"I beg you, Herr Franz, if you ever had a decent bone in your body . . . put his death on the list of my many . . . *atrocities*. What does one more vile nobleman matter to you?"

Heinrich shook his head. "Don't worry, Peter. I expected you might say that, and I commend you for taking priority as a father—however long it might have taken you. I will put the boy's death on your hands."

"Thank you," Peter said. Placing his forehead on the bars, he exhaled. It felt strangely ironic to be thanking a man who had labeled him a murderer. He couldn't help but grin.

"Killing a baron's son and a hero's daughter . . . this will surely be a trial for the ages, Peter," Heinrich muttered, bringing the farmer back to his dismal reality.

Peter shrugged. He felt content for a completely unrelated reason: In his final confession—that of killing Johannes von Bergheim—and possibly the last days of his life, he had finally found the strength in his heart to accept the love and union between his daughter and Father Dieter Nicolaus.

Peter Griswold's trial was a complete spectacle and fiasco. It was a grand show, put on by Archbishop Ernst, Lord Werner, and Bishop Solomon. And, as expected, the citizens of Bedburg came by the thousands to watch it all, to condemn and vilify the treacherous werewolf who for years had stalked their countryside.

During the week preceding the trial, Peter was displayed like a trophy in the town's marketplace. He was placed in a pillory on a raised platform. Passing townsfolk ridiculed and spat on his exposed head, while others threw rotten food and rocks at him. Several daring kids even shaved his head, then ran off giggling.

The trial itself drew the most esteemed and recognizable figures of the German aristocracy. Lords, ladies, and noblemen—most from outside Bedburg—clamored for the best seating. Everyone wanted to bear witness to the grand carnival.

Peter's nickname became his *only* name—Peter Stubbe—due to him missing his left hand. It was predicted that the trial would be drawn out and lengthy, to attract as many spectators as possible.

Baron Ludwig von Bergheim, whose son was one of Peter's murder victims, was the lead magistrate in the case.

With such egregious charges, it was no surprise that Peter's fate was sealed even before he set foot in the courtroom.

He was charged with killing no less than eighteen people, over a span of twenty-five years. His preferred victims were children and women, some of them pregnant (including, apparently, Josephine). He also ate many of his victims—either their brains, parts of their body, or, in extreme cases, their fetuses.

Witnesses claimed they'd seen Peter gorge on the flesh of beasts, such as goats and sheep.

As various accusers and barristers described the sensational details, they became more and more vivid and grotesque, causing many spectators to vomit or faint

At one point in the trial, as Peter was stretched on a rack, nearly to death, he "confessed" to eating fourteen women and children, three of them pregnant, and his own daughter (who was believed to be dead at the time).

The crowds gasped in horror when they learned that, before killing Sybil, he'd engaged in an incestuous relationship with her.

He was also accused of having a sexual relationship with his own sister, whose trial would follow.

He admitted to practicing black magic since he was twelve years old, after obtaining a belt from Satan—the same belt that was actually given to him by his father. Satan's belt allowed him to transform into an evil, bloodsucking werewolf, under the cover of night. Random gasps and groans from the crowd could be heard throughout these "confessions."

The more Peter listened to the repulsive accusations, and felt the pain of his torture, the more numb he got. He stopped listening. All he could do was hope that his daughter, son, and sister were safe.

And then, finally, came the day of his execution.

It was October 31, 1589—All Hallows' Eve. As dawn broke, people were lining up in the marketplace. After relishing in the depravity of Peter Stubbe's trial, the crowd now seemed to share an even higher level of hatred for the farmer. It was nothing more than a crazed mob, hellbent on seeing this man ripped apart for what they believed he was: a vicious, vile monster.

Peter Griswold was guilty by public demand.

Heinrich Franz knew Peter was much less a demon than given credit for. An unfortunate scapegoat, he'd been caught in the politics of warring Catholics and Protestants.

That morning, Heinrich went to visit Archbishop Ernst, who had taken residence in Castle Bedburg during Peter's months-long trial.

"My lord," Heinrich began. "I believe it's time you hear the words I was going to say when you first arrived in Bedburg."

The archbishop was holding a pipe. He looked down his beak of a nose at the investigator. "What are you still doing here, Herr Franz? Don't you have a massive estate to attend to?"

"I believe you have the wrong man in custody for the murders."

Ernst fumbled his pipe and nearly dropped it. His eyes went wide, but he quickly composed himself. "Why are you telling me this, *now*? Are you telling me that you were wrong . . . *again*? If that's the case, it seems I should take your rewards from you."

"Well," Heinrich said, "I believe it makes no difference. This man has to die, I'm sure you know, so that the Protestants are too frightened to attack again."

"They are in shambles," Ernst agreed. "We will make an example out of one of their leaders. But, if you know that, then why have you come to me? What is it you wish to say?"

"I've come to benefit you, in fact."

Heinrich could see the archbishop's eyes sparkle. "Continue," Ernst said.

The investigator cleared his throat. "As you know, I only took this case at your discretion, my lord. As such, I was hurried to make a quick resolution, by Lord Werner and Bishop Solomon. I may be at fault, partly, for my investigation, but it was those two who pulled the strings."

The two men stared at each other. They both knew that, in truth, it was Archbishop Ernst who had been pulling Heinrich's strings. But that didn't need to be said—not in the presence of an official scribe, who sat in the corner of the throne room, writing down their conversation.

The truth was conveyed in their eyes as they gazed at each other. As elector of Cologne, it was no secret that Ernst held the power in Bedburg. But he still couldn't publicly vocalize the misconduct and ruination of one of his colleagues, as much as it pleased him to hear. It would raise suspicion. Heinrich and Ernst understood all of this, in their silence.

So Heinrich had come to him with an alternative. "After the Protestants attacked," he continued, "I was further pressured by Lord Werner to find the werewolf, by any means necessary. So I did, but after further inspection, I believe I may have been . . . wrong."

"How were you wrong? And why are you telling me this?"

Because Bishop Solomon is an old wretch, and Lord Werner is a little weasel, Heinrich thought. "Because I seek the truth," he said.

Ernst looked frustrated, but waved him on. "Go on, Herr Franz. What is it you believe?"

Heinrich cleared his throat again. "Peter Griswold may be at fault for many of the murders," he said, making sure to smother any wrongdoing on his own part. "But . . . I believe it was Georg Sieghart, also known as Sieghart the Savage, who was responsible for many of these treacherous acts. I think that the man we first believed to have *killed* the Werewolf of Bedburg was in fact the werewolf all along."

The archbishop's eyebrows rose. "What evidence do you have?"

"The spy you sent to follow him, Konrad von Brühl, he—"

"You are quite resourceful, investigator."

Heinrich smiled. "It wasn't difficult to uncover. Anyway . . . Konrad's body was found with his throat torn out, in a tunnel beneath my jailhouse, just a short time ago. My man, Ulrich, told me of an unbearable stench rising into the jailhouse, and so we discovered Konrad's body. I believe Georg killed him, after some dispute. Perhaps he lured Konrad to the underground tunnel.

"Furthermore, I believe he killed Josephine Donovan, the courtesan, as he was the last client seen with the woman. Peter could not have killed her, because I am almost certain that he was away—convening with the Protestants—at the time of Josephine's death."

"Why would Georg kill the prostitute?" Enrst asked.

Heinrich shrugged. "Perhaps she denied his advances. After some research, I discovered that Josephine physically resembled Georg's deceased wife. They were both Irish, and redheaded. And, as you eloquently pointed out, Georg was a crazed savage."

Archbishop Ernst started tapping his chin with his pipe.

Heinrich crossed his arms over his chest. "I believe the same fate befell Margreth Baumgartner, who also declined his advances, as Peter was away with the Protestants during her time of death, too."

"This all sounds very circumstantial, investigator," Ernst said, shaking his head.

"True, but I would not be doing my job properly if I did not bring it to your attention."

There was a long lull in the conversation as the archbishop

puffed on his pipe.

Finally, Archbishop Ernst sighed and stood from his chair. "I appreciate your candor, Herr Franz. I will dwell on this new information, but, for now, I have an execution to witness."

Heinrich Franz bowed to the archbishop and was escorted out of the castle. As he rode by the marketplace, passing the bloodthirsty townsfolk and judges charged with deciding Peter's fate, he frowned. *What a circus.*

But once away from the town square, a smile crept to his face. He thought of the seed that he'd just planted in the archbishop's mind, though he wasn't entirely sure whether that seed would sprout.

Heinrich Franz didn't stay in Bedburg for the execution of Peter Griswold, though he heard plenty about it from numerous sources. And as tales of the execution traveled and were repeated, the more outlandish they became. In fact, many of the accounts were printed in woodblocks, to showcase the execution's morbidity.

Before being condemned as a werewolf, a devil, a sorcerer, a cannibal, and a murderer, Peter Griswold looked out at the swelling crowd of hateful townsfolk and felt a sense of remorse. *Shouldn't I be feeling hatred toward these faces? Shouldn't I be damning them with my last breath?*

Instead, as he scanned the faces, he swore he saw two familiar ones under hooded guise: his daughter and Father Dieter Nicolaus.

He blinked. *Surely my mind is playing tricks on me.*

But as he stared at the two, a strange and wonderful sense of calm overtook him. He felt no hate. He forgave them all. Just as Dieter would have asked him to do. He now knew that in the afterlife, God would surely see the falsity of his alleged crimes. He would be forgiven for his sins and trespasses.

It was later reported that he was lashed to a wheel, and that the flesh was torn from his body in ten places with hot pincers. Then the flesh was ripped from his arms and legs, and the people cheered wildly. Despite taunts for more pain and writhing, Peter would not oblige, staying deadly silent throughout the ordeal, resigned to his fate. Looking up, he thought he saw an angel—or God—in the cloudless sky.

His limbs were then broken, crushed by the blunt side of an axe, to prevent him from returning from the grave.

He was probably dead at that point, but, for good measure, he was then beheaded and burned on a pyre.

The only silver lining to Peter's death was that it prevented him from witnessing his sister's similar fate. Though he'd been guaranteed her safety, such was not to be. Another bloodthirsty jury deemed her a succubus and witch—for, among other things, luring her own brother to her bedside—and she was burned alive at the stake.

And with the death of Peter came the death of the Werewolf of Bedburg. For the first time in years, the good people of Bedburg would be safe and free from the werewolf's treacherous curse.

EPILOGUE

The deaths around the countryside of Cologne and Bedburg ceased after the execution of Peter Griswold. Even so, Archbishop Ernst ordered a secret search party to find and arrest Georg Sieghart for unspecified reasons. Only Ernst and Heinrich knew that Georg was being blamed for many of the murders attributed to Peter Griswold.

The archbishop excommunicated Bishop Solomon for his misuse of power and for leading a false investigation, banishing him from Bedburg. It was said that he lived the rest of his life in poverty. Since he'd spent his entire life knowing only the path of the Lord, he became a wandering beggar, traveling from city to city, before finally succumbing to either an unknown illness, or old age.

He never became a saint and was largely forgotten.

Archbishop Ernst replaced Solomon with his Jesuit missionary, Balthasar Schreib, as the new bishop of Bedburg.

Lord Werner, though originally endorsed and chosen by Archbishop Ernst to govern Bedburg, was also deposed and stripped of his title, for the same reasons as Solomon. With his position vacant for a time, it was left to Bishop Balthasar to find a suitable replacement.

Ernst's religious and political hold on Bedburg became absolute.

Georg Sieghart's body was never found at the death site of Johannes von Bergheim and his three guards. In fact, Georg's body was never found *anywhere*.

The archbishop's scouting troop followed a trail of blood that led away from the bodies of Johannes and his men, but they returned empty-handed.

As gossip traveled, Georg's alleged crimes—and the hunter himself—took on legendary proportions in the taverns of Bedburg. People who'd never met him claimed to have known him personally. Tales of his deeds grew larger than life and it was quite some time before "Sieghart the Savage" was forgotten.

Many believed he died from his massive wounds. How could a man live with such a thick trail of blood in his wake? Others believed the blood wasn't his—that it belonged to someone else. Some believed that, on various hunts, they'd seen him roaming the countryside in the fog, as a hermit, or werewolf, or worse—maybe a ghost.

Then, after a while, no one cared.

With Peter Griswold's death, and the end to the murders, the hysteria that had plagued Bedburg for so long ultimately died as well.

Dieter Nicolaus, Sybil Griswold, and Martin Achterberg managed to traverse the countryside west of Bedburg, over the hills and through the woods, eventually making their way to Amsterdam and the Dutch coast. From there they booked passage to England and, while on board, managed to find a Protestant minister who conducted their marriage. Martin became the de facto brother to both Dieter and Sybil.

Dieter didn't lose his leg or fingers. He made a full recovery from his wounds.

In England, they went to Windsor Castle in Berkshire, the home of Queen Elizabeth and her court. Their lavish tales of the Werewolf of Bedburg drew in great audiences and acclaim, and though both Dieter and Sybil thought that would earn them a place in the Queen's court, that was also not to be.

As their tales became old news, their audience of fickle nobles soon lost interest, leaving them to roam the streets to find a place of their own.

Fortunately, before their banishment Sybil went into labor and was lucky enough to remain in the care of Queen Elizabeth throughout the birth, with the best nurses and physicians at her disposal. Had her timing been different, she no doubt would have died giving birth.

The baby's features were soft, with a hint of dark hair and the pale face of Dieter. There could be no doubt who the father was.

When Sybil asked Dieter what they should name their boy, his reply came quickly.

The name of the father who had finally accepted them. The protector who had rescued them.

And together they hugged their new child, Peter Sieghart.

Months after the events in Bedburg and far from the Cologne principality, a young girl—no more than fifteen years of age—walked from her town's cathedral to her family farm in the country. She was fair skinned, with curly blonde hair and a plush, red face.

It was nearing sundown. Walking alone, she'd prayed and gossiped with some of the nuns for far too long and had lost track of the time.

A man came up alongside her, seemingly out of nowhere. The girl jumped, clutching her chest.

"Hello, my dear," the man said cheerily.

"Oh my," the girl replied, "you startled me, sir."

The man smiled. He was tall and thin, and had his hands clasped behind his back. "I see you're alone, and I'm sure your father wouldn't like you walking alone at this hour. May I escort you home?"

The man had a charming smile, and though he was much older than the girl, he was somewhat handsome.

The girl smiled shyly, and the man walked beside her, draping his hand over her shoulder. He wore black gloves, his spindly fingers resting on her thin collarbone.

"That's very kind of you, my lord," the girl said. "But it's my mother who told me it isn't safe to walk alone so close to night." The girl blushed. "I . . . lost track of time at the church."

The man smiled and said, "I know the feeling." The two continued west toward the sunset. He looked to the sky. "I love when it's bursting with orange and pink. Don't you?"

The girl smiled, looked up at the man's gaunt face, and nodded.

The man gestured toward the rolling hills and trails in the distance. "Look how beautiful it is out there in the wilderness! If you ask me, my dear, you shouldn't be too frightened about stories your mother tells you."

Then the man's hand moved to his face, and he started twirling a wispy mustache on his upper lip. With his other hand, he squeezed the girl's shoulder tight. He looked down at her. His lips curled and his gray eyes flashed.

"Besides, my dear, I doubt the Devil's in the countryside."

Fact or Fiction?

The Werewolf of Bedburg is based on a true story that took place in Germany, during the Catholic Counter-Reformation. The span of killings happened from around 1564 to 1588. Though the gruesome murders and the "werewolf's" trial actually happened, not all of the characters or events in this book are based on fact —actually, most of them aren't.

Heinrich Franz, Georg Sieghart, and Dieter Nicolaus are completely fictional characters. So is Dorothea Gabler, Josephine Donovan, Baron Ludwig and Johannes von Bergheim, Margreth and Arnold Baumgartner, Konrad von Brühl, Pastor Hanns Richter, Lars, Cristoff, Tomas, Ulrich, Bishop Solomon, Balthasar Shreib, Claus, and Karl, Bertrude, and Martin Achterberg.

Peter Griswold (or Peter Stubbe) *was* real. A Rhenish settler, he had two children (Sybil, and an unknown son), though Griswold might not have been their surname. Katharina Trompen was supposedly a distant relative of Peter, but I used creative license and made her his sister.

Archbishop Ernst was the actual prince-elector of Cologne during this time. Lord Werner was his truly appointed Lord of Bedburg. Archbishop Gebhard von Truchsess was the Protestant archbishop and prince-elector before Ernst, and the Cologne War most definitely happened. Ferdinand of Bavaria, Count Adolf von Neuenahr, and Duke Alexander Farnese of Parma were all real as well.

The Werewolf of Bedburg's trial was the most popular trial of the times, attracting all the lords and ladies of the land, and this story stems from the simple question: Why was this particular werewolf trial so much more important than any others?

Despite pretty intense research, I could never find an answer to that one. So I wrote this book instead.

Thanks for reading it. And stay tuned for the sequel!

About the Author

Cory Barclay lives in San Diego, California. When he's not writing novels (such as the sequel to this book), he's probably playing guitar, or engaged in other shenanigans.

Subscribe to CoryBarclay.com for news on his upcoming releases!